Praise for *Knowing Me Knowing You*

'*Knowing Me Knowing You* was so real I feel as if I know Alex and Gihan as personal friends. Jeevani Charika has the perfect touch with character, story and sensitive subjects. I'm ready for her next book already.'
Sue Moorcroft, *Sunday Times* bestselling author

'A love story as warm and comforting as a wearable blanket . . . So enjoyable and engaging it got me through a bout of covid. (Are you allowed to put "Better than paracetamol" on a book jacket? Because this really worked.)'
K.J. Charles, author of *The Secret Lives of Country Gentlemen*

'I totally loved this book . . . I was completely drawn into the story and fell deeply in love with Gihan – honestly I felt if Alex didn't want him I'd have him! A beautiful tale of true love overcoming all obstacles.'
Kathleen McGurl, author of *The Girl from Bletchley Park*

JEEVANI CHARIKA (pronounced 'Jeev-uh-nee') writes multi-cultural women's fiction and romantic comedies. She spent much of her childhood in Sri Lanka, with short forays to Nigeria and Micronesia, before returning to England to settle in Yorkshire. All of this, it turned out, was excellent preparation for becoming a novelist.

She also writes under the name Rhoda Baxter. Her books have been shortlisted for multiple awards.

A microbiologist by training, Jeevani loves all things science geeky. She also loves cake, crochet and playing with Lego. You can find out more about her (and get a free book) on her website www.jeevanicharika.com.

Also by Jeevani Charika

Picture Perfect
Playing for Love

Knowing Me
Knowing You

JEEVANI CHARIKA

ONE PLACE. MANY STORIES

HQ
An imprint of HarperCollins*Publishers* Ltd
1 London Bridge Street
London SE1 9GF

www.harpercollins.co.uk

HarperCollins*Publishers*
Macken House, 39/40 Mayor Street Upper,
Dublin 1 D01 C9W8

This paperback edition 2024

2
First published in Great Britain by
HQ, an imprint of HarperCollins*Publishers* Ltd 2024

ISBN: 9780008605858

This book contains FSC™ certified paper and other controlled
sources to ensure responsible forest management.

For more information visit: www.harpercollins.co.uk/green

Printed and bound in the UK using 100% renewable electricity
at CPI Group (UK) Ltd

*To everyone whose dream died
because the money ran out.*

Content note:

This book is a light-hearted romance, but it contains references to cancer – from a survivor and from someone who lost a loved one to the illness. If this is something that would hurt you to read about at this time, please feel free to put it aside. Come back to it if and when you're ready.

Chapter 1

Five years ago

Alex bounced on the balls of her feet. Even wrapped up in her big coat, she was freezing. Her knee-high boots, though pretty and comfortable, weren't exactly warm either. It was ten o'clock on New Year's Eve and she had been waiting for Todd for fifteen minutes already. She double checked the time. He was definitely late. She was often early, so maybe this was a normal amount of lateness. She checked for messages. Nothing.

'Oh, for heaven's sake, Todd.' She called him.

It rang – two rings. Three. Her mind whirred as she waited. For the first time doubt wriggled. They'd had a stupid argument a couple of days ago, but . . . well, couples argued, it was healthy. He couldn't still be angry. Besides, she'd sent him all those cheery texts yesterday and this morning. This date had been arranged weeks ago and he knew she was looking forward to it. Him being late was just rude.

The call stopped ringing and went to answerphone. Odd. She hung up and tried again. This time he picked up.

'Alex.'

'You're late,' she said. 'What time are you going to get here?'

1

There was a beat of silence, then a muttered curse.

Alex rolled her eyes. 'Are you sulking because I thought you should meet my parents? You don't have to. We can leave it a few more weeks.'

'I can't do this anymore. You're too full on. I thought I made it clear.'

'What?'

'I'm breaking up with you. Stop calling me.'

A click and he was gone. Alex stared at the phone in her hand. Had he just dumped her? By phone? After standing her up?

She called him again. It cut off after one ring. Alex shivered.

Something wet landed on her cheek. And then on her phone. Sleet. Another cold splat and then another and another. The onslaught unleashed suddenly. Around her people ran for cover. Sod it. She ran into the lobby of the hotel where she'd arranged to meet Todd.

A blast of warm air greeted her. Oh. Bliss. She stretched her neck to let the warmth spread, but it wasn't enough to warm her.

The door to the bar, a few yards ahead of her, opened and music spilled out. She peered in. It was busy, but not heaving like most pubs were. She had suggested this place to Todd because it was more upmarket than the pub and more likely to be quiet. Crowds stressed her out. She retreated to the lobby.

She tried calling Todd again. It rang and then cut out.

The argument hadn't been so bad as to split up over. She'd tried to persuade him to meet her parents, he'd said it was too much pressure. He had stormed out. At no point had either of them mentioned splitting up. If he'd been feeling pressured, he should have just mentioned it.

Hmm. Maybe he had and she'd missed it. Todd was a chronic over-sharer on social media – even though she rarely paid attention to it. With a sigh, she opened Twitter and searched for his profile. Maybe he'd told strangers what he couldn't say to his actual girlfriend.

This account has blocked you.

What?

She tried Facebook. Instagram. He had blocked her on them all.

Her face burned. How was this possible? There must be some mistake. The first time Alex was ghosted, she was fourteen and she'd put it down to the boy being an insensitive dumbass. But Todd wasn't fourteen. He was a twenty-four-year-old graduate student, the same as her.

She navigated over to his best friend's page. If Todd wasn't with her, he was usually with his friends. Oh, there. They were all going out to ... London Bridge? Fingers trembling, she scrolled through some photos. There he was, in the background. She zoomed in. He had his arm around a girl! Todd had his head turned slightly and was laughing. The girl had her head on his shoulder.

Alex lowered her phone and exhaled slowly. Emotions boiled up inside her, but she wasn't sure which ones. Anger, for sure. Quite a lot of humiliation. And sadness. She had liked Todd. They'd been together for two months now and she had hoped ...

But she had clearly been wrong. Todd had dumped her and moved on effortlessly.

She put her phone in her pocket. What now? Her choices were – go home and drown her sorrows on her own or go into the bar and drown her sorrows in the company of strangers. Of the two, home was by far the most attractive. She looked at the weather outside again. Sleet splattered down. Okay. Going in was a viable option. She took a step backwards. And trod on someone.

'Ow.'

She turned around to find a man, standing on one leg, rotating the other foot, with a pained expression on his face.

'I'm so sorry,' she said. 'Is your foot okay?'

She glanced at him and registered details. Tall, light brown skin, smart casual clothes, neat.

He put his foot down, as though testing it. 'It's okay. I've got another one.' He smiled.

3

She added 'handsome' to her list of observations.

There was a pause as his gaze flicked from her face to her damp coat and back again. Given her past experience of lone men outside bars on New Year's Eve, he would hit on her any minute now. She braced herself.

Instead, he said, 'It's snowing?' He peered out of the glass in the door. 'Oh, sleet, that's worse. That looks nasty. I think I'll go back to the bar.' He gave her a friendly nod. 'See you later.'

She watched him walk down the foyer and disappear into the bar. Alex stared after him. While she hadn't particularly wanted the guy to try to flirt with her, it was a bit disconcerting that he hadn't. Here she was, dressed up on New Year's Eve and to get nothing more than polite disinterest from a handsome man was . . . disappointing. Was there something wrong with how she looked? Was that why Todd had so summarily dumped her?

More minutes went by. Alex told herself off. No. She couldn't let Todd's behaviour get her down. She couldn't stand here like a leftover doughnut, she had to move. If Todd could move on in the space of a couple of days, she bloody well could too. The voice of reality pointed out that she wasn't really that sort of person. Hah. Maybe, but tonight, she could be. Maybe tonight, she could be the sort of woman who could punch life in the face.

Alex gathered her strength. Fine. Into the bar it was. Maybe she could buy that poor man a drink to apologise for crushing his toes.

She checked in her coat at the cloakroom on the other end of the foyer, took a deep, fortifying breath and went in. The bar was busier than it looked from the outside; she had to weave her way through the crowd. The guy from earlier was standing alone at one of those tall tables, looking at his phone. She headed for the bar to get herself a glass of wine.

'Hello, darling,' said a male voice.

She turned to glance at the man who had spoken. He seemed young and very drunk. She ignored him. The anger fizzled out of her. Maybe she should have gone home to lick her wounds. Maybe coming into a bar on her own on New Year's Eve wasn't her smartest move. She was suddenly aware of how the neckline on this dress plunged. Normally, she wouldn't have worried about it, but right now, she felt vulnerable and very, very alone. She glanced out of the corner of her eye to check if the drunk man was still there. He was.

'Hey, don't be rude. I'm being nice here.' He came closer.

She continued to ignore him and tried to catch the server's eye.

'You know what would look good on you? A smile.'

'I'm here with my boyfriend,' she snapped, not turning. Maybe she didn't need a drink that badly. The crowd was pressing closer near the bar.

She felt a warm hand on her bum and pain as he grabbed and squeezed. 'Hey.' She spun to face him.

He grinned at her, holding his hands up. 'What?'

He had groped her, but it was her word against his and he could always claim he was jostled.

Anger and fear flared through her. To her horror, pressure built up behind her eyes. *Don't cry. Don't cry.*

'There you are,' said a different voice. 'I'm so sorry, I was tucked away over there and I didn't see you come in.' A light touch on her shoulder.

She turned to see the man from the foyer. One of his eyes twitched – a small hint of a wink.

'It's . . . fine,' she said. 'You're here now.'

'I've saved us a table,' he said. 'This way.' He moved back, one arm extended, so that he was a barrier between her and the guy who had harassed her.

The other guy had backed away. She gave him a death glare before she followed her new friend away from the bar.

'You okay?' he said, out of the corner of his mouth.

'Uh-huh.'

There was barely enough room for two to stand around the

5

table. He had left his pint and a pair of glasses on it to 'save' it. She stood between the table and the wall and leaned back. Her heart was still racing, but the threat of tears had subsided. She breathed out slowly. 'Thanks.'

He picked up his pint and leaned his elbows on the opposite side of the table, his back to the bar. 'Do tell me if that guy is coming up behind me with a blunt instrument, won't you?'

She peered behind him. 'No. You're safe.' She focused on him again. 'Seriously. Thank you.'

He shrugged. 'I have a sister.'

A bit random. She didn't know what to say to that.

'So, how come you're alone?' He frowned thoughtfully. 'Okay, that sounds creepy. I meant . . . are you waiting for someone to come join you? Do you want me to hang out with you until they show up? I'm not being creepy, I promise. I'll go away if you want me to.'

She smiled. 'That's a lot of questions. So . . . yes, I was waiting for someone to join me.' She checked her phone. 'But it appears that he's dumped me.'

'Ouch,' he said. 'I'm sorry about your date. He's clearly not good enough.'

'I mean, I didn't realise anything was wrong until a few minutes ago.' She pushed away from the nice, safe wall and joined him at the table. 'But he says it's over. He's blocked me on everything and is right now . . . out with some other girl so . . .'

'That sounds pretty conclusive. Dumped on New Year's Eve. That sucks.' He gave her a sympathetic smile. He had nice eyes. Dark brown and very clear. They were framed by unfairly long eyelashes.

'So, if you don't mind, a bit of company would be nice,' she said. 'I'm sure I owe you a drink for standing on your foot anyway.'

'Ah excellent. I was getting a bit bored drinking by myself, so I appreciate the company.'

'How come *you're* alone?'

6

'Ha. Good question.' He placed his pint down with exaggerated care. 'My family thinks I'm spending New Year with my girlfriend. My girlfriend . . . is no longer my girlfriend and she's spending New Year with her new partner.'

'So, you got dumped too. I'm so sorry.'

'Oh, don't be. We weren't together for that long. I don't think we were right for each other anyway.'

She studied him, trying to work out if he was putting on an act or if he really was fine. There was no way of telling. 'I need a drink,' she said.

He glanced over his shoulder. 'Given your last experience, do you want me to go to the bar for you?'

She looked at the crush near the bar. Mr Handsy and his group were still near too. 'Yes please.' She got some cash out and handed it to him. 'I'll have a double JD on ice, please. And could you buy yourself something as well?'

'You don't have to—'

'I would like to.' She looked up and caught his eye. He smiled and the sad and angry part of her responded to the warmth. 'So, please.'

His smile widened to a grin. 'I'll be right back.'

She waited, with her back against the wall again. His half-drunk pint was next to her. Marking her as 'reserved', she felt. She wasn't reserved for anyone though. She took her phone out and looked at the photo on Todd's friend's feed. Why had Todd done this? Why this way? Couldn't he have talked to her and tried to work it out? Even if they weren't meant to be, he could have been less brutal.

The anger that had fueled her entrance into the bar had ebbed away now. She turned over Todd's last few words in her mind. 'Too full on'? What did that even mean? Okay, maybe she'd been a bit hasty suggesting that he meet her parents, but she'd thought she and Todd were getting along really well. It seemed silly to wait for some arbitrary length of time. Clearly,

Todd had felt differently. Was she being unfair? *Was* she too hasty with relationships?

Speaking of hasty, she was in a bar she didn't know, hanging out with a man she didn't know. She glanced up at where her new friend was trying to get the attention of the bar staff. 'New friend'. She didn't even know his name. She sniffed. She'd known Todd's name. She had thought she knew him rather well. They'd been together for two months. Turned out, she didn't know him at all.

Picking up her phone, she started typing a text to a friend. Everyone was out doing something for New Year. If she got in touch, they'd have to stop what they were doing to talk to her. Or come and find her.

She deleted the text.

At the bar, her friend got served. He glanced over, caught her watching and smiled. She smiled back. He was attractive. And kind, as far as one could tell with first impressions. Alex looked back at her phone, thoughtfully. She knew the right way to do things. You met a guy, you liked each other, you spent some time together, grew closer and closer until you couldn't imagine a life without one another. But that wasn't how things worked out for her.

Perhaps she should go with the flow. Flirt with this stranger, with no expectation of a future relationship. Playing by the rules hadn't helped her. Maybe breaking a few rules would work better. Screw it all. Why not? At the very least, it would be fun.

Her friend walked over carrying two glasses of whiskey. 'Here we go,' he said and handed her one. He dug a meagre amount of change from his pocket and passed it across to her. Alex was glad he hadn't insisted on paying for drinks.

She raised the glass. 'Cheers.'

He left his tumbler untouched and picked up his pint again. 'Oh, I guess I should introduce myself. I'm—'

'No.' She held up her hand. 'Let's not. Right now, I have a small window where I don't have to think about explaining the whole humiliating story about being dumped to anyone. I want to just stay anonymous and talk to a stranger. So don't tell me your name. I don't want to know.'

He stared at her for a second, then shrugged. 'Okay, mysterious lady. Strangers it is.'

They clinked their glasses together.

She took a big sip. The whiskey warmed her, burning as it went down. Her hair, newly cut and coloured a mix of brown and deep red, brushed at her chin. She tucked it behind her ear. 'So, stranger, you didn't really explain why you were here all by yourself. Can't you go hang out with your family?'

He gave a small sigh. For the first time, his expression showed discomfort. 'I haven't told them yet. It's all a bit new and my dad and stepmum can be . . . a bit much. Family. You know how it is.'

She did. She would have to tell her parents about Todd breaking up with her. They would be sad on her behalf. She took another sip. Tomorrow. She would deal with it tomorrow.

'I'll tell them in a few weeks.' He looked up, the pain gone from his expression. 'I thought I'd come down and see the old year out. It seemed less lame than seeing it in while playing SyrenQuest.'

She must have looked confused because he clarified, 'It's a computer game.'

Ah. She nodded. 'I came in here because it was better than getting wet. Besides, I don't have anything exciting waiting for me at home, apart from quite a lot of leftover Christmas pudding.'

'Christmas pudding is always exciting.'

'No it's not. It's horrible stuff. No one ever eats it apart from on Christmas Day.'

'I love Christmas pudding!'

She wouldn't normally diss anyone's favourites, but right now, she was nameless and free. She could be whoever she wanted to be. 'It tastes like greasy raisins and disappointment.'

He made a shocked face. 'I can't believe you just said that!'

She laughed. 'What can I say? I'm a woman with strong tastes.'

They fell into an easy conversation. They finished one set of drinks and got another. They ended up on the same side of the table, leaning on it, their heads bent towards each other so that they could hear above the ambient noise. They talked about how she didn't seem to have any luck with guys, despite trying so hard. They discussed how it was weird that he wasn't more upset that his ex had met someone else, and perhaps that was because he hadn't been in love with her in the first place.

'I'm not sure what I think about love anymore.' She swirled her drink round the glass. 'Whenever I meet someone, I do my best to keep the love alive, but they always leave me.' She knocked back her drink and reached for the next one. This one was a diet cola. 'I mean, was there even a sign that Todd wasn't happy? He didn't say.'

At the back of her mind, a voice said that maybe he'd tried, but she'd been so keen to keep it alive, that she'd kept suggesting they go for dinner or on another date and see if things got better.

He nodded thoughtfully. 'The guy is clearly a fool. Worse, it sounds like he's a fool with no emotional vocabulary.'

She wasn't sure how to take that. The implication that her boyfriend was an immature idiot stung more than she'd expected. Why was she even thinking of Todd as her boyfriend? He clearly wasn't.

'What about you?' she said. 'You were with a girl that you didn't love. Don't you believe in love?'

'Oh, I believe in it,' he said. 'I know what real love looks like. That wasn't it.'

He told her about his parents and how well they loved each other and how his mother's death had destroyed his father and the whole family along with him. She told him about her own parents and how they had fallen in love at first sight and married three months later. Pulling out her phone, she showed him a photo of them, sitting together in their new garden. 'They took early retirement last year and moved to Cornwall. They're so happy. They're treating it almost like a second honeymoon.'

He leaned closer to look, bringing with him warmth and a faint smell of aftershave. 'They do look happy.'

'They are. And they're still in love.' She looked affectionately at the photo. 'Perhaps the way they complement each other so well has given me unrealistic expectations.' She gave a little laugh. She was only half joking. She believed in true love. Unfortunately, every man she'd been with had managed to disappoint her in some way. The only one who had managed to come close was Todd . . . and look how that turned out. 'Your parents mess you up, even though they never mean to.' Alex took another sip.

He was watching her, his eyes so dark in the dim light that they were almost black. 'Ain't that the truth,' he said.

When he smiled, lines appeared at the corners of his eyes, as though he smiled a lot and his skin knew exactly what to do. Everything about him lit up. It was mesmerising.

Somehow, as they talked, they'd moved closer, moving unself-consciously into each other's space. She felt . . . comfortable. Which was something she rarely felt in dating situations. Having spent so much of her 'normal' teenage years ill in hospital, she didn't really know the rules of dating. But this wasn't dating. This was something else.

She nudged him with her shoulder. 'Thanks for this,' she said. 'I started the evening feeling miserable and you've cheered me right up. I'm sorry if I unburdened myself on you too much.'

She expected him to smile and make a joke of it. Instead, he looked at her for a long moment, his expression serious. 'I think sometimes, it's easier to talk to a complete stranger. Someone who comes to you with no expectations. No judgement.'

'That's true. Especially if you're never going to see them again.' She met his gaze. It pulled her in towards him. They were already standing close together, but she had to fight the urge to move even closer. She tore her gaze away from his eyes only for her attention to move to his mouth. She swallowed.

11

Thankfully, a cheer distracted her. She looked at the crowd around them. 'Oh. The New Year countdown.'

He didn't say anything, but she felt his weight shift a little. Her brain finally caught up. The countdown. After which people traditionally kissed each other. Did she want to kiss him? Oh god, yes. She did.

Five . . . four . . . Her heart pounded louder with each number. Three . . . Her shoulder tingled with awareness where it pressed against his. Two . . . But what happened after that? Did she want it to be more than a New Year kiss? One. She turned to face him. And he kissed her.

It was a slow kiss, not deep enough to be presumptuous, but long enough for her to want more. When he drew back and whispered, 'Happy New Year', his face was still millimetres from hers. She closed the gap and kissed him back.

This kiss was different. Sensation rushed through her, lighting her up from head to toe. He slid his arms around her and pulled her closer until her body was pressed against his. His mouth was warm and soft against hers. The gentle pressure of his arm against her back made her feel safe and cocooned. She ran her fingers into his hair. His breath hitched and the kiss deepened. Everything else – the cheers, the fireworks outside, the lights going up – none of that mattered because she was lost in that kiss. It felt like something that was meant to be. Like she knew him on a whole different level. He kissed her like his life depended on it. No kiss had ever felt like that before.

When they drew apart, she stared at him, breathless, and felt like her chest was full of stars.

His eyes were wide and his lips were parted. He seemed to be just as struck as she was.

Reality filtered back in. Around them the party was changing tone. Breaking up. Her phone buzzed. A reminder.

'Oh,' she said. 'I pre-booked a taxi for half past.' She didn't remove her arms from around his neck. His hands were still a warm caress on her back.

'I live a couple of streets away,' he said. 'I guess I'm walking.'

There was another pause and for the first time it was awkward. Alex ducked her head. 'I . . . don't do one-night stands with strangers.' She didn't. She really didn't. Right now, she needed to remind herself of that.

He blinked. His arms loosened around her. 'Me either,' he said. 'Also, you broke up with someone only a few hours ago. Rebounds are never a good idea, right?'

'Right.' She fought the urge to pull herself closer again.

He took a small step back. 'I'll wait with you for your taxi.'

She moved her arms and suddenly didn't know what to do with them anymore. It was like they'd been removed from their rightful place. 'You don't have to do that.'

'I don't want you to have to wait alone.' He was fussing with his stuff, putting his glasses in his pocket, not making eye contact.

Alex sighed. 'I don't think I'd be able to resist kissing you again.'

It was only when his head shot up and he smiled his brilliant smile that she realised she'd said that out loud.

'I have no problem with that,' he said.

She laughed, half embarrassed, half delighted. 'No. But I really don't do one-night stands.' Her hair swung forward. She let it. All the better to hide whatever signals her face was giving out.

He reached out and gently tucked the strand of hair behind her ear. His fingertips left a trail of warmth where they brushed her skin. It was such an intimate gesture that she stopped breathing.

He stepped back and looked into her eyes. 'Who says it has to be anything more than kissing?' He put one hand over his heart. 'I promise I won't try to stop you from leaving. Or try to come with you.' He held his hand out to her. 'Okay?'

She took his hand with a little, self-conscious laugh. 'Okay.'

'Brilliant.' He pulled her close and kissed her again.

Sometime later, when she finally left him to get into her taxi, he leaned in at the door and said, 'Can I see you again? Later, I mean.'

'I don't know. I like . . . how we don't know each other.'

His face fell. 'Okay.'

'Bye.' It would be a shame to never see him again. Maybe she should . . .

The taxi started to move. Alex said, 'Stop. One second.'

The taxi driver tutted, but he stopped. She scratched around in her bag and found a pen and scrap of receipt, and scribbled her number on it, her handwriting skittering as she balanced the paper on her knee. When the car had stopped, her new friend had run up to it. She opened the door and thrust the piece of paper at him. 'Call me.'

He beamed at her. 'I will.' As the taxi drew away again, he pressed the piece of paper to his heart and blew her a kiss.

Alex flopped back into her seat in the taxi, her heart singing. Going out drinking alone and kissing a random stranger was not the sort of thing she did. It was the sort of thing that could have gone disastrously wrong. She'd been lucky. She smiled. Oh boy, was she glad she'd tried it. He was fun and interesting and kissed like a dream. Maybe Todd dumping her tonight was the best thing that could have happened. Maybe this was the beginning of the rest of her life.

Between alcohol and post-kissing delight, she fell asleep and only woke up when the taxi driver shouted, 'We're here, love' at her. She paid up and staggered up to her room.

*

The next morning, she woke up with an achy head and an even achier back from standing for too long. Having had back surgery as a teenager, she had to be careful. Sometimes, like last night, she just went with the flow and dealt with the aftermath. As she hobbled around, finding painkillers and gingerly doing her stretches, she thought about the man she'd met the night before.

He had been special. Her memories of him – his smile, his laughter, his kiss – were all seared into her mind. She had barely given Todd a second thought.

Her mysterious stranger was handsome and kind and chivalrous in a way that was thoughtful and not condescending. And he was an astonishingly good kisser. The memory sent a little shiver of delight through her. As far as she could tell, he was perfect. Her ideal man.

She wished she'd asked him his name. The whole anonymous stranger thing had felt like such a good idea at the time, but it was stupid to throw away something that special. Thank goodness she'd come to her senses and given him her number at the last minute. Now he could call her. This could be the beginning of her true love story.

She waited all day, snatching up the phone every time it rang, hoping to see an unknown number. He didn't call. Nor did he call the next day. Or the next. Or the one after that. Eventually, Alex had to admit to herself that he wasn't going to call. Her wonderful stranger wasn't all that wonderful. He was just as unreliable as any other man.

Chapter 2

Present day

Gihan finished hanging up his work clothes and shoved his empty suitcases under the bed. This room was tiny. He sank down onto the single bed and leaned on his elbows on his knees. It had been a turbulent few months. Leaving a job in the Middle East was always stressful. Thankfully, there wasn't much that he was attached to. He thought ruefully of Helen. At least they were still friends. She would meet someone else. Who knew, maybe she had already. It wasn't like she'd tell him if she had. He pulled out his phone and checked his messages.

He took a photo of the room – with its bare walls and the ratty old armchair in the space where his cousin Niro's work desk used to be. When Niro moved out, she'd taken that with her. She'd also taken down all the photos that used to be stuck up on the walls. Well, all but one. It was a photo of the three of them – Niro, Gihan and his sister, Sam, taken the last time he'd been there, six months ago.

'All moved in,' he typed. 'Looking forward to hanging out with Sam. Just like old times.' He sent it to the family WhatsApp group. Downstairs, he heard Sam's phone ping.

He genuinely was looking forward to spending more time with his sister. He'd missed her. He glanced out of the window where he could see clouds scurrying across the sky. It looked like rain. Unbelievably, he'd missed England so much that he'd even missed the weather.

Right on cue, Sam shouted up the stairs. 'Gihan Aiya. Do you want a cup of tea?'

'Yes please. I'll be right down.' He got back to his feet. This room would do for now. Hopefully finding a new place to rent wouldn't take too long. He could have used the relocation budget his new job had given him to rent a place temporarily, but why bother? This way, he got to be somewhere that actually felt like home. God knows he needed it after the shakeup he'd had.

Sam's place was fairly compact. He clattered downstairs and into the living room where Sam was pouring hot water into mugs. Her boyfriend, Luke, leaned against the work surface scrolling through his phone.

Since Sam's handbag insert business had taken off, she had started to look more grown up, even to him, her big brother. The older she got, the more she looked like their mother.

'All unpacked?' Sam asked, as she got the milk out.

'Pretty much. I didn't have much stuff.'

Luke looked up. 'What did you do with the rest of it? That can't be all you have.'

'That really is everything that I needed to bring back,' he said. 'I wasn't exactly settled out there. I'd only been there three years.'

Luke glanced at Sam as though to say, 'Three years is a long time'.

'The rest is in the attic at Thatha's house,' Sam said. It was funny that she called it Thatha's house and not home. They'd grown up in that house, but it had stopped feeling like home some time ago.

Luke seemed to be satisfied with this answer. He turned his attention back to his phone. 'Okay, so I've added my gaming

17

days to your calendar,' he said to Sam. 'And I've got your work events in mine.'

Sam moved around him and passed Gihan a mug of tea, before standing next to Luke, with her own phone, synchronising diaries.

It was all so impossibly domestic. Gihan smiled down at his tea. At least Sam didn't have any problem embracing this true love stuff. He was happy for her.

'I guess I'll leave you guys to finish settling in,' Luke said. 'What are you going to do this evening?'

Gihan and Sam exchanged a glance. 'Takeaway,' said Gihan. 'Probably wine.'

'Niro's coming round later,' said Sam.

'So, definitely wine, then.' Luke stuffed his phone into his pocket. 'When do you start work at the new job, Gihan?'

'Monday,' said Gihan.

'Are you nervous?'

He shrugged. 'A bit. But I'm sure it'll be fine. I'm looking forward to doing something different.' He had changed jobs before, but not in a hurry like this. This job was a move sideways for him. 'I'm hoping there will be less politics here than there was working on one big project for years.'

Luke nodded. 'Office politics is hard. Having employees is hard.' He looked wistfully into the distance. 'I miss the days when it was just me.' When Sam nudged him, he said, 'Still, onwards and upwards, eh?' He gave Sam a hug and a kiss. 'I'll see you tomorrow.' To Gihan he said, 'I'll see you later, mate,' and he left, with Sam trailing after to see him to the door.

Gihan sat down on the sofa and cradled his tea in both hands. Ah. This was nice. He liked Sam's place. It felt cosy in a way that his rented apartments never did. Mind you, he mainly used them as places to sleep. He'd barely used the place in Dubai, preferring to stay at Helen's whenever he could. Her place was closer to the bars they liked to go to and it was bigger than his. They'd maintained their separate addresses simply because they'd both held on to the fiction that their relationship was 'casual'. Until Helen didn't.

He took a sip of tea and picked up the remote control.

Sam returned and sat down next to him. 'So, what're you planning to do until food time?'

'I'm young, single and back in London. I can do whatever I want.'

She gave him an indulgent smile. Yes. She definitely looked more and more like Amma with every passing year.

'I'm going to start by watching some crap TV,' he said and turned the telly on. 'God, I've missed British daytime TV.'

Sam shook her head and laughed, but she didn't object. Sometimes, he supposed, even highly driven little sisters had to unwind.

*

Alex stifled a yawn as she poured the coffee. She hadn't slept last night. Her eyes stung and her back felt sore. She could really do without the Tuesday morning meeting today.

'Tired?' Leila, her friend and colleague, sidled up next to her. 'Late night, was it?'

Alex rolled her eyes. Leila wasn't even bothering with being subtle about digging for information. But then again, Leila had a tattoo that covered her shoulder and back and wore cherry-red Doc Martens with everything. Subtle wasn't her forte. Alex passed the coffee over to Leila and started pouring her own.

'Seriously.' Leila looked concerned now. 'What happened?'

Someone else came into the little office kitchen. Alex silenced Leila with a small shake of the head. She didn't need her personal life becoming office gossip before she'd even had time to process it. They walked down the corridor towards the main meeting room. Other colleagues passed them, heading to the coffee machine.

The smaller meeting room was empty. Leila pushed open

the door and pulled Alex into it. 'You have to tell me.' Her eyes darted as she took in Alex's expression. 'What happened? You look terrible.'

'We don't have time.' She didn't want to talk about last night's disastrous date.

'We do. We're early. We're always early.'

Someone knocked on the door. Alex's other technical assistant, Ray, poked his head in. 'What are you two doing?'

'Alex had date number three with bookshop guy last night, remember?'

Ray came in and shut the door.

Alex sighed. May as well get it over with. Rip it off like a plaster. 'He tried to choose my meal for me . . .'

Leila and Ray exchanged a glance. Ray sucked his teeth sympathetically.

'Oh, honey.' Leila put down her coffee and gave Alex a hug.

Ray, less tactile, said, 'That sucks. I'm sorry boss.'

Alex looked down at her coffee. 'Yeah. When I objected, he said I was too intense. He didn't see it working out.' She sighed. 'Just as well because I didn't see it working out either.'

Leila rubbed Alex's shoulder. 'Straight men are the worst.'

'Hey,' said Ray.

'Not you,' said Leila. 'You're okay. Probably.'

Alex said nothing for a moment and took a sip of coffee. Getting to date number three had felt like an achievement; she hadn't made it past two dates for ages. 'Too intense' came up quite a lot. Every time she went on a date, she got her hopes up and it was exhausting. 'I've had enough,' she said.

The other two stared at her.

'What do you mean?' said Leila.

'I keep being told that I'm too intense. I'm doing my best, but clearly something is off. I should probably listen to feedback, right?'

'I . . . don't think it works like that,' said Ray.

'You wouldn't know though,' said Leila. 'You married your first love.'

Ray shrugged. Despite being younger than Alex, Ray was married and they were expecting their first child. Leila had been with her girlfriend for years. They were both vicariously invested in the tragic wasteland that was Alex's love life.

'When you say listen to feedback, what do you mean?' said Leila cautiously.

'I'm too intense. I come on too strong. I'm trying too hard to find love. I don't know how else to be and this is clearly not working. I haven't been in a relationship since . . .' Since Todd. Five years ago, and that was only two months long. 'So . . . I give up. I'm going to stop looking for love. No more men.' Honesty compelled her to add, 'For a bit, at least.'

The other two considered for a moment, as though she had put a work proposal in front of them. Ray held up a finger. 'What if you meet someone wonderful unexpectedly?'

That would be great. 'How likely is that though?' said Alex.

Leila narrowed her eyes. 'What if you see New Year's Eve Guy again?'

Alex rolled her eyes. She really regretted telling them about New Year's Eve Guy and how he'd made her feel like she was full of light and stars. She should have kept him a precious secret. A private reminder of how someone could make you feel, even when you didn't know enough about them to find them again. 'I'm not going to see New Year's Eve Guy again,' she said, stiffly.

'Okay, but say you experience the same "spark" with someone.' Ray did air quotes with his fingers.

'We had better go to this meeting,' Alex said, firmly. She headed for the door before they objected. She wasn't going to see New Year's Eve Guy again, but maybe she could find that same spark with someone else. Eventually.

'Yes boss,' Leila said, and trailed behind her. 'We haven't given up discussing this though. Okay?'

21

Alex ignored her and marched into the main meeting room. The room was already filling up. Her usual seat had been taken. 'See,' Alex hissed to Leila. 'You made us late.'

There was a seat left at the end of the table, where you tended to draw attention from the CEO, when he was standing at the front. Still, sitting was more comfortable on her back than standing, so Alex took it. Ray and Leila stood behind her, leaning against the sill of the window that ran along the side of the room. The CEO's assistant came in and put three packets of biscuits on the table.

'Ooh, biscuits.' Leila leaned past Alex and snagged a packet. She peeled the pack open and took out a couple. 'Anyone else?'

When one of the guys sitting opposite waved, she slid the pack across to him.

'This doesn't bode well,' Ray said. 'We never have biscuits at these meetings.'

'They must be sweetening us up for bad news,' someone else said. There were a few worried nods around the room. The biscuit theory was a popular one.

'Or, we're celebrating,' Leila's voice was slightly muffled through biscuit.

'Supermarket own-brand, though,' Alex observed. The biscuit theory suggested that the quality of biscuits that the company provided directly reflected how well the finances were going. There was a beat of silence as everyone considered this.

'We must be really stuffed,' said one of the others.

Alex nodded. More people came in. Ryder Flow Tech only had about fifty employees. Not all of them came to these meetings, but there were still more people than there were seats. That's why Alex liked to come in early.

Isobel, one of the other senior scientists, walked past to take a spot leaning against the windowsill too. Both Isobel and Alex ran R&D projects developing new tests for the lateral-flow blood test kits that the company made. They weren't technically in competition, but they had to fight for the same resources, so sometimes it felt like it. Alex gave her a nod and said, 'Morning, Isobel.'

Isobel muttered, 'Morning' and avoided eye contact.

The hum of conversation around the room got louder as people chatted. There were still a few minutes to go before the meeting started.

'You know,' Leila leaned down to whisper to Alex, 'you can't really let that Todd guy being a shit get in the way of all your future relationships.'

Alex frowned.

'Do you think that's what she's doing?' Ray whispered, also leaning down.

'Guys,' Alex hissed. 'Now is not the time.'

It was one minute to nine o'clock. The door opened and the management team came in. The CEO, Daniel Harrington, stood at the head of the table and looked around at the group.

'Is everyone here?'

People shrugged and murmured. One of the team leads from engineering was missing. Someone was sent out to fetch him. Daniel stood at the head of the table, looking through his notes.

Alex exchanged glances with Leila. Daniel was normally an ebullient man – prone to blurting out management speak and trying to rally the room with bluster. If he was being quiet . . . something important was going on.

The missing engineer was found and the meeting finally started. Predictably, Daniel started with some waffling. Alex waited for the actual substance. Someone pointedly rustled a biscuit packet.

Daniel put down his notes and surveyed the room. 'I'll be straight with you,' he said, earnestly. 'I'm sure you've guessed. We're running out of money. We've had an ideation meeting with the investors and they've given us an ultimatum . . . The long and the short of it is that we've lost sight of the strategic roadmap and wandered into the thicket.'

Alex tried to translate that in her head. From where she was standing, she could see one of the interns scribbling something down. There was a running tally of Daniel's 'managementisms' that they added new ones to. The one about roadmaps and thickets was new.

'We've engaged some consultants,' Daniel continued. 'They're going to get us a helicopter view of everything and help us get laser focus on core deliverables. They'll be arriving later today. You'll each have a face-to-face with them. Please be honest and give them whatever help you can.'

Someone put their hand up. 'Does this mean some of us are going to lose our jobs?'

Daniel looked at his notes again. 'Not necessarily. There might be some realignment necessary to make sure we're all on the same direction of travel, but we won't know that until we see the report.'

That didn't answer the question. Alex glanced at Isobel and noted how her lips had set into a thin, hard line. Given that Isobel and Alex were in research and development, they were the ones most at risk.

'How long before we get their report back?' Alex asked.

Daniel hesitated for a moment. His gaze rested on Alex, switched to Isobel and back to Alex. 'It's difficult to concrete that. Obviously, there needs to be added time for the steering committee to run it round the block and see if the wheels stay on—'

Sally, the HR manager, leaned forward. 'We expect it to be a timeframe of weeks. Three to six weeks. If that changes, we'll let everyone know.' She gave them all an apologetic smile.

Daniel and the HR lady left first. As soon as the door shut behind them, noise erupted. Even through the confusing jargon, it was clear what Daniel had meant.

'Shit,' said the chief engineer. 'We really are stuffed.'

Alex had to agree.

Chapter 3

Gihan sat in the passenger seat and read the brief on the company iPad. His colleague, an older man called John, was driving the car the company had rented for them. He had met John for lunch before, by way of introduction. They would get to know each other much better over the next couple of weeks. Technically, Gihan was experienced enough to lead this project with a junior to help him, but he understood that the firm was testing him out first, by sending him out to assist an experienced colleague. He reminded himself that he should look upon this as a learning opportunity rather than an insult. He was new after all, and still on probation. Although, if there were too many more of these 'tests', he'd have to do something about it.

He skimmed through the description of what the client company made. Blood testing kits. One product near to market, testing for kidney disease. Thankfully, he didn't need to understand the technology in detail. He had been working on one large project for a logistics firm for several years now and it was nice to get back to working on something smaller. You could see the edges more clearly. The business was completely different. Human nature, on the other hand, was exactly the same.

'Is it just me,' he said, scrolling back to look at the introduction, 'or do they already know the answer to their own question?'

John shrugged. 'I think they do. My feeling is that they want someone else to come in and tell them what they already know, so that we're the guys bringing the bad news, not them.'

Gihan refrained from comment. He didn't like these sorts of projects, it usually meant someone at the company was going to lose their job. But then, that was the way it worked. His job was to evaluate everything objectively and come up with an answer, then dispassionately step away.

He could do that.

*

'Alex. A moment, if you will.' Daniel caught up with her as she was heading back upstairs to the lab with a fresh cup of coffee. 'Step into my office.'

The management offices were downstairs, as was all of the administration and the vast factory floor that was the domain of the engineering department. The research labs were upstairs.

The CEO had a corner office. It would have been impressive if it hadn't been looking out over the car park. A huge artwork of a wave adorned one wall. Daniel had been a keen surfer in his youth. It was hard to tell that from looking at him now, though.

'Please. Take a seat.'

Alex sat down. What was this about? Had they decided to make her redundant even before the management consultants got here?

Daniel smiled. 'No need to look so worried,' he said. 'I need to ask you a favour. That's all.'

She relaxed a fraction. 'Oh. Okay.'

'When the management consultants get here, I'm going to need someone to show them around the place and make sure they've got everything they need at their fingertips. I was hoping that could be you.'

Her first instinct was to agree, she was a helpful person after all, but her brain caught up with her before she said yes. 'Why me? Wouldn't someone from admin be better?'

'Oh yes. Ben from accounts will be dealing with most of that sort of thing. But you can be a help on the technical side.' He leaned forward. 'You're an intelligent woman,' he said. 'I'm sure you already know that your position is at higher risk than others.'

Alex stilled. 'I know that Isobel and I are the two R&D project leaders, which are non-essential to the core of the company, yes. Was there something more?'

Daniel gave a huge sigh. 'I shouldn't mention this, really, but . . . it's a zero-sum game.'

She stared at him. She was pretty sure she knew what he was getting at, but she was never certain because of his weird phrasing.

He sighed again. 'It will be a close-run thing between your project and Isobel's. If you can pull a rabbit out of the hat in the next two weeks, it would make it much easier to choose you.'

She narrowed her eyes. 'So you're saying that unless we get the sensitivity and precision to where we need it in the next two weeks, you'll choose Isobel's test over ours?'

'Essentially.' He looked down at his desk and straightened a piece of paper.

Alex sat very still, not knowing how to respond. She had known this to be the case, but to have it stated baldly like that was somehow horrifying. Her throat felt dry. She swallowed. 'Okay. I'll bear that in mind.'

She wasn't sure what she could *do* about it. It wasn't like she or her team could work any harder. Still, it focused the mind.

A frown flickered across Daniel's brow. 'This conversation is strictly off the record, of course. I don't mean to imply that I can influence the consultants in their decision either way.'

He turned to his computer. That was the most information she was going to get out of him.

Once outside in the corridor, Alex stared into space for a second. Why had Daniel even said that? Probably to see if he could wind her up to do even more work. She loved her project, but did she really want to work like this? Even if she and her project survived this cull, what happened the next time? Did she really want to be swinging from crisis to crisis?

She should probably have a look at polishing up her CV. She was young(ish) and single. Finding a new job would probably be okay for her, but what about her team? Leila and her partner were starting the long road to fertility treatment. Ray and his wife were expecting their first child. What would happen to them?

She was still thinking about it as she went up the stairs. Her team couldn't lose their jobs, not right now. There was nothing else she could do. She would be super nice to these consultants and make sure they saw her work in the best possible light. Whatever it took.

*

Alex was in the lab, transferring the results from her lab book into a spreadsheet, when the consultants turned up. At first, Ben from accounts showed them the lab from the outside. Alex ignored them until she'd finished what she was doing. Her handwriting was messy and she had to be careful to copy her numbers correctly. It wouldn't do to mix up a one and a seven because she was in a hurry. When she finally turned around, Ben was pointing out something at the far end of the lab.

There were two men in suits. The formality of their clothes made them stand out on the office floor. You rarely saw a suit around here. Even the management team wore fleeces and jumpers on a day-to-day basis. Suits were for serious meetings with external people.

The man next to Ben was square-shouldered, white-skinned and short, with salt and pepper grey hair. The one nearest her was taller, brown-skinned and had black hair that was cut short. As always, her brain flitted towards New Year's Eve Guy. Five years and she still thought every tall Asian guy she saw might be him. She gave herself a mental shake. *Get it together, Alex. Not actively looking for romance, remember.*

Ben, continuing to talk, pointed to her. The consultants turned around. The recognition registered so strongly that Alex's whole body twitched. *It was him.* It was him.

Rationality took over. It couldn't be. She must be imagining things. Her memories of him were hazy at best, it was very unlikely that she'd really recognise him, even if she did see him. She looked away and pretended to be focusing on her work. She'd been talking to Leila about him that morning, so obviously, her mind was primed to think about New Year's Eve Guy. This had to be a different man.

Ben knocked on the glass and beckoned for her to come over. She swallowed.

The labs were separated from the open plan office space by an anteroom – with lockers, sinks for handwashing and hooks for lab coats and other safety equipment. Alex threw her gloves in the bin and stepped into the anteroom. At the same moment, Ben arrived with the visitors.

Now she could see the consultant clearly. New Year's Eve Guy's face surfaced in her memory. This guy was a bit tidier, a bit older – understandable after five years – but it really looked like him. Her heart picked up pace.

'This is Alex, she's one of our R&D scientists. She heads up the early cancer biomarker test research.'

'Let me just wash my hands.' She used the few seconds while she washed her hands to compose herself. Professional face on.

'We have this anteroom to keep the wet areas apart from the office area,' Ben explained, behind her.

She took a deep breath and turned round. Ben introduced the first man as John. It took effort to focus on the older man. She shook hands with him. 'Nice to meet you, John.' Her eyes were screaming to move across to his colleague.

When she finally did look over, he smiled. That smile. Her pulse roared in her ears. She didn't hear what Ben said.

'I'm sorry, I didn't catch that,' she said. Her voice sounded strange and far away.

His hand closed over hers. 'Gihan Ranaweera,' he said and shook her hand. She knew that voice. There was no doubt it was him.

His expression flickered briefly, eyebrows twitching together, then went back to one of polite interest.

'Gihan,' she said. 'Hi. Er . . . I'm Alex.' She spotted Ben's confused expression. 'But, you already knew that.' She felt light-headed. This would never do. She had to pull herself together. Producing her most professional and polite smile, she said, 'It's nice to meet you both. If there's anything I can do to help you, just shout. I'm usually in the lab.' She gestured towards the door to the lab, feeling a bit like an air stewardess. 'Or, out at my desk.'

'Yes,' Ben jumped in. 'Alex has kindly agreed to be your contact for the R&D team.'

Alex tried to look helpful. She risked a glance at Gihan, who was nodding politely at what Ben was saying. There was still no recognition in his expression, only curiosity. Maybe she was wrong. Maybe it wasn't New Year's Eve Guy. Maybe this was someone who looked like him. She wished he would speak again. Or laugh that low laugh that she heard sometimes in her dreams.

'We'll be talking to everyone at some point,' said John. 'I look forward to catching up with you.'

Alex managed to hold her smile in place until the men left. She went back into the lab, closed the door and leaned against it.

Leila, Ray and a couple of others crowded round. Here, in the small space between the door and the main lab floor, was one of the few places where they couldn't easily be seen by anyone looking in from the office floor.

'What was that all about?' said Leila.

Alex breathed out, slowly. 'Er . . . just the consultants they told us about. They are going to be talking to some of us. Daniel asked me to help them with anything they need tech info wise. So Ben introduced us.' She couldn't tell them of the risk to their jobs. Not without having a go at saving them.

'Why did they ask you?' said one of the technicians from Isobel's team. 'Why not Isobel?'

A good question. Not wanting to stir up any more disquiet than there was already, Alex shrugged. 'I don't know. My desk is closest to the office they've been given. Maybe that's why.'

A few unconvinced nods.

'I think they're going to be introduced to Isobel next anyway.' Alex peeled herself away from the door and grabbed a fresh pair of gloves. 'We'd better get back to work. Look busy.'

At her bench, she sat on her special lab stool and stared at the screen. Her brain whirred. Was it him? If it was, he hadn't recognised her. Had he forgotten her? She raised a hand to her hair, but didn't touch it. Her hair was its natural black now. She'd met him in her red and brown phase. Also, she was in a lab coat with her hair tied back. It was possible he hadn't twigged. Or he was a different person.

'Aargh.' She leaned her forehead on the benchtop.

'You okay?' said Leila, peering at her from the other side of the bench divider.

'I think that's him.' Alex looked up.

'Who?'

'New Year's Eve Guy.'

'No way.' This was Ray. He rushed over to the window to look out. 'The younger one, right?'

Alex sat up, alarmed. 'Ray, get back here. God. They'll see you!'

'Sorry.' He came back and leaned on the end of the bench. 'What are you going to do?'

'First, are you sure?' said Leila.

'Not 100 per cent,' said Alex. 'I haven't heard him speak properly. That would help. But I'm almost sure.'

31

'Was there . . . a spark?' said Ray, a chuckle in his voice.

Alex really regretted telling them about New Year's Eve Guy one evening after too much wine. Even more than that, she regretted going on and on about this spark she'd felt with him. He obviously had felt nothing of the sort, since he hadn't even called her. She felt like such a loser now.

'Shut up, Ray.' Thank god for Leila.

'If it was him, he didn't recognise me. I have to pretend not to recognise him either, right?'

Leila patted her arm. 'I hate to break it to you, honey, but your hook-up might not have had the same impact on him as it did on you.'

'Not a hook-up,' she mumbled.

'Yeah. He's probably married with kids by now,' said Ray.

Leila continued to pat her arm. She was right. Alex had to get a grip. Be professional. Her job was at stake here.

'You're right. I . . .' Alex shook her head. 'Sorry. It threw me for a second seeing him—'

'Or someone that might be him,' Leila said.

'Or someone that might be him. It doesn't matter either way. I'm okay.' She sat up straight and gave her lab coat a sharp tug. If the usefulness of her job was being assessed, this was not the time to be seen sitting around moping. 'Right. Back to work.'

*

There was something familiar about the scientist they'd just met, but Gihan couldn't place where he might have seen her before. Alex. The name didn't ring any bells, but he had definitely met her before. It was like seeing an actor you knew from one thing in a completely different show with different hair and makeup. A feeling had swept over him the minute she smiled. It was something warm and familiar. He knew her, he was sure of it. He liked her. A lot. It nagged at him the whole time while he set up his laptop in the small office that he and John had been given.

His colleague, sitting at the table, tapped on the list of names and times that Ben had handed to them. He had already arranged meetings.

'Looks like we start in twenty minutes with . . . Isobel McLeesh. Senior scientist. R&D.'

Gihan forced himself to focus. He would figure out who the other woman reminded him of later. For now, he had a job to do. If past experience was anything to go by, he had to prove himself on this project before he was fully trusted to be competent. He pulled up the briefing notes and the company organogram. 'Okay. So she's on one of the expansion projects.' So was Alex, he recalled, but a different one. Those were two areas that they would have to look at very closely.

He sat down and tried to regain his professional composure. It would have been nice to have started with something that didn't involve real people's livelihoods being axed, but his job was his job and he was good at it.

He rested his temples on his fingertips and started to read.

*

Gihan was still typing up notes when Alex knocked on the door. He looked up to see her standing in the doorway.

'We're heading downstairs for lunch,' Alex said, addressing John. 'Would you like me to show you where the staff room is?' She paused and then added, hesitantly, 'You're welcome to join us.'

Gihan and John exchanged a glance. Eating lunch with the team was a mixed blessing. On the one hand, you got to observe the team dynamics. On the other hand, it was better to keep some distance, especially if you were going to recommend people being made redundant.

'Thanks for the offer, but we'll work through lunch.' Gihan stood up and gathered up the coffee mugs. 'But if you don't mind showing me the way to the kitchen, I think we could both do with a refill of coffee.'

She gave him a strange look, almost like she was annoyed, before she seemed to recover herself. 'Sure. I'll show you the way.'

He followed her across the open-plan office. People looked up and quickly looked away. It was awkward being the interloper, but he was used to this.

'It's quite out of the way here, isn't it?' he said, making conversation as they went downstairs. 'It feels like the countryside.'

'There's regular trains to London, so you can get there and back in a day,' she said, not looking at him.

'Ah, yes. John mentioned it. He said Oxford was the nearest big station but getting out of Oxford was a bugger.'

'Always,' she said. 'It's easier to go to one of the smaller stations and change at Didcot.'

Why was she so familiar? He knew her from somewhere. He got the impression it was somewhere cold, but he couldn't think where that would be. They carried on going down to the ground floor without speaking.

'So are you staying in Oxford?' Alex said, her tone neutral, like she didn't really want to know.

'No. Actually, we're staying in a village not far from here . . . in a pub.' He held the door open for her.

'Sawdon Green? I live there. It's nice,' she said. When she passed him, he got a trace of perfume. A memory stirred. Winter. Music in the background. A burst of pure joy. As quickly as it appeared, it vanished. The receptionist stopped her to say that someone was looking for her. Alex smiled, a proper smile, rather than the polite but distant ones she'd been giving him. It was a very nice smile. Cute. Also, familiar.

He held the next door open for her and it took everything he had not to try and recapture her scent again.

*

Alex's skin prickled with awareness. The kitchen was small. While Gihan got his coffees, she took her lunch out of the fridge. Now that she'd spoken to him, she was even more sure that he was the same guy. Clearly, though, he had no recollection of her. Why would he? He probably got off with strangers all the time. She was just a conquest to him.

'Can you pass the milk?'

She handed him the carton of milk. Up close, there was no doubt it was him. There was so much about him that was familiar. The creases around his eyes when he smiled. The way he smiled when he nodded. Even the way he stood.

She watched him pour some in and stir. Those long fingers. She remembered them against her face, the thumb caressing her cheekbone. When he handed the milk back to her, a quizzical expression flitted across his face. Oh god, she was staring.

'Sorry,' she said. 'I was miles away.'

He smiled politely. 'Well. Thank you for showing me where to get more caffeine.'

'You're welcome.' She made herself look busy searching for a fork in the cutlery drawer.

'For future reference, is there anywhere around here to get a sandwich? We've brought our own today, but . . .'

The company was in a science park in the middle of fields. The village was about twenty minutes' walk away. Although there were decent bus connections in the mornings and evenings, if you needed to pop out to anywhere quickly, you really needed a car.

'There's a sandwich van that comes round at about ten every morning,' Alex said. 'Someone usually announces it over the tannoy.'

'I'll make a note of that.' He raised the mugs in a salute. 'Thanks again. I'll see you later.'

Alex watched him leave and exhaled slowly. It had to be him. And he definitely didn't remember her at all. That was disappointing. Actually, no. It was insulting. She walked, still thinking, to the staff room on the opposite side of the corridor.

Ray and Leila were already sitting together, bickering about something, in the way that they did. She took the seat next to Leila. They both stopped talking to look at her.

'Did we see you go into the kitchen with that nice management consultant?' said Leila.

Alex nodded. 'I'm pretty sure it is him. Also, I'm pretty sure I mean nothing to him. Not a hint of recognition.'

Ray winced. 'Ouch. I'm sorry, boss.'

She had asked him many a time to stop calling her 'boss'. She was only about five years older than him. But, he had insisted – mainly because when they'd first started working together, he'd been twenty-two and at that age a twenty-six-year-old was impossibly grown up. Now that, two years later, he was married and about to become a dad, he seemed far more grown up than she did.

'So . . . what are you going to do?' Leila checked the folding on her wrap before she bit into it.

'I don't think I have any choice,' said Alex. 'I have to pretend it never happened and carry on as normal.'

'But what about this spark?' said Ray. 'You've been subconsciously sabotaging all your possible relationships because of it.'

'A – I have not been subconsciously sabotaging anything. All men are bastards or idiots,' said Alex. 'And B – even if what you said were true, which it's not, then it's time I broke the cycle and stopped.'

'Wait, that's not fair. I'm not a bastard or an idiot. I'm delightful.'

'Okay. All the men I attract are bastards, then.'

'Do you have data for that?' said Ray. 'How many men have you surveyed? What was your method?'

Alex looked at Leila. 'How much damage do you think I could do if I stab him with this fork?'

Leila laughed. 'Seriously, though,' she said. 'Moving on is good. Giving up on everyone completely . . . not so good.'

'That last person I had a proper relationship with was Todd and he was a prat. So what does that tell you?'

'Just because he dumped you—'

'He didn't just dump me though, did he?' said Alex. 'He dumped me on New Year's Eve. After standing me up. And then he moved on immediately.' Thinking about it still made her face heat up with a mixture of anger and shame. The worst bit was that he had tried to dump her before, but she hadn't even noticed!

'Ouch.'

'My love life has been a disaster ever since. So . . . you can see, there's a pattern there. It seemed the obvious conclusion to come to.' Even New Year's Eve Guy. He was just as bad as everyone else. The strength of her disappointment surprised her. She'd been angry when he didn't call, but now she realised that she'd been holding on to a small hope, a fantasy where he had lost her number or somehow been prevented from calling her. The fact that he didn't remember her at all squashed that idea. She felt small and stupid for hanging on to a dream for so long. There was no more hope. The fresh sense of loss felt like real grief.

One of the other scientists came and sat down in the empty seat at their table. 'Hello peeps. What's new? Have you been in to see the suits yet?'

They all shook their heads.

'I'm scheduled for this afternoon,' said Alex. All the more reason to get her head sorted out. She had to be on the ball when they spoke to her so that she could paint the project and the results they were achieving in the best possible light. The guy didn't remember her. It was probably a good thing. Imagine how awkward it would be if he did.

Chapter 4

Gihan worked it out in the middle of Alex's interview. She was talking about her work. He was doing the talking for this one and John was taking notes so that he could concentrate on what she was saying and the way she was saying it. With these interviews, people often said what they thought the consultants wanted to hear. He was used to that. He had to listen to how they said things and spot the gaps. It was an art to work out what was going on. So far, he gathered that Alex was passionate and, possibly, a perfectionist. She demanded a lot. It would be interesting to see what came out of the interviews with her team.

She was talking about the importance of detecting cancer early, leaning forward and using her hands to add emphasis to what she was saying. 'Normally, we wait until the patient has found a lump – which they might not find for ages . . . or they might try to ignore for a while before they contact the doctor. And if the cancer is an aggressive one, by the time they do get checked out, it's too late. Sometimes it's a matter of weeks.'

As always, the mere mention of cancer pulled at his memories. He forced himself to think about numbers instead. This was work. He glanced down at his notes. 'You mentioned that you were improving the accuracy of your tests.'

She turned her attention to him fully. The quick turn of her head dislodged a strand of hair from her ponytail. She didn't appear to notice. 'No. We're improving the *precision* of the tests. We have to have at least the same accuracy and sensitivity as the devices currently on the market. In the test tube, we can easily better it. But in the device, there's more variability. We are tweaking the formulations and we're very close. The level of accuracy is nearly where we need it to be. To get closer, we have to improve the precision.'

He blinked. The strand of hair curved towards her cheek as though pointing out her cheekbones. She had nice cheekbones.

She gave a tiny impatient sigh. 'If you think of a number of darts around a bullseye. Accuracy is how close they are to the bullseye—'

Oh. Right. Focus. 'And precision is how close they are to each other. Gotcha.'

Her eyebrows rose a fraction. 'Exactly that,' she said, as she tucked her hair behind her ear, her head making a curious little dip as she did so.

Recognition hit him all in one go. Of course. That's where he knew her from. Her hair had been a different colour then. She'd been wearing a dress and red lipstick. No wonder he hadn't recognised her. For a second, all other thoughts emptied from his head, crowded out by a hundred micro-memories of her in that one evening that seemed to last a lifetime. He looked down at his notes, frowning. What had he been doing? Then at his colleague, who gave him a curious glance.

Gihan cleared his throat and reached for his glass of water, all the while trying to work out where he was with his standard questions. Head back in the game. Back. In. The. Game.

He found his place again. 'And . . . er . . . how do you see your work fitting into the company's vision?'

'Cancer is a serious illness, especially when it isn't caught until late. Clearly, it's better to catch the cancer early and remove it or kill it with chemo than not find it until it's started to spread. Current tests have a very high false positive rate when cross referenced against a scan, which is obviously distressing for patients. My . . . I mean *our* test has a very low false positive rate in the lab. We're working on integrating it with the rest of the device to reduce errors there.' She spoke quickly, as though trying to get as much information out as possible.

'Tell me how your test is better than what's already out there.' He was getting back into his stride now.

So was she. Alex leaned forward as she described her testing method. She knew what she was talking about. Clearly, she knew about the market research, too, which was unusual.

'Our goal is to get to comparable accuracy with the competitor test. Our test is more sensitive, so it will detect the cancers even earlier. Which should make it the test of choice.'

He calmly waited for her to continue. Most people, when faced with a silence, would rush in to fill it. That was usually where the more interesting stuff came out. When faced with a void, you said more of what was at the top of your mind.

'It's important,' Alex said. 'In order for our test to be approved, it has to be at least as accurate as the test that's currently on the market.'

Gihan nodded. He knew that.

She pushed her hair back, tucking it behind her ear again. The action brought back another flash of memory. He forced himself to focus.

'I know that Isobel's work is nearer to the market competitor than ours is, but we just need a bit more time to get it to work properly when it's in the device.'

Bingo. In that one sentence she'd told him that she considered Isobel to be a rival, rather than a colleague. What was interesting was that Isobel had said almost the same thing. Both were good scientists, but neither felt like they had earned their place as part of the company's vision.

'Is there anything that you feel is stopping you from doing your job?'

She rolled her eyes. 'Meetings. So many meetings and they go on for so long.'

That wasn't new either. Just about everyone had mentioned that.

At the end of the interview, since he was the one leading the meeting, he had to see her out. He stood by the door and she passed him with only a polite nod. No flicker of any recognition beyond that. Perhaps she didn't remember him either. It had been a long time ago. It was only one evening, in which she had insisted that they stay anonymous.

He shut the door and hesitated. Now he remembered how he'd called the number she'd given him, heart hammering. How a man had answered. He had hung up then, because he didn't have a response to 'Who is this?' or even a name for the person he wanted to speak to. He had called twice more, only to have the same guy answer. She had clearly got back together with her boyfriend . . . assuming the whole story about being dumped was even true! No wonder she had wanted to be anonymous. His New Year's Eve Lady had clearly been out to have a good time. More fool him for thinking it was anything more than that. He had been more upset by this than he'd expected. Two years later, he'd been seconded to the Dubai office for a long-term project, met Helen and slowly forgotten about his random New Year's Eve Lady.

'So, what do we think so far?' John leaned back in his chair and steepled his fingers together.

Gihan dragged his attention back to the task at hand. He couldn't let John see that he was distracted. 'Well, as far as I can tell . . .' He pulled up his notes. 'The business is stretched beyond its resources. They're going to have to retract to the core technology and maybe one R&D project.' He tried not to wince as he said this. That meant that one of two projects had to go. Isobel's or Alex's. 'Or perhaps put R&D on ice completely for a couple of years.'

John nodded. 'That's the impression I'm getting too.'

'We can't really know for sure until we've spoken to the guys in engineering.' Gihan stretched his neck to the side. 'Man, I feel like I've been interviewing people forever.'

John checked his watch. 'It's a bit after four. I guess we should make a start on all the write-ups. We can do that at the B&B. Good with you?'

'Yes. That's fine.' He stretched out his wrists. 'Oh, just had a thought. They all mentioned the meetings cutting into the working day. As a quick win, we could suggest a bit of training on meetings – help them get the number and duration of their meetings back under control.' It wasn't strictly in the remit. 'It's an easy thing to do. It doesn't hurt to over-deliver.'

John studied him for a moment, then nodded. 'That's a good idea.'

'I'll write something up now and send it to the CEO.'

John stood up. 'I'm going to get one last coffee.'

'Oh god, yes. Please.'

Once John had gone, Gihan went back to his laptop. John seemed to have no problem remaining detached and impartial, almost to the point of being cold. Gihan himself tended to be friendly. People opened up to him because of it. It was a difficult line to tread to be approachable, but not have people think that they were friends. Normally, he had no problem maintaining this line. But lately . . . He sighed and wished he wasn't wearing contact lenses so that he could rub his eyes. That thing with Helen had messed up his equilibrium more than he'd realised. Not, he reminded himself hastily, that it was Helen's fault. Somehow, that made it all worse.

He would have to deal with that in due course, but right now, he had to focus on what he was doing. He had to impress John and prove that he was great at this job. The last thing he needed was to be unemployed as well as living in his little sister's spare room.

He opened a new email and drafted a message to the CEO, Daniel.

*

They were staying in the nearest village to the science park. The only available rooms were upstairs in the local pub. It wasn't ideal, but at least the wifi was good. Gihan had a single room, which was clean and warm. From the window he could see the road and the turning into the pub car park. He hoped it wouldn't be too noisy with punters coming and going. The area was so pretty it was almost surreal. He should go for a walk later and take some photos or something. He hadn't seen an olde worlde English cottage in ages and the village had at least two in it.

The pub had a surprisingly good restaurant, so half of the pub was given over to dining tables. The other side of the pub, the bit that you walked into when you came in, seemed to be more for the locals. Everything was soft and muted. It was atmospheric in a way the local near Sam's place, a chain pub, wasn't.

Gihan and John ate an early dinner and tried very hard not to talk about work. Since they barely knew each other, it made for a very awkward meal. Gihan wondered if he should mention that he'd had some sort of involvement with Alex before. Was it a conflict of interest? He genuinely wasn't sure. He had no real connection to her apart from a random snog five years ago. That was hardly worth mentioning. But ever since he'd realised who she was, she kept cropping up in his head. How was he supposed to dispassionately assess the viability of her work if that kept happening? So perhaps it was relevant.

What would he say though? There was no way to put it that didn't sound silly. It was only one encounter. It seemed so trivial. The only one who had seen significance in it was him. Silly, really. He debated with himself while he ate and was relieved when they finished the meal.

'Do you fancy a pint before we head up?' said John.

Ordinarily, he would have been tempted, but with the thoughts whizzing around his brain, he needed a bit of space to think. 'I was hoping to go for a walk around the village before it got dark and then get a bit more done before bed,' Gihan said, ruefully.

'Ah, that's a pity,' said John. 'But I suppose you're right.'

He looked genuinely sad about it, so Gihan said, 'But tomorrow we should.'

John brightened. 'Great. I probably won't get to do stuff like having a pint at last orders soon, so . . .'

'Oh? Why not?'

They both headed towards the stairs.

'We're expecting a baby soon.' He practically glowed with pride.

'Oh, nice. Congratulations,' said Gihan. 'When's the baby due?'

'In about six weeks. So . . . not long.'

'Wow. Is it . . . your first?' There was something in John's manner that suggested it was. Gihan had assumed he would have teenagers.

'Yes, it is,' John said. 'For both of us. My first wife and I didn't have children.'

Gihan didn't know what to say to that. 'That's exciting.'

'We're very excited. A bit daunted, but mostly excited.' John beamed. 'My wife's starting maternity leave in a couple of weeks. I'm going to work right up until the birth obviously, and then take some time off.'

They reached the landing. 'I guess I'll see you in the morning,' said Gihan and pulled the key to his room out of his pocket.

As he was unlocking the door, John said, 'Gihan. Can I ask? Earlier today, when we were talking to that scientist – Alex – something seemed to be bothering you? Has something piqued your professional instincts? Something about the company or the research that we've overlooked maybe?' His tone was friendly and curious, but Gihan recognised where the question had come from. John had noticed his moment of distraction in the meeting with Alex.

Gihan's conscience poked him. Oh dammit. 'Ah that. It's nothing really.'

John paused, the door to his room open. 'Yes?'

'The scientist, Alex. I know her. Well, I knew her . . . a long time ago. It's not a problem. It was in the meeting that it clicked as to where I knew her from, that's all.'

'Knew her? How?'

He rubbed the back of his head. 'Bit embarrassing really. Sort of had a date.' A date sounded better than 'met in a bar and ended up snogging furiously without ever finding out her name'.

John frowned. 'Are you seeing her now?'

'No.'

'Did you break up acrimoniously – like she could think you had a grudge?'

'Nope. In fact, we never even went out at all. It was just . . . an almost thing. Five years ago. I'm only mentioning it for the sake of transparency.' She was even less likely to mention it than he was, anyway.

John gave him a shrewd look. 'You're mentioning it because I asked,' he said. 'Will you be able to maintain your professional detachment?'

'Oh absolutely. I was a little surprised when I recognised her, but that's all it was. It's not relevant at all. Which is why I didn't say anything earlier.'

John's expression was neutral. Maybe he didn't believe it. Gihan bit back the urge to say anything more. It would only make things look worse.

'Well,' said John. 'Let me know if it becomes an issue.'

'I will.' Gihan pushed his own door open. 'I'm going to go for that walk. Get a bit of fresh air and stretch my legs.'

'Good idea. I'm off to call my wife. See how she's doing.'

'Oh yeah. I hope everything's okay.'

Gihan took out his phone and checked his messages. One message from Sam, reminding him that he was going to dinner at their father's house at the weekend. One from the estate agent. Another from a friend, wishing him luck in his new job. He would deal with those later.

After a quick detour to his room to grab his coat, Gihan stepped out in the evening air. It wasn't that far from London out here, but it felt like he was in a different decade. The pub faced a small green with a pond in it. The main road split into two around the green, giving him a choice of two paths. He picked one at random. If he stuck to this road and didn't take any turnings, he would be able to find his way back, even with his rubbish sense of direction. He patted his phone to check it was there. If all else failed, he could rely on Google Maps.

*

Alex finished her supper and loaded her plate and the one pan she'd used into the dishwasher.

Jake, her housemate and landlord, wandered in with a couple of takeaway containers full of food. He owned a private gym. Normally he wandered around in shorts and the official gym T-shirt, but he was currently in his running gear – a vest that showed off his muscles and running shorts. Leila, who used to live in the room Alex had now, had introduced them to each other, because Jake had a spare room. Alex had been a little intimidated by him when she'd first moved in, but now she knew he was a big softie under all that muscle.

'You've eaten already?' he asked.

'Yes, why?' Alex shut the dishwasher and wiped down the kitchen surface with a damp cloth. She always washed and tidied up after herself. Jake did too. Which meant that the cheerfully decorated kitchen was always pleasingly tidy. Jake had decorated most of the house in very dull shades of beige, black and grey. But he had let Leila decorate the kitchen. It was a warm yellow with cream cupboards and wooden surfaces. After her bedroom, this was Alex's favourite room in the house.

'Mal's got a couple of new low-carb meals for us to try out and give feedback on,' Jake said. 'He's coming round later.'

'Aw. I'll take one for lunch and email him notes tomorrow.'

'Sound.' Jake shut the fridge door. 'Would you have time later to go through my investor presentation with me? I've cut it down to fit the ten-minute slot, but I need to check it still works.'

In the time she'd been here, she'd seen Jake expand his gym business from one gym to two and had sat at the dinner table while Jake and his best friend Mal hashed out the business plan to double it again.

'Sure. I'm around this evening.'

'Great.' He secured his phone to his bulky forearm and slipped his ear buds in. 'Right, mate. I'm going for a run.'

'And I am going to go walk Penelope. So take a key with you.'

Jake waved his water bottle at her and set off. A few minutes later, Alex followed him out. Having locked the front door, she walked out the gate and then down next door's path. The door opened almost before she'd finished knocking.

'Hello duck,' said Maureen, leaning on her walking stick. 'She's been waiting for you.' A little yip from behind her told Alex that Penelope was indeed waiting. Maureen unhooked the lead from a coat peg and passed it to Alex before shuffling carefully out of the way. 'Go on then, Penelope. Walkies.'

Penelope, a small, white-haired Maltese who was getting quite old herself, came out, wagging her tail so hard that her entire backend was moving.

Alex knelt to clip the lead onto Penelope's collar. 'How are you getting on, Maureen?'

'Not bad, really. Every day is much the same as the other, you know. How about you?'

'We've got management consultants come in at work. They're trying to make the company more productive.'

Maureen made a face. 'That sounds like bad news. Whenever I've heard "productivity" mentioned, that usually means someone's going to lose their job.' Before she retired, Maureen had worked in HR for a large department store.

Alex gave Penelope an extra pat and stood up. 'That's what I'm worried about.'

'You've been there for a good long while now, though,' said Maureen. 'I'm sure you'll be fine.'

'A little over four years now,' said Alex. 'I suppose that should count for something.' Penelope pulled on the lead, so Alex waved to Maureen and set off for their walk. Maureen's comment replayed itself over and over in her mind. Although her natural instinct was to hope for the best, it was hard to avoid worrying about her job. Her work was part of the company's pipeline, but if they didn't get the main product off the ground, there would be no pipeline. So if they had to prioritise, her work would be the first to go. She corrected herself. Hers or Isobel's.

When she had taken the job four years ago, she had based her interview presentation on the breast cancer test she was working on now. She'd had visions of seeing her work out on the shelves in pharmacies. These days she had a better idea of how much time, effort and money it took to get something from idea to product. Especially medical products. It would be years and a lot of money before her early cancer diagnosis test reached the market. Ryder FT didn't have that kind of money right now.

She hated the idea of all her hard work being mothballed, but the idea of dusting off her CV was a good one.

The walk took her out of the village and through a small wood. Penelope rushed ahead, sniffing the hedges and puddles. Alex was still deep in thought when someone said, 'Excuse me.'

She didn't need to look up to know who it was. The voice had been living in her head rent free for years.

Gihan was standing at the edge of the woodland, taking his earphones out of his ears. 'It's Alex, isn't it?' He waved his phone. 'I'm afraid I'm a bit lost and I can't get my Maps to update . . .'

Penelope went up to sniff him and he leaned down to pat her. 'What's his name?' he said, looking up.

Be cool. Be cool. 'Penelope. *She* is called Penelope.'

Gihan knelt and scratched behind Penelope's ear. The little

dog was delighted and rolled over to have her tummy rubbed. He obliged, making little 'good doggy' noises.

'She's not mine,' Alex blurted out. 'I walk her for my neighbour.' Walking Penelope had come as part of the agreement when she rented the room from Jake. Jake had started walking Penelope when it became too difficult for Maureen, but it turned out he couldn't do both morning and evening. So Alex did the evening walk. When she couldn't, Jake got Mal to do it.

Gihan stood back up. 'That's very kind of you.'

There was an awkward silence for a minute. She pulled herself together. This guy should mean as little to her as she did to him. She had to be civil and helpful to him because he had the ability to shut down her work. That was all there was to it. 'Oh. So, directions . . . Where were you heading?'

'Back to the pub.'

She looked behind her and decided it would actually be quicker for him to go on rather than back the way she'd just come. She pointed ahead. 'You keep going that way until—'

He shifted, looked uncomfortable.

'Actually. If you're heading back to the village, would you mind if I joined you? I have a terrible sense of direction.'

'It's a small village. You can't really get lost around here. You can see the church from pretty much everywhere.'

'You clearly don't know me very well. I can get lost anywhere.'

That was true. She barely knew him at all. Their past meeting was barely a blip on the radar. Right now, she had to be helpful. 'Sure. Penelope needs her run around, but you're welcome to tag along.' She might be able to get some information out of him about what was going on at Ryder FT. Or at least put in a good word for her project. Maybe make him see how important it was that her test went on the market. It could save countless lives.

She pointed towards the woodland and indicated that they should carry on walking. Penelope was happy to be off again. 'I thought men were all supposed to have a great sense of direction.'

'I thought so too,' said Gihan. 'But then I kept getting lost and I had to accept the sad truth.'

That made her smile. His sense of humour was one of the things she'd noticed when she'd met him before.

'So . . .' she said, cautiously. 'How are you getting on with your assessment?'

He gave a rueful click of his tongue. 'I can't really talk to you about that,' he said. 'Confidentiality and professionalism and all that . . . sorry.'

'Oh. Of course.'

'But thanks for asking. Everyone has been really helpful, which is nice.' So polite and distant. He must not remember her at all.

'That's good.' She nodded. They walked along a bit more, entered the woodland and followed the tree-shaded path. The silence between them was awkward. She wished she hadn't agreed to let him join them. It was hard not to look at him. At least once, when she glanced at him, he was looking at her, which made it all even weirder. It was almost a relief when Penelope hunkered down to relieve herself.

Alex busied herself getting out the plastic bag and doing what was necessary. Gihan checked his phone while he waited for her a few yards up the path. They resumed walking, only now there was an awkward silence and she was carrying a bag of warm dog poo. Great.

There was a bin at the other side of the woodland. Alex disposed of the little bag and opened the gate that led into the next field.

'I usually let Penelope off the lead for a bit here,' she said, more to break the silence than anything else. 'It's fairly secure. She doesn't often run off.' That wasn't strictly true, but Penelope never ran far.

He was looking at his phone again. 'I'm trying to work out which direction the church is. I can't see it from here.'

'That way.' She pointed back towards the village.

He tilted his head. 'Oh. Yeah. I think I get it.'

'Do you really not know where you are?' The village was so small, it seemed impossible to her that he could be confused.

He shrugged. 'It's like a weird mental block. Used to be a real pain when I was playing computer games that involved maps and landscapes. I used to have to leave myself little road signs all the time. Then my brother and sister would nick them or turn them around and I'd get lost all over again.'

She laughed, despite herself.

He put his phone away, smiling. 'Siblings are such a pain.'

She remembered him saying 'I have a sister' with a protective older brother edge to his voice. 'You've got a sister, right?'

Oh shit. Should she admit to knowing that? He didn't remember her, so she should pretend not to remember him either. He'd mentioned a brother and a sister a few seconds ago. Okay, phew.

He nodded. 'And an older brother. You?'

She knew he was making conversation to be polite. He genuinely didn't remember her, so he was treating her like someone he'd met for the first time. They walked along the top of the field.

'No siblings,' she said. 'Just me.'

'Was that lonely?'

'I'm good with my own company.'

He gave a little chuckle. 'Sometimes I think I do a job where I have to spend so many nights away, alone in hotel rooms, because I never got any time to myself when I was young.'

'What do you do of an evening?' She considered her own question. 'Is that a safe question to ask? Don't answer if it's not.'

This time he laughed out loud. It was a glorious sound that made her smile too. 'I wish!' he said. 'I mainly just work. Or, if I'm really tired, play SyrenQuest online.'

'Computer game, right?' She remembered.

The laughter dimmed and he gave her a thoughtful look. 'Right.'

Was it weird that she knew that? Surely not. It was a well-known

51

game. There had been some buzz about it in the newspapers a couple of years ago.

They reached the gate at the other end of the field. Alex called for Penelope, who came up with a stick in her mouth. The little dog looked up at her hopefully. Alex sighed. 'Fine. Come on then.'

She took the stick off Penelope and threw it for her.

As she stood watching Penelope, Alex was hyper aware of Gihan standing next to her. She had spent years being angry about the way he'd treated her. Now, here he was, acting as though none of that had happened. It was humiliating. What made it worse was that, even though she knew she should leave it alone and walk away from it all, another side of her wanted to bring it up. To confront him.

All the men she'd ever been attracted to had been pathetic. She had thought he was different. No, she had *hoped* that he was different, because she'd liked him so much.

Penelope brought the stick back. She took it off her and threw it again, with a little more force than necessary. The silence was becoming excruciating.

Clearly, he thought so too, so he said, 'Have you been living in this village long? It seems very idyllic.'

'About four years,' she said. 'I moved here when I started work at Ryder.'

He nodded.

'How about you?' she said, in what she hoped was a conversational tone. 'How long have you been . . .' *Don't say hatchet man. Don't say hatchet man.* 'A management consultant?'

'Years,' he said. 'It feels like forever. But I've only been in this job a few days.'

'Oh? Where were you before that?'

'Middle East. I worked in-house for a big logistics firm.'

'Must have been a bit of a shock – coming back, I mean?'

He tipped his head to the side. 'It was, I suppose. But not in a bad way.' His eyes met hers briefly. 'Not all shocks to the system are bad.' He looked away again.

What was that supposed to mean?

Penelope returned with the stick again. Alex crouched to retrieve it. The little dog refused to let it go. 'Penelope, let go. I can't throw it for you, if you don't let me have it back.' In response, Penelope trotted off, stick still in her mouth. Alex shook her head and followed.

'Penelope has you very well trained,' Gihan observed, following her.

'She has us all very well trained,' Alex muttered. This wasn't the first time that the dog had done this. Alex knew exactly where she was going. Penelope disappeared into a thicket of something with dark leaves. 'Penelope, come back here. Now.' The little dog didn't reappear. Alex spotted the gap she'd gone through and squeezed in herself. Inside the thicket was a small hollow. The leaves filtered out the evening light, leaving it dark. Penelope sat in the middle, a ghostly white in the gloom, wagging her tail. 'You little tyke.' Alex crouched to attach the lead back onto the little dog's collar. 'Come on you, it's time to get back to Maureen.'

She stood up and turned to find Gihan right behind her. Surprise made her lose her balance and clutch at something. That something was his arm. He steadied her with his other hand on her elbow. There wasn't much room in there, so he had to hunch down a little, which all had the effect of bringing his face very close to hers. For a moment, the world froze. All she could think about was the last time she'd been that close to him. His mouth was close enough to kiss and she remembered exactly what that felt like. Her pulse rose and filled the hollow. Her skin tingled, as though there were sparks dancing on it.

Penelope tugged the lead. They both moved back.

'Sorry.' Gihan stepped back. 'Ow.' He twisted. 'I . . . think I should back out first.' He did, crouching and moving backwards.

Alex took the few seconds of being alone with Penelope to get her breath back. What was her body playing at? She knew he wasn't good for her. He had taken her number and never called.

She was angry with him. Angry. Except, a few seconds ago, with heat radiating off her face, and her pulse still galloping, she hadn't felt angry. She'd just wanted to kiss him.

She told herself sternly to get a grip and followed Penelope out.

'Why on earth did you follow me in there?' she demanded, as soon as she was out.

Gihan picked a dead leaf out of his hair, which mussed it up. 'I didn't know there was a hollow there. I thought it was more path. You're my guide home.'

'But she likes running in there to hide. It's one of her games.'

'I didn't know that, did I?' He sounded annoyed too.

That was a fair point, but she wasn't in the mood to concede it. She really needed to get away from him. Much as she would like to storm off, leaving him in the woods, she had to keep being nice to him, so that he thought twice about axing her job. Charming him, even. She let out a breath.

'Let's . . . Shall we head back?'

'Good idea.'

It was getting darker now. Soon they wouldn't be able to see where they were going without a torch. Time to get back to the roads with streetlights. She said, 'Now we walk round the back of the houses until we loop round the village and back to the pub. Okay?'

Gihan nodded, solemnly. 'I am entirely in your hands.'

She tried not to think about what that could mean. She certainly remembered the feeling of his hair underneath her fingertips. They walked along in silence for a bit. The route meant that they had to walk a little way on a pavement that ran alongside a road. There was no sound but the swish and hum of cars going by.

She glanced sideways at him. He was walking along, with his hands in his pockets, looking thoughtful. She checked in with her gut, which was full of butterflies. She was definitely still attracted to him. Dammit. Treacherous body. That was so inconvenient.

54

She was still clinging to the memory of their connection, when clearly, he had forgotten all about it.

Gihan cleared his throat, making her jump.

'So, er . . . do you like it here?' he said. 'It's quite a way from Cornwall and your friends in London. Don't you miss London?'

Grateful to talk about something else, she said, 'A bit. Although, my memories of London are all student memories, so maybe I miss being a student.'

He nodded. 'I can see how that would confuse things, yes.'

The road they were walking along entered the village. Streetlights made pools of clarity in the gathering gloom. High hedgerows gave way to front gardens. Gihan looked around, peering down the road.

Amused, Alex asked, 'Don't tell me you don't know where you are.'

He frowned and had another look around. 'I can't see the church,' he said, reproachfully.

This surprised her. She turned to look around. Surely, there was enough light to see the church spire against the sky . . . but no. He was right. Where they were right now, you could not see the church. She walked forward a few yards and pointed between the houses. 'There.'

'I wouldn't have known where to look,' he said. 'But I suppose I would have known that I was in the right village.' He pointed to the back of the 'Welcome to Sawdon Green' street sign they'd passed.

They walked a little further into the village. Now she could see the green ahead. 'My place is down here.' She pointed. 'And the pub is a little way beyond that.'

'Assuming that's the green that's in front of the pub,' he said, 'I can find the way from here.'

They walked the rest of the way, chatting about the village and how it was a strange mix of thatched cottages and modern houses, as most villages in the Cotswolds were.

'It's nice that you can go for a walk and find a field,' he said. He swung his arms. 'It really has made me feel better.'

'That's good.'

He looked at her from under hooded lids. 'Thank you for letting me join you and Penelope,' he said. 'I hope I didn't inconvenience you too much.'

'Not at all. Penelope likes you.'

'And I like Penelope,' he said, giving the dog a pat. 'I guess I'll see you around. At work, tomorrow.'

'Yes. Bye.' She turned into Maureen's garden. He walked away towards the pub. Jake, back from his run, jogged past Gihan going in the opposite direction. He stopped to pat Penelope.

'Hey, Lady Penelope. Been for your walk with Alex?' Penelope was delighted to see him and wagged her tail into a frenzy, prompting Jake to hunker down and pet her, saying, 'Who's a good girl, then? Who's a good girl?' in the special voice he reserved for talking to Penelope.

Alex watched with amusement. Jake looked like a musclehead, but he was one of the most caring people she'd ever met. When he'd interviewed her about renting the room in his house, he had mentioned Penelope. That was one of the things that had persuaded Alex to take up the room. This big man, who was kind enough to do the shopping and walk the dog for his elderly neighbour, would be a good person to live with.

Jake straightened up and tilted his head to one side. 'Oh. What happened to you?'

'What? What about me? Nothing's happened to me.' Her mind flashed back to standing in the hollow, looking into Gihan's face. A telltale heat started creeping up her face.

'You look . . . a little wide-eyed and excited, my friend.' He reached up and tapped a finger on her cheek. 'And if I'm not mistaken, you're blushing . . .' He looked over his shoulder. 'That guy I passed a minute ago. Is there something you want to tell me about?'

She gaped at him. How could he possibly tell what was going on in her head? Were her thoughts that obvious?

Jake grinned and waggled his eyebrows. Wait. It wasn't obvious. He hadn't deduced anything from looking at her. He already knew. That could only mean one thing.

'Leila. Leila called you.' Of course, Leila would want to share gossip with Jake. 'I'm going to kill her.'

'Aw, come on. It's exciting news. You have to tell Uncle Jake all about it.' He patted her shoulder. 'I'll see you inside.' Still grinning, he carried on jogging down the path to the house. When Alex looked up the lane once more, Gihan had gone.

*

Gihan sat on the bed at the B&B and hit send on another email requesting to be shown round a rental property next week. He lifted his glasses and rubbed his eyes. Looking at properties to rent was more depressing than he'd anticipated. He was too old now to want to house share like he'd done before. Which meant that he couldn't live in central London or even anywhere near it. He was going to end up in the suburbs. His younger self would have been horrified by that, but having hung out at Sam's flat, which was in the suburbs and very nice, he was less bothered by it now. Thankfully, he had more money now than his younger self.

He yawned and closed his laptop. It was late and he had to be up early tomorrow. Even though the window to his room was closed, he could hear voices from the pub downstairs. This assignment was a million miles away from the work he was used to. Accommodation on work trips at his old firm involved a hotel that had a decent gym downstairs. He could have gone down and worked out, instead of going for a walk after dinner.

But he'd genuinely enjoyed walking outside, even with the chill and the darkness. He'd missed all of that. Living in the Middle East it was warm and dry and, if you left it until the evening, pleasant to walk by the sea or in a park. Yet he'd missed the dark and the chill and the damp, dripping woodland. It made no sense at all.

He realised that he had half hoped that he'd run into Alex, which was next level self-sabotage. He tapped the lid of the laptop, thoughtfully. He had thought about her a lot in the weeks after they'd met. There had been something there. An unexpected connection between them. Something that felt strong and . . . right. But she'd got back together with her ex after she left in the taxi.

What would have happened if she had picked up the call instead? Maybe they would have seen each other again. Maybe gone out for a bit. Would he have still taken the secondment in the Middle East? Would the relationship have lasted? When it came to the crunch, wouldn't he just have screwed it up like he did with Helen?

He sighed, put his laptop down on the floor by the bed and got under the covers. Working right up to the minute he fell asleep was a bad habit. Helen had always told him off for it. Pulling the chintzy duvet up to his shoulders, he turned off the light. He missed Helen. Not as his girlfriend particularly, but in a more vague sense. She had been his friend first. They'd drifted into their relationship by accident, and kept things as casual as they could, which had suited them both fine at the time. Until the week before Helen's thirtieth birthday.

She had suggested dinner in one of her favourite restaurants. The food had been great and he'd had too much wine. He remembered sitting across from her thinking that the soft lighting and candles made her glow. They'd just finished their main meal. The waiter cleared away their plates.

Helen sat up a tiny bit straighter. She always did that when she was about to say something important, so Gihan paid attention. He was organising a party for her birthday. It wasn't a secret exactly, but there were things that would be a surprise to her.

'Gihan,' Helen reached a hand across the table to him.

He smiled fondly at her. 'Helen.' He curled his fingers around her hand. There were many things that he and Helen had in common. Their sense of humour, the feeling of being far from home, the fact that neither of them wanted a committed relationship. He was really lucky to have found her.

'We've been together for a few years now . . .' she said.

'Well,' he said. 'Sort of together.'

She raised her eyes heavenward in a gesture of affectionate exasperation. 'Come on now,' she said. 'I know we like to tell ourselves it's casual, but . . . I haven't seen anyone else for . . . well, not since I met you, really. Have you?'

He hadn't either. He shook his head, smiling. 'We're busy people, right?'

She gave a soft laugh. 'We are, that's true.' She held his gaze for a moment, then nodded, as though she'd come to a conclusion. She let go of his hand.

'One second.' She dug into her handbag and produced something.

Okay. This was strange. Some of the warmth from the wine drained away. 'Helen? What's going on?'

She took out a small jewellery box. 'Gihan,' she said, solemnly. 'I like you. A lot. I'm going to be thirty soon and I need to . . . think about my future. With that in mind . . .' She opened the box. 'Will you marry me?'

He stared at the two rings in the box. One thin with a baguette cut diamond on it and one plain band. His vision darkened at the edges. Helen's voice sounded muffled and far away. He tried to look away, but the rings had his gaze trapped. He couldn't breathe. Couldn't breathe.

'Gihan?'

He should look at her, but he couldn't move. There wasn't enough air. He had to focus on pulling in a shuddering breath.

'I see.' She snapped the ring box shut and stood up. 'I should have guessed.' She stood up, grabbed her coat and left.

He tried to say 'Helen, wait', but his throat had closed up. He didn't know what he would have said to her anyway. All he knew was the sight of those two rings, and all they represented, had filled him with abject terror.

Even now, remembering it made his chest feel tight. He rubbed where he thought his heart was and willed it to be calm. The whole incident with Helen had shaken him at the time and he still wasn't over it. Not, he realised, because he was devastated about breaking up with Helen, but because he'd thought he was doing okay. He'd thought that he was taking life as it came and not being an emotional disaster zone like certain other members of his family. Then suddenly he was the sort of guy who had a literal panic attack because a woman asked him to marry her.

As soon as he was done settling into this job and finding a place to live, he was going to try and find a decent therapist. He had hurt someone he cared about. Helen deserved better than that. He should have sensed the change in what she wanted and extricated himself sooner. He hated that he'd hurt her like that.

All his adult life, he had resented his father for hurting the people around him by being weak. Now he was doing the same thing. He couldn't stand for that.

His phone buzzed, a welcome distraction from his thoughts. It was his sister.

Quick chat?

He propped himself up in the bed and called her back. 'What's up?'

'I just wanted to check that you hadn't forgotten that we're going to Thatha and Aunty-Amma's for dinner on Saturday night.'

'I haven't forgotten. I'll be there.'

'Good, because you can't leave me to face the life questions all by myself,' said Sam.

'Of course. Plus, proper Sri Lankan food.'

'Exactly.' Sam laughed. 'How's the new job going?'

He looked at the twee little bedroom. It was warm and cosy. He couldn't really complain. 'Not bad. They've sent me to a

60

medium-sized tech start up.' He thought about how he was technically 'assisting' John. 'I think they're testing me.'

'That must be quite different from the sort of big corporation stuff you did before,' said Sam. 'Is it still interesting? Or are you bored?'

The unspoken question was, 'Are you regretting the move?' He might be thrown by the changes, but he wasn't regretting the move. 'It's okay,' he said. 'I quite like the start-up vibe. As you say, it's very different to the big corporate environment. Different frustrations, I guess.' He didn't particularly want to talk about it. 'How did your supplier meeting go today?'

'Not bad,' said Sam. 'At least I'll have something interesting to talk about at dinner. You know what Thatha's like for quizzing about careers.'

'I thought he was being supportive now.'

'He is. I mean, it's nice and all, but . . . he still tries to give me advice and it gets a bit annoying. I'm hoping he'll be too distracted with your new job to bother much about my business.'

Gihan groaned. Their father had been confused by Gihan's decision to leave a big company that had sent him on a lucrative secondment where he got expat perks as well as being paid his usual salary. He had explained that he'd got fed up with the work. His old job was demanding. He already knew that he had to decide whether he wanted only work and travel in his life, or whether there was a better balance to be struck. The thing with Helen had only hastened the inevitable.

He was fairly sure now that he wasn't cut out for having a family, but he would like other things in his life. Amma had once joked that when her life flashed before her eyes, she was glad she'd had so many fun things to look at. At the moment, his life was mostly work. There had to be more to it than that. Good friends, family, maybe even a hobby. He wasn't sure what was wrong right now, but something was. He was far more broken than he'd realised. Moving back was a step in the right direction. He needed some space to think. Besides, it wasn't like he could stay where he was. It seemed that the incident with Helen had polarised their entire social circle. Everything was awkward. When he'd said he was leaving, there had been a sense of relief all round.

'I really don't need that right now.'

Sam chuckled. 'Well, you could always distract yourself with Aunty-Amma's worry about how you're single now.'

That made Gihan snort. 'Oh yeah. We've had a chat about that already. She is all for getting the aunties to find me a nice girl. I love her to bits, but when she's with the aunties, she's as much of a menace as the rest of them.'

'That's what the aunties do,' said Sam. 'You're single now. You're next.' The giggle that followed was almost malicious.

Gihan clicked his tongue. 'Just because you're all settled and free from interference.'

'Ha!' said Sam. 'I'm not free. Luke and I have been together a while now and I'm always being asked when we're going to get married. Then it'll be kids. Face it, I'll never be free. You might, once you're married, you know. It's different for guys.'

'I'm not going to get married,' said Gihan. 'So they're wasting their time.'

There was a beat of silence as Sam worked out how she was going to respond. Everyone in his family thought that he and Helen had drifted apart. Sam was the only one he'd shared the details with. She hadn't said anything apart from, 'You know I'm here for you whatever you decide.'

'I hope,' she said, after a few seconds. 'That you have reason to change your mind.'

'I don't think I will, but thanks.'

'Helen wasn't the right one for you. Who knows though, you might meet someone who is. Someone who reaches you in a way that no one else did,' said Sam. 'Someone who makes it worth the risk for you.'

An image of Alex flashed through his mind, which was ridiculous because he barely knew her. 'I doubt it,' he said.

They talked a bit longer until a yawn interrupted Gihan mid-sentence. 'Listen, Sam, I'd better get some sleep. I'm going to try and get a bit of reading done before breakfast tomorrow.'

'Okay. Don't work too hard. I'll see you at the weekend.'

He hung up, plugged his phone back in to charge and lay back. Why had he thought about Alex, when Sam said 'someone to change your mind'. It was most likely because he'd seen her that evening. Top of his mind and all that.

Another sudden memory flash of her smiling at him as she tucked her hair behind her ears. He had been so pleased to make her laugh and forget about the idiot who'd dumped her. He remembered the way his eyes seemed to get dragged back to her whenever he looked away. How, as the night wore on, he'd drunk in the details of her smile, the way the light caught her eyes, the shape of her lips. For weeks afterwards he'd kept seeing people that looked a bit like her and being disappointed when it wasn't her.

Logically, he'd known it was a meaningless encounter, but the way she'd burrowed into his mind in those few hours had made him think it was the start of something bigger. Even now, after all the intervening years, there was something. When he had followed her into that leafy thicket thing earlier that evening, for a moment, she had been so close that he could smell her perfume and feel the warmth from her body. His own body had been assaulted by memories of how she felt pressed against him, his hand on her back, her arms around his neck. The taste of Jack Daniels on her lips. It was as though the intervening five years had never happened.

He shook his head. No, he couldn't think about that. It was a long time ago and they had both moved on from that. Alex was living with her extremely well-muscled boyfriend now. He had seen them together when he'd looked back at her before turning off the street to come back to the pub. He'd seen the way that guy had affectionately stroked her face. Was that the same man she'd been with when he'd met her five years ago?

He rolled over again and punched his pillow into a more comfortable shape. Good for her. She had a boyfriend and she was happy. That was great. He was happy for her.

This feeling of loss when he thought about Alex was just a quirk of fate. Fate was probably telling him he needed to move on from his cosy, long term hook-up type relationships and work out what he really wanted. He couldn't carry on having a panic attack every time someone asked him for a commitment. He hated that he'd hurt Helen like that. He needed to work his issues out before he hurt someone else.

Gihan believed in fate. He also believed that fate could be a real bitch.

Chapter 5

Alex's computer was taking a while to boot up. The office was always quiet at this time of day. The only people there were her and Isobel. She glanced across to where her fellow scientist was eating her breakfast at her desk while reading her emails. Isobel had got in before her again. This niggled. There was no one else here to see which one of them came in first, but Alex wanted the satisfaction of being the earliest. On the other hand . . . did she really want to get up any earlier?

The computer was still chugging through its updates, so she stood up with a sigh and stretched. She had prescribed exercises she was supposed to do every day. It stopped her back from stiffening up over time and hurting her. Most of the time, she was very good about doing them. Besides, if she looked like she had back pain, Jake would always know that she hadn't done her stretches and tell her off.

Crossing arms and placing her hands on her shoulders, she twisted round to stretch. This meant that she could see right into the office the two consultants shared. It was behind her normally, so she couldn't see them when she was sitting at her desk, but, disturbingly, they could see her and probably read what was on her screen.

Not that Gihan would care what she was looking at. She slowly released her stretch and twisted the other way. Why would he? If he'd remembered her, he'd had plenty of opportunity to talk to her about it yesterday and he hadn't. Their encounter clearly didn't mean anything to him.

Annoyingly, he didn't let her quiz him about work either. That would have been a useful thing to have done. All that had happened was she'd embarrassed herself by going weak at the knees over a guy who clearly didn't think much of her.

The computer finally got to the login screen. She sat back down, typed in her password and took a sip of coffee while her emails loaded. It was silly to get perturbed about a guy right now. Especially a guy who was hired to work out who in the office should be sacked. She glanced across at Isobel again and resolved that she would get up earlier tomorrow. There was no way she could let anyone think that Isobel worked harder than she did.

The office slowly filled up. Leila turned up at nine and came straight over, just as Alex was getting ready to go into the lab.

'So . . .' said Leila. 'You had an interesting time walking the dog last night?'

'Oh my god, you and Jake are such gossips.'

'Yeah. Sure. But what happened?'

'Nothing. Nothing happened. Nothing at all.'

'Methinks the lady doth protest too much.' Leila raised her eyebrows.

They both shrugged on their lab coats.

'Honestly,' said Alex. 'Nothing. I was walking Penelope and he was looking lost in the woods. I showed him the way back to the village centre.'

'That's cute. What did you talk about?' Leila pulled out a pair of latex gloves from the 'small' box and passed them to Alex before getting herself a slightly bigger pair. 'You must have talked about something? Or did you walk in silence?'

'We talked. Casual stuff.'

When Leila continued staring at her expectantly, Alex sighed. 'He told me how he'd been in the Middle East and he's really new to this job. I told him I'd lived here a few years. He asked if I missed London and Cornwall . . .' She stopped and frowned. Wait. She hadn't told him about her family living in Cornwall yesterday. Her parents had moved after she'd gone off to uni, so he couldn't have worked it out from her CV. 'Well, damn.'

'What?' said Leila.

Alex held up a hand, still thinking. 'I didn't tell him about Cornwall yesterday. He knew already. The only time I mentioned "home" being Cornwall was . . . five years ago.

Leila frowned. 'So . . . he remembers? That's good, right?'

She nodded. 'But he pretended he didn't. He must really want to forget all about it. On purpose.' The thought made her feel terrible. How humiliating.

'Oh. Honey, I'm sorry,' said Leila. 'That's very low. He should at least man up and own up to it.'

'Arguably, so should I,' she said. 'I guess I could drag it up, but I'm not sure I even want to now.' It made her feel soiled. Like she'd been used and discarded. She knew this sort of thing happened, but she'd assumed it wouldn't ever happen to her. Thank goodness she hadn't given into temptation and slept with him. She would have felt so much worse if she had.

Leila patted her arm. 'I guess you could lay low for a while. Focus on work.'

'I can hardly avoid seeing him. I'm supposed to be helping him, remember?' She pushed the door open. 'But you're right. I should get to work. That's what's important here.'

The churn of disappointment turned to anger. If he preferred to pretend that the whole evening five years ago hadn't even happened, then so would she. All this time, she'd thought of him as the one who'd got away. She had been wrong. So very, very wrong. The only reason he had seemed perfect back then was precisely because he was a stranger. He hadn't revealed enough of himself for her to be disappointed in him yet. And now he had. It was a blessing, really. She needed to keep her focus on her work. If these consultants were going to choose a project to axe, she had to make sure it wasn't hers.

*

Gihan crossed another interview off the list.

'How many more do we have to do?' John asked.

It took him a few seconds to count up the appointments. 'Another ten or so.'

John stretched his arms above his head. 'How much more data gathering do we need to do?'

'I . . . can't find the right folder for the KPI summaries from this year. I was going to catch Alex and ask her to show me where they're kept. I have access to the folder, I just can't find it in all the noise.' He tried not to give any emphasis to Alex's name. Especially now that John was watching him. He had dreamt about her last night and had woken up still thinking about her.

John tapped his fingers on the edge of the desk. 'So . . . we're on track to get this done by the end of week three?'

Gihan considered the question. Working evenings, as he and John were doing, they should be done by the end of week two, but having a bit of leeway was always good. Things always took longer than you expected them to. 'Sure. Easily.'

'Great.' John stood up. 'I'm going to go stretch my legs before the next interview, I think.'

Someone knocked on the door and Daniel, the CEO, leaned in. 'Hello, chaps. Can I have a minute of your time?'

John gestured to the empty chair across from them. 'Sure.' He sank back into his seat. Gihan flipped his notebook open again.

'It's about your interim notes,' Daniel said. 'Can I ask, would you guys be able to provide some training on meetings?'

They looked at each other.

'Not . . . really what we do,' said John. 'But we have a training department. I can ask a colleague to get in touch with you.'

'It might be better, if the push for shorter, more appropriate meetings came from inside the culture,' said Gihan. 'Maybe put a small group together and get them to work out how to do it? Give them a small-ish budget.' Then, remembering who he worked for, he added, 'I'm sure we could facilitate something like that.'

Daniel winced. 'Budget is so tricky right now.'

'I'll ask someone from the office to call you,' said Gihan.

'Yes. Please do that,' Daniel stood up. 'And I'll look into forming a meetings task force.' He nodded, almost as though talking to himself. 'That's a good idea.' Still nodding, he turned to leave. 'Thank you.'

John waited until the door clicked shut and rolled his eyes. Gihan smiled and looked down at his work. That sort of conversation happened all the time. With big corporations, they tended to just add more budget. With smaller companies like this, it was a matter of saying no.

Whenever they were brought in to look at teams like this, the management sometimes forgot that they were part of the assessment too. Daniel Harrington was the sort of guy who thought he was good at reading his people. But he tended to treat people as walking skill sets rather than individuals.

Gihan's gaze fell on the notes from Isobel McLeesh's meeting. Both she and Alex had mentioned being in competition with each other. 'Interesting management style,' Gihan observed, quietly. 'Pitting the teams against each other to make them work faster.'

John nodded, but didn't reply for a minute. Gihan worried whether he should have kept his opinions to himself. He turned back to his work.

After a few more minutes, John said, 'Right. I really am going out for a minute.' He took his phone out of his pocket. 'My wife is texting me about pushchairs.'

'Oh yeah. The baby's wheels are a big decision.'

'They all look great, to me. But she's the expert. I'd best call her back before she gets wound up enough to call me.' He grabbed his jacket.

'I'll go see if I can find Alex.' Gihan stood up too and followed his colleague out.

When he looked at the open-plan office he spotted Alex immediately. She was reading her emails, while putting her hair back into a bun. It took a second before he caught himself looking at the long slope of her neck. Not appropriate. While he was working here, they were colleagues. Maybe friends at most.

He strode over to her desk and knocked on it to get her attention. She turned. She had a hair grip held in her teeth. It was adorable. She removed the hair grip and shoved it into the bun.

'Hi,' she said. 'Can I help you?'

'I . . . am looking for some files. I have access to your reports folders, but I can't find the ones I need. I'm trying to find what the KPIs were and progress towards them over the last couple of years.'

Alex frowned. Her lips contracted into a moue as she thought. 'I think I know which ones you need.' She leaned forward and pulled up a file menu, then paused. 'Shall I show you on your laptop? So that you can bookmark it and find it quicker when you need it?'

He walked back to the office, feeling weirdly self-conscious about her following him. He didn't normally get self-conscious, but these days he didn't even know what was normal for him anymore.

Ever since he'd worked out how he knew Alex, he kept wanting to bring it up. Why had she given him her number if she was still with her boyfriend? It had been years ago; he should just move on. Why was it bothering him so much? In the office, he unlocked the laptop and gestured for her to take a seat.

'Right then.' She sat in his chair and leaned forward, searching the screen. 'Here we go. This folder. Then this one. Then the year that you want.'

He made a note of the folder path.

She opened one of the documents. 'They're always the same format, so if you go to section three . . .' She scrolled to the right place. 'There you go. Separated by department and project. See?'

He leaned forward. This brought him very close to her shoulder. He could see the tiny loose hairs at the nape of her neck now and smell her perfume, mixed with the faint hint of latex gloves and laboratory hand soap. It should be weird, but it wasn't. 'Yes, I see,' he said.

She turned and suddenly, her face was very close. Too close to ignore. So close that he could see her pupils dilate and her lips part.

A thousand hoarded memories from the one evening he spent with her crowded into his head. The way she dipped her head when she laughed. The smile she'd given him as the taxi drew away. The sensation of her skin against his lips.

In the office outside, someone announced they were doing a coffee run and brought him back to reality. He was at work. He breathed in sharply and pulled back. 'Thank you.' He cleared his throat. 'That's very helpful.'

She blinked and looked down at her hands. 'Anytime.'

There was a moment of awkward silence. He could see a flush brightening on her neck. Had she noticed his momentary lapse in professionalism?

'Was there anything else?' she said.

'Er . . . no. No. Thank you.' He made himself take a step back, away from the temptation to touch her.

She stood up, still not making eye contact. 'If you need anything else, come find me. Always happy to help.' She managed to make scant eye contact and give him a quick smile before she left and headed towards the lab.

He watched her leave and carried on staring at the door for a few minutes after she'd left. Someone else walking past the glass door gave him a puzzled look. He pulled himself back together and looked down at the computer. Heat radiated off his cheeks.

What was wrong with him? He was normally so good at being in control. He had an excellent poker face. Why did this woman get him all flustered?

He had to nip this flicker of interest in the bud. Except, he remembered, this wasn't a new flicker of interest. It was a whole flame that he'd convinced himself to extinguish. He couldn't rekindle it now.

He sat back down and gave himself a stern pep talk. He had the files he needed. He should get to work. Getting involved with a client's employee was not advisable. Never ever. He had a job to do and it depended on his ability to remain objective. John was watching him, he was sure of it. He couldn't afford to slip up.

Clicking on the first of the files, he skim-read the report. Even if all the reasons he'd just thought of went away, there was always the issue that his report may well end up costing Alex her job. That was definitely not romantic.

Chapter 6

Alex had gone down to put some samples in the cold room and was on her way back, when Daniel stopped her by stepping out of his office and calling her name. 'A moment of your time?' he said.

Puzzled, Alex went in. He gestured with his hand to shut the door. She did so.

'I thought it would be good to catch up with you for a quick thoughtopsy on how things were going with the consultants,' he said.

Thoughtopsy? Oh good grief. 'Don't you do autopsies on dead things?'

'Oh, we're hardly dead yet.' He smiled, without mirth and waved in the direction of the chair opposite him.

Alex sat down.

Daniel steepled his fingers like a Bond villain and peered at her. 'So anyway. Thoughts?'

'I . . . don't really know what to say. They seem to be doing their job. I'm helping them whenever I can.' She thought about Gihan leaning closer to look over her shoulder and the way her treacherous body had responded. Helping was awkward. 'I'm not sure I have anything else to add.'

'You're facilitating, I hope.'

'Like I said, I'm helping them with whatever they ask for.'

'Hmm. Quite so, quite so.' He nodded and stared at her over his fingertips.

Where was this going? She was so tired of Daniel's games. 'Look, Daniel,' she said. 'My team and I are working as hard as we can. Experiments take as long as they have to take. I don't know what you expect me to do here?'

Daniel shook his head. 'I don't expect anything more. I know you always give 110 per cent.'

She bit back her instinctive response to that. 100 per cent was the maximum – 110 per cent effort was just nonsense.

'Everything to play for,' Daniel said. 'From what I can tell, you and Isobel are neck and neck.'

'That's interesting, but there isn't much I can do even if that wasn't the case.' It was an effort not to shout.

Daniel hesitated. 'I can see that this situation is causing you some stress.'

'Of course it is.' Her voice rose. 'We're talking about the jobs of me and my team, here. Not to mention my project!' And her past connection to Gihan wasn't helping.

Her boss nodded, as though he'd expected her to react that way. 'Try not to worry. Even if the conclusion is against you, we will do our best to make sure you're looked after.'

'How?' she snapped.

'There are wheels we can put in motion,' said Daniel. 'Of course, it's possible that the consultants come up with a way to square the circle after they've got a helicopter view of things. They are experts in this sort of thing after all.'

Now she felt like she had overreacted. She forced herself to breathe slowly. 'Is there anything else?'

Daniel leaned back. 'No, no. I wanted to check on the troops, that's all.'

'Good. I'll get back to work then.' She stormed out, only just preventing herself from slamming the door.

She marched outside. Ugh. When she got home tonight, she was definitely going to get her CV updated. This was no way to work. She barged past the reception desk without even bothering to nod to the receptionist, like she normally did. Daniel's vagueness infuriated her. The situation was bad enough for her as it was, but he'd somehow managed to make it worse.

At the top of the stairs, she decided that she had to do something. So far, she'd played carefully by the rules, being as professional as possible, but clearly if she was going to save her project, she needed to do more than that.

Fine. If she had to beg, she'd beg. She marched up to the office the consultants were in and peered inside. There was no one in the room with them, but both men were busy at their laptops.

She rapped on the door and walked in. Both men looked up.

'Have you got a minute?' she asked, addressing her question to John. 'I need to talk to you both.'

'Of course . . .' He paused, then added, 'Alex,' as though he had to dig her name out of his memory. 'Take a seat. What can we do for you?'

She glanced at Gihan, who had taken his notepad out again and leaned forward. She didn't sit down, choosing to stand. 'I need to make you understand how important my cancer diagnosis test is.'

John tilted his head in a dismissive manner. 'Alex—'

'No. You don't understand. Breast cancer kills over 11,000 people a year, most of them women.' She rattled off the statistics. She had seen them often enough to be able to know them by heart. 'My test is a simple finger-prick blood test that detects breast cancer at a really early stage. If we can diagnose it early, we could prevent thousands of deaths. This is really important. There is a clear clinical need.'

She noticed that Gihan looked down at that, while John remained impassive. She directed her comments at Gihan. He might be more sympathetic.

'If people could buy a test over the counter, or take a quick finger-prick blood test at a pharmacy to check for cancer markers, it would be so much easier for them. If there are any signs of trouble, we'd be able to catch them so much easier. The test is so close to—'

John put his hand up. 'What you're saying is completely true, Alex, but there are so many wonderful things that haven't made it to the shelves. The kidney-function test panel the company makes is important too. Unless the company can make its core product, it can't support anything else.'

'But—'

'Our job is to work out how the company can still be in operation two years from now,' John said, firmly.

She turned to Gihan, hoping for help. He had sympathy in his eyes, but he gave her an apologetic shrug. 'It's a very good technology,' he said. 'And important. But . . .'

She stared at him for a few seconds and he had the decency to look away. 'So, does that mean you're going to close my project down?'

'Nothing is decided yet,' said John. 'I'm really sorry Alex, but we can't tell you any more than that until after we've finished.' He stood up, one hand extended towards the door.

Once again, she glanced at Gihan, who said, 'Thank you for coming to talk to us, though. You're clearly very passionate about your technology.' His expression was pleasant but neutral – as though they were talking about the weather rather than a matter of life and death.

The anger that had propelled her sputtered out, squashed by a feeling of defeat. 'Right,' she said. 'Okay. Well, thanks for listening.'

As she walked back to her desk, she glanced through the big window into the lab, where Isobel was testing the latest version of her work. Did this mean Isobel had won? The guys had implied that wasn't the case. Isobel was devoted to her research, but Alex doubted that Isobel would have managed to make such an impassioned plea for her work. She would just have to wait and see if it did any good.

John had been completely unmoved, but Gihan had shown glimmers of sympathy. She could work on him a bit, maybe. Especially if she could catch him without John. Maybe he would be going for a walk again this evening? She could try and talk to him then.

She was annoyed with him for pretending not to remember meeting her, but she had to park those feelings and be nice and polite to him for the sake of her work. If she didn't do her very best to save her test, she could never forgive herself.

*

Gihan and John finished their last interview for the day and compared notes. While Gihan was filling in the data sheet, John checked his phone. 'I've got a missed call from the wife,' he said. 'That's odd. I only spoke to her a few hours ago. I'll just go check what's going on.'

'I hope everything's okay.'

John laughed. 'To be honest, I wouldn't be surprised if it's something vital like what colour the nursery curtains should be. She's obsessed at the moment.' He left, phone in hand. The building was a unit on an industrial estate, which meant that it was basically a giant metal box, so the phone signal was better outside.

Typing up his notes, Gihan felt another stab of discomfort. The last guy they'd interviewed had been in engineering. From his responses, it was obvious that the R&D projects weren't being given much input from the engineering and manufacturing teams. Which meant that no matter how well they worked in the lab, a lot of work would have to be done (or undone) when it came to making sure the chemicals survived the manufacturing process. Despite Alex's impassioned speech earlier, things were not looking good for Alex's team. Or for Isobel's, for that matter.

Alex clearly cared a lot about her work and he knew better than anyone how important it was to diagnose cancer early. If a test like the one Alex was developing had been available, would his mother have taken it earlier? Would it have saved her life?

No matter how much he wanted to be able to save Alex's project, John was right. They had a job to do. If the company didn't make some changes, it would go under.

He rubbed his temples. This was why he couldn't get involved with people he worked with. Not until the project was over at the very least. He leaned back and sighed. This was never usually a problem. He generally got on well with people he worked with. Sometimes, he ran into them again and got on well with them all over again . . . and those ended up in friendships.

This was different. It wasn't a case of merely becoming friends with a client; it was more than that. He was attracted to Alex. The way he was drawn to her had taken him by surprise. Sure, they had some history, but that was five years ago. It hadn't even gone anywhere. It shouldn't matter so much to him.

Even five years ago, the strength of his attraction to her had surprised him. It had to be purely a physical thing. He didn't know her. Now, a whole five years after she should have become irrelevant – a one-off evening of fun and kisses – being near her still scrambled his brain. All he could think about was kissing her again.

Against his better judgement, he stood up and, under the guise of having a quick stretch, moved to the other side of the room. From here, he could see Alex's desk. She wasn't there. Probably just as well, because he had no idea what he was going to do next. He didn't have an excuse to go and talk to her. Nor did he have a reason to stand by the coat stand. Isobel, who was sitting at her desk, looked up and spotted him. Oh dear. He did a bit of theatrical stretching and went back to his desk, feeling silly.

It didn't matter how he felt about Alex, he was here to do a job and he was far too much of a professional to fail at it. Besides, he wanted to keep this job, didn't he?

He reopened his document and had barely started work when John came rushing back in. One look at his pale, wide-eyed expression told Gihan something had gone very wrong.

'She's gone into labour,' John said. 'She tried to call me, but I'd put the phone on silent.' He grabbed his coat and dropped it on the floor. 'Her colleague took her to hospital.' He picked up his coat and dropped it again.

Gihan stood up. 'John.' When he didn't get a response from his colleague, he said more sharply. 'John!'

The other man's head snapped up.

'Let me drive you to the station.' Gihan held out his hand for the keys. 'Do you need to go back to the B&B to pick up anything?'

'I. No. Yes.' John paused for breath. 'Yes.'

'Great. Get your stuff. Let's go. I'll drive. You find what time the next train is.' Gihan strode to the door. 'If you need anything and you've left it behind, I can always bring it to you on Friday, when I finish here.'

He ushered John out of the building. Being calm in a crisis was something he was good at. He had always been practical, even as a teenager. He'd had to be. They all had. He had been fifteen when his Amma died. With their father consumed by grief, Gihan, his brother and his sister had had to look after themselves. It was a miracle they'd turned out as normal as they were.

Right now, it was nice to have something important to take his mind off his frustrations.

He adjusted the rear-view mirror to his height. 'Which is the nearest train station?' he asked, as he drove out of the car park.

*

Alex checked her hair before she went out. From her window, she could see the road outside the house. Gihan hadn't been past yet. She was hoping to catch him on his walk and join him, so that she could talk to him some more, maybe drop some more hints about the importance of her project. He had said he couldn't tell her anything about the review, but there was no reason why she couldn't tell him stuff.

Would a touch of makeup be too much? She picked up her lipstick then thought better of it and put it back down. It would look silly to be glammed up to walk the dog. Besides, she had to go to the village fair committee meeting afterwards and there would be questions. She was trying to persuade Gihan of the importance of her work, not trying to seduce him. She didn't even know if he was going to go for a walk again that evening. This plan to talk to him was based entirely on supposition and hope.

All the waiting and watching the road meant that she had to rush out of the house so that she could pick Penelope up at seven, just like she normally did. There was no sign of Gihan when she reached the top of the drive. She hesitated at the gate. Should she wait a few minutes to see if he showed up? She had assumed that he would go for a walk around the same time again. Maybe he wouldn't? After five minutes of waiting around, she went down to Maureen's door and got the little dog.

When she got up to Maureen's gate, Gihan still hadn't shown up. She took out her phone and checked her messages, using it as an excuse to linger. Penelope was getting impatient, so she gave up and went for the walk instead.

She glanced at her watch. Clearly, her plan to talk to him without John around had failed for tonight. There was always tomorrow. She frowned as she followed Penelope towards the woods. Maybe it wouldn't make any difference if she did see him . . .

Much as it annoyed her, Alex wasn't so clueless as to not see that Gihan had to have some sort of objectivity to do his job. That's why he got hired. She was pretty sure that the consultants wouldn't tell Daniel anything he didn't already know. But they would have enough distance to be brutal about it. Firing strangers was easier than firing colleagues.

She shoved her hands deeper into her pockets, making sure

Penelope's lead was wrapped around her wrist. The conversation with Daniel drifted to mind. Maybe that was why. Daniel had suggested that he had to choose between her project and Isobel's. He had always hinted at that before, but never stated it so explicitly. Most of the time, Alex tried to ignore the suggestions about competition between the labs. It wasn't useful to her to worry about what Isobel was doing. Why on earth did Daniel feel that the threat of redundancy would make her work harder? This project meant a lot to her. She'd argued vociferously to be allowed to try it. The fact that she had got it so close to a viable test in only a few years was testament to that. She always gave 100 per cent to her work. It wasn't like she could give any more.

The company was struggling. That was obvious – and not just from the quality of the biscuits and coffee. She really should move on to somewhere more stable. The problem was, if she moved on, the work on her early cancer diagnosis test would stop. She wanted to see it turned into an actual product that hospitals could use. The threat of it disappearing had highlighted exactly how much that meant to her.

She shifted her shoulders inside her jacket. The scar on her upper back pulled at the movement. She had been lucky. Her osteosarcoma hadn't reached the stage of spreading. But there were so many others who hadn't been so lucky. She thought of Jude, who she'd met on the ward. For a second, the familiar guilt of surviving when other people she knew hadn't gnawed at her. It was stupid to feel that way. She knew that. But still. Sometimes she remembered the other kids in the support group and shrank away. She had only been twice after Jude had died. Both times she'd come away feeling like her problems were insignificant compared to those of the others.

Penelope gave a sharp bark, pulling her away from that train of thought. They were nearly at the field. Alex let Penelope in, shut the gate behind her, and let the little dog off the lead.

Her plans for the cancer detection test were one thing, but her need to have a stable job was another. If she was to keep herself safe, she had to start looking for another job.

She walked down the field. The evening was darker and more chilly than the night before. Looking up, she could barely see the sky for clouds. She pulled her head torch out of her pocket. It had been a present from Maureen last year – entirely self-serving she'd said, but still useful nonetheless.

'We should probably get this done quickly,' she called to Penelope. 'I think it's going to rain.'

When she got back to the house, Maureen looked past her. 'No young man accompanying you today then?'

What? 'No.' Alex removed her head torch and turned it off.

'Shame,' said Maureen. 'He seemed nice, that young man yesterday. Tall.'

Alex let this sit for a second. He was tall, yes. 'O-kay.'

'Don't stand in the cold. Come in.'

'Only for a few minutes.' She stepped inside and shut the door. Warmth from Maureen's too-warm house seeped in through her coat.

'Someone who goes for a walk as a first date is always nice.' Maureen rested one hand against the wall, so that she could lean down and scritch Penelope behind the ears with the other. 'Old-fashioned, I suppose, but nice.'

'It wasn't a date,' said Alex. 'He's not . . . well, he's not anything really. Not even a friend. He and his colleague are doing some work at the office. He got lost yesterday and Penelope and I showed him the way back, that's all. So, you can stop with the gossip. There's nothing going on.'

Maureen slowly straightened back up. 'I see,' she said. 'But you like him. You waited for him today, didn't you? I saw.'

Alex, pulled at her scarf, her face hot. 'I . . . had a message I had to check. I wasn't waiting.'

Maureen beamed at her. 'I see,' she said. 'You don't like him? Not even a little bit?'

'He's trying to shut my project down,' she said. She checked the time. 'I have to go,' she said firmly. 'The town fair committee is meeting in the pub in a few minutes and I need to get my notes.'

'Of course, duck, of course.' Maureen's mouth twitched with barely concealed amusement.

'Listen, Maureen. If I got my CV and updated it . . . would you give me some feedback on it?'

Maureen's face lit up. 'Of course I will. I would love to help. You're wasted on that place, you know. I've thought that for ages. Leila too. You're both staying there out of habit.'

'Really? You feel that strongly about it?'

Maureen had said something to that effect a few times, but Alex had never really taken it seriously. She had assumed that it was Maureen's way of being supportive or something.

'I do,' said Maureen. 'I'll do a bit of research and see what sort of keywords are being used these days. You send me your CV when you're ready. A print copy, if you can, please. I like to make notes.'

Alex blinked, surprised at the enthusiasm. 'I will. Thank you.' She pulled her scarf back round her neck. 'I really do have to go. I'll see you tomorrow.'

'We'll see you tomorrow, same time. Won't we, Penelope?'

Penelope wagged her tail so hard her entire backend wagged too.

'Yes. See you tomorrow. Bye Penelope.'

Alex walked back to her house. She would be a few minutes early for the committee meeting. She grabbed her notepad and the notes from the last meeting that she'd hastily printed out at work. Being early was good. She much preferred to do that than to leave someone sitting there worrying about whether or not she was going to turn up. She locked the door after herself. Besides, if she hung around in the house, she'd only dwell on the fact that Gihan and John might close down her project.

Chapter 7

The village fair was another one of those things that Alex had got involved in because of Leila. When she'd first arrived, she had thrown herself into her work. She was new to the area and didn't know anyone, so there was nothing to balance out her life, until Leila found out that she was living in a B&B and looking for a place to live. Within a week, Alex was living in a cosy double bedroom in Jake's house and being dragged to the pub to 'help' Leila with her organising committee role at the fair. Now Alex was officially the note-keeper for the village fair organising committee.

The Star Inn had thick white walls on the outside and low ceilings inside. The front end of the pub was still very much a local. The bar was at the centre of the large room, next to the stairs. A small fire crackled cheerfully at one end. A large part of the room still had the old stone floors, so radiators were dotted about the place to keep it from turning into a huge fridge. The restaurant part of the pub, at the back, was much fancier. Alex had been in there once, when Ryder FT still took everyone out for lunch at Christmas.

Alex spotted the fair committee sitting at one of the bigger tables at the back. She waved to the landlady, as she went through. She couldn't help peering into the alcoves, in case Gihan was sitting in one. Nope. Maybe he was still working. Or maybe he'd gone out for a walk without her. She hoped he got lost. No. That was unkind. She hoped he didn't.

The only seat left at the table had its back to the room. She sat down and shifted around a bit, annoyed that she couldn't keep an eye on who came into the pub.

The committee was a random assortment of people, all of whom lived in the village. Leila was already there, as was the vicar, the lady who ran the local café, one retired guy, Fred, who was into everything, and a couple of the wondermums who were now bringing their particular brand of ruthless efficiency to the village fair. If she was being completely honest, Alex found the wondermums terrifying. They were all a few years older than her and seemed to have worked in the City for some years before throwing it all in to make sure that their offspring had textbook-perfect childhoods.

'Are we all here?' said Violet, chief of the wondermums. 'Shall we start?'

Alex pulled out her notes from the last meeting.

'Okay, Alex,' said Violet. 'What do we have on the agenda?'

Violet expected the meetings to have agendas and minutes, just like at work. It felt a little over the top. They'd already agreed on the minutes by email, so the meeting started with actions. Pulling her thoughts away from the pub behind her, Alex read out the completed actions and moved onto the ones that needed updates.

'Sponsorship and raffle donations.' Alex looked at Leila, who was in charge of that.

'We have the usual stuff from the local shops. Jake is donating a month's gym membership. Ada Moon is donating one of her home-made fruit cakes and some traditional fruit tarts for the raffle. Michael is donating a couple of T-shirts with funny slogans on from his shop . . .' Leila faltered. 'Not really much more to add since last time, really. The raffle is looking good though.'

'Have we had any luck trying to get sponsorship money from

anyone?' Violet asked. At the last meeting she'd given them a lecture on being proactive in fundraising.

'Nothing local,' said the vicar, sadly.

'Nope. I tried all the companies in the industrial estate,' Leila said. 'Nothing more than we've already got.' Violet stared at her. Leila threw a glance at Alex and shifted in her seat. 'I did ask my boss. He said no.'

'The company is not doing so well at the moment,' Alex added. 'They're cutting back on everything.'

There was a murmur of sympathy around the table. 'Are your jobs safe?' the vicar asked.

Alex and Leila exchanged a glance and shrugged. 'No idea,' said Alex.

'They've got these management consultants in at the moment,' Leila added. 'They're interviewing people and looking at stuff and generally being annoying.'

Alex nudged her. 'They're staying here, in the pub,' she whispered.

Everyone at the table looked around, as though expecting to see them.

'Can we please focus?' Violet rapped a knuckle on the table. 'Stalls. Do we have enough food ones?'

'Erm . . . yes.' This was part of Alex's remit. 'In the refreshments tent we have the apple cider guys, the farm shop selling jam and home-made cakes, the WI doing a tea and cake service and Jake's gym stall is doing a barbecue and sample low-carb lunches. I believe there's a fish and chips van coming to park up for the day.'

'That's right,' one of the others said. 'They've paid for their pitch already.'

'We should have a stall doing things like cans of soda and chocolate, I guess . . .?' She glanced at Violet.

Violet frowned. 'We shouldn't really encourage that sort of thing. It's not healthy.'

There was a general murmur around the table.

'But I like a fizzy pop,' said Leila quietly.

Violet sighed. 'So do I. Ugh. Go on then. Let's do that. Who's going to run it?'

There were no volunteers. They were already all doing something.

'Maybe a rota?' Alex suggested.

They discussed a few more things and drew up lists of who was doing what for when. When the meeting ended, Alex closed her notebook. 'I need a diet coke. Anyone else?'

'I'll come with.' The vicar stood up and came around the table.

Standing at the bar, Alex sneaked a look around again. No Gihan. She wasn't sure what excuse she'd use to talk to him if he had been there, so it was probably just as well that he wasn't.

The vicar was chatting to the landlady, Hannah, as he ordered. So Alex leaned back against the bar. The pub wasn't very busy that evening. There was nothing much happening in the village on a Wednesday night, she knew. The runners met Monday and Thursday, the choir was on Tuesday, almost everyone showed up on Friday . . . but Wednesday, that was quiet. It was one of the reasons the committee had chosen to meet that night. The village had a pulse, she realised, and she was aware of it. How strange to be part of that?

Back at the table, the two wondermums were laughing at something. Everyone else was involved in an animated discussion. The vicar paid up for his drink.

'What can I get you, dear?' said Hannah.

Alex startled. 'Oh. A diet coke please.'

The landlady smiled and got a glass down. 'Did you have a good meeting?' she said, nodding towards the table.

'Yes. Really good.' Feeling something more was required, Alex said, 'I think we're on track for the weekend, you know.'

'Oh, that's great. And how's Maureen?'

'Er . . . same as always.'

'And Jake? I haven't seen him in here for a while. He's normally here on a Friday, but I haven't seen him for the last couple.'

'He's pitching to investors to get some money to expand the gym franchise,' Alex said. It was hardly a secret. 'So he's been working on that most nights.'

Hannah nodded and slid her drink towards her. 'I hope that goes well. When is he doing his pitch?'

'Tomorrow and Friday. It's a two-day event, which includes a couple of pitch sessions. He's very nervous.'

'I bet he is. Tell him we're all rooting for him.'

As she paid up, Alex reflected that she might be linked to this village, but she wasn't part of it. Not like Leila and Jake were. She was . . . around, but not properly embedded. She wondered what it would be like to be genuinely a part of something.

Growing up, Alex hadn't had many friends. Her cancer had been spotted just when she was starting secondary school, so she'd missed large swathes of school time. Even when she was better, it had taken her a while to build up her stamina enough to do normal things, so she didn't have much of a social life. She'd thrown herself into her studies instead. Looking back, she knew that this single-minded studying had helped her get to where she was today. If she could use it to make a cancer test that found other people's cancers early, then it all felt like part of a grand plan.

Ryder FT mothballing her work was definitely not part of that plan.

She picked up her drink and went back to the table. Leila was talking about work again.

'So, as far as we can tell, they're getting them to look at everything and evaluate what they feel the company should keep and what they should shed.'

'Are you worried?' Violet said.

Alex quietly sat down.

'Well . . . yes. We're doing R&D that isn't linked to the core product.'

Violet grimaced. 'That's hard. I know from experience that they'd probably look at that first. Mostly, they would try to redeploy staff into different areas, I should think. At least that's how we used to do it when I worked in the sector.' That was an interesting idea. Alex tried to work out how that might pan out. Ray only worked on her project a couple of days a week. The rest of the time he was a technician for one of the other teams. Perhaps they'd be able to move him over there full-time. Leila was a skilled technician too. But where would Alex herself fit in? Besides, regardless of all that, her project would be shut down.

'I suppose that might happen,' she said. 'But it still wouldn't be very good for my project.'

Violet extended a hand across the table and touched Alex's arm. 'I'm so sorry. This must be a very stressful time for you all.' She moved her arm back.

Alex blinked, surprised at the moment of gentleness from the normally formidable Violet. 'Thanks.'

'Anyway,' said Leila. 'We have a more interesting thing to talk about. Alex has this thing going with one of the consultants.'

The mood changed instantly and everyone's attention swung to Alex.

'What sort of a thing?' said Violet.

'A non-existent sort of thing,' Alex said severely.

'There's a "frisson".' Leila did air quotes with her fingers.

Violet chuckled. 'You should get to know him a bit. Make it more difficult for him to axe you.'

Alex shook her head. 'I don't think—'

Leila nudged her. 'That wouldn't be so bad, would it? Flirting with the hot man that you like.'

She didn't want to flirt with him. What was the point? She would only end up being disappointed all over again. She should have known, really, from the fact that he hadn't called her. For some reason, her stupid romantic heart had held on to the image of this perfect, nice man. But . . . even if it wasn't going to go anywhere romantically, she still wanted to try and talk to him to impress upon him how important her test was.

'I really don't think he's interested,' she said. 'I wish you guys would stop going on about this.'

Leila rolled her eyes. 'Okay, okay. I still think you should soften him up so that he doesn't shut our group down, but I'll stop talking about it if that's what you really want.'

'Thank you.' Alex took a sip of her drink.

The conversation moved on to safer topics. Normally, Alex would be careful to listen to the gossip, so that she knew what everyone was talking about and knew which topics to avoid with whom. But today, her attention wandered. She shifted her chair round a little bit, so that she could see who came into the bar. Just in case.

When it came to time to say goodbye, Alex waved Leila off and took the empty glasses to the bar. She was heading for the door when Gihan came in, shaking the rain from his hair. He was alone. Alex froze mid-step. How did she deal with this? Should she grab him for a quick chat while she had the chance? How awkward was this situation?

The decision was made for her when Gihan stared at her and said, 'Oh. Alex. Hi.' His voice sounded strained.

Now she noticed that he looked wide-eyed and exhausted. Her confusion evaporated, to be replaced with concern. 'Is everything okay?'

He shook his head. 'Not really.' He ran a hand through his hair and grimaced at the wetness. 'Long story. Do you mind if we just . . .' He gestured towards the bar. 'I'm starving.'

'Oh. Sure. Of course.' She turned and followed him. Was now a good time to try to talk to him? It might be that his defences were down. On the other hand, he might not look kindly on her trying to force him to talk about work when he was clearly tired.

'Is the kitchen still open?' His voice was urgent.

'I'm sorry,' said Hannah. 'We closed half an hour ago.'

'Damn.' Gihan dropped his head forward.

Hannah looked at Alex, then back at Gihan, who was rubbing his eyes now. She softened. 'Let me go and see if there's something we can do. If nothing else, we can probably rustle you up a sandwich.'

'Thank you,' said Gihan. 'You are a godsend.'

Alex hovered uncertainly, wondering if she should sit down on the bar stool next to him. Having followed him in, she was feeling a little awkward now. What did she do next? Her grand plan seemed less well thought out than she'd hoped.

'Do you . . . want me to sit with you for a bit?' she said.

He looked up and she saw the exhaustion on his face. No. Now was not the right time to ask about work.

'A bit of company would be nice. Thank you.'

That sounded familiar. Had she said that to him when they'd first met? Even if she had, he didn't give any indication of recognising it. She took the bar stool next to him. 'So, what happened?'

'John got a call to say his wife was in labour. It was all very unexpected. He wasn't in any fit state to drive, so I drove him to the station.'

'Oh. Wow. That's . . . Is she okay?'

'I don't know. Hang on . . .' He dug his mobile phone out of his coat pocket and checked it. 'Nope. Nothing. So . . . I don't know. Anyway, I was going to take him to Oxford to catch the next train down to London, but there was a road closure of some sort and I ended up driving through all these back lanes to get him to Didcot Parkway instead. Then I got lost trying to get back. It's been an evening.'

No wonder he hadn't gone for a walk. She knew first-hand how confusing the tiny back roads around here could be. 'That sounds stressful.'

'There was a bridge,' he said, in the tones of a man who had been haunted. 'An actual toll bridge. It was such a tiny thing.' He held his fingers inches apart to indicate how small the bridge was.

'I half expected there to be a troll involved.'

Alex nodded. 'Near Eynsham,' she said. 'I know the one.'

'The toll is only a few pence,' he said. 'What's even the point?'

Yes. Definitely not a good time to bring up work.

He shook his head and ran both his hands through his hair again. 'Listen to me going on. Sorry.' He drew a long breath and let it out. 'How're you? This is your local, I expect.'

'It is,' she said. 'I had a meeting here. We only finished a few minutes ago.'

He nodded encouragingly.

She carried on, 'We're doing the village fair on Saturday, so there's a lot to check off.'

He shrugged his coat off his shoulders while still sitting on it. It flopped down onto the stool either side of him. She saw he was still in his suit. Clearly, he hadn't had the chance to get changed.

'I'm impressed you made it back here,' she said. 'Especially in the dark.'

He turned to look at her. 'I had to follow the sat nav.' He gave a little shudder. 'I would have been completely stuffed without it.'

'Your sense of direction thing is okay with sat navs?' she asked.

'Thank goodness. Otherwise John would still be here. Or lost in the countryside around here.'

Hannah reappeared. 'Ham and cheese toastie okay for you? You're okay with pork, right?'

'All good,' said Gihan. 'Thank you so much.'

'Five minutes. Can I get you a drink while you wait?'

Gihan ordered himself a pint. 'Can I get you anything, Alex?'

She was about to decline, but thought better of it and requested a soft drink. Since she was going to sit here, she may as well have a drink.

'Excuse me for one minute.' He slid off the barstool and headed towards the loos. Alex leaned her elbows on the bar. It was weird enough that she was sitting with him right now. He had invited her to. Sort of. But he looked so hungry and harassed. She couldn't bring up her project now. It might annoy him and make him look at it less favourably, which would defeat the object. She could leave, but some part of her still cared about him and she didn't want to leave him by himself when he was clearly having a difficult evening. She chewed her lip. Why did she care? There was no helping her sometimes.

Gihan came back just as Hannah returned with his meal. He was wearing his glasses now. The familiarity of him hit her like a body blow.

His face lit up when he saw the food. 'Oh, that looks like the best meal in the world, right now. Thank you so much.' He unwrapped the cutlery and tucked in.

Alex watched him eat for a minute, feeling increasingly awkward. She cast about for something else to talk about.

'Is it . . . John's first child? His wife's, I mean.' It wasn't like John was having the baby.

He frowned and finished chewing. 'Yes, I think it is. I imagine it's very stressful. He said she wasn't supposed to be going on maternity leave for a few weeks yet.'

'Oh.' What was the right thing to say to that? 'So, the baby is early? But not that early. From what I've heard, that's usually okay. They catch up.'

He shrugged. 'I hope so. I don't have much experience with that sort of thing. I mean, my brother and his wife have a couple of kids and I love them to bits, but . . . I didn't really pay that much attention to their birth stories. I do remember them saying it was overwhelming though. The first one was about five years ago.'

Five years ago. Huh. That seemed like a long time. 'Five years ago, I wouldn't have paid much attention either,' she said. 'But now I seem to be surrounded by people who are getting married and starting families.' She thought about Ray. There were a few other people at work who had had children in the last year or two. The company had a lot of young graduates.

He grinned. 'It's a stage of life, right? First, everyone's getting married. There's weddings all over the shop. Then they start having kids. I've reached the age where you've either got to try and be interested in kid-related things or start hanging out with freshly graduated twenty-somethings.'

Alex laughed. She recognised that feeling. 'So which did you choose?' she said, teasing him.

'Hanging out with bright young things, obviously.' He gestured to the pub, where there were no freshly graduated young people. He gave her a mischievous grin. It was so familiar, she felt something warm ignite in her chest.

She looked down, still smiling. The warmth spread. This was what it had been like when they'd first met. That thrill of attraction, but a feeling of calm along with it. 'I imagine you get to meet a lot of interesting people.'

His gaze met hers briefly. 'I do,' he said. 'I like talking to people.'

'It must be useful that you're good at talking to people . . . and making them talk to you.' Oh no. She shouldn't have said that.

He didn't seem to find it odd. He gave it some consideration. 'I am good at getting people to talk,' he conceded. 'But that's mostly because I'm genuinely interested. That's just me. It's a bonus that it's useful for the job.' He paused. 'Especially if I'm working with someone who is a lot more taciturn, like John is. Speaking of whom . . .' He pulled his phone out. 'Still nothing from John. Poor guy. He was so flustered by the whole thing.'

'I imagine it's a big deal.' She turned her attention back to her drink. Hannah had returned from whatever she was doing in the back, and was watching them talk from the other end of the bar. No doubt the fact that she'd been talking to the nice young gentleman staying in the pub would be round the village in no time. She was going to have to answer questions tomorrow.

Gihan pushed his plate away and sighed. 'I really needed that sandwich. I didn't realise how hungry I was until I started eating.'

The landlady came over. 'Do you need anything else?'

'No, that was perfect,' Gihan said. 'Thank you so much Hannah, you are an angel.'

Hannah beamed at him. 'I'll put it on your tab.'

'Thank you.'

'You got your friend to the station okay then? Any news about the baby?'

Gihan checked his phone again. 'No. Nothing. I'm sure it's all fine though.'

'Let me know if you hear anything,' Hannah said.

'Of course.'

When Hannah had disappeared into the kitchen, Gihan said, 'Listen, Thanks for sitting with me and listening to me. I tend to babble a bit when I'm tired. Sorry about that.'

'Don't apologise. You had a good reason.'

They looked at each other for a moment and Alex felt that same pull she'd felt five years ago. A tug of something in his eyes calling to her. Her heart picked up speed. Suddenly all she could think about was his lips. The memory of what it was like to kiss him.

The moment stretched. Hannah returned to pull a pint, making Alex jump. The spell, whatever it was, broke. Gihan looked away and cleared his throat. She looked at her nearly empty drink, then at the window. The rain seemed to have abated. It was probably best if she left now, before she started thinking about kissing him again.

'It's stopped raining,' she said. 'I should get home. I told my friend I'd help him go over his presentation later.' She drained the rest of her drink and slid off her stool.

Gihan tilted his head to the side. 'Can I ask you something personal?'

'Sure.' Her heart kicked up a notch again. It was probably something really normal and boring. Nothing to get excited about.

'Why do you care so much about your project?' There was a small furrow in between his brows. 'You clearly care a lot and feel that an early diagnosis test is very important. It feels like it's more than just academic interest. Why are you so invested?'

Oh. She'd spent all that time hoping to talk about work and he was handing it over to her on a plate. How wonderful.

'It's a really important thing. It could save thousands of lives every year and—'

'I know all that,' he said. 'What I want to know is why is it important to you, personally?' He pointed at her to emphasise his point.

'Honestly. I was always going to care, because I like my job and I'm good at it,' she said, stalling. She didn't like talking about being a teen cancer survivor, because it tended to overshadow everything else about her. It was much better not to mention it and be recognised for her skill and knowledge, so she kept it quiet. But maybe this was an occasion where she should speak up. Making her plea more emotional could only be a good thing. She could tell him the truth without mentioning her own involvement. 'I had a friend . . . Jude. She had cancer – not breast cancer, something else – as a teenager. She died.' She hadn't known Jude for very long, but friendships formed in the ward had been intense. She'd carried on visiting Jude after her operation, but Jude's cancer was far more aggressive and as Alex got stronger, Jude got weaker. Alex remembered the time she had with Jude as bright spots of laughter and connection. She missed her. Alex had been lucky, in that her cancer had been caught early, before it metastasized. Jude had been less lucky. 'If her cancer had been diagnosed at an earlier stage, she might still be here.' She looked him in the eye. 'How can I not care about it?'

He held her gaze again, but this time it was different. His expression was thoughtful, intense. She felt . . . understood.

'Thank you for telling me that,' he said. 'I like that you care. It's . . . important.'

'Why did you ask?'

He raised his eyebrows. 'I talk to a lot of scientists and

engineers. It always fascinates me why they are into what they're into. It takes such dedication to be focused on the same thing for so long. Me? I'm easily bored. Which is why this job suits me. I get to go in, get properly into the weeds of a business for a few weeks. Then, I can hand over the project when it's finished and forget everything and start over with something different.'

The idea made her shudder. 'But there's nothing familiar. It's like the first day of school every time. How can you stand it?'

'I like it,' he said. 'My mum used to say, "It would be really boring if we were all the same".'

'True.' She zipped up her jacket. She wanted to ask him questions about what might happen to her project, but sensed that she wouldn't get anywhere. 'Thanks for the drink.'

'Not at all. Thank you for the company.' He smiled and her stomach fluttered in response.

'I'll see you tomorrow.'

For a split second, it looked like he was going to say something else, but he merely said, 'See you tomorrow.'

Alex walked to the door of the pub before she gave into temptation and looked back. He was watching her. He gave her a solemn nod. She nodded back and went outside. Once out in the damp air, she blew out her breath. Well, that evening had taken an interesting turn.

She had got the chance to talk to him about work after all, even if it wasn't exactly as she'd planned. Did it make a difference?

He seemed to have understood what the cancer test meant to her, but was that enough? She needed a better plan. It was just so hard to do because every time she was near him, her thoughts got all scrambled and her body dragged her back into this fantasy where he really was as perfect as she'd hoped he was and he wanted her as much as she wanted him.

It was so annoying. Right now, her hormones needed to calm the hell down and help her save her job.

Chapter 8

Gihan's boss Dorian called him the next morning. Thankfully, Gihan was already in the office. After all the excitement last night, he had slept surprisingly well, so he had gone into the Ryder FT early. Isobel had let him into the building.

'We don't have anyone we can send to help you this week,' Dorian said. 'But I'll have someone join your project to take up some of the slack on Monday.'

'John and I were almost done with the interviews and data gathering,' Gihan said. 'I can probably finish the last few by myself. I could do with some help with the analysis.'

'Good. Good.' There was a thoughtful pause. 'Are you sure you want to carry on with the interviews by yourself? Will you be able to . . . maintain objectivity?'

Alarm bells. Gihan ran through several scenarios in his head at lightning speed. Had John mentioned that Gihan had a preexisting relationship with Alex? Had he suggested that it would be a problem? 'What exactly is your concern?' He made sure his voice was neutral. He didn't know exactly what John had said.

'There's a reason we send two people out to jobs like this one,' Dorian said.

'I'm still gathering data. I have four interviews left – all with

98

the engineering and admin departments. I can record them if you need to have corroboration.'

'That won't be necessary. We have the interim report you and John produced. You can contact me directly if you find anything that contradicts your initial assessment. Just . . . be aware of your own blind spots.'

He gave Dorian a brief update, which John normally did, and hung up. He drummed his fingers on the table, thinking. It was a little insulting to be honest, to suggest that he might not be able to do his job because he'd had his head turned by a pretty woman.

It had been nice, last night. Sitting at the bar, chatting to her. It had given him the chance to unwind a little from the adventure that was Cotswold back roads. It reminded him of the night he'd met her for the first time. There had been a feeling of inevitability about chatting to her, as though they were meant to be talking, side by side, for the rest of their lives. He had felt it then and he felt it now.

He shook his head. He was being ridiculous. She had clearly not felt anything of that sort. He needed to forget that he knew her from before. Focus on the here and the now. He considered what she said about the friend who died. That would explain why she felt so passionately about it. His heart went out to her. He, of all people, understood what it was like to see someone you loved suffer and not be able to do anything to change things.

Unfortunately, it wouldn't really make a difference to his assessment. The conclusion to that was looking inevitable too. Unless some miraculous piece of information appeared when he talked to the engineers, he was going to have to suggest they closed both the non-essential R&D projects for the short term and focus on getting their primary product on the market. Most of his report was going to be trying to find recommendations to make that journey easier. He made a note of Alex's story anyway. You never knew when it might come in handy.

*

It was lunchtime before Gihan heard from John. He was busy working in the room that he'd been allocated at Ryder FT, when the text arrived. The baby, a boy, was in neonatal intensive care, but was stable, which was a relief.

Gihan felt a small knot of anxiety unravel. He hadn't realised he was worried about the welfare of John's baby. Now he knew everything was okay, he wished there was someone he could talk to about it. The landlady in the pub would be curious; he supposed he could call the pub and tell her.

He looked up to see Alex walk past, heading for the lab. Alex. She knew all about John and the baby. Not stopping to think, Gihan raced out and caught up with her at the lab door.

She smiled at him. 'Hello. Everything okay?'

Now he was here, he felt self-conscious. 'I heard from John,' he said. 'They had a baby boy.'

'Oh, nice. Is he . . . Is everything okay?'

'Well he's early, so he's being kept in hospital for a few days, but . . . he's out and John's wife seems to be okay.' He pulled up the message and showed her the photo. 'Look.'

They both looked at the picture of the baby, a tiny little thing with a tube coming out of his nose. In order to look, Alex had to stand very close. Gihan could smell her shampoo and a hint of perfume. It was all he could do not to try to breathe more in.

'He looks . . . thin,' she said.

'I think newborns tend to,' he pointed out.

She tipped her head to the side and it almost brushed his shoulder. He drew a sharp breath. Alex looked up and, as if surprised by how close she'd got, stepped back. Her face flushed. Gihan fought the urge to touch her.

She was looking puzzled now, a small furrow had appeared on her forehead.

Now that he'd told her about John's baby, there was no other reason for him to hold her up. He took a step back too, putting a good amount of space between them. 'I'll let you get on. I just wanted to let you know about the baby.'

She nodded. 'Thank you. I did wonder if everything was okay. I guess I'll see you later?'

'Yes. Sure.' He took another step back.

She smiled. 'Listen, I walk Penelope every evening at around seven. You're welcome to join us, if you want a walk with no risk of getting lost.' She raised her eyebrows. 'Emergencies permitting.'

His heart gave a little skip. 'I'll have to see how work goes,' he said. 'I might see you later, then. Emergencies permitting.'

When he got back into his office, he sat down and waited for his pulse to calm down. This was ridiculous. She was just being nice because he'd told her about how often he got lost. It wasn't an invitation for a romantic stroll. It was just an offer to help.

He shook his head. It was all very well telling himself that he could keep his distance from Alex and treat her with professional detachment, but his body hadn't got the memo. Every time he was near her, he wanted more. Like a paperclip near a magnet, he was pulled towards her, no matter how hard he tried not to be.

It was so frustrating. He was supposed to be maintaining a professional attitude. She was dating that big muscly guy.

Even if all of that were not true, he wasn't capable of sustaining a long-term relationship. Look what had happened with Helen. Guilt stabbed at him. Poor Helen. He didn't blame her for being angry. He felt terrible about hurting her.

Damn. He had to get this project wrapped up and get away. Once it was over, he could spend some time and work out what on earth was wrong with him when it came to commitment. Perhaps after that he could get back to dating again. Assuming he was capable of dating without having another panic attack by then.

Ah well. Back to the here and now. He opened the report he'd been working on and sighed. Actually doing his job was probably

101

the best antidote to his problems. Once Alex saw what his report had to say, she might never speak to him again.

*

Alex ate alone before going out to take Penelope for her walk. Jake had gone to Bristol for his big pitch event, so she was alone in the house that night. Walking through the silent living room, she wondered what would happen if she had to move. She paused to sit on the black leather sofa. She'd lived here with Jake for so long, it felt like home. What would it be like to have to start again? Her brief search for biotech jobs earlier that day had shown that there were places within commuting distance, but nothing that was really near. She'd emailed Maureen her CV that morning and made a list on her phone of likely-looking jobs, so that she could discuss them with Maureen after she got back from Penelope's walk.

Things were settled here – she had a place to live, friends in the community. She didn't want to lose that. At the same time, she couldn't share a house with Jake forever. She had to move out at some point. Maybe Gihan's investigation would force her to take the plunge.

Gihan. She thought of how close he had been standing when they were looking at his phone. She'd thought her heart was going to beat itself right out of her chest. She knew she liked him. That night, five years ago, she'd definitely felt some sort of connection with him. At the time, she'd thought it was a product of the night – the atmosphere, her own heightened emotions, the excitement of sharing something with a stranger – but in the days that followed she'd carried on thinking about him. And now . . . now she was getting to know him. He wasn't the person she'd imagined he'd be, not really. When at work, he was distant and reserved. He pretended he hadn't met her before, even when he remembered. It was exactly the sort of behaviour she'd expect from a man who snogs a stranger and then doesn't call the next day. But last night, she'd caught a glimpse of the more relaxed man she'd thought him to be. When she'd told him about Jude, he hadn't given her a fake look of pity or jumped in with a story of his own. He just seemed to understand. But then again, he was very good at getting people to tell him things. He'd as good as told her that. She didn't know what to think anymore.

She wanted to be angry with him. He had treated her abominably in the past and now he was threatening her job. She should be furious at him. At one level, she was. On another level, she just wanted to hurl herself into his arms. Which made her furious at herself.

For all that Gihan seemed to want to keep their relationship purely professional, he didn't have to come bounding out to show her the photo of John's baby. So maybe he wasn't as ambivalent about her as he made out either? It was all so confusing.

Frowning at her own thoughts, she stepped outside and locked the house. She could hear Penelope barking next door. That was strange. Penelope wasn't a very barky dog. She only usually made a racket when the postman came by. Alex pocketed her key, walked up her drive and back down Maureen's drive on the other side of the fence. Penelope was still barking.

Perturbed, Alex rang the doorbell. Penelope's barking took on a more frantic tone. No one came to the door.

'Maureen?' Alex called through the letterbox. Odd. Had Maureen gone out? She normally told Alex and Jake if she was going to be out, so that they knew to use their spare key to get Penelope out. 'Hang on a minute, Penelope,' Alex said. 'I'll go get the key.'

When she got to the gate, Gihan turned up. Apparently to walk Penelope with her.

'I think Maureen must have gone out,' she told him, instead of a greeting. 'I'm just going to get the spare key, so that I can get Penelope and take her for her walk.'

He smiled at her and she felt it in her chest. 'One minute,' she said, suddenly breathless. She hurried into the house and found Maureen's key on the hook by the back door, right underneath their own back door key. The light outside was fading slowly. As she locked her front door once more, she noticed that Maureen hadn't drawn the curtains or turned the lights on. She was definitely out.

Alex hurried back up one drive and down the other. Gihan hovered by the gate. Penelope went wild as she unlocked the door. Alex expected her to leap out to greet her, but instead, the little dog kept barking and ran into the house.

'Penelope, walkies.' She stepped into the house and immediately felt something was wrong. 'Penelope. Maureen?' She followed the dog into the living room. 'Maureen!'

The old lady was on the floor, one leg sprawled awkwardly. She groaned. 'Oh my god, Maureen.' Alex knelt by her friend's head. 'How long have you been here like this?'

Maureen opened her eyes. 'Hit my head,' she said. 'I think I've done something to my leg.'

Light flooded the room. Alex turned her head to see that Gihan had followed her in and turned the light on. He already had his phone held to his ear.

'Ambulance please. My name is Gihan Ranaweera. There's an elderly lady, Maureen. She's taken a fall.' He smiled at Maureen and mouthed 'hello' to her. Turning his attention back to the phone, he told them where they were. He tapped Alex's arm to ask for the house number. She rattled off the full street address.

Alex turned back to her friend to see that the old lady's eyes were huge and frightened. Alex picked up her hand. 'It's okay. We're here now,' she said quietly.

'It hurts,' Maureen whimpered back. 'My leg.'

The emergency call operative asked to speak to Maureen, so Gihan knelt on the floor too and put the phone on speakerphone. After a few questions, the paramedic asked if Maureen could lift her head, so that Alex could check for bleeding. Gihan fetched a glass of water so that Alex could help Maureen take a few sips.

Since they didn't dare move her, the best they could do was make her comfortable and sit with her until the paramedics turned up. Maureen kept a tight hold of Alex's hand. Gihan did all the fetching and carrying, carefully listening to instructions and responding without hesitation. By the time the paramedics arrived, Maureen was covered by a duvet and, after being fed cooled tea with a tablespoon, a little revived. A bag containing all of Maureen's medicines, a change of clothes and other essentials that Alex had guessed at, was packed, ready to go. Penelope had been let out to go do her business and fed an early dinner. Gihan even tried to take her for a walk, but the little dog refused to go beyond the front gate.

Maureen was reluctant to let go of Alex's hand. 'Come with me?' Her voice was reedy, as though she had aged a decade since the night before. Alex's heart cracked, just a little. She was used to Maureen making smartarse comments about her love life, not lying on the floor looking frail.

'I'm her next-door neighbour,' she explained to the paramedic. 'Can I come with you? She doesn't have any family nearby.'

The paramedic agreed that she could come in the ambulance. 'You're going to have to let go of her hand for a minute or two, Maureen,' he said. 'She's coming with you though, I promise.'

As they took Maureen out of the door, the enormity of what she was about to do hit Alex. She was going to go and sit in a hospital. She hadn't done that since she was a child. She shuddered.

'Are you okay?' said Gihan.

She shook her head. 'I hate hospitals. They bring back difficult memories.'

For a second his face went slack. For the first time she realised that there was always a small smile on his face, which she'd only noticed because it had disappeared right now. 'Same here,' he said.

She turned back. 'I promised Maureen . . .' She wasn't sure

which one of them she was trying to convince. She didn't want to go to hospital, but at the same time, she didn't want Maureen to be alone.

'I can come and meet you there,' Gihan said. 'If it helps . . .'

It would be better if someone else could be there with her. It would stop her from falling too far back into her memories. 'Would you?' She looked up at him, hope dawning slowly. 'That would be so good if you could.'

'Of course. I'll follow in the car,' said Gihan. 'If you tell me where you're going. Alex, can I have your number? I can call you when I get to the hospital and find out where Maureen's been taken.'

There was a moment of silence. The last time she'd given him her number he hadn't called. He took out his phone and didn't meet her eye. Perhaps he remembered that too.

That didn't matter now. She rattled off her number, which he dutifully typed into his phone. Her phone rang twice in her pocket and then stopped.

'Now you have mine as well,' he said.

They stood together while Maureen was wheeled onto the ambulance. Alex felt helpless watching. Gihan placed a warm hand on her shoulder and she allowed herself to relax a fraction. There was something reassuring about Gihan. He was calm and practical. He had been focused and helpful the whole time, doing what was necessary without drawing attention to himself. She was unbelievably grateful that she didn't have to do this alone.

When it was time to lock up the house and go, she looked up at him, standing under the streetlight. 'Thank you,' she said.

His expression was serious. 'I'll see you at the hospital.'

She clambered into the ambulance and sat where she was instructed. Maureen turned terrified eyes towards her and grabbed her hand again.

'It's okay, Maureen,' she said. 'I'm here now. I'm going to stay with you until I know you're settled. It's okay.' She glanced over her shoulder, to see Gihan talking to the other paramedic. He looked up. Their eyes met and he gave her another small, comforting smile, just before the doors shut.

Chapter 9

It started to rain. Great. Gihan stopped at a traffic light. His hands were gripping the steering wheel so hard that they hurt. He flexed his fingers as he waited for the lights to change. There was no reason for him to tail the ambulance there. If he spent too long thinking about it, he was likely to not go there at all.

'Ugh, hospitals.'

The lights changed and he drove on. When he'd found the hospital, got lost driving round it, found a car park and parked up, he called Alex. She didn't answer. The tight feeling in his chest was entirely psychosomatic. He knew that. This was a completely different type of visit to the hospital than he'd had before. He was here to support Alex. But . . . but right now, he was sitting in a dark car park, with the rain drumming on the roof and windshield and . . . he was not okay. There was only one person who would understand.

He took a couple of deep breaths to remind himself that he still could, pulled out his phone and called his sister.

'Hey Sam. It's me.'

'Aiya? You sound weird, where are you?' she said.

Hearing his sister's voice so close to thinking about hospitals made a wave of nausea wash over him. For a second, he was transported back to that awful 'family waiting room' outside palliative care. The three of them had clung to each other, while Thatha spoke to the doctor. Their older brother had been a cranky, disagreeable mess, much like their father, so Gihan had been strong for his sister. They had sat together, sharing his headphones, watching their favourite YouTube gamer walk through games. It was the only way to get through the day. He could almost feel her bony shoulder digging into his. The faint wetness that sometimes soaked into his shirt, because she cried, tears trickling down her face unchecked, almost as though she didn't even realise they were there. His eyes did that too, sometimes.

'I'm going to a hospital,' he said. His throat felt tight.

'Shit. What's wrong? Are you okay?' Sam's voice went up an octave. He sensed the panic in her.

'I'm fine,' he said, quickly. 'It's someone else. One of the people in the village had a fall. Alex has to go in with them. She asked if I could come with her.'

'Are they . . .'

He knew the rest of the sentence was 'going to die', because that's what he would have said. 'Maureen, that's the lady who fell. I think she might have hurt her leg. She's quite old. I don't think it's life and death, though. Just . . . worrying and more long term, if that makes sense.' He thought about how pale Maureen was. She didn't look well. She had quite clearly hit her head and that might have done more damage than was obvious. But there was no point saying that to Sam. 'She'll probably be okay.'

'What happened?' Sam's voice was back to normal now. He was glad he'd called her. There was something comforting about having his sister to hand.

He told her what had happened.

'So, you ended up on another mercy mission? Two in two days.'

He rubbed his forehead. 'Taking John to the station was hardly a mercy mission,' he said.

'Probably felt like it was to John.'

109

'Yeah, maybe, but it was only giving a guy a lift.'

'And this time?'

'I was there . . . so I helped.'

'But why are you going to the hospital if the lady already has someone with her? You don't know her.'

'Alex asked me to.'

'Who's Alex? A work guy?'

He closed his eyes. He shouldn't have mentioned Alex. 'Not a guy. She's a woman. Works for the client.'

'And she's special, is she?'

'Don't be ridiculous, Sam. There's nothing like that going on. I was talking to Alex outside of work because . . . we've met before.' He wasn't going to be able to get out of this without telling Sam everything. He could see it with the inevitability of an oncoming train. 'Five years ago. New Year's Eve.'

There was a beat of silence as Sam processed this. 'Shit. New Year's Eve girl? You found her.'

'I did. It has been . . . interesting.'

He half expected Sam to start probing him for details, but instead she said, 'So, this woman Alex asked you to come to the hospital with her. And . . . you said yes.'

'I had to. She told me yesterday that she had a friend who died when she was young. I guess she has terrible memories of hospitals too.' Probably almost as bad as his and Sam's. 'You should have seen her face. She looked so lost and worried. I couldn't say no.'

Sam gave a small chuckle. 'You really like her, huh?'

It was becoming obvious to him that yes, he really did. 'Yeah. Awkward.'

She made a sympathetic hmm noise. 'How long until you hand in your report and the company stops being a client?'

'Well, given that John's out of action . . . probably a couple of weeks. Three at the most.'

His phone beeped. When he looked at the screen he could

see another incoming call. 'Listen Sam, I think she's trying to call me.'

'Go. Go. Text me if you have any news. Good luck at the hospital. It won't be like when we went. It'll be okay.'

'Thanks.' He hung up and quickly accepted the new call before it went to answerphone.

'Hi. Gihan speaking.'

'Hi.' Alex sounded tired. 'I had a missed call from you. I guess you're here?'

'I am. I've found a place to park. How's Maureen?'

'She's busted her kneecap. They think she might have a bit of concussion from when she hit her head. We are still in A&E. They're going to take her in for a scan, to check for bleeding inside. And then they're going to move her to a ward. I . . . I don't know where yet . . .'

He could hear the wobble in her voice. It was hard to know what to do when you were inside a hospital. He did what he always did in times like this. He made a decision and ran with it. 'Tell you what. I'm going to go to the hospital café and grab us both a coffee. If you find out which ward you're going to, call me. If not, just tell me where you are and I'll bring your coffee to you. Does that sound like a good plan?'

The phone rustled as she exhaled. 'Yes. That sounds great.'

'How do you take your coffee?'

'Flat white, please. No sugar.'

'Okay. I might be a while because I've got to find my way through the hospital, but I'm on my way.'

'Gihan,' she said, quietly. 'Thank you.'

'No problem. I'll see you in a bit.' He hung up and put the phone in his pocket. The rain had eased a little. Outside, the lights from the hospital complex winked through the wet glass. He breathed out and forced his phone-free hand to unclench from the fist it had formed. He could do this. His mother wasn't in that hospital, nor were any other members of his family. Maureen was just someone he vaguely knew. And she wasn't dying. He could do this. Alex's eyes, huge and scared, came up in his mind. She needed him. He could do this.

He got out of the car and flipped the hood up on his coat. Blipping the lock on the car, he set determinedly off towards the hospital.

*

Alex sat on a chair in the waiting area outside the side ward. Maureen had been taken away for her brain scan, leaving Alex sitting alone with Maureen's overnight bag on her lap. She had lost track of time – there were no windows visible from where she was. Even though there would be some if she got up and walked along the corridor a bit, she couldn't bear to move.

Hospitals always smelled the same. Disinfectant, floor cleaner and after a few hours, stale coffee . . . and if you were stuck there for long enough, it settled on your skin, making you feel permanently clammy and sour. It reminded her of nausea and pain. In the daytime, through a haze of discomfort and pain, her mother had been there, reading to her. Or her father, telling her about his day. But the nights. Especially after the operation, when she'd been moved to the teen ward. Those were the worst. That was where she'd met Jude. Lovely Jude who managed to be cheerful most of the time, but whimpered when her pain meds ran low at night. The sound of Jude crying had been horrible. The silence when she stopped had been worse.

The idea that Maureen might die was too huge to contemplate. It had always seemed impossible. Maureen was a fixture. A fact of life. But now . . . Maureen suddenly seemed fragile. She needed someone to be strong for her and there was only Alex around.

Alex had already tried Leila, but her phone was off. Ordinarily, she would have called Jake next, he had known Maureen for longer and was a huge part of her life. Alex took her phone out and glared at it. Should she? Jake was at his conference. He had

112

his big pitch meeting tomorrow morning and if she told him, he would come rushing back. What would that achieve? It would only ruin his chances of expanding his business. On the other hand, if Maureen died . . .

Alex shivered. The responsibility felt huge. There was no one who could share it. Her parents were away on their big holiday around Australia. None of her friends in London knew Maureen. Right now, there was only her. She felt so alone.

People had been walking up and down the corridor the whole time. Alex had stopped noticing them. Her usual optimism had deserted her, so that all she could think about was the possibility of Maureen dying. How long had she lain there on the floor? Maureen had seemed genuinely frightened. Did she think she was going to die too?

Alex sat, with her hands clasped around the overnight bag on her knees, oblivious to everyone else, until someone stopped next to her.

'Here. I've brought you coffee.' A hand, holding the disposable cup, appeared in her field of vision.

She looked up to find Gihan standing next to her. The sight of him sent a ripple of relief through her. Thank god. Someone was here. She wasn't alone anymore. She was so relieved that before she could think about what she was doing, she stood up and threw her arms around him.

For a second, he didn't move, his arms held outwards. Oh no. He wasn't hugging her back. She tensed. Then he exhaled and just . . . relaxed. His arms remained held out, but she felt the tension leaving his torso. It took some of her own bleak anxiety with it. He bent his head to rest his cheek on the top of her head – an acknowledgement of her hug. Relieved, she rested her cheek against his reassuringly solid shoulder, glad of the human contact.

'Hey,' he said, softly. 'You okay?'

Alex released him and pushed her hair away from her face. 'I'm . . . glad you're here.'

'Well, me too,' he said. 'If I'd known I'd be getting a greeting like that, I'd have tried to get here sooner.'

Was he laughing at her?

When she stepped back, he handed her the coffee. Of course. That was why he hadn't hugged her back. He didn't want to spill hot coffee on her. It was a kind thing to do. In fact, he had been nothing but kind all evening.

'Are you sure you're okay?' There was no teasing in his voice now, only concern.

Alex nodded. 'I . . . don't like hospitals much.'

He gave a sniff of mirthless laughter. 'I know that feeling. I don't like them either.'

She resumed her seat and he took the seat next to her. After a moment of awkward silence, Gihan took a sip of his coffee. The action reminded Alex that she was holding a hot drink too. One sip and warmth spread through her. She hadn't realised how much she'd needed caffeine.

'Thanks for the coffee,' she said.

'Oh, it was nothing.' He took another sip. 'It's not the greatest coffee in the world, but I've had worse.'

She tasted hers again. 'It's not bad.'

'The café was still serving.'

They sipped in silence for a while. The warmth and stimulation of the coffee made her feel better. So did having some company. 'Maureen's been taken away to have a scan to check for internal bleeding. They did an X-ray earlier. She's broken her knee. They're putting her in a cast, poor thing. Under ordinary circumstances, she would have hated that.'

'She doesn't hate it now?' He frowned.

'I think she's just too scared to think clearly right now. I reckon she genuinely thought she was going to die on the floor.'

'Poor lady,' he said. 'I don't know her, obviously. But that sounds like a horrible situation to be in.'

Alex nodded. 'She . . . Her children don't live nearby. So she's all alone. She's only got me and Jake and a few people in the village to help her and if she—' Tears that had been lurking for hours ambushed her now. She wiped them away with her free hand and tried again. 'We—' A sob cut her off, punching up from her solar plexus and making her gasp.

'Oh.' Gihan quickly put his coffee on the floor and put an arm around her shoulders. When she gave up her fight against the tears and leaned into him, he wrapped his other arm around her as well, giving her the hug that he hadn't done before. She buried her face in the warm space between his neck and shoulder and let herself feel everything she'd been holding at bay. 'I'm so scared,' she said, into his collarbone.

He didn't answer, but gave her a gentle squeeze. Somehow, it was enough.

They sat like that until her tears stopped. She said, 'I'm sorry,' without lifting her head.

'No need,' he said. 'It's been a scary day for you. And it isn't over yet.' His arms tightened around her. 'I'm here for as long as you need me.'

'Thank you.' She closed her eyes for a moment. If she hadn't liked Gihan before, she would definitely fall for him now. He was kind. She hadn't thought that kindness was something she'd have on her list of desirable characteristics in a man, but now it was obvious that it should be. Maybe he still was the man she'd thought he was at first. Kind, thoughtful and chivalrous in a non-creepy way. Also, a small part of her mind supplied, he smelled really nice. With her arms wrapped around him like this, she could feel the muscles on his back. Sinewy. Built for elegance, not bulk. If this had been a different place and a different time . . . but it wasn't. She reluctantly let go of him and sat back.

'I spent a lot of time in hospitals. I didn't know if I was ever going to leave. Being here is a bit . . . triggering.' She found the tissues she always kept in her pocket and wiped her eyes. 'I'm sorry,' she said. 'I don't normally cry.'

'I refer back to my comment about it being a scary day,' he said. 'And don't worry about crying. Hospitals make you do that.' There was something in the way his gaze flicked to the corridor and back that made her think he was speaking from experience.

He shuddered and leaned down to retrieve his coffee.

'You don't like hospitals much either, huh?' she said. 'How come? Were you in hospital with an illness?' She was desperate for a bit of distraction.

'Not me,' he said. 'My mum.' He kept his eyes on the corridor, but she could tell he wasn't really seeing it. 'She had cancer. By the time we found it, it had already spread. She died . . . very quickly. But she spent a lot of her last days in hospital.' He finally looked at her again. His eyes were dry, but she could see the vestiges of the pain in them.

'I'm so sorry,' she said. She wanted to ask what kind of cancer, but it seemed intrusive to ask, so instead she said, 'You must hate hospitals.'

'I'm not a big fan, no. But they're there for a reason, I guess.'

It seemed that hospitals scared him as much as they did her, maybe even more, and yet he was here. She almost started crying again, this time out of gratitude. 'Thank you.' She reached out for his hand and squeezed it. 'I really appreciate you being here.'

He wasn't smiling. His gaze rested briefly on her mouth, then flicked back to her eyes. Her own breath caught in response. He breathed in, as though to say something, then seemed to remember himself and exhaled again. The smile returned, but it was tinged with sadness now. 'That's what friends are for, right? To be there, when you need them.' His gaze slid away.

Friends. Of course. She couldn't mean anything more to him – that's why he was pretending he couldn't remember how they'd first met.

She removed her hand from where it was sitting on top of his and settled back in her chair, so that she wasn't looking at him anymore. They sat together in silence for a moment. Alex tried to reconcile the mental image of a cad who snogged her on New Year's Eve and then ghosted her, with this kind man who was sitting beside her. It didn't make sense. Suddenly cold again, she folded her arms.

Since he was so good at the enigmatic silence when it came to work interviews, she expected the silence to stretch. But after less than a minute, he said, 'Was it something I said?'

She knew he remembered. This pretending it hadn't happened wasn't getting them anywhere. 'New Year's Eve. Five years ago,' she said. 'I know you remember.' She sneaked a sideways glance at him.

'Ah,' he said. 'Yes. I remember. I'm surprised you do.' He turned his head and met her gaze.

There wasn't a hint of apology in his expression. In fact, he was doing that thing where his face went blank so that it was impossible to see what he was thinking. This annoyed her. How dare he.

'You didn't call!' It came out louder than she'd intended. She looked up and down the corridor. Two women sitting further down the corridor had both turned to look and hurriedly looked away, pretending that they weren't listening. Alex lowered her voice. 'You didn't call,' she said.

Gihan looked at first taken aback and then annoyed. 'I did. A man answered.' He looked away and took a sip of his coffee. 'I assumed you'd got back together with your ex.'

'But—' Why would some guy answer her phone? She had watched her phone all day that day. No one else had been near it. 'You definitely didn't call.'

'I definitely did.' He looked at the wall opposite, his back stiff, pointedly not looking at her. 'I called the number you wrote for me on the back of a bookshop receipt.'

She thought about herself, in the back of the dark taxi, scribbling out her number on the back of a receipt, balanced on her knee. Her handwriting was awful at the best of times. Had she somehow written it so that he got the number wrong? Her phone number had three sevens in it and a one. Given her scrappy

117

writing, he could have read any of them wrong and ended up calling some random person instead. He wouldn't have been able to ask for her . . . because she hadn't bothered to write her name on the piece of paper.

Oh. Alex chewed her lip. All this time, she'd thought that he hadn't bothered to call her. But he had. And he'd thought that she'd either maliciously given him a fake number or that she'd got back together with Todd. No wonder he didn't want to bring it up now. This changed everything.

'I have pretty bad handwriting . . .' She turned and found him staring at her.

'You do,' he said. His shoulders dropped a fraction. He turned to look at her. 'It's possible that I read your number wrong.'

'I thought you didn't call. It was all a dreadful misunderstanding.' Emotions bubbled up inside her, but she couldn't work out which yet.

The familiar smile was back. 'Looks like it,' he said.

She felt something loosen in her chest. Now it all made sense. What a terrible thing to happen. She forgot where she was for a second as a wave of elation swept through her. He hadn't snogged her and ignored her! He must have felt that connection between them too.

'So . . . what does that mean now?' she asked.

He started to smile, but stopped as though he'd remembered something. He looked away. 'Not much, I guess,' he said, tightly. 'It's nice that we're not tiptoeing around it anymore. I didn't mean to be rude to you and you didn't mean to be rude to me. Makes it easier to be . . . friends.'

Disappointment crashed over her. She felt silly for even thinking that it could be anything more. 'Yes,' she said. 'Of course. That's good.'

They sipped their coffees, the silence now strained and awkward. She wished she hadn't brought up the past now. It seemed to have messed up the present. Things had been going well despite the desperately sad circumstances. Oh. Maureen. For a few minutes she had forgotten about her neighbour. Now the fear and worry came swirling down again, making her want to cry.

'I hope they bring Maureen back soon,' she said.

Gihan patted her hand. 'I'm sure they will. It'll be okay.' He removed his hand.

'What if it's serious? What happens then?' She shook her head. 'Jake's going to kill me for not telling him.'

He looked confused, but said, 'I'm sure she'll be okay.' After a second he added. 'Who's Jake?'

'My housemate. He's away at a big investor event thing. I didn't want to tell him.'

'Oh,' said Gihan. 'Jake's the big guy. He's your housemate. Of course.'

She frowned. 'Why? Who did you think he was?'

'Your partner.'

That was so ludicrous, it made her laugh. 'Ha! No. Just my housemate. Well, landlord, I suppose. Nothing else going on there. He's gay.'

He stared at her for a moment, his eyes wide, his mouth a little 'o'. Then he gave her a rueful smile. 'I seem to have made a lot of assumptions about you that are untrue.'

She nodded. 'Looks like it.' She had made a lot of assumptions about him too. 'Maybe we should start again.'

His gaze held hers and she knew he was thinking about that night, five years ago. He gave a small shake of his head and looked away. 'If only. We are where we are.'

Another beat of silence. A nurse came to talk to the other two ladies further down the corridor. Alex's thoughts returned to Maureen. She chewed her lip.

Gihan nudged her gently. 'Hey, tell you what? Want to help me find a place to rent in London?'

'Sure.' Why not? It's not like she had anything else to do but worry.

He opened an app and started showing her apartments with enormous price tags. It made her realise exactly how lucky she had been to find a room with Jake. She moved closer so that they could both see the screen better. Their bodies leaned into each other, faces close. His presence was warm and comforting. It was a good distraction.

She watched Gihan's long fingers as he scrolled through apartment listings. He kept up a steady stream of comments about what he was looking for and the quirks of each of the places. At first, Alex barely listened to what he was saying, and sank into the lull of his voice. Clearing up the misunderstanding about what happened had changed everything for her. Everything. All this time when she'd been wondering how something that had felt so perfect had gone so badly wrong. Had she been such a terrible judge of character?

It turned out that he really was the man she'd fallen for that evening. The perfect man for her. Okay, now she knew him better and she knew he wasn't perfect, but . . . he came closer than anyone else so far. He was here, wasn't he? Sitting next to her in a bleak corridor, just so that she didn't have to do this alone. He was even trying to distract her by talking about his search for a home.

Just her luck that he only wanted to be friends. She wanted to wail and ask him why, but even she could see how that was too intense. There was nothing she could do but accept friendship as an alternative. It was better than being without him at all, especially now, when she didn't want to be alone.

'Oh, calling that an apartment is just taking the mick,' he said.

She paid attention to what was on his phone. This place was really a bedsit with a screen to partition off the 'bedroom'. Gihan shook his head and clicked onto a different listing. This one looked familiar.

'Have we seen that one before?' she said.

He checked the listing. 'No. But I think we saw another place in the same building. I guess they're identical.'

'What are you looking for, exactly?'

'Commuting distance for work. One bedroom, maybe two.' He shrugged. 'I don't know, practical things.'

'Your budget is a pretty good size. How many have you seen?'

'Only a few so far. I kinda ruled out the area they were in after visiting it. I've got a couple of viewings lined up for the weekend. In a different neighbourhood.'

'They all look quite similar,' she said. 'How would you choose?'

'I don't know,' he said. 'I'll probably take the first one that meets the criteria.'

'What if you see one that doesn't fit your criteria so well, but you absolutely fall in love with it?' She turned to look at his face and her thigh pressed against the side of his.

He didn't look at her, but swiped down to look at another property. 'It's a flat, Alex, not a puppy. If it doesn't meet the criteria, there's no point taking it because I'd have to live in a place that isn't quite as convenient as it could be for years.'

'You have no romance in your soul,' she said, meaningfully.

He raised his eyes so that he was staring at the wall opposite. 'No,' he said, finally. 'I guess I don't.'

He shifted position, putting a small slice of space in between them. The loss of the warmth sent a ripple of disappointment through her.

Had she offended him? Or was this his way of reminding her that they had to keep their distance from each other because of work? She looked down. Maybe he had a point. They couldn't start again. They were where they were.

*

Gihan watched Alex standing at the foot of Maureen's bed, wringing her hands as she spoke to the doctor. Maureen was asleep, sedated, maybe. The gist of the conversation seemed to be that she would be okay. Gihan wasn't listening to the doctor. He was watching Alex.

121

He wasn't at his best in hospitals. It was hard to think because at the end of every line of thought was a horrible memory that he didn't want to revisit. He didn't want to give into the memories.

Luckily, what he'd found out this evening was helping to distract him. There was a lot to process. Five years ago, Alex hadn't used him as a stop gap until she got together with her boyfriend . . . and she was single now. Two things that he'd been holding onto as facts were gone, just like that.

There was nothing stopping him from handing in his report and then asking her out . . . which should fill him with happiness. It did, but it also filled him with terror. Alex wasn't someone to see casually. She was a romantic at heart. She threw herself into things – a house would always be a home, a relationship would always be true love. He knew how sad she'd been when he'd first met her. The idiot that she was dating had dumped her on New Year's Eve and she was full of anger and sadness. They'd been together for two months and she thought it was the real thing. At the time, he'd been torn between feeling sympathy for the poor guy who was out of his depth and feeling delighted that Alex had been thrown into his path. She had been churned up with disappointment that night. He could never be the guy who made her feel like that again.

Except . . . he couldn't be a good boyfriend to her. He couldn't handle commitment. At the first sign of things getting serious, he would have a panic attack and bail on her. If he couldn't manage to talk to Helen, whom he'd known for so long, how would he talk to Alex? No. There was no way he could be anything more than a friend to Alex. No matter how much he wanted to. He watched her tuck a strand of hair behind her ear. Oh, but how he wanted to.

The best thing, the right thing to do, would be to walk away from her and let her get on with her life.

See, this was why he thought fate was a bitch. He'd thought fate was unfair five years ago, when he met a stranger he'd really liked only to lose all hope the next day. But for it to happen again, this time when he knew he was incapable of being with her without hurting her – that was just cruel.

Losing people was hard. Just like . . . He breathed in and smelled that hospital smell of disinfectant and plastic. A wave of nausea rolled through him. All he wanted to do was to run away.

He swallowed. No. Not thinking about that now. He had to be here to ride out this crisis. This is what he did. He focused his attention on Alex.

Alex asked the doctor a question and her voice trembled. Every instinct in Gihan called him to go to her and comfort her. To protect her as much as he could. How could he walk away when she still needed someone . . . and the only someone available was him?

So he stayed. When the nurse told Alex that she may as well go home and get some sleep, he put a hand on her shoulder and guided her out of the ward. He walked beside her. Wanting to hold her hand, but not trusting himself to let go if he did.

Chapter 10

It was late by the time they left the hospital and Alex was shattered. Maureen had been settled into a ward and they had been asked to leave. Alex sat in the darkened car and rubbed her hand over her face. Maureen had been nodding off to sleep when they left. She'd been less confused and a bit more like her normal self. Alex sighed.

'She'll be okay,' Gihan said, as though he had read her mind. He was driving.

She glanced at him, lit by the eerie glow from the sat nav. He had been a solid presence the whole time – not interfering, just there when she needed him to be. He had fetched and carried and done as he was asked. The only time he had taken charge was when she'd had a moment of utter blankness when told she could leave. He had thanked the nurses, made sure they had her mobile number in case anything changed overnight, and then led her out to the car. With only one or two wrong turns. It was like he was actually paying attention to what she needed and acting accordingly.

She liked that. Guys she'd dated before had either let her take charge and do everything or liked to tell her things she already knew. There seemed to be no in between. She liked how Gihan seemed to know when to step in and when to hold back.

They came to the slip road leading onto the dual carriageway.

She watched as he twisted in his seat to check for traffic and changed gears as he sped up. He moved so smoothly. She could watch him all night.

Embarrassed at her own thoughts, she looked back out of the window. The memory of how it felt to hold him resurfaced. It had been a reassuring and comforting feeling at first, but then, it had been more than that. She remembered all too well what it was like to kiss him, to be free to want him. He had pointed out that they were friends. And earlier, he had been careful to maintain some space between them. He had made it clear that there was a line he wouldn't cross. He obviously didn't want anything more than friendship.

So that was it. There was no point imagining a future with him. Since she knew that already, she could try to prevent herself from getting hurt.

Alex closed her eyes and let herself sink into the memory of that one night five years ago. It had been a few hours outside of real life. No worrying about what was going to happen next. No worrying about sending out the wrong signals or coming off as desperate. Nothing she did would matter. It was supposed to be a one-off, disposable event. A snippet from a life outside her own. And it had been so great. She had conveniently ignored the fact that it had ended badly and kept just the memory to warm her when she needed it.

Gihan turning up in real life had messed everything up. Before, she had been able to imagine that one day they would meet again and she would find out that some catastrophe had prevented him from calling her, that her one night *had* been perfect, and that she could finally recapture the love that got away. Now, they'd met again, they'd cleared up the reason he hadn't called, she had thought that the chemistry was still there, but he had friend-zoned her so quickly that it made her dizzy.

It made her want to curl up in a ball and cry.

*

Gihan threw a glance at Alex, sitting next to him, with her head resting against the window. Her eyes were closed. She had fallen asleep. Good. She must have been exhausted. He knew first-hand how tiring it was worrying about someone and waiting for news.

He frowned at the dark road ahead. Now that she was asleep, he could let his guard down a little bit. He shifted his shoulders to loosen them. Hospitals made him tense at the best of times. Add to that having to fight the urge to wrap his arms around Alex and protect her from everything and it had been almost unbearable. When she'd hugged him so unexpectedly, thank goodness he'd been holding the coffee. It had given him some valuable seconds to process it all and work out that he could comfort her, without letting her know it meant more to him than that.

He took one hand off the wheel to pinch the bridge of his nose. He wished he was wearing his glasses instead of contacts. It was so late now, his eyes felt sore.

Alex shifted in her seat. He glanced across. Still asleep. Good.

He couldn't have her, he knew that. All he could do now was to work out how to minimise the damage he would cause to her.

The report he was drafting was looking clearer and clearer. Alex's project had to go, as did Isobel's. From what he could see, the rest of Alex's small team could be moved to other parts of the company. But Alex and Isobel were both too senior to be shuffled into someone else's group. From his interviews, he could see that neither of them would take kindly to that, anyway. So they were obvious candidates for reducing head count – which was one of the things he had been asked to identify.

He glanced at her again. What would she do? She was so passionate about her cancer test, would she be happy looking for another job working on something else? Would she have to move? Seeing how much she cared about Maureen, he knew that she had a special connection to where she was right now. It wasn't the family or 'home' she'd been born to, but it was the home she'd chosen. He didn't hold with the theory of blood being thicker than water. Sure, his sister was one of his favourite people, but then so were his stepmother and his stepcousin. Blood had nothing to do with it.

He'd found out today that she was single. In the past he would have thought that he might be able to get her out of his system if he dated her for a bit. But he saw that when Alex loved someone, she loved with everything that she had. He wasn't going to be good for her. He couldn't handle serious relationships. Ha. When he was younger he'd thought he stuck to casual relationships through choice. If his girlfriends looked like they were wanting more from him, he gently broke up with them. But he'd got careless with Helen and drifted into something deeper and look how that turned out. He felt awful for Helen. He felt worse for himself. To go out with someone like Alex, when he knew full well that casual was all he was good for . . . He couldn't do that.

Yes, he liked her. He sneaked a glance at her sleeping face. He liked her a lot. Maybe too much. This was dangerous for him too.

The sat nav kicked in to tell him to take the next exit. The village was only about fifteen minutes away, according to the display. Gihan sighed. He would just have to keep a tight lid on his feelings until he had handed in his report. Once the project was signed off, she would lose her job and her research project that she cared so deeply about would be closed down. He was pretty sure she wouldn't want to talk to him anymore after that. He had tried to think of other things that his report could suggest, but short of a miracle, there was nothing he could say. Not suggesting cutting back on R&D would bankrupt the company, cost him this job and only postpone the inevitable for a few months for Alex.

If only there were some way he could make this better without putting the whole company at risk. He sighed again and indicated that he was coming off the motorway.

*

Alex woke up with a start. The car had stopped. She sat up, instinctively running a hand over her mouth in case she had drooled. Out of the window, she recognised her house. Gihan pulled the handbrake up with a loud crick and turned to her.

'Here you are. Are you going to be okay by yourself?'

'Why? Are you offering to spend the night?' She regretted it the minute she said it. It sounded so flirty. What if he thought she was propositioning him? Oh, Alex.

His expression flickered briefly before he smiled. 'Only as moral support,' he said.

Embarrassed, she busied herself gathering her stuff, letting her hair hide her face so that he couldn't see how red she'd gone. Not that he could see much in the shadowy recesses of the car. She could feel him watching her though.

She looked up and her mouth went dry. He was leaning towards her, a look of concern on his face. One hand rested on the steering wheel, the other was at the edge of his seat. He was so close. All she had to do was lean a few inches . . .

She cleared her throat. 'Listen, er . . . thank you. Thank you so much for coming to the hospital with me. I don't know what I'd have done without you.'

'You would have managed, I'm sure,' he said, with a small smile.

'Having someone there really helped.'

She looked up and their eyes met. Silence stretched and flexed between them, changing the mood in the small space. Her gaze rested on his mouth. Just an inch . . .

A dog barked frantically. They both jumped and looked towards the houses.

'Penelope,' said Alex. 'Poor thing must be frantic.' She pulled her handbag towards her. 'I'll pop in and see her before I go home.' She opened the car door and stepped out before the temptation to kiss him took hold again. From the relative safety of being outside the car, she leaned down and said, 'Thanks again for helping me.'

'That's what friends are for,' he said. There was a tiny emphasis on the word 'friends'.

Alex shut the door quietly, in deference to the late hour, and walked up to Maureen's door. She still had the key. It took her a minute to find it. When she looked over her shoulder, she could see that the car was still there. It wasn't until she'd got the door unlocked and stepped in that he drove away. He must have been waiting to make sure she got in.

Penelope yipped and whined at the sight of her. Alex dropped to her knees and stroked Penelope. 'She's okay. A little fragile, but she'll be home in a few days, I'm sure.' She gave the little dog a hug. 'Shall we let you out for a wee?'

While Penelope was outside, she checked the kitchen and living room and tidied up a mug and a plate. Maureen's 'Meals on Wheels' dinner was in the fridge, which meant the old lady had fallen after delivery time had passed. She made a mental note to let Meals on Wheels know that Maureen wouldn't be home for a while.

Going to the back door, she whispered Penelope's name. The little dog came running back in, her tail still at half-mast. When Alex tried to leave, Penelope looked so woebegone, that she didn't have the heart to go. So she found herself a blanket, curled up on the sofa and fell asleep with the worried dog on her feet.

*

Gihan got back to his room, having woken up the landlord with his attempts to let himself in. He crept around his room, resisted the urge to have a shower to wash the hospital feeling off him and got into his pyjamas. He flopped into bed. Now he was wide awake. Bloody fantastic. He had about four hours before he had to get up and drag himself to work and his brain had decided it was wakey time. Ugh.

He turned off the light and lay there in the dark. He didn't want to be thinking in the middle of the night. There were only two things that he could think about right now. One was Alex and how small and vulnerable she'd looked, and how much he wanted to hold her. The other . . . well, he never wanted to think about that, but, without anything else to distract him, it caught him anyway. Grief accosted him at the strangest of times. Like now. In the anonymous dark of a B&B, he had the most vivid memory of his mother telling him to look after his sister. He remembered the dark circles under her eyes, the way her skin seemed all dry and wrong, the tubes in her arm. And Sam, next to him, crying and crying like she'd never stop.

Tears pricked at his own eyes and he blinked them back. He had cried for his mother at the time. He didn't need to do any more of that. Losing her had been a cataclysm. What had been worse was the way it took out the rest of the family as well. Their father's grief had been enormous and all consuming. He had retreated into himself, unable to cope with the loss of his wife. Gihan and his siblings were . . . managed. There was always food and if they asked for anything, he provided, but he hadn't been *there*. So the three of them had coped, leaning on each other for comfort and solace. In losing Amma, they'd lost Thatha as well.

Until Upali Aunty, one of Amma's friends, arrived one day, took one look at the haunted children and their father and took charge. She would turn up around the time they got back from school. She helped them cook proper meals, rather than the sandwiches and beans on toast they'd come to have more and more often. She asked them about their days. Gihan loved her for that. When, eventually, inevitably, she and Thatha fell in love, Gihan had been overjoyed and started calling her Aunty-Amma. Maybe now, they would get their father back. But they didn't. Thatha remained distant and dutiful. Aunty-Amma was there for them though. She was the parent they needed. Not so much for his brother, who went off to uni soon after, but for Gihan and Sam.

Gihan sighed and rolled onto his side. Sam had reached some sort of understanding with Thatha of late, but he hadn't. Not yet.

He punched the pillow into shape. He'd much rather be thinking about Alex. Which, of course, was equally unhelpful because as much as he liked her, he couldn't have her.

Chapter 11

Alex was woken up by an insistent knocking. And barking. Barking? She surfaced, aching and groggy. What—? Memory came crashing back. Oh yes. Maureen. She was in Maureen's house. She had fallen asleep on the sofa. She tried to get up, but her back was so stiff she couldn't. Pain gripped her back like a vice. She sat up very, very slowly.

More knocking on the door.

'Hang on. Hang on.' She rolled off the couch so that she was on all fours on the floor, then used the side of the sofa to haul herself upright. Spikes of pain jabbed up her back with every movement.

'Maureen? Is everything okay? Hello?' It was Mal, calling through the letterbox. Of course. He had agreed to do Jake's Penelope shift. 'I can't find the spare key.'

'I'm coming!' she shouted. Holding the wall, she made it to the front door and unlocked it. 'Penelope, darling, please stop barking.'

Penelope looked up at her. The barking subsided to a low 'wurf'. Then a whine.

Alex pulled the door open. 'Morning Mal.' Her voice sounded gravelly. She cleared her throat. It didn't help.

Mal was dressed for a run, his black hair scraped back into a ponytail, his white headphones glowing stark white against his dark skin. He stared at her. 'Alex? What's going on?'

Penelope gave another little 'wurf'. Mal looked down. 'Sorry Penelope.' He hunkered down to give her a scritch, but then looked up. 'Alex?'

Alex took a few steps back and leaned against the wall. It was still dark outside. Maureen and the boys kept unholy hours. She quickly explained what had happened.

Mal slowly stood up. 'Shit. Is she going to be okay?' He tipped his head to the side. 'Are you?'

Alex leaned her head back against the wall and groaned. 'My back is killing me. I should have known not to sleep on the sofa.'

Mal grimaced. 'You go home and get some painkillers. I'll take Penelope out and make sure I feed her before I leave.'

'She's a bit upset.'

The little dog was making little jumps towards Mal's shoes. He reached past Alex and unhooked the leash from its hook. 'We'll be fine, won't we Penelope?' To Alex, he said, 'I'll see you when I get back.'

'Wait. You'll need a key.' She took her key out of her pocket and handed it to him. 'I'll take the back door key. You can let yourself into ours?'

She didn't know why she bothered asking. Mal had a key to their house. It was ridiculous. He practically lived with them.

'Go home.' Mal told her. 'Come on Lady Penelope.'

She watched the man and dog disappear and closed the door. Ow. Painkillers. She hobbled off to grab the back door key.

By the time Mal turned up at her house, she'd had a very hot shower, got changed and was filling up her special long hot water bottle for her back. She tied it around herself like a bandolier, so that it rested across the place where her back was most sore.

Mal watched her with consternation. He opened his mouth.

She held up a hand. 'Do not ask me if I'm okay. I have taken my drugs. I am having some food so that I don't throw up said drugs. I am moving around. It will pass.'

He set his mouth in a hard line. 'Fine,' he said. 'I'll make coffee.'

'Thanks.' She lowered herself into her chair.

'Is it the scar that hurts?' Mal asked. Like Jake, he was fascinated by the idea of spinal surgery. They both knew a fair bit about muscles and skeletons, although Jake was the more knowledgeable of the two.

She finished her mouthful of cereal. 'No. Muscles in my lower back. It's fine if I sleep properly, on a decent mattress, but that sofa . . . not to mention the hours of sitting on a plastic chair . . .' She shrugged and winced. 'I don't think I've damaged anything. I'm a bit stiff, that's all. Like I say, it'll pass eventually.'

There was relative silence as Mal made coffee. He slid hers across the table and sat down. 'So, Maureen . . . how is she?'

Alex outlined everything that happened. 'She's hurt her knee – but that didn't need surgery, just a cast. They're worried about concussion. She was pretty shocked at first, but I think she was more coherent by the time we left.'

'Is Jake staying with her in the hospital, then? He's very fond of Maureen. She was so kind to him when he first moved here. Back when he was the only gay in the village.'

Ah. Alex looked down at her coffee. 'I . . . haven't told him yet.'

'Why the hell not?'

'I didn't want to mess up his big pitch today. Maureen would have killed me once she came round. I'll tell him later.'

Mal shook his head. 'I don't want him to blow his chances with getting some seed capital, believe me. But I don't think this is your call to make. What if something happens to Maureen? He'll never forgive you.'

This was true. Jake would be furious with her for not telling him immediately. But this pitch was important to him. To Mal too, because more gyms meant more customers for him. 'But it affects your business too, Mal.'

Mal faltered. 'Yes, but . . . you should still tell him. People are more important.'

'But there's nothing he can actually do.'

He scowled down at his mug. 'The last investor pitch is at 11.05. He'll definitely be done by lunchtime. Tell him at lunchtime.'

'Which is what I said in the first place.' Men. Honestly.

They chatted for a few more minutes, arranged a few practicalities, like Mal taking Penelope out that evening, because Alex had to go and help set up for the fair. After Mal left, Alex did her physiotherapy exercises very gently. Her back was sore. Lately, she had been a little less diligent with her stretches than she should have been. Ow. Ow. She called work and said she was taking the day off due to extreme back pain. Then she took herself back to bed.

*

Gihan felt like death warmed to tepid. He'd never been good with not sleeping. He tried to do some work in the morning before heading into the Ryder FT site. He needed to do a couple more interviews, which were already in the diary. It was tricky getting through them without John there to be a foil, but he'd do his best. He yawned so hard that his jaw clicked. He'd just have to drink a *lot* of coffee.

Today was his last day there. The company had estimated that that was all the contact time they'd needed. Now that he was down to one person doing the work, it would take a little longer to do, but that was manageable. Once the interviews were done, he should have everything he needed to do a decent analysis. The rest he could do in the office in London. He rubbed his face. The sooner he was done with this project, the better.

When he got to the company site, he sat in the car and messaged his sister to say he was okay. He had sent her an update the night before, but it had been very short. After a moment's hesitation, he messaged Alex, too. He would be seeing her in the office, but it was probably better to check in in private.

Sam responded with 'Keep me posted. I'm home tonight, so I'll see you when you get back to London.'

Nothing from Alex.

He went inside, signed in and asked the receptionist if Alex was in yet.

'No. She said she's not feeling very well.'

The spike of alarm in his chest took him by surprise. 'Is she ill?'

The woman shrugged. 'She wasn't too specific, but I think it's only a temporary thing.'

'Oh. Right. There was some drama with her neighbour last night,' he said, cautiously. He didn't know how much people knew and didn't want to cause Alex any trouble.

'Oh yeah. Maureen. I heard she was taken to hospital yesterday evening. Did you see the ambulance then?'

Of course everyone knew. Of course they did.

'Yes. Something like that,' he said. 'Did Alex mention how Maureen was getting on?'

'No. But if I hear anything, I'll tell you.' The receptionist's eyes sparkled.

'Thanks.' He stifled a yawn. 'I need to get more coffee.'

'Late night?' Her voice was all too innocent.

'Yeah.' He lifted up his briefcase. 'I'd better get back to it.' He practically fled to his office.

*

All morning, Gihan kept checking his phone. Nothing from Alex. The first interview of the day took longer than normal, because he kept looking down to make notes and then forgetting where he was. One down, one more interview to go.

An email notification popped up. Alex. His heartbeat rose when he clicked on it. It was a group email, sent to Alex's colleagues and to him. Maureen was doing well. She'd been stable overnight.

There was some memory loss of the day before and she had some concussion, but everything else was okay. Alex was going to go and visit Maureen later and would send another update. There was a reminder about the fair happening at the weekend.

It was just news. Nothing personalised. Nothing for him.

He checked his phone. No other messages either. Right. He put his phone away and stood up. A bit of fresh air was called for. If he stayed on site, he couldn't get lost.

Outside, he put his hands in his pockets and walked. Of course she wouldn't have to message him. Why would she? She had imparted all the relevant information in her email to everyone. He didn't need a special message, did he? He was being ridiculous.

Last night, in the car, he had been so tempted to kiss her. He was fairly sure she would have kissed him back. Thank goodness for Penelope. Gihan shook his head. He had to stop acting like a hormone-driven teenager and get over this. Alex was out of bounds. Even if she did like him back right now, she wasn't going to like him when she found out that he'd cost her her job.

He reached the main entrance to the science park and stopped, waiting for a lorry to pass so that he could cross over to the other side and walk back.

That night five years ago was meant to be a one-off. It should have been forgettable. A drunken snog on New Year's Eve. Except, he hadn't been that drunk and it had been . . . special. He couldn't put his finger on why, but something had clicked. Maybe it was because they'd been so sure they'd never see each other again. The anonymity had given him the freedom to talk about himself in a way that he didn't normally do. He had given up more of his real self in that one evening than he had done in years with Helen. Or with any of his past girlfriends. Perhaps that was what was pulling him towards Alex. Whatever it was, the attraction was strong. He honestly didn't know how to deal with it.

He walked back to the company building and went back to his

office. On the way past, he glanced at Alex's special, high-backed office chair. He wished he could see her. He missed her.

Inside the office, he hung his coat up and frowned. He really, really had to get over this. And soon.

One surefire way to end the whole thing would be to tell her what his review was going to say. But that wouldn't be ethical. Daniel had specifically asked that they didn't tell the staff anything. He wanted to review the report before he took any action and he didn't want to cause unnecessary upset. Gihan would have argued that the staff were probably already upset, but it wasn't his place to say, so he'd kept his mouth shut.

Gihan sighed. Despite the emotional reasons for his leaving the Middle East, he'd been glad to leave his job because it had felt so repetitive. The projects all felt the same and he no longer felt like he was making a difference. It was hard to care when the outcomes were basically 'make more money for people who already have far too much money'. He had wanted to feel like he was making a difference. For small businesses, a restructure or pivot meant the difference between success and closure. He could care about what he did now. The thing he'd forgotten about caring was that it sometimes hurt. Perhaps this hadn't been such a wise move after all.

Chapter 12

Alex felt better after a decent amount of sleep on her own mattress. It was mid-afternoon, but she still had time to go and visit Maureen in hospital before she had to help with setting up for the fair.

Maureen was looking much more like her normal self, sitting up and reading a magazine. She peered over her glasses when Alex showed up at the top of the dorm.

Alex rushed over to the side of the bed. 'Oh, you look so much better today. How are you feeling?'

'I'm fine. Bruised. And obviously, there's this.' She gestured to the cast on her leg. 'But other than that. I'm fine.'

Alex shook her head. 'Other than those small things.'

'What about you?' Maureen said, giving her a concerned look. 'You look like you're a bit stiff.'

'A bit,' said Alex. 'My back is playing up a little.'

'Was it being here all that time last night?'

Alex grimaced. 'I fell asleep on your sofa last night, with Penelope. So I'm a bit stiff today. I'll be alright though.'

The look Maureen gave her was sceptical.

'No. Seriously Maureen, I'll be fine.'

'If you say so.' Maureen looked down at her hand and tracked the line inserted into the back of it back up to the drip. She sighed. 'I believe that it's you who found me? My memory is a little hazy on that point.'

'Yes. I came to take Penelope for her walk and she was barking.'

'The nurse said you were here with your boyfriend . . .' Maureen's eyes narrowed. 'Either I hit my head harder than I thought, or I'm missing something. Boyfriend?'

Heat rushed to her face. 'I don't have a boyfriend. Gihan was with me when I found you. He came here with me. He's not my boyfriend.'

Maureen held her gaze without saying anything.

'He's not,' said Alex. 'He's just a friend.'

'He sat here until the small hours, waiting to ensure the welfare of an old woman he hasn't even met? To keep you company?' Maureen nodded slowly. 'Well, that's a very dedicated "just a friend".'

Alex felt the heat climb up her face. She looked away, so that Maureen didn't notice. 'He's a nice guy. We know each other through work. That's it.'

'Are you sure about that?' Maureen smiled. 'Anyone who makes you so flustered sounds like he should be much more than that.'

Well yes. She wished he was too. But . . . 'Pretty sure,' she said. 'At least . . . he is.'

The smirk dropped off Maureen's face. 'Oh, Alex. I'm sorry.' She raised her hand and winced. It had a cannula leading to a drip attached to the back of it. 'Blasted thing.'

The sympathy on Maureen's face hit Alex harder than anything else so far. Maureen, who was all bruised and in a cast, was feeling sorry for Alex. That's how pathetic her life was. She looked down and blinked back the tears that had suddenly appeared.

'Oh Alex,' Maureen said again. 'I'm sorry. I didn't mean—'

'Don't worry about it, Maureen. I'm fine. Look. I picked up a couple of magazines for you on my way in.'

'But—'

'Jake's on his way home and he'll come and visit you soon.' Maybe the mention of Jake coming back early would be enough to deflect her.

It worked. Maureen frowned. 'Now why did you go and tell him? He had his big pitch and everything.'

'I called him after his pitch. Don't worry. He's only missing drinks and social stuff.'

'From what my husband used to tell me, the drinks and social stuff was where the real business happened.'

Alex had heard that before. 'But Jake insisted. I had to tell him, Maureen. You really gave me a fright.'

They talked about her injury for a few minutes, before Maureen managed to circle back to her again.

'I made some notes on your CV. It's on the kitchen table. I was going to talk to you about it when you came for Penelope,' she said. 'I expect it's still on the kitchen table.'

Yes, it probably was.

'Oh, don't worry about that—'

Maureen cut her short. 'I haven't got anything else to do. Besides, you'd left a lot of things off. Like how you help with organising the village fair. That's project management skills, you know. Making sure you get the food tent up and running with enough variety of food and drink to keep everyone happy, arranging the furniture so that people can sit down, setting up the queueing system so that there's less milling around. You did all that. You should mention it. Even if you don't put it in your CV, keep it in your back pocket for an example of delivering a project on time and budget.'

It hadn't occurred to Alex that this was a relevant skill, but now that Maureen pointed it out, it was obvious that it was. She made a quick note on her phone. 'That's a good point. What else did I miss?'

'You do have people management experience. You have a small team.'

141

'I don't do their appraisals or anything. Technically, I don't think I do manage them.'

'They report to you. You look at their work schedules. I'd say you do some people management at work.' Maureen shifted her leg and winced. Talking about something else had livened her up even more. That was good.

'I don't—'

'You have a good CV,' said Maureen sternly. 'Go look at it. Start applying for jobs. You don't know what those consultants will recommend.'

The words felt like a weight in her stomach. Trying not to think about it was all very well, but Gihan was there to tell the management how to streamline the company. She knew all too well that R&D was often the first to go. In her opinion, it was short-sighted. You needed a pipeline of new products and her test was important. But . . . clearly they couldn't support it all, which was why they'd brought these guys in.

Alex faffed around changing the water in the flower vase. It was hard to imagine Gihan would *really* suggest making her redundant. That was his job, but . . . they were friends, weren't they? Except, it was only a limited sort of friendship. When it came down to it, he still had to do what was right by his client.

She must have been scowling when she returned to Maureen's bedside with the flowers, because Maureen gave her a puzzled stare.

'What's the matter? Has something happened?'

She forced herself to unscrunch her forehead. 'No. No. It's nothing. I just . . . don't want to think about it.'

'Not thinking about things won't make them go away, will it?' Maureen glanced down at her leg. 'Unfortunately.'

'Does it hurt?' Alex asked.

'Sometimes, but they've given me painkillers. It's more . . . uncomfortable.'

'Is there anything I can do?' She fluttered her hands, searching for something to do. A pillow to plump or something.

'Alex. What's going on?'

She stopped moving around and finally looked up at Maureen. The exhaustion from the night before came crashing down on her. Alex sighed and sank down onto the hard plastic chair by Maureen's bed.

'What if he says they have to fire me, Maureen?'

'That's why you must start applying for other jobs. In case—'

'But what if *he* says it?'

'Who?'

'Gihan.'

'Wh— oh. The man who was here with you last night? He's the consultant from work.' Maureen nodded slowly. 'Of course he is. I'd forgotten. You've only known him a couple of days, Alex. Why has he had this effect on you?'

'Actually, I've met him before.'

Maureen's eyes widened. 'Oh?'

Alex sighed. 'We . . . It's a long story.'

Maureen gestured to the hospital around her. 'I have time.'

'We met once before. It was . . . a weird night. I'd just been dumped and then ghosted by my boyfriend. It was New Year's Eve. I went to a bar. He was there, alone. He helped me out with something and then we talked. A lot. It was really weird, because I told him all sorts of things that I wouldn't normally tell anyone. Especially not a stranger. I didn't even know his name.'

Maureen reached across and patted her hand. 'Sometimes, it's easier to talk to a stranger. They've no need to judge you.'

Perhaps that was it. Just the mere fact that he had been a stranger. Maybe she'd imagined the chemistry. The tug from the core of herself to the core of him. Maybe the kiss had felt so magical simply because she was drunk.

'Maybe,' she said. She put her chin in her hands and rested her elbows on the side of the bed. 'I gave him my number, but he didn't call because my writing is so terrible, he'd called the

143

wrong person.' She sighed. 'The morning after that evening, I would have done anything to find him again. I really liked him. Now that he's back in my life, I can't seem to get anywhere with him. It's frustrating.'

'Maybe,' said Maureen. 'He needs time. Right now, he's limited by how much he can say or do because he's working for your boss. Perhaps, with time, things might change.'

This was a good point. 'That's annoying.'

Maureen gave her an indulgent smile. 'Patience isn't your strong suit, is it?'

Alex sat up straight. 'What do you mean?'

The older woman's eyes twinkled. 'From what I've heard of your dating history, you do tend to invest rather early.'

Leila had said something similar to her in the past. 'But if you like someone and they like you, why would you waste time dancing around the issue? Life is short.'

'Oh, I agree with you,' said Maureen. 'But not everyone is as in tune with their feelings as you are. Some people need time to let their feelings mature. Besides . . .' She tweaked the blanket on her bed. 'Life isn't that short. A week or two won't make that much difference.'

Alex felt bad. What was she thinking going on about life being short to Maureen? In a hospital no less! 'I'm sorry. I shouldn't have said that about life being short.'

Maureen gave a little laugh. 'I'm not dying, Alex. At least, I don't think I am.'

'You'd better not be,' said Alex. 'Because if anything happens to you on my watch, Jake is going to murder me.'

*

Gihan made it to late afternoon before he caved and texted Alex. She had given him her number to use in relation to Maureen, so he started with asking after both her and Maureen.

She texted back almost immediately.

I'm fine now thanks. Went to see Maureen. She's looking much better – leg in a cast and still a bit muddled about last night, but otherwise good.

That was good. He was still deliberating what to send next when another message arrived.

Thank you so much for all your help yesterday. I really appreciate it.

This was easier to reply to.

You're welcome. I did what anyone else would have done if they'd been there. Glad Maureen is okay. Are you around this evening? Walking Penelope?
   Not walking Penelope. Helping set up things for the fair, so I'll be around in the village.
   Great. Have a good evening.

Feeling buoyed by a text interaction, he took out the fruitcake left over from the lunch parcel the pub landlady had made for him. He may as well take a break and browse letting agency websites properly. He had arranged to go to view a flat on Saturday, but the estate agent had emailed to say that the flat was gone already. He should look at a few more places.

When Sam rang, he was mid-bite – cake in one hand, laptop open so that he could carry on searching. He put her on speakerphone.

'Just calling to check how you were.' Sam said. 'Did everything go okay in the hospital?'

He closed his laptop. 'Nobody died, so yes.'

A sharp intake of breath from his sister pulled him up short. 'Sorry, Sam. I didn't mean—'

'It's okay. You're right. That's a win.'

There was an awkward silence as they tried to work out how to work around their mutual grief.

'Are you okay?' He was furious at himself for his thoughtlessness. 'Did I upset you?'

'It's fine,' Sam said. 'You deal with it your way, right?'

'Yeah.' He had always favoured being blunt when it came to talking to his sister. They'd spent enough time tiptoeing around their father. They didn't have to do it around each other as well. 'As far as I know, Maureen is still okay. I didn't get home until the small hours, though.' He rubbed his free hand over his face. 'I'm shattered.'

'You're at work like normal?'

He looked at the laptop. 'I have to get everything done today. The information gathering bit, at least. Work is going to allocate me some help for next week, but by the time they catch up, it's going to be another day. I don't think they'll be moving the deadline.'

'Will you be okay? Are you going to get it done?'

'I'll have to, won't I?' He was all too aware that the unfortunate timing of John having to leave, and him having to carry the rest of the project, wasn't going to be taken into account when people looked at his performance. If he failed to deliver on his first project, that would follow him around for as long as he worked for the company.

'Oh,' said Sam. 'That sucks.'

Gihan took a deep breath and pulled himself together. 'Meh. It is what it is. I'll get it done.'

'Is . . . her job going to be okay?'

He knew exactly what Sam was talking about. 'I can't talk about that. You know I can't.'

Sam, being Sam, understood. 'I see. Hmm. Tell you what. When you get home tonight, we'll get takeaway and some beer and play some SyrenQuest. That should cheer you up. You can borrow my headset.'

'Is Luke going to be there?' He idly opened a browser tab with his free hand and entered the name of the village. The first thing that came up was about the village fair. Of course. That was this weekend.

Sam laughed. 'No. He's working. Besides, he doesn't like gaming at mine. Too weird, apparently. So you'll have to be content with hanging out with me.'

A yawn ambushed him. He tried to stifle it, but failed.

'You do sound tired,' Sam said.

'I am.' He stared thoughtfully at the computer screen. Once he left the village, he might never see Alex again. Despite his pep talk to himself about keeping his distance, the idea of not seeing her hollowed him out. He should say goodbye, at the very least. 'You know. I might stay here an extra night and come back home tomorrow.'

'Oh.'

'It's a couple of hours' drive and I don't want to fall asleep at the wheel.'

'Uh-huh.' He could hear the smile in her voice. Sam was not easily fooled. 'That's the reason you're not coming home?'

'I haven't got anything to do tomorrow until late afternoon . . .'

'Right. Right. So you may as well stay an extra day in the village where the girl you clearly have a massive crush on lives. Totally normal.'

'Coincidence.' He was smiling too.

'You're just tired.'

'So tired, Sam.'

'So, are you likely to see her tonight?'

'I might. There's a village fair tomorrow. A fundraiser type thing. And she'll be helping to set up. I might pop round and see if I can help.'

'Oh yeah. It'd be rude not to, right?'

'Exactly.'

Sam laughed. 'Okay, Aiya. Good luck with that. I guess I'll see you tomorrow. Don't forget we have dinner with Thatha and Aunty-Amma.'

Gihan groaned. 'Yes. I know.'

'It'll be okay.'

'So long as they don't start going on about setting me up with a wife.'

'I'll be there,' said Sam. 'I'll back you up.' There was the low rumble of a voice in the background. 'I have to go. Take care of yourself. Good luck with the woman you're definitely not planning to run into by accident.'

'Thanks. I'll see you tomorrow.'

He hung up and immediately dialled the pub and asked to book in for an extra night. He would pay for that night separately.

He hung up and opened his files again, feeling more buoyant and optimistic. The mere thought of seeing Alex filled him with happiness. It was probably a bad idea to go back, but if he simply disappeared again, she might think she'd said something wrong. It wasn't all about her either – it was about him as well. The way he felt powerless in the face of his attraction to her was a little bit frightening. He usually had a better grip on his feelings than this. He would see her once more to say goodbye. That way, he could leave her life with clarity. If he didn't, he'd spend weeks beating himself up, just like he had done five years ago.

Chapter 13

After visiting the hospital, Alex went home and crawled back into bed. She would have preferred to simply stay there until morning, but she'd promised to help with setting up the fair, so she forced herself to get up after an hour and walk, cautiously, down to the green. The village green was really a small grassy field next to the church. Normally, all it had of interest was a small rope swing tied to a branch of an oak tree which hung over from the next field. Now, marquees were being put up – three small ones and the main one for the food stalls.

When she reached it, Leila was there already threading the cords through eyelets in the tent canvas, ready to fix the sides down. Violet the wondermum was standing in the middle, holding a clipboard. In her 'working outside' wear, she looked like a model for Hunter wellies.

Violet looked up as Alex approached. 'Hello there. You made it. How's Maureen?'

Alex ignored the twinge of guilt for not having been there earlier and the even bigger twinge from her back reminding her that she was only there at all due to painkillers. 'She's stable, but they're keeping her under observation. She'll probably have to stay in hospital for about a week.'

Violet pulled out her phone and started typing with one hand. 'I'll organise a rota to make sure she has visitors every day. Are you okay looking after the dog?'

Alex nodded. It was nice to have someone swoop in and be all organised about things. You could always rely on Violet to organise a rota. 'Yes. Jake, Mal and I have Penelope covered. We'll feed her and walk her. If she'll let us, we'll have her come and stay with us for a bit.'

Violet finished tapping on her phone with a firm nod.

'What needs doing most urgently?' Alex said. Honesty compelled her to add, 'I've hurt my back, so I can't do much lifting. But if you've got anything that I can do sitting down . . .'

Violet consulted her clipboard. 'The tables need setting up. The sides of the marquee need securing. We have a box of bunting which . . .' She trailed off, staring at someone standing behind Alex.

'Hi. I thought I'd come to help,' said Gihan's voice.

Alex turned. He was standing in one of the open sides of the marquee, his hands in his pockets.

'What are you doing here?' she demanded. 'Aren't you supposed to be going back to London tonight?'

He shifted his weight. 'Change of plan. I'm here tonight, so I thought I'd make myself useful.'

'Excellent,' said Violet. 'Always grateful for a helping hand,' she beamed at him. 'And you are?'

'I'm Gihan. I'm a friend of Alex's.' He spotted Leila and gave her a little wave. 'And Leila's.'

Violet gave him an assessing look. 'You're tall. You can help me bring in the trestle tables. Alex, you can help Leila finish tying the marquee sides up, please. And then make up signs for the tables, so that people know which one to set up on tomorrow morning.'

Alex glanced at Gihan, annoyed that she didn't get to spend time with him. He gave her a quick grin and said, 'I'll catch you later,' before following Violet outside.

Leila stared after them. 'What was that all about?' she whispered to Alex. 'She should have put you two on the same job. Cowbag.'

'To be fair, she'd have had to take you off your job and I really can't carry tables today.' She sat down next to where Leila was.

'Here. You finish this. You can do it sitting down.' Leila handed her the cord she was threading and pulled down the next flap. She had to stand on a chair to reach the top and begin threading. 'How's your back now?'

Alex shifted her shoulders a little bit. 'Still sore, but improving.'

'Did I hear that Violet is organising a Maureen rota?' Leila said. 'Probably for the best, huh? You and Jake both have your own things to do. It's not fair for you two to end up doing all the care for Maureen.'

Alex nodded and kept her eyes on her work. Jake often worried about what would happen when Maureen needed more care. They had spoken to Maureen's son about it and he had promised that he would hire carers – but Maureen was adamant that she didn't need them. She would also have to be persuaded to have a panic button, in case she fell again. There were a lot of difficult conversations looming. She suspected they were going to have to talk Maureen's son more often from now on.

Leila leaned down. 'So, what happened with Mr Cutie last night?'

'Nothing! We were in the hospital. Seriously.' Speaking quietly, she outlined roughly what had happened, again. Leila already knew most of this.

'That's so disappointing,' Leila began, not bothering to lower her voice.

'Shh.'

Gihan and Violet came in carrying a table. Violet was chatting away, talking about leaving London, by the sound of it.

'I don't regret leaving the rat race one little bit,' she told him.

Gihan nodded. His eyes met Alex's. He smiled and quickly looked away. 'I'm hoping it's the right move for me too,' he said. 'I'm certainly enjoying the increased variety.'

They left the tent again.

'Disappointing,' said Leila, loudly.

*

They worked on their different tasks diligently. Alex could feel Gihan's presence as he moved around, carrying tables and setting them up according to the floorplan she herself had created last week. Her senses seemed to track him. It was lucky her job didn't require much concentration.

When they'd finished, Leila left to help with something else. The tables now had labels taped to them so that people knew which table was theirs. Alex contemplated the box of bunting and wondered if she felt up to all the stretching involved with hanging bunting. She looked around for the stepladder. She may as well get this done. No stepladder. Oh well, a chair would do just as well. She didn't need to get it too high up. She experimentally lifted her arms up to see how much it hurt. Ow.

Her sixth sense screamed at her to tell her that Gihan had come back. She turned her head to see him walk in. Whatever he had been doing had made him hot enough that he had discarded his coat and his jumper, which were now in a bundle under his arm. He dumped them on one of the tables. He was now in jeans and a plain green T-shirt.

He came over. 'Can I help with that?'

He was a few inches taller than her, so she gestured to the bunting. 'Can you do the tying please? I'll pass the tape up to you,' she said. 'It's fiddly trying to do that while holding the bunting up.'

'Okay.' Looking around, he grabbed a chair, dragged it over to one of the central poles and stood on it.

She passed the end of the bunting up to him. 'So how come you stayed an extra day?' she asked him. 'Do you need more data or something?'

'No. I'm just tired after the late night, so I thought it would be safer to have a good night's sleep before I drive off.' He raised his arms above his head. This made his T-shirt ride up a bit, leaving her a glimpse of flat stomach at eye level. She tried not to stare. Her house was often full of exercise fanatics, so she was no stranger to muscular male bodies. Jake, especially, had a tendency to walk around without a shirt on. But his broad shoulders and sculpted abs were so familiar they did nothing for her. Gihan was slim and apparently, that was her type.

'Can I have some tape?'

Oh yes. Tape. She quickly focused on her actual task and cut off lengths of tape. He secured the ribbon between the flags to the cross pole and got off the chair, then moved the chair a few feet to do it all again.

As they moved across, systematically putting up the bunting, Alex gave him an update on what was happening with Maureen. She left out the discussion about job-seeking and CVs for obvious reasons. It wasn't easy keeping her focus when her brain kept wandering off and noticing things about him. The corded muscles of his forearms. The set of his shoulders. The rather attractive bottom.

The bunting in her hands ran out. 'We're done,' she told him and handed up extra tape so that he could secure the end. He smiled down at her, his eyes glowing warm and brown in the light from the bulbs strung up inside the tent. Alex's brain shut down completely. Handsome. He looked back at the bunting that now zigzagged across the tent. 'That looks great,' he said.

She had to agree, the view from here was pretty great. Because she wasn't paying attention, she didn't move out of the way to make room for him when he stepped down. Which meant that when he landed, he was too close. She stepped backwards too quickly and overbalanced. His hand shot out and he caught her around the waist.

They were standing so close together that she could feel the heat coming off his skin. It felt like his fingers were burning into her back. She looked up and met his eyes. For a second, she saw a longing so fierce that she forgot how to breathe. Her gaze fluttered down to his lips, brown fading to dark pink. They looked so soft and welcoming. She leaned a little closer and rested her hand against his chest.

He drew a sharp breath and stepped back. 'I'm sorry,' he said.

Oh god. He was rejecting her. Again. This was so humiliating. Heat flared up Alex's face. She stepped away from him and turned away so that he didn't see the tears that sprang up.

'No. Alex, wait.' He reached for her arm, touching it just above the elbow.

She turned. 'It's fine,' she said. 'I was out of line.'

'No. No you weren't. It's me,' he said.

She turned to look at him. He rubbed a hand through his hair. 'I like you,' he said. 'But I'm not really in a space to . . . I'm not ready for a relationship right now. Besides, you work for the client and I really don't want to lose my job.'

She frowned, the elation of hearing the words 'I like you' turning to confusion at what he said next. She liked him too. And she was all for doing something about it. He was the one behaving inconsistently. 'But you keep doing this sort of thing,' she said. 'You turn up to walk Penelope. You stay an extra night to help with the fair.'

He looked up at the ceiling. 'I know. I'm a terrible person,' he said, with conviction. 'I should keep my distance, but I just . . . can't seem to.'

She crossed her arms. 'So, what happens now?'

The look he gave her was wistful. 'I came to say goodbye,' he said. 'I've finished my work on site.'

'Oh,' she said. 'Okay.'

'Can we stay in touch?' he said. 'I would like to know how Maureen's getting on. I know it's not really my business, but I feel invested. So can I email you? I promise I won't spam you.'

She noticed he hadn't mentioned texting her, even though he had her number. He really was keeping his distance as much as he could without cutting ties. She didn't know how she felt about that. It was something to think about later.

They stared at each other for a moment, the unsaid things spreading between them. There was a crash from outside. Alex pulled herself together. 'Shall we go see what else needs doing?'

Gihan grabbed his jumper and coat. 'Let's do that.'

When they walked out, there was a careful space between them.

*

'Have you eaten?'

Gihan hadn't. He had changed into jeans and rushed out so that he could be sure to catch Alex, so he hadn't had time. 'Nope. You?'

'Me either.' She looked across in the direction of the pub.

They could go and have something in the pub. Most of the others were heading there for a drink. He and Alex were lagging behind a bit because Alex was walking slowly. Despite his assertion that he'd come to say goodbye, he couldn't bring himself to leave just yet. He opened his mouth to suggest a pub meal, but she said, 'I have leftover pasta at home. I could heat up a bowl.'

He could think of nothing he would like more. All he had to do was avoid the temptation to touch her. He could do that. Especially now that they'd established the ground rules properly.

'It's nothing special,' she said. 'Only pasta with pesto, bacon and cabbage. I made a load the other day . . .' She frowned. 'Yesterday. It *was* yesterday wasn't it? It feels like it's been days and days. Anyway. I made a load and have plenty of leftovers.'

'That would be lovely,' he said. 'I've been eating pub meals and shop sandwiches all week. The food in the pub is wonderful, but . . . it would be nice to eat something that's normal food. If you know what I mean.'

They walked across the field and headed off in the same direction as everyone else who was going to the pub.

'Jake and his friend are both obsessed with health food,' she said, with a small laugh. 'So some days I make a big pan of carbs, just to wind them up.'

'Of course. You said your housemate was away at an investor thing.'

'He was. But he's probably back now.' She checked her watch. 'He probably went straight back out to see Maureen.'

They walked along in silence for a while. The village was so quiet at night. He was used to cities and lack of car noise felt strange. Other sounds seemed to come to the fore. The sound of their footsteps. The voices of the people walking ahead of them. An owl. The throb of his own pulse.

They came out of the cutting and he could see the pub.

'Guys,' Alex raised her voice. 'I'm heading home.'

There was a chorus of 'see you tomorrow's. No one commented on Gihan staying back as well. He mentioned it to her as they walked away.

'Oh, they'll all be discussing it in the pub,' she said. 'Trust me.'

It wasn't particularly late. Only around nine. It was dark and cooler, but still not cold. Alex opened the front door and he followed her in.

He wasn't sure what he had been expecting, but the first word that popped to mind was 'masculine'. The furniture was black leather. The pictures on the walls were black and white. Even the rug in the middle of the living room was white and grey.

She saw him looking at the pictures on the walls and rolled her eyes. 'Jake's,' she said. 'It's his house. I just live here.' She pointed to a suitcase that was standing in the middle of the living room. It was black and silver. 'Looks like he's home.'

Gihan looked around. 'It's very . . .'

'Monochrome?' she said. 'Yeah. Come through to the kitchen. It's much nicer in here.'

It was. The walls and even the plates were delightfully colourful. There was a lemon-yellow tablecloth on the tiny table and a bunch of dying flowers sat in a cobalt-blue vase.

156

Alex opened the fridge and took out a tupperware container. She looked over her shoulder. 'Take a seat.'

He moved a stack of business books off one of the two chairs and sat down.

Alex moved around the kitchen and he watched her – standing on her tiptoes to get a couple of bowls down, pouring two glasses of orange juice, pushing the cutlery drawer shut with her hip. She looked different here. More comfortable.

He had seen her in all kinds of contexts now and he was yet to find one where he didn't feel drawn towards her. He could watch her all day. He leaned against the table and dislodged an avalanche of paper and books. 'Oh shit.'

Alex threw him an amused glance and carried on with what she was doing. He went down on his hands and knees and gathered up the stuff. He picked up one folder and what looked like CVs fell out. He pushed them back in, expecting them to be Jake's, but her name caught his eye. She was job-hunting. That was good. Maybe she was expecting there to be bad news when he finished his report. The idea should make him feel relieved, but it only made him sad. Quickly, he shuffled the papers back into the folder and picked everything up.

'Just shove all that in the living room,' Alex said. 'We can eat at the table.'

He did as he was told. When he came back in, he asked, 'How come you ended up living here?'

The microwave pinged. Alex took the bowls out. 'When I first moved here, Leila sort of took me under her wing. I told her I was looking for somewhere to live and mentioned my budget, which wasn't huge. She told me that she was moving in with her girlfriend at the end of the month and that Jake was looking for a new lodger. I could afford what he wanted, so she brought me round and introduced me. We went to the pub for drinks and . . . here we are.'

'You were so lucky,' he said. 'Everything in London is so much more expensive than I'd hoped. I'm pushing my budget out as far as I can, but I've still not seen a place that ticks all the boxes.'

She put a bowl down in front of him.

The smell of pesto made his mouth water. 'Thank you so much. I didn't realise how hungry I was until now.'

She took her own bowl and slipped into the seat opposite. He noticed that she winced when she settled in. 'I didn't have a proper lunch. It's been a weird day,' she said.

They ate in silence for a few minutes. Alex's phone pinged. She took it out, read the message, smiled and put the phone away again. 'Leila,' she said. 'She and her partner are trying for IVF. They've finally got an appointment.' She added, 'It's not a secret. Leila's happy to tell people.'

Gihan looked down at his rapidly disappearing meal. It wasn't only Alex who was going to be affected by the changes. Leila was too. See. This is why it was a bad idea to get involved. His conscience kicked him. He really shouldn't have come here. He should have said goodbye and got out at the first opportunity.

'Everything okay?' she said.

'Yes. Yes. Everything's fine.' He took a sip of his juice. 'I was just thinking how nice it is to belong somewhere like you do here.'

'Oh, I don't—' She frowned and looked around. 'I suppose I do, don't I? I have friends. I guess those are roots of sorts.'

'Do you think you'll stay here? Like, forever.'

She laughed. 'That's a big question. I don't know. Honestly. I like it here. As you say, I have friends and I'm involved with life. But forever is a very long time.'

He laughed too. 'I guess it is.'

He didn't have roots, he realised. He had family, he was connected to them no matter what, but there were no other people to keep him in one place. It was like he'd floated through life making as few links as possible. Was that why Helen's proposal had come as such a shock?

He finished his meal. Pasta and pesto, it turned out, was exactly what he'd needed. 'That,' he said, 'was perfect.' He pushed the plate away and leaned back pleasantly full. 'Thank you.'

She lowered her drink and smiled at him. His world melted a little round the edges. He had set himself a line that wouldn't be crossed. It had seemed like such a simple solution at the time but now . . .

Alex blinked, the smile faded. Her eyes met his.

Now . . . keeping his distance seemed like an impossible task.

Alex said, 'Gihan—'

But whatever she was going to say was lost to the sound of the front door opening. 'Alex?' A few seconds later, Jake walked into the kitchen, pulling his coat off. 'Maureen says—' He stopped at the sight of Gihan. 'Oh. Hi.' He smiled. 'Maureen mentioned that you were there to help yesterday.' He moved forward with his hand extended.

Gihan scrambled to his feet and found his own hand engulfed in a firm handshake.

'Thanks, man,' Jake said. 'Maureen is a special lady. So is Alex. I'm horrified that I wasn't there for them. I'm glad someone was, you know.'

'Er . . . yes. I just happened to be in the right place at the right time.' Gihan retrieved his hand. This Jake guy was big. Strong. He flexed his fingers to get the circulation back into them.

Jake put a hand on Alex's arm. 'You alright Alex? How's the back? Do you need to see a doctor?'

'The back?' He could see that Alex had a stiff back, but Jake's voice seemed disproportionately concerned. Was there more to it than that?

Alex shifted in her seat. 'I had a bad backache earlier. When I got home last night, I stupidly ended up sleeping on Maureen's sofa to keep Penelope company. It's much better now, thanks. Painkillers are great.'

He thought of her sitting on those hard plastic chairs for hours, waiting for Maureen. That must have been agony. 'That sounds intense,' he said.

She gave an embarrassed shrug.

'Yes, you need to be mindful of your back. Get back to doing your stretches as soon as possible. You don't want to lose the mobility you've got.'

That sounded a bit more than a plain backache. He gave Alex a quizzical look.

She gave Jake a stern glare. 'I had surgery on my back, when I was a teenager,' she said to Gihan. 'I have a small bit of my spine reconstructed. It's fine most of the time, so long as I keep up with my stretches and things.' She stood up and gathered up the plates. 'Jake worries too much.'

'Someone has to keep an eye out for you. Until you get yourself a man, I'm it.' Jake looked meaningfully at Gihan.

Gihan pretended not to notice. His attention remained on Alex. Last night, when she'd mentioned spending time in hospital, he had assumed it was because of her friend who died of cancer, and that the pain she'd mentioned was emotional. Had she been talking about physical pain?

'When you said hospitals reminded you of pain yesterday, that's what you meant?'

She frowned. 'Yes. Did I not tell you about that?'

'Not really. You said you hated hospitals.' In fairness, he hadn't been thinking clearly yesterday. He'd been rambling, talking about houses in London in an attempt to keep them both distracted. 'You didn't give any context, so I thought you were talking about losing your friend Jude.'

'Jude? Oh. I see.'

Jake paused from banging about in the cupboard to turn and say, 'Have you done that thing again where you forget that people can't read your mind?' He glanced at Gihan again and said, laughing, 'She does that. You get used to it.'

Gihan smiled nervously at him. He wanted to know more. Wanted to be the one to understand and comfort her. He wanted so much more than they had. This woman was precious to him.

The realisation was a shock. He had planned to say goodbye. That was never going to be enough.

'That sounds bad,' he said to Alex. 'Were you in an accident?'

Alex looked up from where she was loading the plates into the dishwasher. He noticed she was bending very carefully. 'No. Not an accident. I had a cancer removed. They did an en bloc resection and reconstructed one of my vertebrae. Got rid of all the cancer tissue. Pretty clever stuff.'

She was still talking, but Gihan no longer heard her. At the word cancer, blood surged to his head. His heart raced. He felt the pasta he'd just had trying to climb back up his throat. The room was suddenly very hot and there wasn't enough air.

No. No. This couldn't be happening. Was this damned disease coming after all the women he cared about? He stood up, making his chair scrape on the ground behind him. 'I . . . should go,' he said. 'It was a bit of a late night last night and I really should catch up on my sleep.'

Alex's eyes widened. 'Oh. Of course.'

Jake looked from one to the other. 'I'm sorry I broke up the party.'

'Oh, no. You didn't.' He grabbed his jacket off the back of the chair, where he'd hung it up. He had to focus fiercely to speak without giving away his internal clamour. 'Thanks for the food, Alex.'

'You're welcome. Will you have time to pop into the fair before you head off tomorrow?'

'Sure. Yes.' He backed out into the black and white living room. 'It was nice to meet you, Jake.'

Gihan left the house and practically ran out of the gate. The fresh air helped a little. As he got close to the pub, he slowed down, breathing slowly. The nausea receded. He paused outside the entrance and put his hand over his heart, willing it to slow down. His pulse was a low buzz in his ears now. He felt drained and shaky.

Connections pinged in his brain. Alex had survived cancer. No wonder she was so dedicated to early diagnosis. The friend she mentioned who'd died – he had assumed it was someone she'd known at school. But they could well have been someone she'd met while being treated. In fact, that was more than likely.

The word cancer reverberated in his thoughts. Feelings he couldn't handle towered precariously above him. He had to get to his room before he had a full-blown panic attack out here in the car park. He forced himself to move, the edges of his vision clouded, so that he could only see what was in front of him. Path. Door. The entranceway to the pub.

When he walked through the pub, someone called his name. A group of people sitting at the bar waved at him. The people who were helping set up the fair. It took some effort to make his hand move and wave back. He stumbled up to his room.

The wave of grief caught him as soon as he shut the door. It was hard to breathe. He crawled onto the bed and curled up in the foetal position, his arms folded over his head, and forced air in and out of his lungs. He was fifteen again, peering past his father at his mother's lifeless form. The feeling of loss was so vast it encompassed the whole world. He couldn't go through this again. He just couldn't.

*

'What just happened?' Jake said, staring at the space where Gihan had been. 'Did I scare him off?'

Alex shook her head. 'I don't think so.' But what else could it be? Gihan had been relaxed enough when he came in. 'He seemed okay until we started talking about . . . my back pain. That's weird. Why would that scare him?'

Jake frowned. 'Did he somehow think he'd hurt your back?'

'Don't be ridiculous,' she said. There was something she was missing. A connection. What had he told her last night? She would have to try and remember. Right now, everything was a little fuzzy.

Jake looked worried. 'Maybe he thought I was serious about you needing a man to look after you?'

Maybe. He had said he wasn't looking for a relationship right now. But then, he had voluntarily come round for dinner . . . She shook her head. 'I'll text him in a minute and check that everything is okay.' There were more important things to think about right now. She turned towards Jake. 'How did your pitch go?'

Jake grinned. 'Pretty well, actually. Two of them were not great, but one was brilliant. You only need one, right? And we've got one investor. I need to talk to Mal about it and make plans, but I'm optimistic.'

'That's fantastic. Well done.'

Jake put the kettle on and got down his box of herbal tea blends. 'Now then, you and I need to have a little talk about Maureen.'

Chapter 14

Gihan woke up the next morning feeling completely wrung out. His head hurt and his eyes felt gritty and horrible. It took a shower and several cups of coffee before he felt human again.

He sat at a table in the restaurant section of the pub, where they served breakfast, and stared out of the window. The weather had been kind – it was a clear autumn day. The morning mists had burned off, leaving everything painted a mellow orange and yellow. He tried to sort out what had happened the night before.

Alex's casual revelation that she'd survived cancer had shaken him and he wasn't sure why. She seemed perfectly relaxed about it, so she wasn't likely to be in any danger of a relapse. His reaction had basically been because he'd remembered Amma's death. But why had it affected him so strongly? Another panic attack. Was it the idea of Alex suddenly falling ill and dying?

He took another sip of coffee. Was that a flash forward of what it would feel like? A shudder ran through him. He never wanted to feel as helpless and angry as he had done when his mother died. There were so many shades of grief and he'd rolled through most of them at one time or another. He had thought he was doing okay, but clearly something was catching up with him. If his father's reaction was anything to go by, losing your spouse was at least as hard as losing your mother. He knew himself well enough to know that he was his father's son. He would crumble just as badly.

If the remote possibility of losing Alex gave him panic attacks now, imagine how much worse it would be if she actually fell ill. He couldn't bear that. He had to protect himself. And her, really, because if she fell ill, she didn't need a man who would fall apart. His initial instinct that he should stay away had been the right one.

With a heavy heart, he finished his coffee and went upstairs to pack.

Before long, he was lugging his bag downstairs to the car again.

'Are you heading straight off? Or are you going to pop into the fair first?' Hannah said, when he checked out.

Gihan checked his watch. It was around ten-thirty. 'It's started already?'

'Oh yeah. We popped round earlier to help with the stalls. We can't really help during the main part of the day because the fair tends to bring the punters in here for lunch as well.' She handed him a receipt. 'You should go have a look before you head off.'

He didn't have to be in London for a while. He had run away rather rudely from Alex's house and hadn't replied to her polite text last night. He should at least apologise.

When he reached his car, he hesitated. The sound of voices and music drifted down from the fair. He could see the green from here. Colourful flags fluttered in the breeze. Kids ran around. It was so idyllic it was almost funny.

Part of him longed to go over and be part of it, but it was just postponing the inevitable.

He took his phone out of his pocket and sent Alex an email. It seemed less immediate than text.

I'm heading back to London now. I hope the fair goes well and Maureen continues to recover. Best, Gihan.

Then he got in the car and left. Back to London, where he could get his head down and do his work. And try to forget all about Alex.

Chapter 15

Gihan was still thinking about Alex when he got back to his sister's apartment and threw his clothes in the washing machine. What was it about this woman that had got under his skin so much?

He got out some bread to make himself toast. Toast was always cheering.

'Oh, are you doing toast? Make me a slice, will you?' His cousin Niro was lying sideways on the armchair, her legs slung over the side, laptop balanced on her stomach. On the sofa next to her, Sam was sitting with her laptop, also working.

Gihan got more bread out. 'What are you doing here?' he said to Niro. 'You don't live here anymore.'

Niro grinned at him. 'Force of habit,' she said. 'Besides, I wanted to come and see if you guys needed any moral support before your family dinner tonight.'

'You're all heart,' said Gihan.

'Have you come up with a good excuse for not wanting to get married yet?'

'I don't want to. That's going to have to be good enough.'

'You poor deluded fool.' Niro shook her head.

'Are you coming this evening?'

'Nope. Just you Ranaweera kids. I am going out for dinner with my boyfriend.'

'Should you be having toast?' said Sam, not lifting her head. 'You'll spoil your appetite.'

It wasn't clear which one of them she was talking to, so Niro and Gihan both pulled faces at her. Without looking up, Sam made a rude gesture to them both.

Gihan smiled. This was one of the reasons he had wanted to come back to England. He'd missed these two. Of course, things weren't the same now. Niro didn't live here anymore and Sam was a busy woman with a successful business and a serious boyfriend. Soon they would both move on and have families and he would be relegated to being the cool uncle that visited from time to time. This moment in time was fragile. Easily lost. He would miss them.

The toast popped. He got it out and buttered it.

'I'll have the new jam, please?' said Niro.

'Any other instructions, your ladyship?'

'You could bring it over, if you like,' she said, grinning at him over the top of her computer.

'Get it yourself.' He slid the plate to the edge of the counter towards her and went back to sorting out his own toast. 'What're you doing, anyway?'

'Setting up some of the images for the "Influencer" exhibition,' said Niro. 'We did the first photoshoot last week. Felicia and Ronee have only just okayed their images. Look, aren't they lovely.'

Gihan took a bite of toast and leaned against the counter. Niro's art business was finally taking off. This time next year, she would be busy. Sam was already busy. That's how life went. You meet people. You love them. Then they leave. But Sam and Niro were family, they would always be connected to him. They would come back eventually, even if it was just to visit. Even his elder brother, who rarely spoke to him now, would come back at some point. But other people – they didn't.

Alex . . . When he'd met her, there had been no danger of him feeling anything for her. It was the most no-strings meeting ever. He hadn't even known her name. At the time he'd thought it was liberating and safe. But it hadn't occurred to him that it was exactly the opposite. That the fact that she was determined to be a stranger had meant that he'd let his guard down. He hadn't bothered to remind himself that he couldn't let people in, or why she wasn't right for him, because he'd been so sure he'd never see her again.

He thought of her, sitting on that hard plastic chair in the hospital, staring into space. 'I spent a lot of time in hospitals. I didn't know if I was ever going to leave.' How had he not spotted that she'd been talking about herself being ill?

At that moment, all he'd wanted was to hold her and comfort her. He had thought he was just being a good human being. It wasn't until later that he'd realised he would do anything to protect her.

He chewed his toast, thoughtfully. Losing her job would be a blow to Alex, but she was bright. He knew she was looking for a new job and was pretty sure she'd find it. Losing her technology though, would be a bigger blow. Seeing the early diagnosis kit actually get to market was important to her. He understood why now. Promising technologies got binned because of money constraints all the time. If only there was a way to save the project and Alex's work without compromising the job he'd been given to do. There had to be a way.

His phone buzzed, reminding him that he had to set off soon. He quickly polished off his toast. 'Sam, I'm heading off to go look at a flat,' he said.

'Are you coming back before going to Thatha's or shall I meet you there?' Sam turned in her seat.

He considered the distances involved and added a few extra minutes for delays on the underground. 'I'll meet you there. Do you want me to grab a bottle of wine?'

'Yes please. I'll get chocolates. So neither of us will turn up empty-handed.'

He headed to the door.

Niro called out, 'I hope you find the perfect nest for you.'

He looked back at the two of them and smiled. Both women had found partners who complemented them and made their lives better. Despite the terrible frailty of that sort of happiness, he was glad for them. The room around them had been moulded by Sam and Niro over the years. It wasn't a big apartment or a very fancy one, but it was somehow home.

He would be really lucky if he could find that. A place that made him feel like he'd come home.

'I hope so too,' he said.

*

The flat that Gihan went to see was fine. There was nothing wrong with it. It was within his budget, just about. With white painted walls and pale wood floors, it was a perfect blank canvas. It ticked most of the boxes on his list. So why was he hesitating?

He walked idly through the kitchenette. Why did it feel wrong? He remembered the conversation he'd had with Alex about home. He had been dismissive at the time, but maybe she had a point. All the places he'd lived in before had been chosen for convenience and budget. None of them had felt like anything more than a place to sleep. He had thought he was looking for the same this time, but it seemed he wasn't.

The trouble with looking for 'home' was that he'd been sure he would know it when he saw it. But after seeing a few places now, he wasn't so sure. What was he looking for, really? Should he settle for something that was good enough and work on the 'home' part later?

'It's conveniently located for transport,' the estate agent said. 'And it's empty right now, so you can move in as soon as we get the paperwork sorted.'

Gihan stood in the doorway of what would be a bedroom and looked at the somewhat gloomy view of the backs of other houses. The living room looked out onto the nondescript street. He could easily imagine him coming home to this place to sleep. But to live?

His Amma used to say, 'You need strong roots to thrive'. He wasn't sure he even had roots. He was more like a capsule person – he lived as flexibly as possible. When he needed to change, he just removed himself from one place and slotted neatly into another, never really touching his surroundings. But it meant that his surroundings didn't really touch him either. He had no roots.

Something else tried to get his attention. Something about capsules and thriving.

'What do you reckon?' the estate agent asked him.

'I don't hate it,' he said, truthfully.

'A couple came to look at it earlier,' she said. 'They were going to think about it. So, you might want to make a choice and put the deposit down sooner rather than later.'

What was the thought nagging him? He forced himself to focus on the estate agent. 'I need to think about it too. What time are you open until today?'

He promised to get back to her soon and left. Because he was feeling restless, he took the stairs instead of the lift. There was something hypnotic about clattering down flight after flight of stairs. What was the thought that was trying to catch his attention? Something about capsules and fitting into something else. It was something he'd seen. A presentation. What was it? What was it?

He got to the last flight of stairs and jumped the last step, just like he used to do as a child. His mother used to roll her eyes whenever he did it. The memory, suddenly sharp, made him smile. What would Amma make of him now? He crossed the short entranceway and made his way to the street.

He had to buy a bottle of wine to take to Thatha's. Looking around he spotted an off-licence. He was crossing the street when the memory slotted into place. A presentation about potential new directions for a company that made test kits. He had done a piece of work for them some years ago. They didn't make test strips for homecare. They made hospital-based ones. They were called . . . He snapped his fingers a couple of times.

'Swanland.' That was it. Alex's test worked in a test tube, but they were stuck on making it stable enough to freeze dry into the test strip. But what if they didn't need to freeze dry it? Swanland might be able to take Alex's test and fit it into their proprietary kits.

He stood still on the pavement, thoughts whirring as the idea played out in his head. He still had contacts. He'd have to run it by his employers first, but . . . why would they object? It was merely a matter of him introducing the two companies. Yes! That could be the solution. If it worked . . . He paused to admit that there were a great many things that could go wrong. But if it worked, Alex's project would be saved. He could even phrase things in such a way that they might consider hiring Alex as well, to keep hold of her know-how.

He was practically skipping with excitement by the time he got to the off-licence.

Chapter 16

Gihan was standing in his stepmother's kitchen when the estate agent phoned him to say that the flat he'd seen earlier had been taken. There was a hint of reproof in her voice as though disappointed that he hadn't made a decision on the spot. 'These properties are very popular,' she said. 'You have to move fast.'

'It's a pity I missed out,' he said, without a trace of regret.

'We will have a new set of properties going on the website on Monday,' she said. 'I'm sure we'll find something that appeals. You are signed up to our website, aren't you?'

'I am, yes. I look forward to seeing them.'

When he hung up, Aunty-Amma said, 'Flat hunting not going well?' She handed him the wine and a corkscrew.

'Not really. I've seen a few flats so far, but none of them felt right.' He twisted the corkscrew into the cork.

His father came in. 'Your Amma used to say that she got a feeling about a place the minute she walked into it.'

Gihan stopped, his wrist mid-twist. Thatha rarely spoke about Amma. His eyes darted to his stepmother. She took some plates out of the cupboard and passed them to his father. 'She did, didn't she?' she said, as though talking about Amma wasn't a huge thing. 'She was always right.'

Aunty-Amma had been friends with his mother for years before she had fallen for Thatha. She never seemed bothered by her memory. Gihan had always admired how she managed to simultaneously carry the memory of her friend while becoming an integral part of the family her friend had left behind.

'I remember the time Shanthi, Ruvini and I were moving Kumudhini into her new house,' Aunty-Amma said with a giggle. 'We walked in and she said, "Oh, this is a party house". She wasn't wrong.'

Thatha, normally so severe, smiled. 'When I came to pick Shanthi up, all four of you were very, very drunk.'

'Yes. Party house. See.'

Thatha shook his head and turned his attention to Gihan. 'So, how long are you going to be back for this time?'

Ah. There we go. Back to the usual.

'I don't know,' said Gihan. 'Haven't decided yet.'

'You can't just move around on a whim, Gihan. What was the reason—'

Aunty-Amma cut him off by tapping his arm. 'Here,' she said, giving him a meaningful glare. 'When you've put those on the table, can you come back and take the chutney and the coconut sambol in?'

Thatha's eyes flicked towards Gihan and back. He nodded and sauntered off with the plates.

'Thanks.' Gihan put the bottle between his knees and pulled the cork out with a faint pop.

'I'm not letting you off the hook that easily.' She smiled at him. 'I just don't want the dinner to go cold while you two argue.'

He grinned at her, grateful nonetheless.

Dinner was delicious. Aunty-Amma had made chicken curry, lentil curry, butternut squash, coconut sambol and a mallung out of kale. They sat around the table, eating with their fingers.

Gihan had a bit of peace while Thatha quizzed Sam about her business. He had been expecting a more combative atmosphere.

Normally, Thatha asked questions, and Sam gave monosyllabic answers, but Sam and Thatha seemed to have reached a tentative understanding now. She was actually giving him detailed answers. Even more surprising, he seemed to know quite a lot about what went on in her business. After all those years of their father being distant, it was unnerving to watch. He was listening to what she had to say! Without giving advice! Well, not much advice anyway.

Gihan himself was interested in Sam's business. After all, business development was his thing. He had helped her by reading over business plans and pitches here and there. As far as he could tell, she was doing fine without his help anyway.

'So, Gihan putha,' said Aunty-Amma. 'How is the new job going?'

He gave her his standard answer – a bit different, keeping things interesting.

'It is more fulfilling?' his father said, slowly, in the manner of someone choosing his words carefully.

Again, another question he would not have expected. 'It's a bit early to tell,' he said. 'But I think it will be.' Especially if his idea about selling Alex's work to another company came off. 'It's more interesting than my old job.'

He was surprised by how much more invested he felt in the work. In his old job, he'd met people who were broadly similar to each other. They ran big companies and juggled huge budgets. The day-to-day operations seemed abstract, reduced to numbers and graphs. In the last week, he had talked to scientists and engineers and marketing people. He saw how each person had a personal interest in seeing the product succeed. Even if they didn't make money from it, they took pride in it. That kind of passion was nice to see. 'I get to meet some interesting people, too,' he continued. 'Not as many powerful people as before, but very interesting people.'

'Worth the pay cut?' said his father.

Gihan narrowed his eyes. Here came the criticism. 'It wasn't really a pay cut. On paper, it's about the same, even a tiny bit more.'

'But given the perks you had . . . in real terms it's a pay cut.'

This was true. 'Definitely worth it,' he snapped.

'Tell us about the interesting people you meet.' His stepmother stepped in smoothly. Another warning glance towards Thatha.

He told them the whole story about John. 'He texted me yesterday to say they expect to go home next week. The baby is still small, but stable.'

'That's a relief,' said Aunty-Amma. 'I can't imagine how worried they must have been.'

'Have you met any other interesting people at your work?' said Sam, eyes sparkling with mischief.

'A few,' he said, glaring at her.

'No one special, then?' Sam said.

'No one that special.' He served himself more rice and another piece of chicken.

'Have some more.' Aunty-Amma moved the coconut sambol towards him with the back of her wrist. 'Since you're back here, and maybe settling down a bit . . . it would be nice if you met someone special.'

'Are you? Settling down a bit?' said Thatha.

'I don't know,' he said. 'I haven't decided. I know what I didn't want. I'm still working out what I do want.'

'You're thirty-two. Surely you have some idea.'

Gihan glanced at Sam, who was looking remorseful. She should be, stirring and dropping him in trouble like that. Little scumbag.

'Not everyone knows what they want from the get-go,' he said, mildly. 'Some of us take time to work it out.'

'You should be thinking about settling down, though,' said Thatha, in almost the same tone of voice. 'At your age.'

'You know,' said Aunty-Amma. 'Kumudhini was talking about a nice girl whose parents are looking for a partner.'

'Their parents want a partner?' said Gihan, innocently.

175

'No, silly boy. A partner for her.' She nudged him.

'Is Kumudhini Aunty the official matchmaker around here now?' said Sam. 'She set up Niro and Vimal too.'

'She seems to have found an aptitude for it.'

Gihan and Sam exchanged glances. They were both fond of all the aunties, even Kumudhini Aunty – who was a bossy nightmare – but if you really needed help, she was always there for you. When Amma fell ill, the other three members of her group had rallied round, cooked, helped with laundry, done lifts to and from school, and generally taken the load off Thatha so that the family could spend her last days together. Above all, they had spent afternoons sitting with Amma, making her laugh.

'If Kumudhini Aunty has decided you need a wife, you don't stand a chance,' said Sam. 'Best find someone on your own, quick.'

'What if I don't want to get married?' said Gihan. 'I'm happy on my own.'

'Oh darling, that would be such a waste,' said Aunty-Amma. 'I'm sure there's a nice girl out there for you . . . or a boy,' she added, after a moment's thought.

Everyone looked confused.

'Well, Gihan has had several girlfriends, but he hasn't really been . . . very committed,' said Aunty-Amma. 'I thought . . . never mind.'

Sam bowed her head to her meal and snorted.

Gihan rolled his eyes. 'I'm not interested in getting married, okay?' This came out more forcefully than he'd imagined. 'A person can be happy without getting married, you know. Lots of people are.'

'That's true, actually,' said Sam. Finally, she was coming to his rescue, like a good sister. 'I know a few people who are comfortably single and happy with that choice.'

Aunty-Amma looked from one of them to the other. Her mouth twitched. 'I think maybe we should leave the boy alone. He's clearly not ready to talk to us yet.'

Thatha nodded. 'Yes.'

Gihan stared at him. 'What? Aren't you going to tell me that I'm wrong? Tell me exactly where I've gone wrong in my life?'

Thatha looked serious. 'I'm sorry,' he said. 'I have been told . . .' His gaze went to his wife and back again. 'That I am sometimes distant and don't listen to you.'

'Sometimes.' Gihan huffed.

'I am trying,' said Thatha. 'To not be like that. You have to understand that it's hard.'

Gihan glared. After all that he'd put them through! 'You—' No. He couldn't do this. He stood up and took his half-finished plate into the kitchen. Anger felt like flames burning up his neck and face.

He dumped the rest of this meal into the bin and washed his hands. He was drying them furiously on a tea towel when Thatha came in.

'Gihan putha,' he said. 'Can we talk?'

Thatha was between him and the door. He didn't have any choice. Thatha paused to wash his hands. Gihan considered storming past him.

Thatha turned around. 'I'm sorry. I didn't mean to upset you.'

'I'm not upset Thatha. I'm angry. All these years, you've been acting like the big I Am. Telling us what to do, even though you failed us when we needed you the most. And now you're trying to make out like you're the big benevolent father? You expect me to buy that?'

His father raised his hands. 'I know. I know. It took Samadhi's outburst to make me realise just how badly I let you down. I am trying to make amends. Trying. I may not be very good at it.'

What was he supposed to say to that?

His father took a breath and seemed to gather his strength. 'I was . . . blinded by my grief and then I was ashamed. I dealt with it by not dealing with it and that's unforgivable, I know. I've been going to . . . therapy.' He flinched slightly when he said it.

Gihan blinked. They'd all been to grief counselling before. That was what Aunty-Amma did, after all. It wasn't a cure all, but it had helped Sam a lot and Gihan to a certain extent. His brother and father, not so much. Thatha hadn't even finished his agreed sessions, deeming it a waste of time. The fact that he had gone back was big news.

'You're right. I failed you,' said Thatha. 'I'm trying to do better. So, how can I help?' He made eye contact, properly. His eyes looked watery.

Gihan forced down the retort that sprang to mind and took a deep breath. He prided himself on not losing control, but he was doing it a lot lately. He needed to get a grip.

'You can help me,' he said, slowly, 'by being supportive of what I do. I might not know exactly what I'm doing, but no one ever does, do they? You try things to see if they work. I wasn't happy at my old job. I saw where my future was going and it wasn't what I wanted. So I'm trying something different. Just let me . . . find my own way. Okay?'

Thatha looked at him for a long while, then nodded. 'Okay.' He smiled, a half-tug at the corner of his mouth. 'You children have grown up,' he said. 'I missed it.'

'But it still happened anyway,' said Gihan.

Neither of them said anything for a moment. Then Thatha said, 'We should go back out there. Come.' He clapped a hand on Gihan's shoulder in a way that he hadn't done in years.

Gihan let himself be steered out of the room. Perhaps things really were changing. He wasn't sure he bought it though.

Later on, he helped Aunty-Amma with the washing up. She didn't like to put glasses in the dishwasher, so they had to be washed up by hand. She thanked him for listening to his father.

'Speaking more freely with Samadhi has made him see what he's missing with all three of you. He's really trying,' she told him. 'He needs a bit of encouragement from time to time.'

Gihan carefully set a wine glass to dry. 'I'm sure you're cheering him on,' he said. His anger had gone down to a low simmer now. He was calmer and trying not to take out his frustrations with his father on Aunty-Amma. 'You chose a very difficult family to adopt.'

She laughed and, unexpectedly, gave him a hug. 'Oh you,' she said. 'I've always loved you guys. All four of you. Five, because I loved your mother too.'

He couldn't return her hug because he was forearm deep in soapy water, so he leaned his head on top of hers. 'We love you too,' he said. 'We're just very bad at showing it.'

She released him. 'I know that,' she said. 'I'm prepared.' She sniffed and stepped back. 'Just because your father is not criticising you, doesn't mean I'm going to stop nagging you about being open to your feelings.'

'What?' he said, getting back to his task. 'I'm open to my feelings. So open that bits of me fall out sometimes.'

She nudged him. 'Look at your sister. She's so happy with Luke. And Niro too, with Vimal. They'll both tell you that their lives are better for having fallen in love.'

Gihan shook his head. 'I'm happy for them,' he said. 'But it's not for me.' He had fallen for a woman who he had to lose, one way or another. He didn't gamble. Not with money, not with his heart. Look what happened when Thatha lost someone he loved. He fell apart and the rest of the family suffered because of it. Gihan knew himself well enough to know that he wasn't strong either. Pretending he was would simply be a recipe for disaster.

As if she'd read her mind, Aunty-Amma said, 'You're not your father, you know. You would react differently. Besides, you might not need to deal with something as cataclysmic as he did. Everyone is different.'

He couldn't see her now, because she was behind him, busy dividing the food into tupperware boxes. He stared at the sudsy water. He thought of Alex, tucking a strand of hair behind her ear; her shy little smile; the warmth of her when she'd thrown her arms around him. He would like to have that, but . . . the thought of having it and losing it was more terrible than not having it at all. The deeper you fell, the harder it was when it ended. And although Alex said her cancer was gone now, he didn't trust it not to reappear. He knew he wouldn't be able to watch Alex fade away like Amma had done. He would be a useless burden, something else for her to worry about when she should be focusing on herself. She deserved better than that.

'Besides,' his stepmother continued, behind him. 'If you shut yourself off to the possibility because you're scared of the lows, you cut off your chances of experiencing the highs. Life isn't always fun, fun, fun, but . . . the good times are worth it.'

Gihan finished the last glass and reached for the tea towel. When he turned around, Aunty-Amma held up a stack of boxes.

'Will this be enough for you and Sam and Luke?' she said.

'There's enough food to keep us in curry for a few days,' he said.

Aunty-Amma rolled her eyes. 'I've seen you boys eat.'

*

Later, as they took the train home, Sam said, 'I think tonight went okay, don't you?'

Gihan looked up from scrolling through estate agent sites on his phone. 'I suppose. I'm not sure I can get used to Thatha suddenly being in touch with his feelings.'

Sam laughed. 'You get used to it. It's nice.'

Resentment stabbed into him. 'I'm glad you've made nice with him. I'm still not ready to forgive and forget.' The flare of anger took him by surprise. This time, he let it roll over him. 'How dare he?' he said. 'How dare he pretend that he can play the caring dad now? He disappeared on us for over ten years and now he wants to pretend none of that happened?'

'He didn't disappear—'

'Yes he did. He was there physically, sure. But we needed him and he wasn't there for us.' He glared at his sister, baffled that she couldn't see this.

'He had a huge shock to the system.'

'And we hadn't? Seriously?' he snapped.

Sam shook her head. 'Yes, but being resentful and hating him is . . . exhausting. It's much better to move—'

Gihan shook his head. 'No. I can't forgive and move on. I just can't.' He looked down at his hands, gripped into tight fists. 'It makes me so angry.'

Sam fiddled with her bag. She took a deep breath and said, 'Are you sure that this anger . . . isn't misdirected?' She looked up at him, cautiously. 'Are you sure you're not really angry at someone else?'

'What the fuck, Sam? Who else would I be angry at? Amma? For dying? It's not her fault. She didn't want to die.'

'I was thinking more that this might be about what happened with you and Helen. Are you sure you're not angry with yourself?'

He shook his head. 'We needed him. We. Needed. Him.' He pounded the side of one hand into the palm of the other in a cutting motion. 'We were children. He was the adult. He should have been strong for us. He wasn't.'

Sam stared down at his hands for a moment, then said in a quiet voice, 'But you were.' She put her hand over his. 'And you shouldn't have had to be.'

He looked at his sister's hand tucked over his and felt tears threatening. She was right. He shouldn't have had to be the strong one. He wasn't the strong one. At least, if he had been, he wasn't any more. He swallowed the tears that had gathered in his throat.

Sam caught his eye and gave him an apologetic smile. 'Sorry.'

He turned his hand over to squeeze hers and let go. 'S'okay.'

They sat in silence for the next few stops. Maybe she was right. Maybe this anger he was directing towards Thatha was really anger he felt towards the world for putting him in a place where no teenager should have to be. Or perhaps at himself for losing his ability to hold it together. Thatha was trying. That was obvious. But he couldn't let himself forgive Thatha so easily.

He glanced at Sam. She had obviously found a way to be happier around their father. He should at least be happy for her. It should have been a nice meal. He had made it awkward.

He looked down at the bag full of tupperware at his feet. On the one hand, it was just food. On the other hand, it was Aunty-Amma telling them she loved them. 'At least we got a ton of food out of it.' His voice sounded uneven, but it held.

Sam gave him a relieved smile. 'Do you think there's enough to feed Niro and Vimal as well?' Sam got her phone out.

Gihan nodded. 'There's definitely enough to feed us all.'

Chapter 17

Two weeks later

Alex was sitting in Maureen's living room, with Leila. She had just explained to Maureen that Leila would be taking Penelope for walks and popping in to see Maureen that weekend because she was going to London overnight.

'I'm going to the Point of Care device innovation awards,' she said. 'We did a pitch for the device, covering the future R&D and we got shortlisted.'

'That's exciting,' said Maureen. 'Well done, both of you.'

Leila shrugged. 'I didn't have anything to do with it. It was one of those things that the team leads did without us.'

'It's mostly extrapolating from what we're working on now,' said Alex. 'Don't quote me, but I think there were only four applicants – so we're all on the shortlist.'

'It's still nice to go to a fancy dinner in London,' said Leila.

'It'll be full of people who make devices,' said Alex. 'It will probably be so, so dull.'

'It'll be good networking for you,' said Maureen. 'And if you win, you must add it to your CV.'

'Networking sounds terrifying,' Alex retorted.

183

'It's only talking to people,' said Maureen. 'And being memorable.'

Leila laughed. 'In a good way, not for falling over into the punchbowl.'

Alex shuddered. She could picture herself doing exactly that.

'What are you going to wear?' said Maureen.

'I don't know!' Alex said. 'I was going to maybe wear the interview suit with a nice top.'

Maureen protested.

'Well, I don't have anything fancier than that.'

'Stand up,' said Maureen. 'Go on.'

Alex stood, puzzled.

Maureen eyed her thoughtfully. 'You'll fit, I think.' She nodded. 'Leila my love, would you be able to go into the attic and fetch down the brown suitcase. It should have a luggage tag on it with "dresses" written on it.'

Leila's face lit up. 'Ooh. Have you got some old dresses? Party ones?'

'I do,' said Maureen. 'I didn't go out that often, but when I did, I had a preference for a nice dress.' She looked down. 'I don't fit into them any more now, of course, but I couldn't bear to get rid of them. You may as well have them. Either of you. Or if your Marielle wants them, Leila.'

'Oh no, Maureen—' Alex said.

'Nonsense. What use are they to me now?' Maureen gestured to the wheelchair, parked next to her chair. 'Go on, Leila. Go get the suitcase will you.'

While Leila was upstairs finding the suitcase, Maureen quizzed Alex about her latest job interviews. There had been two. One had gone well enough that she was hopeful she might have a second interview.

'See,' said Maureen. 'You'll have a new job in no time.'

Alex nodded. She was more optimistic now than she had been. 'The only thing is that I'll be sad to leave the project. The early diagnosis test is important.'

'Would it have made a difference to you, if your cancer had been diagnosed sooner?' Maureen asked.

'Yes. I mean, this test doesn't work on my sort of cancer. It works on breast cancer and possibly prostate cancer. But in general, any early detection is good.' She thought briefly of Jude. If they'd found her cancer earlier, before it had spread, who knows, she might have survived and gone into remission too. 'I hate the thought that we've got a test that could work if we give it a bit more attention. We're so close, but if I leave and they drop all the patents, it will just die and the test will never get to market.'

'That is sad,' said Maureen. 'But you have to look after yourself too. Maybe you can work somewhere where you can develop an even better test.'

It seemed unlikely, but Alex smiled anyway.

There was a lot of thumping and Leila appeared, lugging a brown suitcase. Alex got up and fetched some kitchen towel, so that they could wipe the dust off it before she opened it. Leila cleared a space on the floor and opened up the suitcase. A strong smell of mothballs filled the room. Penelope sneezed. Inside the suitcase were carefully folded dresses. Leila picked one up with a happy exclamation.

'Oh Maureen! This is beautiful!' She stood. The dress she was holding was a wine-red, floor-length dress with one shoulder and a long, flowing sleeve. 'Is this an actual vintage designer dress?'

'Don't be silly,' said Maureen. 'It's modelled on a Halston pattern. My friend used to be a whizz with a sewing machine. She made these beautiful dresses. I used to be the glamorous wife at my husband's work parties.' She smiled. 'I didn't have the heart to throw them away.' She leaned forward. 'I was thinking, there's a blue one in there that might suit Alex.'

Each dress was taken out and carefully unfurled. One or two of them had discoloured, but most were still true to their original colours.

With each new dress, Maureen's face glowed anew. It was as

though when she looked at the dresses, she was transported to happier times with her husband. Alex watched her, and wished with all her heart that she could have that sort of connection with someone.

'That's the one,' said Maureen.

Leila held up a dark blue sleeveless dress. It had a wide collar, but the back was completely covered. 'Oh yes, I see what you mean,' she said. She held the dress out to Alex. 'Try it on.'

Alex considered refusing, but . . . the dress was beautiful and Maureen wanted her to try it, so she stood up and held it up against her. It fell to her calves.

'I think it needs to be taken up a bit,' said Maureen. 'Go try it on, Alex. You can use my room to change in, if you like.'

Since returning home, Maureen's living room had been rearranged so that she had a bed downstairs. This meant that she could effectively live on one floor. It also meant that she was constantly sending Alex upstairs to fetch things. Alex took the dress upstairs and put it on. It was too long and possibly a bit too big around the chest. Maureen was clearly better endowed in the boob department than she was. The high back meant that the scar on her back was hidden. The velvet fabric was heavy, but the lining inside was soft. She stood in front of the mirror in Maureen's room and moved her hips. The dress swished gently at her calves. It was so glamorous. She had never tried on anything so glam before.

When she went back downstairs, the others fussed over her. Leila was given directions to find Maureen's sewing kit and she had soon pinned up the hem and worked out how much to take the top in by. 'I know who can help with taking this in,' she said. 'Violet the wondermum. She does all the costumes for the kids' school shows. I bet she could take this in with no trouble.'

'Is your young consultant going to be there at this do?' Maureen asked, shrewdly.

'I don't know,' said Alex. She had wondered about that, but short of asking him, there was no way to know. Apart from a few short emails asking about Maureen's health, he had kept his distance. She didn't know what to make of it. 'He might be.'

'In that case,' said Leila. 'You'll definitely have to wear this. You're going to look amazing and he's going to be helpless to resist you.'

Alex grinned. She liked the sound of that.

*

Gihan knocked on the door of his boss's office and entered. Dorian's assistant had already told him he was expected.

Dorian, a wiry older man with a surprisingly robust shock of grey hair, looked up from the screen and waved Gihan towards a chair. 'Give me one minute.'

Gihan sat, flicked a small piece of lint off his trouser leg and crossed his legs. The report had gone in two days ago. He had also included a separate update on his proposal that Ryder FT sold their early cancer detection technology to a bigger company. When he'd spoken to Daniel and the company founder – Professor Ryder – the idea had gone down well. Daniel had asked him to keep it confidential – specifically from the staff. This meant he couldn't mention it to Alex until Daniel did, which was annoying, but he had to oblige.

Dorian turned away from his work. 'So. Gihan. How are you finding it here?'

'I think I'm finding my feet,' Gihan said, smiling.

'How did you find your first project?'

'It was interesting.' He took a deep breath and took a risk. 'I have worked on bigger projects than that in the past.'

There was a beat of silence. Dorian said, 'Noted,' and looked back at his screen. 'I gather the client was happy with your and John's report.'

His report. 'John is still on paternity leave.' He kept smiling, because he knew how conversations like this could descend into awkwardness.

'It seems the client was also delighted with your alternative suggestion.' Dorian read the document in front of him. '"Found an excellent solution that allows us to focus on what's important and solve some of our financial difficulties," it says here. Excellent.'

'Thank you.'

'Can I ask how you came up with this perfect solution? You found a potential buyer quite quickly.'

Gihan uncrossed his legs and leaned forward. 'I had worked with the buyer before and I knew that they had complementary technology. I merely signposted one to the other. I didn't share anything that wasn't already available on the company websites,' he said. 'I did run this by your deputy before I did so.'

Dorian nodded. The corner of his mouth twitched. 'Well. Good job. The client is happy, it's generated a bit of goodwill towards us from the other party and could potentially bring us more work from them.'

'That's great.' He let himself relax a little. There had to be more, though. You didn't get pulled into the boss's office for nothing. He waited. When the pause got too long he said, 'Is that everything?'

'Hmm. No. I've got a new fairly complex project coming in soon. I'd like you to be on the team we put on it. It's more biotech, medical devices.'

'Great.'

'And the Point of Care awards. Heard of it?'

Gihan gave a cautious nod. 'I've heard of it.'

'We usually take a table there. We had John down to go to the award ceremony. He has confirmed that he isn't going. I'd like you to take his place. We have a few consultants and a few clients at the table. Do a bit of networking. That's it.'

'Of course.' His mind whirred. That was promising. All this was looking good for his probation period passing smoothly. 'That sounds great.'

'It's a bit short notice. Tomorrow night.'

'That's fine.' He didn't have any other plans.

'I'll have my assistant send you the details. Well done again.' Dorian turned back to his computer screen.

Gihan left the room, feeling better about life. The job was secure. He had three more properties lined up to look at in the next couple of days. Things were looking up.

*

Alex stared at the email on the screen. Minimised it. Then re-enlarged it and read it again. A second interview from the company she'd had an interview with last week. Wow. Hearing approaching footsteps, she shut the window down and turned.

'Whatcha doing?' said Leila. 'You look guilty as all hell.'

'Nothing. I was just . . .' Ugh. She needed to think faster on her feet.

Leila narrowed her eyes. 'Hmm. Okay.' She looked over her shoulder. 'Listen. Can I talk to you for a second?' She jerked her head in the direction of the empty meeting room behind her.

Puzzled, Alex followed her. The last time she'd been in this room, she'd been talking to Gihan. She pushed the thought out of her mind and shut the door. Leila needed her. She had to focus. 'What's up?'

'I've been offered a job,' said Leila.

For a second, Alex didn't know what to say. Then relief flowed into her. 'Congratulations! Does it pay more than here?'

Leila shrugged. 'Only a bit, but I get an extra day's holiday. And there's a better pension scheme.'

Alex gave her a hug. 'That's fantastic.'

'It's a bit of a commute,' said Leila. 'The . . . main reason we live in the village is because it's sort of halfway for both of us. Marielle can get on the motorway and drive up to work. But with us both being closer to Bicester . . .'

'You'll have to move.' Oh. She would miss Leila, but this wasn't about her. 'Is that okay?'

Leila's shoulders rose for the start of a shrug. 'That would be okay, actually. Because . . . if things go according to plan, we're going to need a bigger place anyway.'

Alex gave a little squeak. 'Have you heard from the clinic?'

Leila nodded. 'We can start natural cycle IVF whenever we're ready.'

'Ooooh. Oh, that's exciting.'

'That's one word for it. Terrifying is another,' said Leila. 'I know it's what we both want, but . . . oh my god, I'm not sure either of us is ready.' She smiled, ruefully. 'We can have a baby. But I don't know anything about *raising* a child. What if I screw it up?'

Alex shook her head. 'You won't. I don't think anyone is ready for taking such a huge step. Sometimes, you just have to have faith and step out into the unknown.'

Leila threw her arms around Alex and gave her a hug. 'I can't imagine not working with you. I'll miss you so much.'

Alex held her friend tight. 'I'll miss you too, but things can't stay the same forever.'

They clung to each other for a moment and stepped apart. 'Speaking of change,' said Leila. 'Have you heard anything from your friend Gihan?'

'He emailed a couple of times to ask about Maureen. And he sent her flowers. It was all very distant though.'

'Has his report gone in?'

'It should have done. But he hasn't said anything and neither has Daniel. I don't want to chase . . .' Alex bit her lip. 'He would have told me when it was done, right? Unless he doesn't actually want to see me. He was pretty sure about being just friends. I was hoping he might change his stance once he handed his report in but . . . what if I was wrong?'

'Alex . . . no. Don't self-sabotage and assume the worst,' Leila warned. 'There must be good reasons for him to keep his distance.' She made a face. 'Maybe his report said they should sack us all.'

Alex nodded, slowly. It wouldn't be that surprising if it had. 'Obviously, I hope he didn't say that,' she said. 'But . . . it's a possibility. If he did say that, wouldn't Daniel have said something by now?'

Leila rolled her eyes. 'You know how long they take to make any kind of decision.'

'True.' Alex checked that no one was within earshot and beckoned Leila closer. 'By the way,' she whispered. 'I've got a second interview.'

'Ooh. Where?'

She outlined the job she'd gone for. 'It wouldn't be in cancer research. But I'd be able to commute from here, which is good. I don't really want to move at the moment.'

'Why the hell not? We go where the work is.'

'I'd have to leave Maureen and Jake and all the people I've got to know here . . . and start again. I dunno . . .'

'You can't let your life pass you by, just because you feel a bit bad for Maureen and Jake. Besides, Jake's going to meet someone at some point and ask you to move out. Then what? You can't put your life on hold for other people.'

Alex said nothing. She liked the way her life was right now. The last few weeks had taught her that she genuinely was part of the village now. The idea of uprooting that filled her with sadness. But Leila had a point. If Leila left and Jake found someone, her life would be significantly different. She couldn't make her choices based on them.

Leila patted her shoulder. 'What you need is a night out,' said Leila. 'Go out and get hammered and forget all about everything. Live in the moment. Do something out of character.'

Ha. The last time she'd done that, she'd snogged Gihan and that encounter had been the standard against which she measured all kisses ever since. Nothing had ever matched up to it. It had ruined all other kisses for her. 'No.'

'You've got the Point of Care device awards tomorrow,' said Leila. 'You should go and pull a hot scientist from a rival company. That should take your mind off things.'

Alex groaned. 'I'd almost forgotten about that. Aargh.'

'Oh, come on. It'll be fun. There will be free food and wine. And you look super hot in that dress.' Leila chuckled. 'If Gihan is there, he won't be able to take his eyes off you.'

It had occurred to her that he might be there. His company sponsored a table, she'd noticed. In the last two weeks, he had never been very far from her thoughts. She shook her head. 'I don't think he will. He didn't mention it.'

'Ah well, then who knows who you could meet,' said Leila. 'Probably not the perfect man,' she said, quickly. 'But a fun man perhaps.'

Alex chewed her lip. She didn't particularly want to meet a fun man. She wanted to meet Gihan again. 'I'll be at a table with Daniel and Isobel. It's going to be so dull.'

'Simon from engineering is going,' said Leila. 'And a couple of the other engineers. The award is for their innovation, mostly.'

When Alex gave her some side-eye, Leila added, 'Obviously, you and Isobel had input too. But the point is, it'll be fun and, as Maureen says, you can network. And if you meet a nice man there, you'll be in the best possible form to seduce him.'

'Are you sure you're not trying to live vicariously through me? Not the man bit, I mean the getting drunk and going out on the pull bit.'

Leila grinned. 'Absolutely I'm trying to live vicariously through you. I adore my Marielle, but once we have kids, that'll be the end of our social life. You're going to have to go out twice as hard from now on.' She nudged Alex. 'So go out there. Have some fun.'

Alex laughed. 'I'll do my best.'

*

On Thursday evening, Gihan managed to fit in two viewings of flats. He walked listlessly around the apartments. Mindful of Amma's comment about knowing when a place felt like home, he tried to pay attention to what each place made him feel. It turned out the answer was nothing. He felt absolutely no sense of anything in any of these places.

The estate agent frowned at him. 'No?' she said.

'I'll have to think about it.'

She raised her eyebrows at him. Her mouth said, 'Okay. Well, let me know,' but her face was saying 'You are wasting my time'.

Gihan felt bad. He knew it was her job, but it must be disheartening coming out in the cold and the dark to show him round these places. 'I'm sorry,' he said. 'I guess I'm not really sure what I want.' In so many ways.

'It happens. You said it's not urgent that you find a place. Maybe you should stop looking for a while. Work out what you want and then come back. I can find you places that match the criteria you ask for, but if you're asking for the wrong criteria . . .' She shrugged. She looked down at her iPad. 'Right. I guess that's us done.'

'Thank you.' He turned to leave.

'Wait.' She was scrolling. 'I have something else. It doesn't really fit what you want. Not quite in the budget, well, really not the same sort of thing. But it's not far from here. Would you like to see it?'

He frowned. Wasn't that a waste of time?

'It's literally round the corner. I have the keys in my bag.'

What the hell. He would only have spent those minutes staring at his phone wondering whether to call Alex or not. He was pretty sure he was going to see her at the awards thing tomorrow and he had no idea how to handle it. A few more minutes of obsessing wasn't going to offer any solutions, so why not? 'Sure.'

The apartment building was innocuous enough. It was across the street from a takeaway pizza place and a gift shop. It was the sort of area that had once been run down, then become bohemian and would soon be gentrified. The apartment was on the second floor.

The estate agent gave a nervous little laugh as she unlocked the door. 'I urge you to keep an open mind.'

Gihan frowned. What was that supposed to mean? When she turned the light on, he stepped inside and understood. 'Oh dear god.'

Someone had lovingly decorated the place in the 1970s. In lime green. The walls were lime green. The carpet was light green with darker green circles. Even the curtains were green. The feature wall opposite the windows had a psychedelic green and yellow design that made his eyes water.

'Like I said,' said the estate agent. 'It's . . . different to what you've seen so far.'

He looked around. There were indents where the furniture had stood, patches of brighter colour where the photos had protected the wallpaper. 'Let me guess, someone died recently and left this to a distant relative.'

The estate agent shrugged. 'Yes. Something like that.' She checked her iPad. 'Owner is in the US.' She went across to one of the doors that led off the main room. 'This is the kitchen.' She cleared her throat. 'It's clean.'

It was also very orange. The floor was lino with a crazy pave design. The cupboards were hand-painted fever dreams. Gihan looked at it, bewildered. Something bubbled up in his chest. For a second he wondered if it was his lunch. Then it popped and he started to laugh. It was the most ridiculous place. So unlike anything he'd seen before. He stepped into the kitchen and looked at the walls. There had clearly been things hung up on the walls here too, but the fading was less obvious. Had someone redecorated this room recently . . . and made it look like *this*?

'I'm sorry,' he said, between giggles. 'It's just—'

The estate agent grinned. 'It is, isn't it?' She made a 'round the corner' gesture. 'You should look in the bathroom.'

He went out of the kitchen and peered into the bathroom. Pink. And orange. He stared at it. The colours offended, but the layout was clean and sensible. The giggling subsided. Someone had loved this apartment. Okay, their decor choices were interesting, but they had put a lot of thought into it. He crossed the living room space again and opened the door to the bedroom. A big window looked out over the street. If you ignored the wallpaper and the swirl pattern carpet, the room was a good size. There were built-in wardrobes. It was perfectly serviceable as a bedroom.

He looked at the carpet, which was thick and springy. Again. It didn't look very worn. As he turned to leave, the ceiling caught his eye. There was a clear rectangle shape where something had been removed. With horrified fascination, he looked at the floor directly underneath it. Yes. The indentations for the bed were just below. There had once been a mirror on the ceiling. It had been removed and the ceiling painted over. This made him giggle all over again.

There was one other room. He looked in. That one was chocolate brown and electric blue, which . . . sort of worked, compared to the rest of the house.

'It would make an excellent study,' the estate agent said. 'Or a child's bedroom.'

'Study,' he replied, without thinking. He smiled into the little room. He liked this place. It felt like someone had once had fun there. For the first time, he'd got a feeling about a place. It felt almost like his mother was giving her blessing.

'How much was it again?'

When the estate agent told him how much, he frowned. 'That's asking a lot, considering the state it's in.'

'But it's in an up-and-coming neighbourhood and you know the going price around here.' Gihan pointedly looked at the migraine-inducing 'feature wall' and raised his eyebrows. The estate agent pursed her lips. It was difficult to argue great value with that wall there.

'How about,' he said, 'if I redecorated the place, at my own cost, would he, or she, consider giving me a substantially lower rent? For two years, say?'

'I can ask.'

'If it would help,' he said. 'I have a cousin who does a bit of creative design work. I'm sure I can get her to mock up what it might look like after I've painted and changed the carpet.' He looked thoughtfully at the floor, which was so psychedelic it was making him dizzy. 'It would have to be a substantial discount.'

The estate agent made a note. 'Okay. I will definitely ask and get back to you.' She sounded relieved. Perhaps he was the only person who had seen it so far, who hadn't run away whimpering.

He left the building and headed towards the underground with a spring in his step.

Chapter 18

Since it was a special occasion, Alex had wanted to stay in the hotel where the event was being held, but the price was far too much for her, so she was staying in a much smaller place round the corner.

It was cold enough that she needed a coat and a scarf for her short walk to the venue. There was a small queue for the entrance. Taking out her invitation, she joined it. Judging by the few admiring glances that were coming her way, she must look as pretty as she felt. She brought her hand up to brush her carefully styled hair off her face, but remembered just in time about her makeup and lowered it again.

Once inside, she checked in her coat and headed to the main ballroom. At the door, she took a deep breath. Tonight was all about networking and enjoying herself. She could try and forget all about job interviews and redundancy and even Gihan. Who knows, maybe Leila was right. Maybe she would meet someone else, entirely unexpectedly, while looking fabulous in this dress.

Maureen's dress was surprisingly comfortable now that it fit properly. Violet the wondermum had found her a bolero shrug, which covered her shoulders and kept the beading on the bodice of the dress from catching the underside of her arms when she moved. She loved the flow of the skirt. Despite Maureen's pointed comments about 'proper shoes' she'd chosen to wear it with shoes that had a low heel rather than stilettos. Better to look slightly less glamorous than to risk agony from her back. The earrings tickled as they dangled. All in all, she felt amazing.

Heading to the drinks table, she grabbed a glass of sparkling wine and took a healthy sip. She was going to need a bit of extra courage.

Scanning the room, she spotted Daniel and Isobel, deep in conversation. Next to them Simon, the chief engineer, was looking a little out of place. She made a beeline towards them.

When she said, 'Hello', Simon beamed at her. 'Hello Alex,' he said. His gaze swept quickly down and up her dress. 'You look great.' He looked down at his suit. 'I feel a little underdressed now.'

Alex immediately felt self-conscious. Her earlier confidence evaporated. 'Is it too much?'

Isobel was wearing smart trousers and a sparkly top. All the men were in suits. The women were in a mixture of party wear and smart work wear. It was too much, wasn't it? She should have stuck with her first instinct and worn a suit.

Simon looked around the room. After a few seconds of silence, he said, 'No. You look nice.'

Which was . . . factually accurate, but not that helpful. 'Thanks, Simon.'

She moved so that she was standing next to him. 'So,' she said. 'What's interesting?'

He leaned down a little and nodded towards a group of people. 'Those are our main competitors. Another lateral flow device. They've got this nifty filter in their kit to stop blood cells getting in and messing up the system. I think they'll win.'

She talked shop with Simon, her shoulders slowly untensing. She agreed that it was unlikely they would win anything. So, she may as well enjoy the evening. Daniel spotted her and beckoned her over.

'I see you've pulled out all the stops this evening,' he said, eyeing her dress.

Alex resisted the urge to shrink into a dot. 'Oh, this old thing?' she said. 'I borrowed it from a friend.'

Isobel was eyeing her with fierce intensity. Alex ignored her. Despite her best intentions, the thoughts about possible redundancy kept intruding. Daniel was here now and his guard was down. Now would be an excellent time to get information about of him.

'Daniel,' Alex said. 'Have you heard back from the consultants? Do we know what's happening?'

She saw the momentary widening of his eyes before he composed his expression into a brilliant smile. 'Ah, come now, Alex. Let's not talk about work tonight.'

'This is a work event.' It was an awards ceremony. Not a party with friends. They were meant to be networking.

'Yes, but you should be celebrating the tech success. Being shortlisted is an achievement in itself. If we win, it would be such a bonus when we go out looking for the next round of funding.' He clapped one hand on her shoulder and the other on Isobel's. 'And you two ladies did such sterling work on working up the reactants and excipients for the test. I'm so glad you're both here to see it being projected up on the big screen. Now, can I get either of you a drink?'

'I'm good, thanks.' Alex politely moved her shoulder so that he had to let go.

Isobel raised her own, still full, glass.

'Right. Right. Well, I'm just off to get myself a top up then.' He gave them each a pat on the shoulder again and wandered off.

Isobel eyed Alex, who eyed her back.

'I . . . uh. I like your dress,' said Isobel, quietly.

What? That sounded like . . . small talk? Did Isobel even *do* small talk? 'Thank you.'

'It's actually vintage, isn't it? Not retro.' Isobel had her head to the side now and was scrutinising the dress with interest.

Alex tried not to fidget. 'It is actually.'

'1960s ish? Formalwear.' Isobel pointed to the beadwork. 'I love that. So hard to do. And you've had to take it in. You did a great job with that.'

Now, Alex was genuinely astounded. 'I . . . The dress belongs to my neighbour and a friend did the alterations.'

Isobel studied the dress with intense focus. 'Well. She's clearly very good with a needle. I'm impressed.'

Alex stared at her co-worker. They'd known each other for years and had been in conflict many, many times. This was the first time she'd seen Isobel talk about anything that wasn't work, without looking like she had a broom stuffed up her spine.

'Do you . . . sew?'

Isobel flushed. 'A bit. I do a bit of historical reenactment. Not battles and things, but 1920s up to the 1940s, really. There's a stately home where I volunteer sometimes . . .' She looked away, as though embarrassed.

Alex was fascinated. 'That sounds really interesting. What sort of reenactment?'

'We . . . do scenes. When the guided tours are on in certain parts of the house, we move around in the actual room, in costume – appropriate for the period the room is decorated in. People ask us questions. It's fun.' She seemed to run out of words and looked slightly panicked. 'Sorry. This is probably really boring for you.'

This was the first time she'd seen anything of Isobel other than the scientist. This woman who seemed to live and breathe science, who ate her lunch sitting at her desk, reading journal articles, had a hobby that no one knew about.

'No. No. Not at all. I don't know very much about that sort of thing, that's all,' Alex said. 'What sort of scenes do you do for the 1920s?' By way of reassurance, she added, 'I'm genuinely interested.'

Isobel's eyes lit up. 'Oh. Well, there's four rooms that are on the tour. We've got two teams of actors and we sort of tag team . . .'

Alex sipped her drink and watched Isobel's face. It was like she'd opened a door and let out a whole new person. How had she worked alongside this woman for so long and never known about this? To her embarrassment, she realised that she'd never made the effort. In fairness, Isobel hadn't made the effort to get to know her either. They had always been at odds with each other – competing for resources and staff time.

'I'll have to go to this place and have a look now,' Alex said. 'Would it be weird if I came along on a guided tour?'

Isobel flushed even brighter. 'Yes. In all honesty, it would be weird.'

'Tell you what, I'll let you know beforehand and check that it's a weekend you're not performing.'

Isobel nodded. 'That sounds like a good idea.'

The conversation ran out of steam and they stood side by side, awkward again. Alex glanced sideways at her colleague. She had been talking to Daniel earlier. 'Isobel? Do you think the consultant's report came in already?'

Isobel side-eyed her right back. 'You're friends with the consultant. Couldn't you ask him?'

'I'm not—' Alex stopped talking. She could ask him, couldn't she? 'Actually, yes. That's a good idea. I'll email him tomorrow.'

Her colleague tilted her chin up towards Daniel. 'He told me a few weeks ago that it was likely to come down to you or me being sacked.'

'He told me the same thing.' They both watched the older man, who was now chatting with another man.

'He's always pitching me against people,' said Isobel, glumly. 'I always believed him. Now I'm wondering if it's a tactic. Like he thinks it's motivating.'

Alex let this sink in. She knew that Daniel had always encouraged competition between teams. She had never really figured out why. 'Does he think we work harder if we think we have to compete? That's ridiculous. Surely collaboration works better.'

Isobel crossed her arms. 'You'd think that. I also wonder . . . if he does the same thing to the male scientists as much.'

Alex stared at her. Did he? How could she find out? It would take some time to figure that out and she might not have much longer at the company, so why bother? That said, there was something she could do right now. 'Listen, Isobel,' she said. 'What if . . . we worked together. Not in the formal team meetings, but just generally. Take a few minutes to troubleshoot for each other, rather than trying to find holes in each other's work all the time? Collaborate a bit. Talk about the things that don't work, as well as what does.'

'Okay.' Curt. This was the Isobel she was used to.

There was only one thing left to say. 'If it does come down to you or me and it's me . . . no hard feelings,' Alex said.

Isobel smiled, a thin, humourless smile. 'We've both been taking a bit of time off lately,' she said, quietly. 'Let's not pretend it was for fun. If we both get better jobs, it'll serve him right.'

Alex didn't even bother to deflect that. She raised her glass. 'Good luck,' she said.

Isobel touched her glass to Alex's. 'You too.' She took a sip. 'I am going to find our table.'

The drink she'd had earlier had worked its way through. 'I'm going to find the loo,' Alex said. 'It was good to talk to you.'

Isobel didn't reply, merely nodded and set off across to the tables.

Alex stared after her for a moment. In the last three or four minutes, she'd learned more about Isobel than she had done in years. There was a lesson in there somewhere about how accessible people could be. She wished she'd made the effort sooner. Still thinking about it, she headed to the exit and went in search of the lavatories.

By the time she came back, people were drifting towards their tables. She headed to the boards with the seating plans. She wasn't sure what exactly made her turn when she did – some sort of sixth sense.

'Gihan.'

He was standing a few feet away from her, holding a glass of wine and peering at a seating plan. He turned when she said his name. Because she was looking straight at him, she saw the exact moment that he saw her. His face went slack, eyes wide. When he looked her up and down, his lips moved as though he'd forgotten how to form words. One hand came up to rest against his heart. Thunderstruck. That was the word. It described exactly how he looked.

When he recovered himself, he beamed at her and Alex felt like the most beautiful woman in the world.

'Alex. You look . . . wow.' He seemed to notice his hand over his heart and extended it. She shook it firmly.

'Thank you,' she said. 'What are you doing here?'

'Apparently, we have a table,' he said. He stepped away from the crush by the board and closer to her. 'John's not here, so I got his ticket. I saw Ryder FT on the award nominations list. You must be here to collect that.'

She gave a little laugh. 'Hardly. We're just delighted to be in the running.' Someone tapped on the microphone. She looked across the room, scanning the table numbers for her table.

'I guess I should let you get to your seat,' he said.

'Yes.' She turned back and her eyes met his. They burned into her with an intensity that made her breath catch. They were standing close enough for her to smell his aftershave.

Neither of them moved. Now that she'd seen him, she didn't want to leave him again. All she wanted was to move closer.

Someone jostled him, making him step sideways. Eye contact broken, Gihan cleared his throat. 'Good luck. I'll be keeping my fingers crossed for you.'

Right. Awards. That's what they were here for. 'Thank you. I'll see you later.' She hurried to her seat, before she did anything embarrassing. Only after she'd left him did she remember that she should have asked him about the report. Had he submitted it? Was he now free to talk to her?

At her table, the one empty seat was next to Daniel. She slipped into it.

'Ah good,' Daniel said. 'We were about to send out a search party.'

As the lights lowered, she leaned towards him and asked in a low voice. 'Daniel. Seriously. Did the consultant report come in?'

He turned to look at her, the few lights reflecting off his glasses. 'We'll talk about it tomorrow,' he said, firmly.

Could this man never give a straight answer? 'So . . . it has come in?'

'It has indeed.' He lowered his voice even more. 'Don't worry. It turns out we had a golden goose and it's about to lay an egg.'

She stared at him. What? 'Is that . . . good?'

'For *you*, yes.' She might have been mistaken, but he seemed to tip his head towards Isobel. 'You enjoy your night.' He patted her hand.

Did that mean that it really had been a choice between her and Isobel and she had been chosen to stay? Poor Isobel. As the speeches happened, Alex sat still, thinking about what it meant. She had a second interview on Monday. If she wasn't going to be sacked, did she really want to move jobs? The job she'd been interviewed for had been interesting, but it wasn't working on her test, and she was settled where she was. If she could get her early diagnosis test to market, that would be so amazing. Their device worked – the fact that they were at this event was testament to that. Her test worked too. She just needed to figure out how to make the two things work together. Something she'd designed would be out there saving lives. That would be the most amazing thing in the world. So why wasn't she over the moon? Had she secretly decided that she'd enjoy a change of scene?

When the starter came round, she snapped herself out of her reverie. She was here now. Despite looking like it was doomed, her project had been saved. Daniel was right. She should enjoy the evening.

Also, Gihan was here. Trying not to be obvious about it, she looked around, searching for him. Eventually, she spotted him sitting far across the room. Even at that distance, he seemed to sense her looking at him and caught her eye. She quickly looked away.

He had been so careful to point out that he wasn't letting personal feelings interfere with doing his job, but she still felt grateful that he hadn't betrayed her faith in him. The last piece of reservation fell away. She wasn't sure she believed in fate, but meeting him again after so many years had to mean something. What's more, after five years, she was just as attracted to him as she had been that first time. She thought about him sitting with her in the hospital. Of him letting her hug him, when he couldn't hug her back. If anything, she liked him even more now.

Now that she knew where he was, it was impossible not to keep sneaking glances. More often than not, he was looking in her direction too. She could feel her connection to him, stretching across the room. It made all her senses sit up. Her skin felt electrified with anticipation.

She took out her phone and texted Leila.

He's here.

Leila replied saying, 'Get in!' followed by a string of rude emojis.

Alex put her phone back in her bag and smiled. Leila kept telling her that she shouldn't rush to think she was in love, but this thing with Gihan, it felt different. He was different and . . . Oh god, he was looking at her again. She flushed and focused on her meal.

The thread connecting her to him seemed to pull tighter and tighter. There was a sense of inevitability about it. Okay, he was inconsistent. He may well disappear again tomorrow, but he was here tonight and if that's all she had with him, then so be it. She'd never felt this drawn to someone before. She had a sudden memory of kissing him, her body pressed against his, her chest full of stars. She wanted that again.

It didn't matter whether they won the award or not, she just wanted this meal to end, so that she could go and talk to him. After that look he gave her, he was almost certainly going to want to talk to her too.

After the main meal, there were more speeches. Presentations. They didn't win. Daniel said something that was meant to be heartening. Alex wasn't listening. She didn't care. All she wanted was to be able to get up from the table and go and find Gihan. Everything else was irrelevant. When finally, *finally*, the coffee had been served and all the awards had been given out, she looked up to see that he'd disappeared.

'Right, everyone. Bar,' said Daniel, rubbing his hands together. 'I'm getting all of you a drink. Come on.'

She followed them out, with no real intention of joining them at the bar. Daniel had confirmed that the report had been received, and it seemed Gihan had not suggested closing down her project. Everything was okay. There was only one more thing she wanted right now to make this the most perfect night of her life. She just had to find him.

Chapter 19

Gihan drained his glass of wine. He had managed to keep up with conversations and sound like a competent professional throughout the meal, which wasn't easy considering a part of his brain was occupied entirely with thoughts about Alex. If he leaned to the side, just a tiny bit, he could see her in the distance, sitting with her colleagues. He found all manner of excuses to lean to the side a little. At one point, she had turned her head and caught his eye and he'd nearly choked on his wine.

All his good intentions of keeping his distance had vanished the minute he'd seen her. He had pictured seeing her again, but somehow he hadn't accounted for the fact that she wouldn't be in her usual work clothes. That dress! It hugged her in all the right ways and the skirt swung at knee length, showing off her legs. She had lovely legs. He'd never seen them before and now he would never be able to get them out of his head. The impact on him had been almost a physical punch to the chest.

He'd fallen in lust before, but this was different. He knew her. She wasn't just pretty, she was clever and charming and capable. He could fall in love with her if he wasn't careful and he couldn't afford to do that.

He touched his fingertips to his chest. He should get away.

Make his excuses and leave. She had been polite earlier, and he had no idea how she felt about his suggestion of her project being sold off. If she was angry with him, then she hadn't shown it, but that was perhaps because she was in company. He wanted to find out what she thought of his solution. At the same time . . . he needed to get away. He liked her too much.

He left the minute the speeches ended. If he saw Alex again, he wasn't sure he could keep his distance. He almost made it through the bar, but someone he knew from a previous job caught up with him. He had to make a tiny bit of small talk to be polite.

He was still there when she came out of the dining hall. Her colleagues all headed off to the bar. Alex caught Gihan's gaze, smiled at him then inclined her head towards the double doors at the end of the bar. He could barely catch a breath. This amazing woman wanted him and he wanted her. They were adults. He knew there was a reason he should stay away, but right now he couldn't think what it was.

A few minutes later, he found her outside in the lobby, standing in front of a painting. His heartbeat grew louder with each step until he could barely hear anything else. He stopped next to her.

'I'm sorry you didn't win.'

She didn't look at him. 'Wasn't really expecting to.'

He cleared his throat. 'I handed in the report,' he said. 'Have you . . . had a chance to talk to Daniel about it at all? About my suggestions?'

'I haven't discussed the details, but it sounds good to me.'

The relief felt like wings. 'That's fantastic.'

'The contract is over now, right? I'm no longer a client.' She looked up at him. Inside his chest, something caught fire. He could barely think now, above his one primal thought of 'I want you'.

'I'm staying in London tonight,' she said. 'I thought I'd treat myself. So I'm staying across the road.'

Was she saying what he thought she was saying? His eyes met hers and he saw his own hunger reflected in hers. Oh. Yes. Yes.

'I was thinking of leaving now that the dinner is over,' she said.

Now. Now was good. He didn't think he could focus on anything else after this. 'I could walk you there . . . if you like?' He managed to keep his voice even.

'Better than waiting for a taxi, right?' The corner of her mouth curled up and it was all he could do not to kiss her right there and then.

'Quite.'

They walked together towards the cloakroom. His hand brushed the back of hers and he felt the spark that arced between them. When he waited beside her while the cloakroom attendant found her coat, he didn't dare look at her. If he did, he might have exploded.

When they walked out into the street, where the damp evening chill was like lotion on his overly hot face, he finally faced her. She gave him a tiny smile. He grinned back in response and took her hand in his.

In the lift, she squeezed his hand. He tried to marshal his thoughts. There was something inevitable about tonight. Normally, he would have just rolled with it and seen what happened. But this was Alex. He cared for her. A lot. And feelings made things complicated. They should talk more about her job. They should discuss how far this was going to go. He should wait until he'd worked out his own problems.

Getting carried away on a wave of lust was one thing, but hurting her was not. He had to pull himself together.

'Alex. I'm . . . not really looking for a serious relationship right n—'

Rising on her tiptoes she stopped him with a kiss that made his brain short circuit. 'Don't care,' she whispered.

Oh. Well in that case . . . cupping her cheek in his hand, he returned her kiss. The press of her lips against his were so familiar. So right.

The doors slid open to her floor. She strode forward, towing him along by the hand. She let go of it to dig out her key card.

'Alex,' he said, making one last effort to be a sensible adult. 'We should talk about the report—'

She turned and held up a finger. Her eyes burned into his. 'I don't want to talk about work.' She pushed the door open without breaking eye contact. 'Not now.'

'But—'

Grabbing a handful of shirt, she pulled him down towards her and murmured, 'Tomorrow.' Then kissed him.

It was almost exactly like it had been before. Everything shifted slightly and fell into place, as though the world had slipped suddenly into focus. He stepped closer and kissed her back, wrapping her in his arms. She let go of his shirt and slid her arms around his neck. There was a feeling of rightness. As though, of all the places he could be in the world, the one place he truly belonged was right here. Kissing her.

*

Alex stumbled backwards into the room, still entangled. Gihan kicked the door shut behind him. He reached around her as though to pick her up. She immediately tensed, fearing for her back.

He froze. 'Did I hurt you?'

'No. But be careful of my back.'

He loosened his arms from around her and kissed her again. She walked backwards into the room, pulling him along with her.

'Show me?' he said.

When she pulled back a bit, puzzled, he said, 'Your back. Can I see? Show me what I can do so that I don't hurt you?'

No one had asked to see her scar before she'd slept with them, although a few had been fascinated by it afterwards. When she was younger, she would just put up with the odd twinge of pain in order to get to the good bit. But she was older now. It had been a while . . .

He was looking at her, with his dark, dark brown eyes. She didn't want to slow things down, but she trusted him. He wouldn't be repulsed by it. Feeling brave, she nodded, very slightly. He kissed the side of her neck as she turned around. He carried on kissing her as he undid the zip on her dress. The cool air against her skin meant that her scar was exposed. His fingertip traced it, making her skin tingle.

'Does it hurt?' He placed butterfly kisses on her back that made her flex her shoulders with pleasure.

'No. Only if you jolt me.'

'Mmm.' He pressed a kiss onto her scar, which made her close her eyes.

He kissed his way up to her neck. 'Then, we'll take this, very . . .' Kiss. 'Very.' Kiss. 'Slowly.'

The noise that escaped her throat was part giggle, part sigh.

'I won't hurt you,' he said, the words a warm ripple against her skin.

She turned around in his arms so that she could look into those beautiful eyes again. 'I know you won't.' Cupping his face in both hands, she rose on her tiptoes and kissed him until there was nothing more in the world than him and her and perfection.

Chapter 20

Alex opened one eye cautiously. Her head was fuzzy but she recognised that she was in her hotel room. There was a warm body next to her. She turned and found Gihan, fast asleep. Everything from last night came back to her in a rush that made her hot from head to toe. She turned over, slowly, so that she didn't wake him, and propped herself on her side. Now she could see his handsome face clearly. It was calm in repose. She studied the long eyelashes, the cheekbones, the faint black layer of stubble, the strong line of his jaw. There was a hint of red on his lower lip, which might have been her fault. If she didn't think it would wake him, she would have kissed it better. There was another mark on his shoulder. She pressed her lips against that.

He stirred, but didn't wake up. Alex smiled and stretched. She felt . . . content. No regrets. He had told her, some time ago, that he wasn't the sort to settle for a long-term relationship. Despite Leila going on about her naiveté, Alex wasn't delusional enough to think that she could change the mind of a man who said he didn't want love. This was good enough, for now. She'd gone for true love and happy ever after before and it had never worked out, so why not try love for today, and tomorrow . . . to be confirmed.

Carefully, so that she didn't wake him, she slipped out of bed to go and wash her face.

When she came back, he was sitting on the bed, dressed in his trousers but no shirt yet. When he saw her, he smiled. 'Hello.'

Suddenly the tranquility had gone and it was awkward. What did you do the morning after you'd essentially jumped a guy that you used to sort of work with? A guy who was not going to stick around long enough to fall in love. 'Hi.'

She was wearing knickers and the hotel dressing down. It had seemed fine a few minutes ago. It felt like not enough clothes now.

He reached up and took her hand. 'How are you this morning? Not hungover?' A gentle tug brought her closer.

'A little. Nothing strong coffee wouldn't clear.'

'And your back?'

'It's fine.' A bit sore, but nothing she couldn't handle. She stood in front of him, looking down, her hands in his. 'What happens now, Gihan?'

He gestured for her to sit down. She chose to sit next to him. He put his arm around her.

'What do *you* want to happen now?' he asked. 'I like you, Alex. A lot. In case it wasn't obvious from . . . last night. But I should warn you, I'm a terrible boyfriend.'

'Are you? In what way?' She didn't know why she was asking. It wasn't like she could change him, any more than she could stop thinking about him.

'I . . . I don't really do serious relationships. I don't mean that I'm super laid back or anything, although I am. I just . . . can't do commitment. It's a bit difficult to explain.'

She pushed back her hair, which was still a mess. 'Well, I don't know what sort of a girlfriend I am now. I haven't managed to keep a relationship going for more than a few months.' She sighed and nudged her head further into his shoulder. 'But I like you. I mean . . . *really* like you.'

213

He looked down at her hand for a few seconds without saying anything. She wondered what he was thinking.

'It looks like,' he said, slowly, 'we might both be thinking of doing new things?'

A flutter of happiness in her chest made her smile. There was hope for them. The man she wanted was willing to take a risk on her. And her job was safe. That was more than she'd dared hope for.

She put her hand in his. He gave it a gentle squeeze.

In which case, there were practicalities to think of. 'Long distance isn't great, but we can make it work,' she said. 'You live in London. I live in Oxfordshire.' She didn't need to worry about having to move now.

'That's not for much longer. You'll be moving to London soon, I expect.'

She frowned and sat up, so that she could look at him. 'What do you mean?'

'Because of the—' He clamped his lips shut and paled visibly. His hand loosened around hers. 'When you said you'd spoken to Daniel . . . what exactly did he tell you?'

A terrible sense of foreboding stirred under her sternum. 'He said it was good news for me . . . which means my project isn't going to be closed down, right?'

'He didn't tell you what the report actually said?' Gihan reached for his shirt.

She shook her head. 'Gihan, what's going on?'

He stood up. 'Alex. The report said that the company should focus on its core product. Both R&D projects are draining resources and effort should be refocused onto troubleshooting the main product. Both your and Isobel's projects should be reassessed.'

She took a second to process that. She gathered up the collar of her bathrobe tighter. 'You mean, my project is going to be axed.'

He nodded, his eyebrows knitted in an expression of concern. 'But your test has such potential that I put them in touch with someone who was looking to expand their own cancer diagnosis provision – for use in hospital labs. I suggested that Ryder FT should sell the IP and your expertise.'

She stared at him, too stunned to respond. The sides fell off her world, leaving her feeling exposed and vulnerable. All the scraps of emotion coalesced into one. Anger. 'What?'

He buttoned up his shirt and pulled on his jacket. Why was he suddenly in such a hurry to leave? Oh, that's right. Because he'd screwed her out of a job.

'Alex, I'm sorry. I thought—'

He'd cost her her job and then she'd slept with him. Her face flamed. 'You told him to fire me?'

He closed his eyes and reopened them. 'No. I advised him to close your project.'

'Same thing.'

'And I found a buyer for your work so that it didn't disappear.'

'So you told them to sell my work. Like that's so much better.' Which wasn't completely fair, but she didn't care right now.

'Well it is,' he said. 'It means your work doesn't go to waste and with your CV, you could potentially end up with a much bigger research budget in a much bigger company.'

'Oh, right. So you had a plan to save me as well? That's big of you,' she snapped back. 'What makes you think I needed to be saved? I could have got a new job myself.'

'It's not like—' He stared at her for a second and his expression closed down in front of her eyes. He leaned against the wall and brought one knee up to put on his shoe. 'Of course you could,' he said. 'You're an excellent scientist.'

She rubbed her hands over her face. Anger, disappointment, embarrassment tumbled inside her. She felt so stupid. How could she have believed that he wouldn't do his job even if he had feelings for her? How could she even believe that he had feelings for her? He'd only wanted to get her into bed and, guess what, he'd succeeded.

215

'You could have told me,' she said, her voice too loud. 'You should have told me.'

He lowered his leg and then drew up the other one. 'I thought you knew.'

The calm in his voice was even more infuriating. This was just a transaction to him. A joke. *She* was a joke.

'You could have clarified.' She gestured at the bed. 'All that time. You could have said something.'

'As I recall, we were both rather busy.' He stood straight, looked around and picked up his tie from the corner of the room, where it had landed the night before. He shoved it in his pocket.

'You still could have—' Her voice cracked.

He took a step towards her, one hand held out. His voice was soft. 'Alex . . .'

She batted it away. 'Please leave.'

'Alex, please. I did—'

'Just go. Please.'

He nodded. 'Okay.' He started moving towards the door and paused. 'I'll call you.'

'No. Don't.'

Something melted in his eyes. He gave the smallest of nods, as though acquiescing. 'Bye Alex.'

As the door closed behind him, her last act of defiance was to shout 'You're right. You would have been a lousy boyfriend anyway.'

When the door clunked shut and his footsteps faded, she sat on the bed and let out a long breath. Shit. The room blurred and distorted as the tears came. 'Shit, shit, shit.' She threw herself down and punched the pillow. Once the first storm of tears had passed, she wiped her eyes, rolled over onto her back and stared at the ceiling, trying to untangle her feelings.

The sense of betrayal was overwhelming. She had liked Gihan. Genuinely liked him. No. More than that . . . There had been something. A spark. A feeling of inevitability about seeing him,

216

as though he was the missing piece in her life. And he had betrayed her.

Logically, she understood that he had a job to do and that her project and Isobel's were the most obvious candidates for the chop. But he'd lied by omission, just to get her into bed. How could she not feel betrayed?

She swore again, using the more colourful vocabulary she'd learned from Jake. The worst part was that she wouldn't have expected that level of duplicity from Gihan. She had thought he was different to the other guys she normally fell for. Kinder. Less of a douchebag. She was clearly a terrible judge of character.

Her alarm beeped, reminding her that she needed to check out soon. Her face felt dry and taut from crying. She probably looked terrible. Wearily, she hauled herself off the bed and went to get herself tidied up so that she could face the world.

Chapter 21

Thankfully, Sam was out when Gihan got back home. He had no recollection of his journey home. When he ran through the conversation from the night before in his head, he could pinpoint the exact moment where they had misunderstood each other.

I haven't discussed the details, but it sounds good to me.

She meant the details of the report. He'd assumed that she was talking about the details of the deal, because that was what he'd wanted to hear. He should have clarified. Or mentioned the sale. Or something. How could he have been so stupid?

He changed into a tracksuit and hoodie, because he couldn't even be bothered with jeans, and flung himself down on the narrow bed.

The room was small and had a sloping ceiling with a dormer window at one end. His life was crammed into the small spare room in his sister's flat.

He knew exactly how he could have been so stupid. He'd been so into Alex, so struck by the sight of her in that dress, that he'd temporarily lost all sense. He tapped a finger against his chest, where he imagined the ache resided. It wasn't only then, was it? Right from the start, every encounter with Alex had made him do something he wouldn't normally do. That first night, he'd agreed to be anonymous and then begged to keep in touch. He never went back on his word. Never . . . apart from then – when the stakes had been so high that he'd broken his own rules.

Then with the past few weeks. He knew better than to get involved with a client. Sure, he'd made a pretence of keeping his distance, but he'd sat with her in hospital. Hugged her. Followed her to help with the village fair, like a lovelorn puppy. Those were not the actions of a man keeping his distance. And last night. Oh dear god, last night.

With the heel of his hand, he thumped himself on the forehead. Stupid. Stupid. Stupid. If he'd just kept it together for a tiny bit longer, he would have been able to talk to her properly and this would never have happened. He paused and rubbed his chest again. It hurt. He barely knew this woman, but her being angry with him *hurt*.

Gihan frowned. If they had the power to hurt each other quite so much now, when he'd only known her for a couple of weeks, imagine how much it would hurt if they'd known each for longer. Imagine in six months, a year, two years. Imagine if her cancer came back and he lost her. The pain would be so much worse. Perhaps this was for the best. Maybe this time of slight discomfort was a blessing in disguise.

He sat up, slowly. Another one of his rules that he'd broken. Always hold a part of yourself back. Somehow, he'd forgotten that with Alex. Oh sure, he'd tried, but . . . even on that first night, when he didn't know her name, he'd told her far too much about himself. Come to think of it, maybe it was *because* he hadn't known her name. She had seemed safe, somehow. A stranger. He had thought about her, and that kiss, often while he was out of the country. But she had remained a stranger. She was a special encounter. A memory that he could take out and examine and marvel at, but not something real. He genuinely had never thought he'd meet her again. And when he had, he'd lost his mind a little.

He pushed himself to his feet. Well, no more. This little misunderstanding had put the kibosh on any romantic notions he might have had. His 'relationship' with Alex, such as it was, was over before it had even begun and that was for the best. She made him act out of character. That wasn't safe. That way lay pain and heartbreak and he wasn't going to go through that again. He'd seen what his father's heartbreak did to the rest of his family. He wasn't going to risk that for anyone else. He couldn't do that to Sam, either. Nope. Nope. He was going to go make himself some comforting porridge and watch Netflix until he got over this gnawing ache and then he was going to get on with his life.

*

Alex didn't cry anymore. Crying would involve knowing how she was feeling and she had no bloody idea right now. She held it together by concentrating fiercely on what she was doing. So, by the time she got back to the monochrome comfort of her living room, she was exhausted. The sofa looked tempting. But if she stopped moving, all the things she was avoiding thinking about would crash into her and it would hurt.

Pulling out her phone, she started to make a list of all the things she needed to do. Prepare for her second interview with JD Forensic, visit Maureen, take Penelope for a walk, find more jobs to apply to—

The phone rang in her hand and she nearly dropped it. For one wild second, she thought it might be Gihan calling her. But no. It was Leila. She couldn't talk to Leila right now. Not until she'd processed . . . her throat closed up. She hit cancel and slowly sank down onto the sofa. The room blurred. Alex groaned. She was going to have to face it, wasn't she?

The phone rang again. Leila. Again. She cancelled the call again. She should turn it off because when Leila got the bit between her teeth, she did not let go. Sure enough, thirty seconds later, the phone rang again. Dammit. A sob made her hiccup. She turned her phone off and slumped backwards onto the sofa.

Why? Why did she always fall for the wrong guys? There were two things that she wanted in her life. To help early diagnosis of cancer and to fall in love with someone who loved her back. Gihan had somehow managed to throw a brick at both.

Alex balled her hands into fists and pressed them against her eyes. 'Why? Why me?' Why couldn't her life just be—

Someone banged on the door.

What? Who was that? Alex swallowed down the next sob. Maybe they would go away. No. More knocking. There was the noise of the letter box being opened and Leila's voice said, 'I know you're in there, Alex. Open this door or I'm going to have to ask Maureen for her spare key.'

Dammit. Leila must have been at Maureen's. Alex stood up and wiped her face. Fine.

By the time she reached the door, fresh tears had taken the place of the ones she'd wiped away. She pulled the door open, glanced at Leila, turned around and walked back into the living room.

'What happened?' Leila followed her in. 'I had a text from Simon to say that you'd disappeared with the consultant. I thought you'd be all loved up. What happened?'

'He told Daniel to close my project. And to sell the IP. And me.' She sat back down and picked up her handbag to fish out tissues. 'That's what happened.'

Leila let out a whistle. 'That's a real buzzkill.'

Alex found the pack of tissues and pulled one out. 'It's worse.'

Leila frowned. 'How can it be worse?'

'He didn't tell me until this morning.'

Leila's eyes widened. 'This morning as in . . . after?'

Alex nodded.

'Bastard.'

Alex tried to agree, but all that came out was a watery mewl.

'Oh, honey.' The sofa dipped as Leila sat down beside her. 'Let it all out.'

Wrapped in Leila's arms, Alex gave into the pain and sobbed.

How could she have been so stupid? When he'd asked her if she knew what was in the report, why hadn't she said she didn't know? Why on earth did she say something so easily misconstrued? Of course he had told them to close her project down. Of course they had. They weren't meeting the targets and the company had to cut costs. She knew that. That was why she was busy looking for a new job. Why had she been so easily persuaded that it wouldn't happen?

Shamefully, she knew the answer to that too. She had wanted him. She had been so needy that she'd ignored every single warning sign and carried on. Then she'd taken out her anger on him.

*

Gihan was startled by the sound of keys hitting the small brass bowl that Sam used specifically for the purpose. He rubbed his eyes. The TV was on and he was sprawled on the sofa with a packet of crisps balanced on his chest. He must have fallen asleep in the middle of *Diagnosis Murder*.

Sam stopped in the doorway and stared. 'Oh shit. What happened last night? Did you crash and burn?'

Gihan sat up. The crisp packet fell off in a flurry of crumbs. 'Um . . . no. Crashed and burned this morning instead.'

His sister frowned. She took in what he was wearing, the crisps and the daytime TV. Her expression softened. 'Do you want to talk about it?'

He knew this scenario. 'No, but you're going to make me talk about it anyway, aren't you?'

'Yep,' she said. 'Aunty-Amma says bottling up feelings never helped anyone, remember.' She patted his shoulder as she went past. 'Let me get some tea. Do you want one?'

'Yeah. Okay.' He gathered up as many crumbs as he could and tidied up. Then he went to the bathroom to splash some water on his face and make himself look less like he'd been wallowing in self-pity.

He stared at his face in the mirror. He had bags under his eyes from not sleeping much last night and his stubble was more than a shadow now. His head hurt, and he suspected only some of that was caused by being upset. The rest was a hangover. He'd had a fair bit to drink last night. Granted, not enough to excuse what happened, but still a lot.

Tea was probably a good idea. He dried his face and hands and went back out to find his sister had taken a small handheld vacuum cleaner thing to the sofa. Wow. When had his baby sister become so organised?

She pointed to the sofa and said, 'Sit. I've made you tea too.'

Sometimes, even though she didn't know it, Sam sounded exactly like their late mother. Gihan sank back into the same spot he'd been in before. 'Can I have a couple of painkillers as well? Please.'

He pulled out his phone and checked it. There was nothing from Alex. No recriminations, no apologies. That wasn't fair. He had asked her about the report. Okay, he had misinterpreted her answer, but he had still asked her.

Sam handed him two painkillers and a mug of tea and then sank onto the sofa next to him. 'Okay. Tell me.'

He told her about the night before, without going into too much detail because there were things you just didn't talk about with your little sister.

'That sounds like it all went well,' she said. 'So why have you got a face like a wet weekend?'

'Because, this morning, we realised that we'd been talking at cross purposes. She didn't know about the contents of the report, not fully. She thought her job was safe and she didn't like it when I told her it wasn't.'

Sam made a face. 'Oh no. Poor her.'

'Then she accused me of tricking her.'

Sam hissed in her breath. 'Ouch.'

'Yeah. I mean, I get that she'd be upset about her job – but I did put a solution in place and . . . I thought she knew.' Now that he was talking about it, he felt indignant all over again. 'Does she think so little of me that she thought I'd lie to her?'

Sam looked thoughtfully at the drink in her hands. 'Well, you don't know what other people have said to get into her knickers in the past.'

He looked at her, surprised. He'd never known Sam to speak so candidly before. But she had a point. He didn't know what Alex's exes had done. He knew that she'd been lied to in the past. 'But still,' he said. 'I was always very clear with her about where I was coming from. Okay, I messed up last night by not following up with more questions, but honestly, she said she was pleased with the report, which . . .'

'Which was what you were hoping to hear, so you accepted at face value,' said Sam.

'Whose side are you on?'

'Yours, honestly.'

'Doesn't sound like it.'

'Well, I know what it's like to think that the guy you like lied to you,' she said, mildly. 'She'll sit down and think about it, just like you're doing, and she'll come to the same conclusion. It was a misunderstanding. You were hasty. What you had is worth saving.'

He let that sink in for a few minutes. 'I . . . don't think she will think that,' he said. 'I don't know her as well as I thought, but I do know her.'

'You should call her and clear the air, though.'

'No. She said not to.'

'So? What? You're going to give up? Seriously?'

He looked up at the ceiling. 'She said not to call her. So yes. I'm going to give up. Maybe . . . it's better this way.'

'Better because . . .?' Sam made a winding motion with her hand.

'I can't be there for her if she needs me. If she falls ill . . .'

Sam gave a noisy and exasperated sigh. 'Not this again. Just because Amma died, doesn't mean everyone will.'

He rolled his eyes. 'Everyone dies, Sam.'

'What if you die first?'

'Then I'm sparing her the terrible grief that will ruin her life. Not to mention her relationship with the kids.' He faltered. Kids? Where had that come from? He had always assumed that family life wasn't for him. But he had slipped up and let himself imagine a future with Alex which might have included family. Thank goodness this misunderstanding had happened. Better he got out of it now.

Sam gave him a shrewd look. He shook his head. She scowled at him. 'Look, just because Thatha went off the deep end and left us to fend for ourselves, doesn't mean that you will do the same.'

'Everyone always used to say I had the exact same temperament as him. And look how I reacted to Helen's proposal. I'm clearly not emotionally stable.' Gihan shook his head. 'I'm not inflicting that on anyone.'

'But you're not Thatha, are you Aiya? We were all suffering when Amma died. Thatha got depressed. Loku Aiya buried himself in his studies. They both disappeared into their own worlds to process their grief. You didn't. You were there for me.' She stared straight ahead at the now dark TV. 'I don't think I'd have got through those months without you,' she said, quietly.

He looked at her and, for a moment, saw the terrified teenager that she had been. He too turned and looked away.

They sat in silence for a bit, then Sam said, 'There's a YouTube live about the new SyrenQuest release happening now, want to watch?'

He shrugged and watched as she pressed buttons to search for the right channel.

'Sam,' he said. 'Do you think you'll have a family?'

She didn't look away from the screen. 'Probably,' she said. 'Luke wants to. I would like a couple of years to get the company onto a stable footing first, but yeah. Probably.' She found the channel. 'Ah, here we go.'

As the familiar chatter of YouTubers washed over him, some of the tension left Gihan's shoulders. He sat next to his sister and watched, letting real life still around him.

This is what they'd done, in those awful months. Gihan would make them something to eat. They would sit in the living room, side by side on the sofa, finish their homework in silence, and then put YouTube on and watch Blaze do video game walkthroughs. Gihan, at only fifteen, wasn't old enough for the responsibilities that life had given him, and all he knew was that grief was terrible and he would do anything to avoid it. He had handled it as best he could at the time, but it seemed that all he'd done was store it up so that it could erupt later. He felt depression and anxiety ticking away inside him, waiting to wreak havoc on his life. He couldn't in good conscience drag someone else into this.

Hot pressure built up behind his eyes. He blinked and tears loosened themselves from his eyelashes and ran down his cheeks. He quickly wiped them away, but more followed. In the end he gave up and let them come.

Next to him, Sam didn't comment, but merely passed him a box of tissues and leaned against him, in the same way that she had done all those years ago, when putting your arm around your little sister was too cringey even in grief. They sat, shoulder pressed against shoulder, silently supporting each other.

On the TV, Blaze and his friends ran around, climbed and shot things. Their chatter filled the room, soothing in its own way. And Gihan quietly mourned all the things he'd lost and all the things he was about to lose.

Chapter 22

'Was it worth it?' Maureen asked.

It was Sunday morning. Alex had related everything again – this time to Maureen. She was sitting in Maureen's cheerful kitchen, with Penelope at her feet. Leila was making tea. After a bad night's sleep, Alex was feeling fragile and achy. At least her headache had gone and she could think through the clouds of anger and self-recrimination now.

'Pardon?'

'The sex,' said Maureen. 'Was it worth it?'

Alex gaped at her, not sure how to answer. Her face heated up by several degrees.

Maureen smiled. 'It was, wasn't it?' She preened. 'That dress *always* works.'

Leila snorted, failing to hide her laughter. 'Maureen, you are incorrigible.'

'It was a relevant question,' said Maureen.

'Was it though?' Leila put mugs down and handed them out to the right people.

'Alex risked quite a lot to spend the night with this man.'

'But she wasn't to know that he was going to stab her in the back.' Leila sat down.

'I don't think he did "stab her in the back" as you say. His report wasn't a surprise, was it? You all knew it was a possibility.' Maureen looked at Alex. 'You were job-hunting because of it.'

Alex sighed. 'I mean, I sort of knew. We all did. I just . . . didn't want to face it.' She dropped her head back. 'Ugh. I feel so stupid.'

There was a moment of silence. Alex raised her head back to an upright position. 'What do I do?'

Maureen gave her an appraising look. 'About which part?'

'Either. Both.'

Maureen and Leila exchanged glances.

'I think,' said Leila, 'only you can answer that. What do you want to do?'

Alex took a deep breath and let it out. What did she want? Thinking about Gihan was too much, so she focused on the more obvious problem of work. 'Well . . . I have a second interview to do. If I get that job, then . . . that makes life easier. I feel bad about you and Ray, though,' she said to Leila. 'Especially Ray. He can't move and he can't afford to lose his job.'

'Don't worry about me and Ray, we're both going to be fine.' said Leila. 'What do *you* want?'

'I want . . . I want to help prevent cancer.' That was easy. 'I know I can't eradicate it, but if my work can help people's survival, then I'd have done something with my life.' The more she said it, the more she realised it was true. She had been given a second chance at this life, she needed to make it count.

'And the new job, would it help with this?' This was Maureen.

'Not really, no. I'd be doing interesting work and developing new forensic tests, but I won't be able to bring the early diagnostic kit to market.' She shrugged. 'Plus, it's quite far to commute to.'

'You don't have to stay here. You're young. You can move to wherever the job is,' said Maureen, as though it was the simplest choice in the world.

Alex stared at her. 'But you need me. So does Penelope. And I'm part of the—'

Leila stopped her by putting her hand over Alex's. 'Are you trying to tell me that if you were offered this job you'd turn it down?'

'Well, I . . . I'd have to think about it. Obviously.'

Maureen fixed her with a stern glare. 'Because of me?'

The obvious answer of 'yes' withered under the glare. 'Well . . .'

'No,' said Maureen. 'You'll not turn down a good opportunity because of me. Or because of some village committee or, indeed, because of Jake or Leila or anyone else. If you're going to turn it down, it's because it doesn't suit *you*.'

Alex sighed. 'I know it sounds silly to you,' she said. 'But community means a lot to me. I spent a lot of time in hospital as a kid. I missed out on a lot of social stuff. I never figured out how to make friends. Even at university, I was either too intense or too weird. I never belonged.' She waved a hand. 'It's the same with relationships. I can get myself into them, but I don't know how to *be* in a relationship. What are the rules? Somehow, I always get them wrong. None of my relationships have lasted. There must be something wrong with me.'

Leila leaned forward. 'There's nothing wrong with you. There are no rules. You're not missing a "relationship" gene. Men are just odd.'

They were all quiet for a moment. Then Maureen said, 'I must admit, I'm disappointed in this last one. He seemed like such a nice chap. After all, he seems to care about my welfare and he doesn't know me from Adam.'

Alex shrugged. 'Maybe he felt bad. Maybe he wanted to impress me.' Even as she said it, she knew she was wrong. He had come to the hospital with her because she'd asked him to. He hated hospitals – he'd told her that. She thought about his manner when they were waiting for Maureen to be brought to the ward and believed that he genuinely did find it upsetting . . . and yet he'd stayed with her until she was ready to leave. That wasn't a guy trying to impress her. That was him being kind.

'You said he asked you if you knew what was in his report, before you got . . . involved?' Maureen said.

Alex nodded reluctantly. She remembered her finger against his lips. *I don't want to talk about work. Not now.* He had asked and she'd given what she'd thought was an accurate answer, but she'd made an assumption. If she'd stopped to think for more than two seconds, she could have worked out that there was something wrong with her assumption. 'Argh. I jumped to a conclusion from Daniel's comment. He said it was good news – and I thought he was talking about the same thing I was thinking of.'

'Hmm,' said Leila. 'You do that sometimes.'

'What?'

Leila put her hands up defensively. 'You have . . . a tendency to jump in and believe what you want to be true. Even when it's not true. When people say you're too intense, I think maybe that's part of it. You go from "we just met" to "and we lived happily ever after" within days. Hours, even. Sometimes, it's not actually true.'

Alex stared at her. 'Why are you only telling me this now?'

'I've only just figured it out,' said Leila. 'I mean, I know you from work. At work, you're all about the consistent results and the null hypothesis, but when it comes to your love life, you're not. It's two completely different mindsets.'

'But work has to be like that, otherwise it's not good science. Love and life . . . that's different. Love is meant to be impulsive and life . . . Life is short.'

Leila shrugged. 'If you're with the wrong person, life can feel very long.'

'But sometimes,' said Maureen, 'you can know you've met the right person from the minute you meet them. I know I did.'

Alex dropped her face into her hands. 'This is not helping,' she said into her palms. Emotions churned. If she and Gihan had talked about things properly, they would have ironed this out. But then last night wouldn't have happened. Last night was wonderful. She had felt powerful and safe and adored. Despite all her anger and confusion, she was clear on that. It was such a shame that it had ended up like this. 'Nothing is helping.' She curled her fingers, so that her nails dug into her scalp.

'You could call him,' said Leila. 'Talk about it.'

Alex lifted her face high enough that she could peek at Leila. She could. But she'd gone on about how she didn't need him to save her. Besides, apparently, *apparently*, she had a tendency to jump in and see love where it didn't exist. Maybe this was what she was doing now. Maybe, if she stopped acting in the heat of the moment, she would find that this pain wasn't so bad.

'I think,' she said, 'I should give it a couple of days and find out whether I got the forensics job first.'

*

The next day, Alex turned up outside Daniel's office early, as usual, and ended up leaning against the wall, waiting. Five minutes after her meeting was due to start, the door opened and Isobel came out. Her mouth was set in a thin line. Alex met her gaze for a second and understood. Isobel hadn't had good news.

The two women nodded to each other. Isobel marched off – heading for the exit, by the look of it. Alex knocked on the door.

Daniel was inside, along with Sally from HR.

'Ah, Alex, sit down. We have some exciting opportunities to bat and ball with you.'

Alex sat down. She'd had a lot of time over the weekend to think. One of things she'd realised was that she really disliked Daniel. He had set her and Isobel up to be rivals, which was completely unnecessary. He had kept the report secret from them. Surely, he must have known the anxiety that they would have been feeling – especially given that he'd dropped so many hints that one of them was going to lose their job. Did he think he got some advantage from doing this? Or was cruelty the whole point?

At any rate, Sally being there was not a good sign.

'What opportunities?' she said, hoping to prompt a response with less waffle than usual.

'Well, as you know, we had the report back from the consultants and now that we've had some time to give it a thoughtopsy . . .' He patted the paperwork on his desk.

The portmanteau word made her cringe again. 'Thoughtopsy?' she said in her most withering voice.

'Aha. A post-thoughtem, if you like.'

She refused to rise to the bait a second time. 'What was the conclusion? I have an experiment running. I need to finish this on time so that I can get back to the lab.'

'Ah. Yes. About that. Well . . .' He glanced at Sally, who kept her eyes on her laptop. 'As you know, we commissioned the report to see where we needed to focus and which deliverables needed to be ring-fenced in the basket. The consultants were very clear that we've overcommitted—'

'Daniel,' she snapped. 'Please can you get to the point?' She was fired anyway, so why bother with the niceties? She didn't have to put up with this nonsense.

He looked taken aback. 'Okay, then. Unfortunately, we have to close down your research project.'

She knew it was coming, but it was still a blow. It took a few seconds to recover. Daniel carried on talking, but she'd stopped listening. She looked at Sally. 'What does that mean, job wise?'

Sally spoke quickly, before Daniel could get in. 'For you, it would mean that we're giving you two months' notice as of now – and I'll email you details of how we work out the redundancy package.'

'But we have an offer for you,' Daniel jumped in.

Alex ignored him. 'What about Ray and Leila?'

'We will move them both onto the team that's testing shelf life and excipients,' Sally said. 'Don't worry. Their jobs are safe.' Her smile was small and apologetic.

Daniel cleared his throat, loudly.

Alex turned her attention back to him. 'Was there something else?' She knew there was. Gihan had told her they were in talks to sell her research. They would need her expertise for that.

'We've started discussions with another company. Bigger fish than us. They might be interested in buying the IP around your work and hiring you as well, to make sure they have your know-how. They want to acqu-hire you.' He paused and looked expectantly at her.

Neither Alex nor Sally responded.

'Who are these people?'

'Big fish,' said Daniel, with pomposity. 'I'm afraid the negotiations are delicate and we're operating on a need-to-know basis.'

'Well, it seems like you need me in order to pass on the knowledge. If you want me to cooperate, I do need to know.'

She noticed the slight widening of Daniel's eyes and the amused smile, quickly squashed, from Sally. They needed her cooperation. Good to know.

Daniel frowned. 'What are you saying?'

'I'm saying, I need to know who we're talking about, so that I can do some research on what else they do. That way I can work out how best to pitch our diagnostic test so that they are convinced that it fits with their existing technology.' She kept her voice level and spoke slowly and clearly, as though explaining it to a child.

Daniel seemed to see the logic in this. 'They're Swanland Corp.'

For a second Alex was speechless. Swanland Corp made hospital-grade tests for all kinds of things, including prostate cancer. If they were interested in her work . . . that would mean the real possibility of her test actually being used in hospitals – perhaps as an early warning system. If they could make it cheaply enough—

No. She was getting ahead of herself. She took a deep breath and focused on the room. 'Do you know what exactly they're interested in? Are there particular parts of the test that are of interest?'

Daniel gave her a blank look. 'That's the sort of thing we'll excavate when we have our meeting.'

'Meeting?' Oh god, getting a straight answer out from this guy was like extracting teeth. 'What meeting?'

'We have a meeting on Wednesday. We're going over to their site. I'm going to need you there to answer any technical questions. Don't worry about getting into the weeds of the negotiation, we'll handle that. I need you to be the science vision in the room.'

'Okay. I'll have to reschedule my work so that I can prepare.'

He shrugged. 'Your focus now should be streamlining the tech ready for the sale, anyway. Can you thumbnail it for me by close of play today?'

Alex translated that in her head. 'You want a . . . summary?'

'By close of business.'

She started to nod, then realised that he was only her boss for two more months. Right now, he needed her more than she needed him. 'It'll take me longer than that. I'll have it for you by 9am tomorrow.'

There was the slightest of frowns from Daniel. 'Of course, I expect you to keep this confidential.'

'I have to tell my team. You're changing everything. I can't not tell them.'

'Leave that to me,' Daniel blustered.

'Actually,' Sally said, 'we'll be talking to the rest of the teams – yours and Isobel's – this afternoon. I've already sent the meeting request. So, please be discreet. I'm sorry. That's going to be awkward for you. But it's only for a few hours.'

Alex already knew that she wouldn't be able to keep it from them. So she said nothing. They would find out sooner or later. Leila would be less bothered than Ray. So she would tell him that his job was safe. Everything else was peripheral to that.

A few minutes later, when she walked out of the meeting and down the corridor, she felt oddly liberated. It was as though the scales had fallen from her eyes. She'd spent all this time trying to be recognised by management in her company, but really, there was nothing wrong with her work. She was just trying to get the attention of the wrong people.

Back upstairs, she found an email from Isobel waiting for her. She glanced across the room to see the other woman watching her. She opened the email.

Isobel: They're closing my project down. I've been given notice and offered a redundancy payoff. What happened to you? Are they keeping your project open?

Looking up again, she jerked her head towards the empty meeting room behind her. As always, the thought of Gihan nudged into her mind. She firmly booted it back out again.

'I have two months and then I'm out,' Isobel said, before Alex had even closed the door. 'They're closing down the research, letting the patent applications lapse. How about you?'

'They're closing the project down,' Alex said, carefully. 'But they're selling the IP from the project – the patent application and all the background info.'

Isobel folded her arms and studied her. 'So . . . you're staying?'

'Not exactly. I think there's a possibility that the buyer might want to hire me too. I don't know the details yet, but . . . either way, I won't be working here much longer either.'

'What about your team?'

This surprised Alex, she hadn't expected Isobel to care about other people. But, she reminded herself, she didn't actually know Isobel. The version of Isobel in her head was formed on incomplete information.

'The team is going to be okay. They'll be reallocated.'

Isobel nodded. 'Mine too.'

'You told them?'

'Obviously.'

They stared at each other for a moment, reassessing their old rivalry.

'You've got a new job lined up, right?' said Alex.

'Yes. I had the week to decide and I guess that's the decision made.' The corner of Isobel's mouth twitched. 'More difficult for you, though.' She uncrossed her arms and leaned against the desk. 'What are you going to do? If you're offered the job with the buyer would you take it?'

'There's nothing certain yet. They might not really want to buy the technology. I only have Daniel's say-so that they do.'

The roll of Isobel's eyes told her exactly what the other woman thought of that.

'So . . .' Alex said. 'Pastures new?'

Isobel nodded. 'I guess this was a blessing in disguise, this whole thing.'

Alex glanced across to the empty desk. Gihan had sat there not so long ago and held the strings of a potentially catastrophic report. Now that it was out, it might not have been as devastating as she'd thought. 'I guess it was.'

Chapter 23

Alex stood in the labs at Swanland corp and tried not to gawp. Their labs were so much better equipped than Ryder FT. The senior scientist showing her around, a pleasant lady called Farnaz, was clearly familiar with Alex's work, which was enormously flattering. They talked about technical details, while Daniel and the marketing manager Brent tried not to look bored. Alex got the impression that the tour had been mainly for her benefit. They had rushed through talking about the company as a whole and focused on the labs. Alex had taken the time to read up on their technology and what they were offering, so she could ask Farnaz some detailed questions.

At the end of the tour, there was a meeting. Alex sat at the conference table, trying not to fidget. She would give anything for her test to be trialed in Swanland's device. Something Farnaz had said set off a train of thought about what she could change. She quickly made a note on her phone and emailed it to herself.

The meeting itself covered a range of topics, some of which Alex could discuss with confidence – like the technology or the patent applications – while the rest were handled by Daniel and Brent. She had always seen Daniel as a bumbling, management-speak obsessed figure, but that day she saw why he had been given the job of CEO. He was smooth. The management-speak, deployed in its proper context, didn't seem quite so ridiculous as it did when he was talking to the team. He answered questions, judiciously gave precisely the right amount of information. It was uncanny to watch.

Finally, they arrived at a point when everything had been said. There was silence around the meeting table. Alex fought her impulse to jump in and say something to fill it.

She looked down at her notes. The people from Swanland had asked interesting questions. The sort of questions they could only have come up with if someone, possibly even Farnaz, had read everything she'd published on the test and read the patent application very carefully. They were not messing about here. The interest was real. She allowed herself the tiniest glow of pride. Even if this sale didn't go ahead, her work was sound. Scientists who had much bigger research budgets than she did were taking it seriously.

Daniel was the one who broke the silence. 'Of course, you'll need time to decide, but I think we've made a compelling case.' He looked at Alex, who nodded. Daniel continued, 'Shall we put another meeting in the diary to circle back?'

The three people from Swanland looked at each other. 'Yes,' said the chief scientist. 'I think that's a good idea. We'll need to get the details ironed out before we can make a formal offer.'

Wait. Did that mean—? Alex glanced at Daniel. Did that mean what she thought it meant?

Daniel beamed. 'That's good to hear. How long will you need?'

Afterwards, in the taxi back, he turned around from the front seat and said to her, 'We mustn't put the cart before the horse. The offer might be very low.'

'But we don't have any other options,' said Alex.

'They don't know that.' Daniel squared his shoulders. 'Thank you for all your hard work on this Alex.' He smiled. 'They were clearly courting you. Even if the sale doesn't go through, I wouldn't be surprised if they make you an offer anyway.'

She nodded. They had made no secret of the fact that they'd expect access to Alex's expertise as part of the deal. Daniel had put it as, 'We will be willing to second Alex to you for a fee.' Even though he knew Alex was working her notice, he was using her to get Ryder to commit to a higher price. Alex hadn't wanted to contradict him, but the negotiating tactic rankled. She might have a firm job offer from JD Forensic soon. She knew now that she would turn that down in a heartbeat if Swanland Corp offered her the chance to work on her own technology. There would be a real hope of seeing her test out in the real world. How could she resist that?

It seemed that the people from Swanland understood this, because they made sure to point it out.

Daniel opened his laptop and started reading his emails.

Alex leaned her head back and looked out of the window and daydreamed of her test saving lives. It would be the culmination of a dream she'd held for a long time. And if one test worked, why not others? There were ways to adapt her test for other cancer types. Last night she had said that work was work and life was different, but was it really? Right now, her work was very important.

But wait. Was she jumping to happy ever after too quickly here too?

You had to allow yourself to dream, didn't you? Nothing could be made if it wasn't imagined first. If you didn't dream about what could be, you wouldn't do anything new.

If she was offered a job at Swanland, everything would change. But she could see now that things couldn't stay the same for much longer anyway. Maureen was going to need more care. Jake was going to be even busier than he was now. He was talking about hiring another manager to take care of one of the new branches. Leila and Ray would have babies to look after. Her world would not look the same.

There was so much going on, she really needed to talk to

someone. But she had no one to talk to. Her boss sat in the front, tapping away. She didn't trust him – if it came to a choice between her and the company, he would choose the company every time. Jake – sure, he was helpful and kind, but he was consumed by his business. Leila would understand, but she would have other priorities soon too. And Maureen – much as she loved Maureen, there were some things she couldn't share with her.

The only person she felt really understood her and where she was coming from, would be Gihan. Talking to him had made her realise how badly she wanted her cancer test to become a real product. Just like talking to him five years ago had made her realise that Todd dumping her wasn't her fault.

Alex sighed. She had been terribly angry with Gihan, but today's opportunity had only come about because he'd connected the dots and put her on Swanland's radar.

That morning in the hotel, he had said, 'You could potentially end up with a much bigger research budget in a much bigger company.' This was what he'd seen when he wrote his report. Those weren't the actions of someone out to mess around. Those were the actions of someone who genuinely cared. She closed her eyes and stifled a groan. She had rushed in and jumped to conclusions again, hadn't she?

Opening her eyes again, she stared, unfocused, out of the window. Why was she holding off talking to him? Pride, she had to admit, was a part of it. She had said he didn't need to save her and that she could save herself. If she got either one of these two jobs that were dangling in front of her, she could call him with her head held high.

Did that really matter so much? She missed him. Right now, she wished she could call him and tell him everything that happened in the meeting to see what he thought. Of course, she couldn't, even if he were still talking to her. Non-disclosure agreements were inconvenient like that.

If she was being calm and rational about what happened, they were both at fault. They had both heard what they wanted to hear because they had both wanted each other so badly. Was that such a bad thing?

So, she should call him. She pulled out her phone and checked her messages. He hadn't messaged her. Or called her. What if he was never going to? She turned the phone down on her thigh and looked out at the motorway sliding past the window. The last time he had ghosted her, it was a mistake. What if this time it was for real? She obviously picked a type of man who did that. What if she thought he was different because she wanted him to be?

Alex sighed again and put her phone away.

Chapter 24

Gihan was supposed to take a taxi from the client's office back to work, but the sun was shining. It was mid-afternoon. Not quite late enough to be dark, but almost late enough that it wasn't worth trekking back to the office only to turn around and go home. His boss had a fairly relaxed attitude towards working from home, so long as the work got done on time, and Gihan's work always got done on time. 'Don't worry,' he told the guy in reception. 'I'll walk to the tube.'

He stepped outside into the autumn light and took out his phone. There was a missed call from the estate agent. He considered leaving it until later to return the call, but decided now was as good a time as any.

'I have great news,' the estate agent said, once he'd said who he was. 'The owner of the flat is willing to discuss your proposal of reduced rent in return for you redecorating the place.'

'Oh. Brilliant.' They discussed details – the owner wanted a more specific list of what he was planning to do. He had only sent some mockups that Niro had made for him.

'I'm amazed,' the estate agent said. 'He's been very clear about the price whenever we've asked before. It must have been your suggestions that made the difference.'

'I would be raising the value of the property while living in it,' said Gihan, dryly. 'If he ever decides to sell it.'

'I did point that out to him,' she said.

He promised to send her a more detailed email and hung up. Yes! A new project. This was what he needed to take his mind off Alex. It had been a week and a half now and he still couldn't stop thinking about her. He needed distractions.

He pulled up a map on his phone – he knew better than to wander around without it. Locating the nearest tube station, he took a few steps to make sure he was facing the way he thought he was. Excellent. Going well so far. He walked, enjoying the evening. Not much was happening at this time of day. It would get busy soon once the schools turned out. The low rays of the sun caught the undersides of turning leaves and made the trees glow. Everything, even the air, felt moist and mulchy. No wonder they called it the season of mellow fruitfulness.

Mellow. That was a good description for how he felt right now. Work was going well. John had decided to take six weeks of paternity leave, which meant that Gihan had a lot of very interesting work. He was getting on well with his colleagues. All he had to do was keep his focus on these good things and he would soon get over Alex.

He came to the top of the road and looked at his map again to get his bearings. Wait, the blue dot hadn't updated. Argh. He refreshed the map and waited. He wasn't familiar with this area, so he amused himself by looking at the things nearby. A street sign caught his eye. Buddhist Vihara. Two streets over. Not far.

For a second it was as though something rippled through him. He looked up.

He had been there before, with Amma, when he was small. He had also been there for at least three pujas in Amma's memory at this temple. Aside from the knowledge that they'd definitely happened, he had no recollection of any details.

On an impulse, he retraced his steps to a shop and bought

a bunch of carnations. Checking the app again, he crossed the road and followed the directions through the back roads until he ended up outside the familiar entrance to the temple. On the outside, it was just a big house. A sudden bout of anxiety made him nauseous. Sweat prickled at his neck. All he remembered was that this place was Aunty Central. They'd never been big temple-goers anyway, but after Amma died . . . The idea of going there and meeting all those sympathetic faces . . ..

Well, he was here now and no longer a child. Onwards. He opened the door and stepped in. The door shut behind him and the noise level dropped dramatically. He breathed in and the smell, with its trace of incense, was all too familiar. He went over to the coat racks, removed his shoes and put them in the shoe rack. Then hung up his coat. Picking up the flowers again, he wandered into the long, narrow kitchen. Vases lay upside down, drying on the stainless-steel sinks. A man was putting tupperware containers into the fridge. He gave Gihan a friendly nod. 'The monks have gone to an almsgiving. They'll be back in an hour or so, if you need to talk to them.'

Gihan smiled back. 'Oh, no. I'll just go to the prayer room and be on my way.'

He splashed the flowers with water, then popped them in a vase with a bit of water in it and padded back out before the cold from the kitchen floor seeped in through his socks.

The rest of the temple had thick carpet on the floor. It muffled any sound and helped with the atmosphere of quiet serenity.

The prayer room was empty. A few lamps flickered with LED candles and the incense from joss sticks was heavier here. The golden Buddha statue gleamed against its backdrop of thick red velvet. All at once, he remembered sitting in this room when he was small, tucked in between his parents. He and Sam had drawn smiley faces into the thick carpet pile. He found a place for the flowers, backed away into a corner and sat down to pray.

He could barely remember the gathas. He'd never really learned them in the first place – just, sort of absorbed them through hearing them over and over. But he remembered the sentiment. He cobbled together a prayer of sorts and whispered it into his hands, which he pressed together in front of his face.

What next? Oh yes, meditation. He lowered his hands onto his lap, right hand nestled in the left, like Thatha had taught him. Thatha as he had been, before heartbreak had made him distant. The father who played and laughed and tried to teach his giggly children how to meditate. Gihan closed his eyes and tried to remember. There was one about spreading kindness. Breathe in. First show compassion to yourself. Be happy, be healthy, be content. Breathe out. Next show compassion to your loved ones. He focused on his breathing and pictured himself in the centre of a glow that spread from person to person as he thought of them. Just the way he had thought about it as a child. As his web extended across the world, he suddenly remembered a discussion with Thatha about whether he could extend his compassion to galaxies far, far away and a long time ago.

Concentration broken, he opened his eyes and looked up. Past the flowers, the incense, the lamps, the small platter of offerings, to the Buddha statue at the centre. Everything looked so peaceful. So timeless. He wondered how many eyes had taken in this scene. In happiness, in sadness, in hope, in fear, in boredom from the daily drudgery. He looked down at his hands. Suddenly, he had the strongest memory of Amma, holding out her hand to him to help him to his feet. He couldn't always remember her face when he tried to, but at times like these, his memories of her were vivid. She was gone, but in all the tiny memories, she was still with him.

He closed his eyes. Something untwisted inside him. Tension slid off. All this time he'd been trying to keep away from getting attached to people, because he didn't want to get hurt. But if he didn't ever get to know them, how would he know what he was missing?

Perhaps you should stop fighting and accept that the world doesn't want you to be alone.

The voice in his head sounded like Amma. His eyes flew open. There was no one else there.

Thoughtfully, Gihan pressed his hands together and bent his head. Then he got up off the floor and left the prayer room feeling much lighter than he'd felt in years.

Chapter 25

Every time Alex's phone rang, she pounced on it, hoping it was Gihan. It had been over two weeks now and although work was keeping her busy, it still wasn't enough to stop her thinking about him. She took it into the empty office nearby to get some semblance of privacy.

Her phone was still ringing. It wasn't Gihan. It never was.

This time, it was Farnaz from Swanland, offering her a job.

'Oh, that's . . . that's great,' Alex stuttered, her words failing her.

'You'll have to wait for the confirmation email for exact details,' said Farnaz. 'But I can give you some ballpark figures.'

She named a sum that was substantially higher than what Alex was being paid at the moment. 'Of course, you know about the lab resources. There's a pension and other stuff.'

'Thank you.' She couldn't accept straight away, could she? This was only the informal offer. The real thing needed the email. 'How . . . long do I have to think about it?'

Farnaz gave a small laugh. 'I think maybe a week? The offer of the purchase of the IP is conditional on you coming to work for us.'

Oof. No pressure there then. If she turned this job down, the test would die. Not that she had any intention of turning it down.

She thanked Farnaz again and hung up. Feeling a little shaky, she walked out of the meeting room and into the open plan office. Across the room, Isobel looked up at her. She gave Isobel a quick smile and texted Leila.

Meet me downstairs in the coffee room. Now.

She hurried down the stairs.

Leila was delighted when she heard. 'Oh my god, congratulations!'

'I haven't had the formal offer letter yet,' Alex said. 'Something could still go wrong.'

'Oh come on,' said Leila. 'It's as good as done.'

'Now who's jumping to conclusions?'

Leila gave her an exasperated look. 'Look, I'm sorry I said all that, okay.'

'Didn't you mean it?'

'I meant it,' said Leila. 'But you weren't ready to hear it and it was insensitive of me.'

'You were right though.' Alex looked thoughtfully at her phone.

'Does that mean you're going to call him?'

She wanted to. 'I think about it all the time.' She sniffed. 'I think about *him* all the time.'

'So you should call him.'

Alex shook her head. 'I can't. I . . . need him to call me. Or email me. Or something. It's been days and he hasn't. I think he's ghosted me and if I call and find out that he's blocked my number I . . .' To her horror, her voice trembled. 'I just can't.'

'Oh, Alex.' Leila pulled her in for a hug. 'If I ever meet any of your exes, they will be going home with their teeth in a bag.'

The idea was so ridiculous, it made Alex smile.

'Ah, who needs him anyways,' said Leila. 'You've got a swish new job offer.'

Alex's phone rang. They both stared at the caller ID. Unknown number.

Deflated, Alex answered.

248

'Hi Alex, this is Lauren from JD Forensic. I'm phoning about the job in the forensic science team . . .'

By the end of the call, Alex had two job offers. She had promised herself she'd call Gihan after one. When Leila stopped jiggling up and down and squeaking, she sobered enough to ask her which one she was going to take.

'Oh, I think I know which one,' said Alex. 'But tonight, I'm going to enjoy being a woman with two good job offers.'

'You should,' said Leila.

'And,' said Alex, 'this weekend, I'm going to call Gihan.'

Leila patted her shoulder. 'That's my girl.'

*

On Saturday, Gihan stood in his new living room. The lease had come together at such a surprising speed that he suspected both the landlord and the estate agent had been keen to see the place off the books. He had picked up the keys on Friday after work and they had spent Saturday painting.

Niro's Instagram influencer friends had asked if they could use the mural as a backdrop for some photos. He had expected them to be annoying, but they'd actually been respectful and efficient. Some of their photos made the place look incredible. He quite liked Niro's new friends. They were completely unlike the people he was used to hanging around with. One of them, Ronee, had kept flirting with him, which while flattering, was a little unnerving because they were so young. Gihan had been polite, but kept out of the way by painting the bedroom first, which had kept him busy until they left.

The very idea of flirting with someone else filled him with a nagging sense of guilt. He and Alex weren't together, but it felt like they were. Like it or not, some part of him belonged to her. He wasn't sure what to do about it.

He shook his head and went back to carefully adding masking tape around the window frames. They were painting the living room white, but the lime green layer underneath still showed through. Even after two coats, it was likely to end up ever so slightly green. Niro had suggested that they leave the window frames lime green. Gihan had been sceptical, but she was the artist. He had to trust that she knew what she was doing.

Niro was looking at the mural on the wall, with her hands on her hips. 'That is really spectacular. It seems such a shame to destroy it,' she said.

'But,' said Sam, who was painting one of the other walls, 'it's hideous.'

Niro turned and pointed to Gihan, who had been busy measuring up the window. 'What do you think? You're the one who has to live here.'

He eyed the mural and noted in passing that he needed to add 'lampshades' to the growing list of things to get when he went to Ikea. 'I think you're both right,' he said. 'Is there a way I could keep some of it?'

Niro tapped her pencil against her lip. 'Actually, I have an idea. How do you feel about a large acrylic picture frame? We'll keep some of it and put the frame over it without a back so that it looks like the mural is framed?'

'Sounds like a plan.'

'I'm done taping up.' He pushed up the sleeves of his paint-stained hoodie and reached for one of the paint rollers.

'Tea break first!' Niro disappeared into the kitchen. The first things they'd brought into the house were a kettle and some mugs.

'Oh, fantastic.' Sam put down her roller and wiped her hands on her old jeans.

Niro brought out the teas and a packet of chocolate Hobnobs. Gihan joined the two women sitting on the floor.

'It's a nice place,' Sam said. 'Once you cover up the puke-inducing carpet, it'll look really nice.'

'If we get a decent amount of the painting done today, I'm

going to do an IKEA run tomorrow.' Gihan dunked his biscuit in his tea, watching it carefully so that it didn't get too soggy.

'At least it's only one flight of stairs,' said Sam. 'Which will make life easier when you buy furniture.'

'We're on the fourth floor; getting stuff up there with no lift was a nightmare,' said Niro. 'The lift is fixed now, thank goodness.' She gestured with a crumbling biscuit. 'I have to get all the photos for the exhibition out in a couple of months. Carrying all of that would have been a complete nightmare.' She dunked her biscuit. 'You guys will help me with setting up for that, right?'

'Of course,' said Sam. 'It's your comeback exhibition.'

'Is everything going according to plan for that?' Gihan asked Niro.

'Touch wood.' She tapped her own head. 'The Instagram influencers have been awesome.' She launched into a story about what was going on behind the scenes of her exhibition.

Gihan watched as his cousin lit up, talking about her photography with a level of animation that would have been unimaginable a few months ago. She glowed, healthy and happy. This change had come about since she'd met Vimal. Even if she was headed for heartache, maybe it was worth it for her to have this window of happiness where everything was glorious.

He wondered what Alex was doing right now. Was she thinking of him? Was she still angry? Had Daniel told her about the deal and what was expected? He had no way to check on the progress of the deal – all he could do was make introductions and hope that things went smoothly from there. Would Alex take the job with Swanland? If she did, that would bring her to London. Would she even come? She seemed happily settled where she was, with Maureen and Jake and the whole village community. He couldn't see her finding a place in London again. He took his phone out and idly looked at it. There were no messages from Alex. Scrolling through, he saw a few words of an old text about Maureen. He could check in on Maureen, couldn't he? He had her number.

'Gihan Aiya?' Sam's voice cut through his thoughts.

'Pardon?' He put his phone away. 'Sorry, I was miles away for a second.'

'I said, have you called her?' said Sam.

'No.'

The others exchanged glances.

'You know you're being ridiculous, right?' said Niro.

'Well, she hasn't called me either. And she did ask me not to call her. Specifically.'

'Oh my god, what is wrong with you!'

'I wouldn't bother, Niro,' said Sam. 'I've said all that. He's being a fool.'

'I know what I'm doing,' Gihan said.

The two women gave him identical indulgent looks. Now, he felt like a fool. 'Oh, bugger off,' he said.

Neither of them took any offence. After a few moments of companionable silence, he offered to get takeaway for dinner.

'Can't,' said Niro. 'I'm meeting Vimal for a thing.'

Sam finished her tea and put down her mug. 'And I,' she said, 'have to do a YouTube live for work.'

'How much do you think we'll get done by the time we have to leave?' Sam asked, looking around.

They had done quite a lot already. The bedroom and the small room looked completely different now that they were painted white. They were making good progress on the living room too.

The flat was looking less and less 1970s with each passing hour. Despite Gihan's initial worries that making it less over the top would make the place feel less like home, the feel of the place hadn't changed at all. If anything, it was even better now because his first memories of the place would be of him hanging out with Sam and Niro.

'If you don't mind a hint of green in the living room, we could probably get all the walls done today.' Niro said. 'That would leave the kitchen and bathroom to paint tomorrow.'

Gihan shifted, took a gulp of tea and then lay down on the carpet. 'I think we could leave the kitchen for a bit. I quite like the way it looks.' He thought of the cheerful kitchen in Alex's house. This kitchen felt warm in a similar way.

'Oh good,' said Niro. 'I love those cupboards.'

'I reckon I could do the Ikea run tomorrow. Is Vimal still okay to come and help me?' he asked Niro.

Niro nodded, her mouth full of biscuit.

'It's all coming together so quickly,' Sam observed. 'It's almost like it was meant to be.'

Gihan looked around his new home. It was still an empty box, waiting for him to stamp his personality on it. But it felt like a home. 'Yes,' he said to Sam. 'It really does feel like that.'

*

Alex spent her Saturday working on handover notes for the Swanland deal. Throughout the day, Daniel had sent her about a dozen emails with questions ranging from the vital to the annoyingly detailed. It seemed he was working through Saturday as well. His questions had helped shape the notes she was drafting for him. She had almost finished it when she went round to Maureen's that evening to take Penelope out. Once she'd done Penelope's walk and had a chat with Maureen, she would send her notes to Daniel. An email sent in the middle of the night would make her look more diligent too, perhaps.

Maureen was in a mood. Her son had arranged for a carer to look in on her once a day.

'I'm not that ill,' she said, indignantly, as she wheeled herself back into the living room. 'I can manage perfectly well on my own.'

Alex, who had been doing a lot of small tasks every time she came round, wondered what she could say that wouldn't lead to an accusation of 'taking his side'.

'I mean, I've got you and Jake to help me. Someone from the village pops in around lunchtime to see if I need anything. I've

253

got more social interaction now than I ever had. I don't know why he's bothering.'

'Perhaps he feels that he's making it so that you have more reliable support.' Alex topped up Penelope's water bowl. 'We're always here for you, but all it takes is one small thing to change and it will become more difficult.' Like if she took a job in London and moved away, for example. She had accepted the job, but she couldn't tell anyone about it until the deal was signed. It was taking ages.

She turned around to find Maureen watching her with a frown. 'Then he should have said that to me, shouldn't he?' Maureen said. 'Not arrange things and tell me it's done. I'm not senile.'

Alex wasn't entirely sure he hadn't tried to tell her, but she didn't say anything. 'I'll take Penelope out for her walk and then we'll have a cup of tea and talk about it, okay?'

By the time she got back, Maureen seemed to be calmer.

'It is a lot that you and Jake do for me,' she said to Alex.

'We don't mind.' Alex put the kettle on. She had made a mark on the side of the kettle to remind her to top up the kettle with enough water for Maureen to have two mugs of tea, but not so much water that the kettle would become too heavy for her to lift and pour. These things you didn't even think about normally, that became extra difficult when you were weak. Since the accident, Maureen seemed more frail and her moods were much more changeable. Alex worried that this was a sign of worse to come. Her son's intervention was a pragmatic one.

Alex wondered how best to support this without annoying Maureen.

'Still though, you're right,' said Maureen sadly. 'It does make sense to pay someone to do it, rather than rely on you two.'

Alex leaned towards her friend and patted her hand. 'Maureen, we like visiting you. But Jake's going to expand his business, he's bound to get busier.'

'And you might get a job that means you have to set off for

work earlier and get home later,' said Maureen. 'I wasn't thinking.' She sighed and rubbed her hands together slowly. 'Not like me not to think of those things, but there you go. I guess that just proves the point. It's no fun, this getting old nonsense.'

Having made Maureen's tea, Alex checked the time. She still needed to go through the report and send it in before meeting Leila in the pub.

Maureen noticed. 'Have you got things to do tonight?'

She wasn't supposed to talk about the deal yet, because they hadn't agreed on the terms, so she said, 'I have this report that I have to send in before eight o'clock tomorrow morning.'

'Ha. You don't owe them anything.'

'I should get it in on time, though,' said Alex, mildly. 'Professional pride.'

'That's fair,' said Maureen. 'It's important to take pride in your standards.' She looked around for Penelope before moving the wheelchair. 'Listen, you go home. I'm fine for the night.' She nodded towards the bed in the corner of what used to be the dining room. 'Penelope and I can watch *Death in Paradise* together.'

Alex checked her watch again. 'If you're sure . . .'

'Before you go, can you get me some fresh bedding down from the airing cupboard, please? If that woman is going to come to help every day, I may as well get her to do something useful.'

'Sure.' She put down her tea and went to the stairs.

'Have you contacted your young man yet?' said Maureen, from the living room.

Alex paused on the second step. 'No. And he hasn't contacted me either.'

'Maybe when you asked him not to, he took you seriously . . .'

Alex fled up the stairs before Maureen started quizzing her some more. Had he taken her seriously? Maybe he wasn't calling because he genuinely thought she didn't want him to. In which case, she should call him. Especially if she was going to take a job in London.

Maureen kept a very organised airing cupboard. Neatly ironed bedding was stored in sets. She should learn Maureen's system. It was certainly better than her chaotic bedding cupboard. She threw the bedding into the small collapsing basket that Maureen kept for the purpose and started down the stairs. She couldn't see where she was placing her feet, but she knew where each step was.

'You're both being very stubborn. I think you should be the bigger person and call him,' said Maureen, who had wheeled herself to the doorway of the living room. 'Penelope, come here.'

Alex carried on down the stairs, trying to work out what to say. She wasn't entirely sure what happened next. Her foot landed on something soft. Penelope yelped. Alex stumbled and pitched forward. She flailed and tried to grab the bannister, but all she succeeded in doing was to twist herself round, so that she fell down the last few stairs, bumping her back on the steps on the way down, her hand trapped in the handle of the basket.

'Oh my god, Alex! Are you okay?'

It took a moment for everything to come back into focus. Alex moved her head. She was at the bottom of the stairs, her legs were above her, still on the stairs. Her head seemed okay. She tried to sit up. Ow. Her back hurt. Gingerly, she tested if she could move. She could, but it hurt. When she tried to push herself up, pain shot up her arm. 'Ow.'

'Are you hurt?' said Maureen, anxiously moving closer.

'Not sure,' she replied. 'My head seems okay.' She checked the back of her head for blood or any pain. That seemed okay. 'I think I've hurt my wrist and . . .' She cautiously rolled her shoulders to test her back. Ow ow ow. 'And possibly my back.'

'Oh, that's bad, isn't it? I'm going to call Jake.'

Before Alex could stop her, Maureen had wheeled round and propelled herself back to the living room. Alex leaned this way and that to see what hurt. 'I can move,' she called out to Maureen. 'But it hurts.'

When Jake burst in, still dressed for his run, Alex was sitting at the bottom of the stairs, afraid to move in case it hurt.

'We should get your back checked out,' Jake said. 'Can you stand?'

It took a few goes, with him helping and her crying out. Once she was upright, she let him sling his arm around her and half carry her to the car. 'Let's get you to A&E,' Jake said.

Alex didn't bother to protest. The pain in her back worried her more than the pain in her wrist, despite her wrist hurting more. Once upon a time, she had lain awake at night worried, despite doctors' assurances to the contrary, that she might never walk again. The fear, long subsided, welled up and rolled around inside her. It was taking a huge effort not to cry.

Chapter 26

Once the others had left to do their fun things, Gihan went back to Sam's and took a cup of tea up to his room. It was funny how his social life had started as a whirlwind of catching up with people he hadn't seen in a few years and then gradually dried up. He should get out there and get himself back into the going out circuit. He looked at the backs of his hands, still flecked with paint despite his best efforts to scrub it all off. Not tonight though. Tonight, he'd chill.

Although he'd been back for over two months now, he hadn't spent that much time in this room. He still thought of it as Niro's room. He sat on the bed and stared at the few belongings he'd brought with him. The things he had which weren't clothes or work essentials amounted to a few photos, a few books and a smart speaker. He didn't have much stuff.

Even though he'd put everything out, the room still felt sparse. It was as though he didn't really live there. His flat in the Middle East had been similar – minimalist. He had assumed that it just meant he was living a clutter-free life, but really, it was because he'd spent a lot of time over at Helen's and only used the flat to sleep in every so often. He tended to drift through life, falling into and out of relationships with relative ease. It rarely hurt to break up, because he never fully invested.

A tightness in his throat reminded him that he was hurting right now. He had split up with girlfriends before. Why was this time different? He hadn't even been going out with Alex properly. He shook his head. He couldn't think about that. He was supposed to be moving on.

He rearranged his books on the shelf. He tended to listen to audiobooks these days, so he had only a few textbooks and a handful of paperbacks. What sort of books did Alex have? She'd said she liked crime novels. Maybe she had a lot of those . . . He should ask—

No. No, he was doing it again. He sank down on the bed and pulled out his phone. Still nothing from Alex. There were so many things he wanted to talk to her about. Everything he saw made him think of her. He wondered what she would think of the flat. It certainly wasn't the most practical option he'd seen. He had gone with his gut reaction to it.

He couldn't call her, when she'd said not to. But he could check in on Maureen. He had Maureen's number from when she called him to thank him. They had exchanged a few texts. Calling her to see how she was would be a normal thing to do . . . He could ask about Alex in passing, but he would simply be checking in on Maureen.

Yes. That was a good idea. It wasn't that late. She would be up. Before he could change his mind, he hit call.

'Hi Maureen. This is Gihan. I'm . . . er . . . Alex's friend.'

'Oh, I remember,' said Maureen. 'What can I do for you?'

'I was just checking in to see how you were getting on.'

'Not too bad, since you ask.' She spent a minute explaining about her leg and how bloody inconvenient it was not being able to walk properly.

Despite his impatience to ask about Alex, Gihan listened and asked questions. 'How's Penelope?'

'She's fine. She's loving having all these people coming over all the time. Alex and Jake and Leila popping round at all sorts of times. She's in her element, aren't you, little pup?' This last bit must have been addressed to Penelope.

'How's Alex doing?'

'Actually, I'm waiting to hear from her. Jake took her to the hospital earlier and I haven't heard anything since. I'm hoping it's nothing serious.'

Alarm buzzed through him. 'What's happened? Why is Alex in hospital?'

'Oh she . . .' Maureen paused. 'Actually,' she said. 'I'm not sure what was wrong. Something to do with her back.'

Her back! His throat went dry. 'Which . . . Which hospital?'

'The same one I was at. The General.'

'Okay. Um . . . I hope your leg recovers really fast, Maureen. I'm sure it will, you being the fit and active person you are.'

'Oh, you're sweet,' said Maureen. 'I'd better let you get on. Goodbye.' There was a click and she abruptly hung up.

Gihan stared at the phone, mind racing. Alex was in hospital because of a problem with her back. He thought of the smooth scar on her back, extending down her spine, from where they'd removed her cancer when she was a teenager. Alex had been adamant that her cancer was gone, but she'd asked Jake to take her to hospital. He knew Alex well enough to know that she wouldn't waste NHS time on something trivial. What if her cancer had come back? No. It was far more likely she'd had a fall or something. But then, wouldn't Maureen have said? Maureen hadn't said A&E, she had said hospital.

He knew how quickly cancer could take you from 'a bit worried' to death. For his mother it had been a handful of weeks. Old, familiar panic rose, pushing bile to his throat. He couldn't bear it if that happened to Alex. The idea was excruciating.

His entire world view shifted. Not being with Alex didn't make his feelings any blunter. He cared about Alex in a way that he'd never cared about a woman before. He hadn't even gone out with her, but he'd got to know her. That frisson that he'd felt the first time he'd met her had never left him. He liked Alex. He might even love her. He was definitely not ready to lose her without at least making an effort to patch things up.

He tried her phone. It was turned off. He could leave a message . . . His mind went blank.

He hung up. Gripped with a sense of urgency like never before, he paced the tiny room a few times, until he banged his head on the eaves. His chest felt tight. What now? What now? The idea that she might be in hospital, in pain, chewed at him. When he finally sat down, he spotted the keys to the rental van on the desk, where he'd put them so that he could find them in the morning. He had a vehicle . . . He could drive over there and see her. Without thinking about it any further, he grabbed the keys and his coat and left the flat.

*

Alex felt awful. Her wrist had been bound up – a bad sprain, apparently. The doctor in A&E had given her a wheelchair and sent her off to have her back X-rayed. The drugs they'd given her were kicking in, so the pain in her back wasn't as bad as it had been.

Jake sat on a plastic chair next to her, furiously typing away on his phone.

Alex shifted her weight and groaned when her back complained.

Jake looked up. 'Everything okay?'

'Yeah. Nothing new. Just the same old pain.'

He shook his head. 'A&E twice in two months. You'll be able to collect frequent visitor stamps soon.'

'The loyalty program nobody wants.'

'If you're making jokes, you must be feeling better.' He smiled, the tense pinching around his eyes loosening a little.

'The painkillers are doing their work.' She gestured to her bound up hand. 'How am I going to do my work? This is such bad timing.'

261

'Why is it bad timing?' Jake looked puzzled. 'You're finishing soon anyway, right? According to Leila, you guys are winding up the project. Surely, Leila and Ray can do most of the work for that.'

Ah. She couldn't talk about the sale of her project because she'd been told to keep it confidential. 'There might be some . . . options at work.'

Apart from Leila, she hadn't told anyone about her job offers. She had intended to tell Maureen, but with the fall and all the excitement afterwards, she hadn't got around to it.

'Confidentially,' she said carefully. 'I might have a job offer . . .'

Jake beamed. 'Mate, that's amazing! Congratulations!'

'I'm waiting for the official confirmation, but thank you.'

Jake's phone buzzed. He was immediately distracted by it. 'That's great news.' He was only half listening now.

Alex looked away. Her own phone had run out of battery some time ago. Not that it mattered. The one person she wanted to hear from wasn't calling her.

A painful spasm from her back made her tense up. She held her breath for a moment and fought the urge to whimper. After a few seconds, the pain subsided, and she allowed herself to cautiously relax.

This visit to the hospital was so much worse than last time. She wasn't as worried this time, but against that, there was the pain. Jake was awesome, but nowhere near as comforting as Gihan had been. She realised now how much of a distraction he had provided. He had told her such an assortment of things – about his sister falling in love with a YouTuber, about various escapades when he was at university, about his mother's illness. Of all those, she sensed that one that meant the most was about his mother's illness. There had been a tightness in his voice when he talked about it, as though he was forcing the words past a lump in his throat. He must have hated being back in the hospital, waiting for news.

While Jake was amazing, he wasn't being particularly comforting

262

right now. But he was clearly busy and was giving up his evening to be there, so she couldn't ask for more.

'What was it that made you fall down the stairs?' Jake's voice made her jump.

She thought back to what had happened. 'Penelope, I think. She was on the stairs, I was carrying some sheets down and I didn't see her.'

Jake looked thoughtful. 'You know how Maureen can't remember how she fell when she hurt her leg? Do you think she tripped over Penelope?'

Alex mulled this over. 'It's possible,' she said. 'In which case, it's a worry. She'll be fine while she's in the wheelchair, but once she's out of it, it might happen again.' She had a horrifying thought. 'What if it happens on the stairs?'

Jake sighed. 'I'll have a word with Maureen about getting a stair gate so that Penelope can't go upstairs. I might ask around in the village if anyone's got one going spare. There's bound to be someone whose kids have grown out of needing one.' He made another note on his phone.

It buzzed as a message came in. 'Ah good,' he said. 'Mal's going to take Penelope for a walk and check in on Maureen tomorrow evening – so you don't have to worry about that.'

'That's good. Thanks for sorting that out.'

'I worry about Maureen, you know,' said Jake. 'I love her to bits, but . . .'

Alex explained her conversation about Maureen's carer, arranged by her son. 'That's why I was carrying bedding down-stairs,' she said. 'So that she could have something for the carer to do.'

'That's good,' said Jake. 'I'll have a chat with her too, make her see that it's a good idea.' He looked up. 'I feel bad, but . . . I'm so glad. I'm not cut out to be a carer.'

'Neither am I. I can barely cope with looking after myself.' She lifted her bandaged wrist. 'I really don't need this right now.

I've got so much to do at work.' A thought occurred to her. She wasn't going to be able to drive with her hand like that. 'Oh shit. How am I even going to get to work?'

'Well,' said Jake, 'if you don't mind going in super early, I can drop you off in the morning. Maybe someone could give you a lift back? Leila would, I bet. She's been popping in to see Maureen pretty often these days anyway.'

Yes. That would work. 'I don't know what I'd do without you guys,' she said, and meant it. How was she going to cope when she had to move away? She'd have to leave all of her support network behind.

'Ha. That's what friends are for,' said Jake.

That's what Gihan had said to her that night. Only, when he'd said it, she had felt disappointed. He had been very kind and patient. She hadn't offered him the same courtesy on Saturday morning. She closed her eyes and once more wished he was there. When she got out of here, assuming she was allowed out after her X-ray, she was going to call him. Not tonight, because it would probably be late by the time she got to leave. Tomorrow. She would definitely call him tomorrow. That would at least give her a bit more time to work out what exactly she was going to say.

*

Driving up to see Alex had given Gihan time to think. The main thing he'd realised was that he was currently panicking about not seeing Alex again. Before, he'd had panic attacks at the idea of being with someone forever. This time it was about *not* being with Alex. That had to mean something.

He wasn't actually having a panic attack either. His heart had picked up speed and he could feel how tense he was, but this was just normal levels of 'very stressed'. He was in control, which was something of a relief. Maybe he was stronger than he thought. Hopefully, strong enough to be a supportive friend for Alex while she was ill – if that was what she wanted.

264

The turn-off to the village was coming up. Gihan was heading for the hospital, but it occurred to him that he had no idea where in the hospital Alex would be. The urgency that had fueled his trip had fizzled out a bit. He could stop, go and see Maureen, and get some more information. It wasn't that much of a detour and an hour or so wouldn't hurt him, would it? Especially if it saved him having to wander round the hospital searching for Alex. If he had to be in the hospital, he needed to at least be able to focus on his purpose.

He indicated and pulled into the correct lane.

Chapter 27

Alex hobbled into the house, her back still sore and prone to spasming.

Jake helped her in. 'Do you want to sit there and rest for a bit?' he said, gesturing to his sofa, with its three grey cushions. 'Or do you want me to help you to bed?'

The idea of stairs was too much. 'Sofa please. I will need to get upstairs at some point, but . . . not yet. Please.' She'd been given a support cushion at the hospital. Jake threw that on the sofa and helped her sit.

'Thank you so much, Jake. I don't know what I'd do without you.' Alex carefully lowered herself onto the sofa, wincing as she had to drop the last few inches. She had to move cushions around to get more support for her back. The leather squeaked underneath her.

'I should make you move in with Maureen,' Jake said. 'That way you can hobble around each other and I can come and look in on you both at the same time.' He hung her coat up for her. 'I must have done something terrible in a past life to have to continually look after old ladies.'

'Hey. Less of the old,' Alex said.

Jake grinned. He put his hands on his hips. 'What else do you need?'

About ten nights' sleep. 'My phone has died,' she said. 'Can you get my charger? It's next to my bed.'

Jake gave a mock salute and disappeared up the stairs.

Alex sank back into the sofa and winced from the back pain. Theoretically, her wrist was the worse injury, but the fall had jarred her back. Thankfully, there was only bruising. 'Only bruising' was still painful, though. She sighed and shifted the cushions around.

Jake returned, plugged her charger into a socket and held out his hand for her phone. She passed it to him. When Jake plugged it in, it beeped.

'What's that?' she asked. The phone was too far away for her to check it.

Jake rolled his eyes and hunkered down to look at the screen. 'Well, without unlocking the screen, all I can tell you is that it's a missed call from a Gihan.' He looked up and smiled at her. 'Well, bugger me.'

Alex stared at him. Gihan had called her? Oh wow. Her heart lifted. 'Did he leave a message?'

Jake checked the screen again. 'Doesn't look like it,' he said. 'But if he's called you, you can now call him back and demand to know what he wanted.' He put his head back and groaned. 'Aw. I owe Mal a tenner now.'

'Why?' Alex narrowed her eyes. 'Wait, did you guys have a bet on which one of us would call first?' She was only mildly annoyed until a realisation struck her. 'Did you bet I'd cave first? I thought you were my friend!'

Jake shrugged. 'Of course. My darling, it's obvious to anyone who has seen you two together, that there's a real spark there. And you've been so bloody miserable, even despite all the drama at work, that it's obvious you're in love with the guy.' He shook his head. 'Besides, I expected it would take him longer to get over you casting him as a villain like that—'

'Hey!' said Alex.

Jake turned to her. 'Well, you did a bit though, right? From

267

what you said, he was upfront with you the whole time about what might happen in the report.'

'But then, he tried to *save* me. Like I couldn't find a new job by myself.'

He frowned and looked puzzled. 'He tried to save your job?'

Oh. Right. She wasn't supposed to tell Jake about the proposed deal. She squeezed her eyes shut.

'I seem to be missing something here,' said Jake.

She could tell him. It would help having someone besides Leila to talk to who knew what was going on. She could trust Jake. 'Okay,' she said. 'You have to swear not to tell anyone. It's really secret.'

Jake came over and took the seat opposite her. 'Oh. Intriguing.' He leaned forward, his elbows resting on his spread knees.

'Swear you won't tell anyone.'

'Of course.' He held up his hand. 'Scout's honour.'

She outlined the proposal to sell her work and her offer from Swanland Corp.

Jake gave a low whistle. 'That's a clever solution. He gets to do his job properly and not completely screw you . . . in a manner of speaking.'

Alex didn't rise to his joke. 'He didn't have to step in and be the saviour.'

'Maybe it wasn't that,' said Jake. 'Maybe he felt bad. I mean, I would. Or maybe he was trying to save your work? You can find another job, but your technology . . . It's clearly important to you and it would be really amazing if your test becomes a real product. Think of the lives you could have saved. Maybe that was what he was thinking about?

The lives you could have saved.'

She stared at him. Gihan's mum had died of cancer. It had been detected too late. Of *course* he would want to save her work on early cancer detection. Why on earth did she not remember this before? She had been so caught up in her own drama that she hadn't considered his point of view at all. 'Shit.'

Wasn't this what Leila was trying to tell her? She had never understood why her relationships always went so badly wrong at the end. She had assumed that she'd always picked shit men, but . . . was it really her? 'Jake,' Alex said. 'Do you think I'm self-centred?'

He gave her a long, sad look. The fact that he didn't respond immediately wasn't a good sign. 'Oh, honey.' He leaned forward and patted her hand. 'You're not self-centred. You're just . . . impulsive. When you like someone, you tend to get ahead of yourself and make assumptions on the other person's behalf. And then, when they disappoint you – which they invariably will, because you've made up this whole scenario that doesn't exist – you get hurt. It means that . . . when things are not going well, it's hard for people to talk to you. Sometimes, for some people, it's easier to run away than make you understand.'

'So my exes who dumped me . . .?'

'Perhaps they saw things weren't working out, but you didn't.'

Alex let that sink in. 'I thought Gihan would find a way to keep my job alive. I knew there was a chance he wouldn't, but I sort of hoped that he would,' she said, thoughtfully. 'And when Daniel said it was good news I jumped to the conclusion that it was the good news I'd imagined it would be.'

'And when it wasn't, you took it out on him.'

She groaned. 'I accused him of pretending so that he could sleep with me.'

'Do you really believe that?'

No. Of course not. She had seen his face when he realised. She shook her head. 'I lashed out.'

Jake winced. 'Poor guy.'

'I should call him back,' she said.

Jake tipped his chin towards where her phone was charging. 'Give it a few minutes to charge and then, yes. You should.'

He turned back towards her. 'Do you think this new company will be able to get your test to market?'

She nodded slowly. Her research into the company told her that her test could potentially work brilliantly in the Swanland Corp device. She was struggling to get her test to work in the Ryder FT device, despite it working fine in the lab. The Ryder FT device had issues brought about by how they freeze-dried the chemicals so that they could transport and store them. Swanland Corps technology would not have that problem. Their tests were carried out in labs. They didn't need to be designed to sit on pharmacy shelves, without refrigeration. 'I'm quietly hopeful.'

'Nice,' he said. 'Things are looking up.'

She sincerely hoped so. She glanced at her phone. *Hurry up and charge.*

*

When Gihan pulled up outside Maureen's house, the first thing he noticed was that the lights were on in Alex's house. Jake must be back. He would know everything Gihan needed to know.

Gihan parked up in the pub car park, silently apologised to the pub for using it in the middle of the night, and walked back to the house. Jake unnerved him. The guy was clearly fond of Alex and would probably be angry on her behalf. Gihan stopped at the gate. What could he say to Jake? Well, there was a version of the speech he'd been practising in his head the whole time. 'I like her. I want to get to know her better. Even if she's terminally ill. The thought of never seeing her again is just too much to bear. So, even if it means breaking my heart later, I want to be with her now. If she'll have me'.

If that didn't work and he got punched, well, then he got punched. It was worth it to find Alex. He puffed out a breath like an athlete about to go into competition, strode up the path and rang the doorbell.

Jake opened the door. He was wearing running shorts and a hoodie and holding a mug of tea. 'Oh,' he said. 'It's you.'

So far, so good. 'Hi. I heard that Alex was in hospital. I was hoping you'd tell me which ward so that I can go—'

'No need,' said Jake. 'She's here.' He looked over his shoulder and shouted, 'It's for you, Alex.' He pulled the door open. 'Come in, Gihan.'

She was home? That was good. Something loosened in Gihan's shoulders. He hadn't realised he'd been *that* tense. He shut the door behind him and followed Jake into the living room.

*

If Alex had any doubt about how she felt, the way her heart swooped when Gihan stepped into the room would have made it clear. She tried to sit up straighter, but winced and slumped back.

He was dressed far more casually than she'd ever seen before – scruffy, faded joggers, a long-sleeved T-shirt and a hoodie. His hair was messed up and his eyes had a certain wide-eyed panic about them. His gaze swept over her, studying her.

'Are you okay?' They both said in unison.

'I am going to my room.' Jake said, loudly. 'Call me if you need me. You kids be good.'

Alex couldn't look away from Gihan. She vaguely registered Jake's footsteps going upstairs and his door clicking shut. The sound seemed to release both her and Gihan from their stasis.

Gihan was still studying her, as though searching for something. 'You went to hospital . . . because you hurt your hand?' he said, slowly. 'Not because of your back?'

That was fairly obvious, you'd think, given that her hand was bandaged up. What an odd thing to say. 'Both, actually,' she said, cautiously. 'I hurt my back when I fell. They had to check everything was okay with my back, but it turns out that's only bruised. The main damage is the sprained wrist.'

'You fell,' he said, faintly. 'That's a relief.'

'Gihan. What's going on? Why are you here?'

He drew a breath. 'When Maureen said that you were in hospital because of your back, she didn't say why. And I thought . . .' His shoulders dropped, as though strings pulling them up to his ears

271

had been cut. He breathed out and his hand drifted up to his heart. 'But you'd just fallen.'

He sat down on the chair opposite her, abruptly, as though his legs had given out.

She blinked. What had he thought had happened? She saw the relief on his face and suddenly she knew. Maureen, for some reason, had made it sound like she was gravely ill. Cancer was what killed his mother. He had jumped to the worst-case conclusion.

'Just a fall,' she repeated, to make sure it was clear. 'What did you think it was?'

He wouldn't meet her eye. 'Oh. I don't know. Something awful, I guess. She didn't say A&E – that would have said 'accident' to me. But she said . . .' He waved a hand, as though trying to be dismissive. His hand shook slightly and he quickly clasped both hands on his lap. 'Silly really, thinking about it.' He looked down at his feet and gave a little laugh. It sounded completely unlike his usual one. 'Bit embarrassing, now I think about it.'

'You came all the way over here . . . to go to the hospital, which you hate,' she said, quietly. 'Gihan, did you think I was dying?'

He tried to rally. She could see it in the way he blinked and tried to swallow down his feelings. 'I—' He shook his head. His hands dug into each other.

All the anger she'd felt towards him was gone. Evaporated in the face of the look of fear he'd worn when he came in. She couldn't blame him for anything that had happened. All she wanted to do right now was to put her arms around him and comfort him. But she was stuck on this sofa and he may as well have been miles away.

'Gihan,' she said. 'I don't have cancer anymore. I'm in remission. You don't have to worry about that. My chances of that are pretty much the same as yours now. Okay?'

He nodded, still not looking at her. 'Listen, I'm sorry about what happened. I'm sorry about your job and I really didn't—'

'I know,' she said. 'I know. I'm sorry too. I should have given you a chance to explain. Can you forgive me?'

Finally he looked up. 'Of course I forgive you. There's nothing to forgive. I wouldn't have come if I was still angry.'

The anguish in his eyes unraveled her. She held her hand out to him. He unclasped his own hands, then leaned forward to take hers.

'I can't move very much,' she said and gave his hand a gentle tug.

He moved across and sat next to her. For a few seconds, he just looked at her, his breathing uneven. It was as though he was trying to memorise her. His eyes glistened. He was slowly coming apart and it was all because of her.

She put a hand to his cheek. 'See. I'm okay.'

He nodded.

'Thank you, for coming all this way to check on me.'

Very gently, he put his arms around her and drew himself to her so that her head rested on his chest. 'The thought of not seeing you again . . . and you still being angry with me was . . . unbearable.' The last word was a whisper, said into her hair. He sniffed. 'I'm sorry.' He loosened his hold on her so that he could wipe his eyes.

She tightened her arm around him and felt the shivers running through him. 'You're having an adrenaline come-down. You were very stressed and now you're not. Sometimes anxiety takes people like that.'

He nodded against her hair. 'That must be it. I'm sorry anyway. I should be comforting you, not the other way around.'

'It's okay.' She nestled her head into his shoulder. It felt so right; like this was the place she was meant to be. 'I'm glad you came.'

They held each other in silence for a few minutes. Gihan's breathing became steady again. Alex's life suddenly felt smoother. She had options. They weren't difficult choices. She loved her work. She'd invented the early detection test. It wasn't the right technical fit for Ryder FT, but it was perfect for Swanland Corp. She would have to move to London, which wasn't such a terrible thing. She could always come and visit Maureen once a month. And Gihan . . . She didn't dare hope that things would work out long-term with him. They had never worked out for her before. But he had come back to find her and that had never happened to her before either. He was holding her so carefully right now, so that her nest of cushions was barely disturbed. It was a level of care she'd never had from a guy. She closed her eyes and sighed. Maybe this time, she should relax and see where this went.

'I think I might be in love with you,' Gihan said, so quietly, she could have persuaded herself she'd imagined it. She tried to move too quickly and her back twinged. She gave a tiny whimper.

'Shit. Are you okay? Did I hurt you?'

That made her giggle. 'No. You didn't hurt me. You just said you loved me? You did, right?'

He gave her his brilliant smile. 'I said that out loud, huh? But yes. I think so. These last few days have been . . . awful. I couldn't stop thinking about you. It's like . . . you were meant to be there in my life and without you, a bit of me was missing.' He grimaced. 'That sounds ridiculous. Sorry.'

'No. It's sweet.' She shifted against his shoulder. How did she feel about him? She fancied him. She missed him. She might even love him. But she had thought she was in love before, and had been wrong. What if she was wrong this time too? 'I'm told that I get ahead of myself when it comes to relationships,' she said, slowly. 'But I'd like to see where this goes.'

He didn't say anything for the longest time. Should she say something? Was she supposed to say 'I love you too'? Was that the right thing to do if she wasn't sure?

'I'm not great with relationships either, so that's good enough for me,' he said. 'We'll figure it out together. One day at a time.'

She closed her eyes. Yes. This felt right. She had no idea how far this would go, but this time, she was ready to enjoy the journey.

'What happened with Swanland?' he said, suddenly. 'Not the details, obviously. But was it a good suggestion?'

She should move back to look at him, but she was too comfortable. His shoulder was warm and comforting. She let her head rest against it. 'It was a good call. They came to talk to us. It went pretty well.'

'Excellent. I thought it would do.'

He didn't ask her for any details about the deal, which was a relief. It was nice that he understood. 'How did you know that they would be interested? I mean, I go to a lot of the conferences and read the journals. I didn't know they were interested in that sort of thing.'

'They have been for a few years, but mostly doing in-house stuff. I did a bit of work for them in my old job. Obviously, I couldn't talk about it with your company, but I could put them in touch with each other. So that's what I did. And how about you?' he asked, carefully. 'How's the job-hunt going?'

'I . . . have two job offers. One not far from here. The other in London. With Swanland.'

'Well done. I'm not surprised. You're brilliant.' The gentlest squeeze across her shoulders. A kiss in her hair. 'Do you know which one you're going to choose?'

'London, probably,' she said.

A small chuckle rumbled through his chest. 'I approve of that choice.'

From where she had her head, she could feel his voice against his throat as well as hear it. His thumb was stroking her shoulder. He smelled nice. Clean. Alex relaxed a fraction more, leaning more of her weight against him. Now that all the excitement was over, she felt heavy and weak.

'I'm sorry I shouted at you,' she murmured.

'I'm glad it worked out well in the end,' he said and she could hear the smile in his voice.

She relaxed against him, her eyes drifting shut. 'I thought you didn't have a car? How did you get here?'

'Oh, I have a hired van. I found a flat to rent and we were getting it ready. I was supposed to go to Ikea in it tomorrow. When Maureen said you were in hospital, I figured I may as well make use of it.'

Maureen. She would have to speak to her about telling little white lies. Although, if Maureen hadn't interfered, Gihan wouldn't be here now. She tried to reply, but her eyes drooped shut.

'You're tired,' he said. 'You should get some sleep. Can I help you get upstairs?'

The idea of moving was too much. 'No. I'm comfortable here.'

'In that case . . .' He removed one arm from around her and moved one of the few remaining cushions to behind his head. Once it was in position, he put his arm back. 'Let's just stay here.'

And that was fine by her. She nuzzled her head against his warm, solid shoulder and drifted off to sleep.

Chapter 28

The next morning, Gihan woke up early and slid out of Alex's bed, quietly, so that he didn't wake her up. Last night, when Alex's pain had subsided enough for her to move again, Gihan had very carefully helped her up the stairs to her room. She had crawled into bed and pointed out that there was plenty of room for him too, so long as he didn't bother her. It wasn't exactly how he wanted to spend time in Alex's bed, but he was so happy to be with her that he didn't care.

He got dressed and went across to her side of the bed. 'Alex,' he said.

She opened her eyes blearily. 'Hmm?'

'I have to go. I'll call you later.'

She blinked sleepily at him. 'Oh. Okay.'

'How are you feeling today?'

She tried to sit up and cried out. 'Nope. Bad. Turn the light on, will you.'

He switched on the bedside light, anxiety stabbing at him. She picked up the glass of water and frowned. 'I think I left the pain-killers on the sofa. Can you go and get them please? I need drugs.'

When he got into the living room, he found Jake already there, sitting on the sofa with a mug of coffee, scrolling through his phone. If Jake was surprised to see Gihan, he gave no indication. 'Morning.'

'Um . . . I'm looking for Alex's drugs?'

Jake pointed to the coffee table. 'There. How is she this morning?'

'In pain again, I think.' He picked up the paper bag with the medication in it. 'Hopefully, these will help. I'll go grab her another glass of water as well.'

He took the water and the medication upstairs, where Alex had pulled herself up into a sitting position. He watched her take the medication.

'What are you doing today?' Alex leaned back and winced.

'Ikea. Then putting together flat-pack furniture.'

'All the fun,' she said, smiling.

'I'd much rather spend it with you,' he said. 'But you probably need to spend the day recovering.'

She nodded. 'And then tomorrow, I have to accept a new job in London.'

Happiness flowered in his chest. 'I'm so proud of you.'

She squeezed his hand. They sat there, her in bed, him kneeling on the floor, for a moment, just content to be together.

Gihan's phone buzzed. 'I should go,' he said. 'My parents messaged me last night saying, "If you're going to Ikea can you pick up these things for us?" So now I'm shopping for twice as much.'

Alex laughed. 'Is that annoying?'

'Oh, very,' he said. 'But my stepmother said she'd give me food, so . . . it's a fair trade-off.' He leaned forward and kissed her forehead. 'I'll call you tonight. Get better quickly.'

'I will,' she said. 'I've been here before. The pain will go down in a few days and then Jake will force me to do my physio exercises.'

He gathered his things and left. She was asleep again by the time he closed the door to her room.

*

When Gihan got to Thatha's house with a van full of Ikea things, the aunties were all visiting. He and Sam were greeted like returning heroes.

Aunty-Amma sent Thatha out to help Gihan bring the boxes in. Gihan watched his father sit carefully on the stairs to put his shoes on.

He hadn't spoken to Thatha since that disaster of a dinner. Looking at him now, Gihan was surprised to find that he was no longer looking through a filter of anger. He had always assumed that Thatha was aloof and distant on purpose, but now he saw a man who was elderly and fragile. His period of mourning had diminished him and, more than that, diminished his relationship with his children. Thatha had apologised to him. The astonishment that he'd felt when it happened was a reflection of how hard it must have been for Thatha to say it. Gihan was suddenly ashamed of his own reaction. He had lashed out, not seeing it for the gesture that it was.

He should apologise too. But how?

'How much do you have left to do at the flat?' Thatha asked as they walked out to the van, with Sam tagging along behind them. A few weeks ago, Gihan would have searched for the veiled criticism in the question. Today, he chose to take it as the question it appeared to be.

'The decorating is pretty much done,' said Gihan. 'I need to change the carpet in the living room at some point, but for now, I've got a couple of big rugs.'

'That's pretty impressive that you've finished painting,' Thatha said.

'He didn't do it by himself,' said Sam.

'No,' said Gihan. 'Sam and Niro and the gang all helped. That's why we got it done so quickly.'

'That's good that you were all around to help,' Thatha said.

They put the box down. Sam disappeared into the kitchen with their stepmother. His stepmother had bought two bookcases, so

279

there was one more big box to bring in. He and Thatha went back to the van for it.

'I'm glad you found a place to rent. Does that mean that you're staying for a while?' Thatha said.

Gihan thought of Alex and hid his smile. 'Yes.' He leaned into the van to pull out the next package. 'I think I will be.'

'That's good. It's nice to have you around.'

He braced himself and said, 'Thatha. I . . . just wanted to say I'm sorry about how I acted that night we came for dinner. I was rude and I didn't listen.'

Thatha looked down at his feet for a few seconds before looking up. 'That's okay.'

They stared at each other for a moment. Gihan couldn't think what to say next, so he took refuge in his standby – random chatter. 'I went to the temple a few days ago.'

'You did?'

'Yeah. I hadn't been since Amma's remembrance . . .'

Thatha nodded. 'I see. It was okay?'

'It was okay. It made me feel better.'

His father smiled. 'That's good then. That's really good.'

Gihan smiled back. 'It is.'

Something between them lifted.

Aunty-Amma popped her head out of the door. 'Bring that in and come and have a cup of tea,' she said. 'Those smaller ones can go in Kumudhini's car later.'

Gihan hadn't realised he was shopping for Kumudhini Aunty as well. He didn't know why he was surprised. They took the second box in. He helped his father put the box down and dusted off his hands.

'Have you got everything for the flat now?' his stepmother said. She and Sam joined them in the living room, carrying trays of tea and cake.

'Everything apart from a mattress to sleep on.' Sam laughed. 'Apparently, he has specific ideas about what sort of mattress he needs.'

Kumudhini Aunty bustled in, carrying a mug in one hand and a chocolate biscuit in the other. 'It's very important, the mattress. It has to be comfortable for him. And his wife when he gets married.'

Gihan braced himself. Sam bit her lips as though trying not to laugh.

'Gihan says he's not getting married,' said Aunty-Amma.

'Oh what? Silly boy. You have to get married. Otherwise what is it all for?' Kumudhini Aunty said.

Before Gihan had time to respond, she carried on. 'Now then.' She pulled out her phone. 'I know two nice girls who could meet—'

'Aunty. Aunty, stop.' He put his hands up.

'I know you young things think we don't know anything. But I think you'll really like—'

'No. Aunty. I'm . . . sort of seeing someone.'

Sam gave a little squeak. 'You called her?' She gave him a look that said she would be demanding a full explanation later.

'It's still very, very new, okay.' He didn't know where the smile came from, but he couldn't stop it. 'So. Please. Don't start searching for a wife for me.'

Aunty-Amma was beaming at him. 'You have to tell us more about this girl. Who is she?'

'Later, please,' said Gihan. 'We've only been together a day now.'

'And you're already smiling like the happiest man in the world,' said Kumudhini Aunty. 'Ah. Must be love.'

Gihan said nothing, but his smile widened.

Kumudhini Aunty nudged Aunty-Amma. 'All the children are settling down. You must be so proud.'

Thatha put a hand on Gihan's shoulder and another on Sam's. 'I am proud of my children,' he said. 'All three of them.'

Gihan exchanged an awkward glance with Sam. He didn't know what to say to that. Perhaps he didn't need to say anything. Just knowing was enough.

Chapter 29

Nine weeks later

Alex followed Gihan up the stairs to the flat. It was January now and she'd finished her first week at Swanland. It had been a whirlwind of new experiences – new house share, new city, new job. At least the boyfriend was only new-ish. What with one thing and another, this was the first time she was able to visit his flat.

'As the estate agent said to me,' said Gihan, 'I urge you to keep an open mind.'

She had seen pictures of the place before the transformation. Nothing could be that bad. He turned the light on as she entered.

The room was white with a hint of green. The floor was covered with an enormous beige rug, centred so that a border of green psychedelic carpet peeped out around the edges. A teal sofa sat facing the windows, which were edged in lime green. Outside, you could see the lights from the pizza shop. Gihan drew the curtains. Alex turned around. The feature wall was behind her. She had seen photos, but it was even more impressive up close. Most of the wall below it was taken up by a white unit. Niro had painted a border of white around the mural, leaving most of it intact, but framing it, so that it didn't dominate the room. It worked.

'That is incredible,' she said, stepping closer. 'It makes it look like this room was designed by a really expensive interior designer.'

'In a way it was,' said Gihan. 'Niro helped me and she's an artist.'

'When you said the Instagram kids took lots of photos with it, I can see why.'

'Come see the kitchen.'

She walked in and immediately felt the same sense of warmth and welcome that she'd felt in Jake's house.

'We changed the cupboard doors,' said Gihan. 'I put the old ones on eBay and they sold for a decent amount. It's surprising what people will buy.'

'I like the crazy paving effect lino.'

'Me too.'

They carried on with the tour. The bathroom fixtures were still pink. 'Pink? I didn't know toilets came in pink.'

'Now you know,' said Gihan. 'The walls were pink and orange before. We toned it down to pale pink. Rose white, I think it's called.' He gave a little laugh. 'It's not the most macho of bathrooms, but it serves its purpose.'

She peered into the smaller room, which had a desk and a fold out sofa in it. Gihan opened the door to the main bedroom. She walked in. This room was blue and white.

'This looks so normal,' said Alex. 'What happened here?' She sat down on the big bed.

'This one wasn't too bad. It was brown and electric blue. So we painted the brown bits dark blue and covered up the electric blue with white.' He sat down beside her. 'I don't think I could have coped with anything too outlandish in here.' He leaned backwards and lay down.

She flopped down next to him. It was comfortable hanging out with him like this. He had been there for her through all the stress of moving and changing jobs. It felt impossible to imagine a time when he wasn't in her life. She reached across and found his hand. He interlaced his fingers through hers. She smiled at the ceiling.

Hang on. There was a rectangular outline on the ceiling above the bed, as though something had been removed. She tilted her head. 'Wait, was there a . . .?'

'It was already gone when I saw the place,' Gihan said. 'Which I'm glad of. I don't think I'd like to see myself when I'm lying in bed.'

Alex laughed. 'The person who owned this place must have been quite a character.'

'All I know about her is that she'd lived here since the Seventies and at one time she was very pretty and had a lot of parties. That bit of gossip is from the guy who runs the shop downstairs,' Gihan said. 'I wish I'd got to meet her.'

'Do you think she approves of what you're doing with the place?'

Gihan was quiet for a bit. 'I think she probably does, yes.'

He rolled onto his side, so that he was facing her. 'So, what do you want to do this evening?' He stroked the side of her face.

She met his eyes. 'Netflix and chill?'

He held her gaze for a few seconds and smiled his glorious smile. 'I'm up for that.' He gently tucked her hair back behind her ear before he kissed her.

She kissed him back. Things were going well until her stomach rumbled.

Mortified, she said, 'I'm so sorry.'

Gihan laughed. 'Let me sort out some food. I could nip across the road to the pizza place. They're pretty good.'

Alex flopped back and let out a soft groan. 'I don't want to move. This bed is so comfy.'

This seemed to perk him up. 'It is? Oh good.' He sat up and patted the mattress. 'I haven't actually slept in it yet.'

She struggled into a sitting position. 'What do you mean you haven't slept in it yet? You moved in weeks ago.'

He gave her a shy smile. 'I wanted to get a mattress that you would be okay sleeping on, with your back. So I asked Jake to find out the type of mattress you had and ordered one online. Then I had to wait for delivery. Then there was a mix-up and . . . basically, this only arrived last week. I've been sleeping in the pull-out bed in the spare room all this time, so I thought I may as well carry on sleeping there until tonight. So that we could try it out . . . together . . . Why are you looking at me like that?'

'You ordered a special mattress . . . for me?' The fact that he had even thought of it was astounding to her. If she had ever needed proof that he loved her, this was probably it. Happiness flooded into her, lighting her up. How on earth could she have mistaken any of her past relationships for this? She felt seen, and loved, and part of something incredible.

'Well, I wanted you to be comfortable when you stay h—'

'I love you.' She interrupted him and pulled him towards her. 'I really, really, really love you.'

Gihan grinned, happiness radiating from him. 'I love you too,' he said and kissed her.

They didn't make it out to get pizza until a long time after . . .

Acknowledgements

There are always so many people to thank. I write the book myself, but researching it involves lots of people.

First of all, huge thanks to Mary Kilgarriff who responded to my plea on Twitter for someone who knew about the aftermath of back surgery. Her notes on how Alex would feel in most everyday situations were all wonderful. I hope I've incorporated them all correctly. Obviously, everyone's experience is different, but I hope I've captured something of what it's like to live with a back injury.

When I needed a name for the dog, who was called 'the dog' for a long time, my newsletter people came to my rescue again. Special thanks to Linda Marion Hill and Jodi Wresh who suggested Penelope/ Penny. Thanks also to Nancy, Cath, Karen, Way, Paula, Kathy, Angeline, Julie, Algernon, Colcam, Manel (and grandson), Philip and Shunthea – all of whom sent excellent suggestions.

In October 2022, a group of authors ran a bookish auction to raise money for the East Yorkshire Food Bank. One of the lots I offered for the auction was the chance to have your (or a loved one's) name in the book. Huge thanks to Michelle McGrath, who gave a generous donation and asked for her great-grandmother's name, Ada Moon, to be included. In the book Ada provides cakes for the village fair.

Writing isn't the most sociable of occupations and sometimes you need to talk to other authors to work out your story issues, so thank you to Jenni Fletcher and Jane Lovering for the regular writing meetings. As always, I wouldn't manage to stay upbeat without the help from the fabulous ladies of the Naughty Kitchen – thank you Ruth, Janet, Alison, Kate, Sheila and Imogen for all the encouragement and for putting up with my terrible puns.

Thanks as always to my agent Jo Bell and the team at HQ for all your help. This book went through quite a lot of changes during the editorial process and has emerged a much better book because of it.

Most of all, thank you to my family, who are very understanding about how much time and effort I put into this job. You're the best.

A letter from Jeevani Charika

Thank you so much for reading *Knowing Me Knowing You* (I always struggle not to add an 'aha!' at the end of it. I shall try and behave). I hope you enjoyed it! If you would like to know what happened to Alex and Gihan after 'The End', you can get a bonus epilogue when you sign up to my newsletter: https://jeevanicharika.com/knowingme/

So, this is the bit where I tell you what inspired the book. At the risk of sounding ridiculous, most of it was inspired by something else I wrote. When I finished writing *Picture Perfect*, I read it back and thought 'Gihan's acting a little shifty, I wonder why'. Pulling at that thread made his story slowly come alive.

The scene in the temple was inspired by a conversation with a seven-year-old about how some religious spaces have really thick carpets. It's amazing how inspiring lunch at Nando's can be!

My day job involves seeing a lot of wonderful new inventions that never make it to market because we don't manage to secure funding to develop it. It makes me so sad when you can see how it could save or change lives. A long time ago, I worked for a medium sized startup company that ran out of funding and had to close. I remember the terrible days when we started to feel the slide towards bad news. I've tried to capture that in showing how

Alex feels caught between the logical understanding that things can't carry on as they are and the emotional tug of denial.

The inspiration for Daniel and his management-speak came from the absolute legend that is Bob Mortimer and his 'Train Guy' sketches. If you haven't heard of them, Google them – they are hilarious . . . or indeed, 'hilario'. I crowdsourced cringey management phrases from Twitter and tried to make them worse (which was mostly impossible because they were so terrible to begin with).

The setting in the Cotswolds is somewhere familiar to me. I lived in Oxfordshire for over a decade. Like Gihan, I have no sense of direction. I'm forever getting lost when I'm driving. Trying to follow a diversion, I once got lost on the backroads between Kidlington and Didcot (I didn't even have a sat nav, like Gihan did, so I was following yellow 'diversion' signs). Somehow, I ended up having to cross the toll bridge near Eynsham. It was completely unexpected. And the toll was 5p. So surreal! It was too good not to put in a book.

I put lots of things in the book that I remembered from being a young person living in the area; most of them weren't relevant to the book and had to be taken out again, but the village fair remained. I love a village fair, me. I mostly go so that I can buy cake.

I hope you loved *Knowing Me Knowing You* (. . . aha!) and if you did, I would be so grateful if you would leave a review. It doesn't have to be long – just a few lines about how you felt about the book will do. I always love to hear what readers thought, and it helps new readers discover my books too.

Don't forget that you can get a bonus epilogue for *Knowing Me Knowing You*, when you sign up to my newsletter. Just visit https://jeevanicharika.com/knowingme/

Picture Perfect

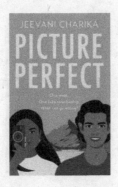

Niro is a photographer who's lost the joy of taking photos. Burned by a bad break-up, she's in desperate need of inspiration.

Vimal is determined to win back his ex-girlfriend. When he hears she's bringing her new boyfriend on a group holiday, he impulsively declares that he's bringing a plus one too.

Their mutual friends have the perfect solution: Niro can pretend to be Vimal's new girlfriend and join the holiday. Imagine the incredible photographs she could take in the Swiss alps . . .

She's not thinking about love. He's thinking about someone else. Can they fake a picture-perfect relationship – or will real feelings get in the way?

Don't miss this funny and uplifting fake-dating romance for fans of *The Kiss Quotient* and *The Love Hypothesis*!

Playing for Love

When Sam's not working on her fledgling business, she spends her time secretly video-gaming. Her crush is famous gamer Blaze, and she's thrilled when she's teamed up with him in a virtual tournament.

But what Sam doesn't know is that Blaze is the alter ego of Luke, her shy colleague – and he has a secret crush too.

Luke has a crush on Sam.
Sam has a crush on Blaze.

How will this game of love play out?

A fun, feel-good romance for fans of *You've Got Mail*, Helen Hoang, Jasmine Guillory and Lindsey Kelk!

Dear Reader,

We hope you enjoyed reading this book. If you did, we'd be so appreciative if you left a review. It really helps us and the author to bring more books like this to you.

Here at HQ Digital we are dedicated to publishing fiction that will keep you turning the pages into the early hours. Don't want to miss a thing? To find out more about our books, promotions, discover exclusive content and enter competitions you can keep in touch in the following ways:

JOIN OUR COMMUNITY:

Sign up to our new email newsletter:
http://smarturl.it/SignUpHQ

Read our new blog www.hqstories.co.uk

🐦 https://twitter.com/HQStories

f www.facebook.com/HQStories

BUDDING WRITER?

We're also looking for authors to join the HQ Digital family!
Find out more here:

https://www.hqstories.co.uk/want-to-write-for-us/

Thanks for reading, from the HQ Digital team